MOONLIGHT FALLS

By Vincent Zandri

First Printing – December 2009
ISBN: **978-0-9819654-0-6**

R.J. Buckley Publishing
Queen Creek AZ

www.rjbuckleypublishing.com

Other novels by Vincent Zandri:

AS CATCH CAN

GODCHILD

PERMANENCE

Of Vincent Zandri novels:

"... certainly qualifies as a high-concept novel ... this former journalist also has the talent to deliver ..."

"... a thriller that has depth and substance, wickedness and compassion."

"... sensational ... masterful ... brilliant ..."

With tough, lurid prose, Vincent Zandri crafts haunting, broodingly paranoid thrillers that move relentlessly to their final, unforgettable twists.

Acknowledgements

The people who took a vested interest in this novel at one time or another during its rather long eight-year incubation reads like a *Who's Who* of the publishing industry.

The list includes Jacob Hoye, Abby Zidle, Jimmy Vines, Suzanne Gluck, Rolf Blythe, and even the American poet, Christian Barter. Why it eventually landed in the hands of agent Janet Benrey and the indie press RJBP, both of whom reside far away from the ground zero of literary ambition and commercial publishing success is a story best told over a quiet drink in one of my favorite dives. However, the author is indebted to the aforementioned agent and publisher for their gracious support and willingness to go out on a very thin limb for me. You guys rock!

In the end, I'm grateful to everyone who read this book, reread it, and who offered their most inspired commentary and who also had to listen to my silly banter along the way.

I owe you a beer or maybe lunch.

For Ava Zandri

"He reached out and took the knife to slaughter."
Genesis 23:10

Prologue

Man's life is flashing before his eyes.

He's a little amazed because it's happening just like it does in a sappy movie. You know, when they run real fast through some homespun super-eight film starting with your birth, moving on to toddler's first step, then first day at kindergarten, first communion, first prom, first Gulf War, first marriage, firstborn son, first affair, first divorce ...

So why's the life flashing by?

Man's about to execute himself.

He sits alone at the kitchen table inside what used to be his childhood home, pistol barrel pressed up tight against his head, only a half-inch or so behind the right earlobe. Thumb on the hammer, index finger wrapped around the trigger, hand trembling, eyes closed, big tears falling.

On the bright side of things, it's a beautiful sunny day.

Outside the kitchen window wispy clouds float by like giant ghosts in a heavenly blue sky. Bluebirds chirp happily from the junipers that line the perimeter of the north Albany property. The cool wind blows, shaking the leaves on the trees. The fall air is cool, crisp and clean. "Football weather" his mortician dad used to call it back when he was a happy-go-lucky kid.

On the not so bright side, a bullet is about to enter his brainpan. But then, as much as the man wants to enter the spirit world, he's not entirely insensitive. He's thought things through. While he might have used his service-issued 9mm to do the job, he's decided instead to go with the more lightweight .22, his backup piece. To some people, a pistol is a pistol. But to the man, nothing could be further from the truth. Because had he chosen to "eat his piece" by pressing the pistol barrel up against his mouth's soft upper palate, he'd guarantee himself an instant death.

A good death.

Problem is that "good death" would leave one hell of a spatter mess behind for some poor slob to clean up after his soul has left the building. So instead of choosing the safe "good death," he's opted for the more thoughtful *no-mess, easy-clean-up* kind of suicide—the assassin's death. Because only a professional killer with a steady hand knows that a .22 caliber bullet hasn't got a chance in hell of exiting the skull once it's made jelly filling of your brains.

Outside the window, the wind picks up.

The chimes that hang from the eaves make haunting, jingly ghost music.

The super-eight memories inside his head have ceased. His life story—the entire thirty-six year affair from birth to this very moment of truth has officially flashed before his eyes.

Roll credits . . .

Man swallows a lump, thumbs back the hammer. The mechanical action reverberates inside his skull.

There's no stopping him; no penetrating the resolve of the already dead. He's happy with himself for the first time in he can't remember how long. So happy, his entire body weight seems to empty itself from out the bottoms of his feet. That's when a red robin perches itself on the brick ledge just outside the picture window, just a small scarlet-feathered robin that's beating its wings and staring into the house with its black eyes.

"Don't look," the man whispers.

He plants a smile on his face a split second before he pulls the trigger.

1

FOUR YEARS LATER
Albany, New York
140 miles northeast of New York City

I'm escorted into a four-walled basement room by two suited agents—one tall, slim and bearded, the other shorter, stockier, clean-shaven. The space we occupy contains a one-way mirror which I know from experience hides a tripod-mounted video camera, a sound man and several FBI agents, the identities of whom are concealed. There's no furniture in the room, other than a long metal table and four metal chairs. No wallpaper, no soft lamp light, no piped-in music. Just harsh white overhead light, concrete and a funny worm smell.

As I enter the room for the first time, the tall agent tells me to take a seat at the table.

"We appreciate your cooperation," the stocky agent jumps in.

Out of the corner of my eye, I catch my reflection in the mirror.

I'm of medium height. Not tall, not short. Not too badly put together for having reached the big four-zero thanks to the cross-training routine I put myself on not long after my hospital release. Nowadays, my head is shaved. There's a small button-sized scar behind my right earlobe in the place where the fragment of a .22 caliber hollow-point penetrated the skull. I wear a black leather jacket over black jeans and lace-up combat boots left over from my military service during the first Gulf War. My eyeglasses are rectangular and retrofitted from a pair of cheap sunglasses I picked up at a Penn Station kiosk. They make my stubble-covered face seem slightly wider than it really is. So people have told me.

Having been led to my chair, I am then asked to focus my gaze directly onto the mirror so that the video man or woman stationed on the opposite side of the glass can adjust the shooting angle and focus.

"Please say something," requests Stocky Agent while removing his suit jacket, setting it over the back of an empty chair.

"There once was a cop from Nantucket," I say to break the ice.

But no one laughs.

"You get that?" the taller agent barks out to no one in particular.

"Okay to go," comes a tinny, hidden speaker voice. "You gonna finish that poem, Mr. Moonlight?"

"Knock it off," Stocky Agent orders. He turns back to me. "Before we get started, can we get you a coffee, a cappuccino? You can get one right out of the new machine upstairs."

"Mind if I burn one?"

Tall Bearded Agent purses his lips, cocks his head in the direction of a plastic *No Smoking* placard to the wall.

Stocky Agent makes a sour face, shakes his head, rolls up the sleeves on his thick arms. He reaches across the heavy wood table, grabs an ashtray, and clunks it down in front of me as if it were a bedpan.

"The rule doesn't apply down here," he says. Then, in this deep affected voice, he adds, "Let's get started, Mr. Moonlight. You already know the routine. For now we just want to get to the bottom of who, what, where and how of this train wreck."

"You forgot the why," I say, firing up a Marlboro Light. "You need to know why, to establish an entire familiarity with any given case."

Stocky Agent does a double take, smiles. Like he knows I'm fucking with him.

"Don't be a dick, Dick," he says.

I guess it's important not to take life too seriously. He laughs. I laugh. We all laugh. Ice officially broken. I exhale some smoke, sit back in my chair.

They're right, of course. I know the drill. I know it's the truth they're after. The truth and almost nothing but the truth. But what they also want is my perspective—my take on the entire Scarlet Montana affair, from soup to peanuts. They want me to leave nothing out. I'll start with my on-again/off-again love affair with my boss's wife. Maybe from there I'll move on to the dead bodies, my cut-up hands, the Saratoga Springs Russians, the Psychic Fair, the heroin, the illegal organ harvesting operation, the exhumations, the attempts on my life, the lies, deceptions and fuck-overs galore.

As a former fulltime Albany detective, I know that nobody sees the same thing through the same set of eyeballs. What's important to one person might appear insignificant or useless to another. What those federal agents want right now inside the basement interview room is my most reliable version of the truth—an accurate, objective truth that separates fact from fantasy.

Theoretically speaking.

"Ask away," I say, just as the buzzing starts up in the core of my head.

"Just start at the beginning," Stocky Agent requests. "We have all night."

Sitting up straight, I feel my right arm beginning to go numb on me. So numb I drop the lit cigarette onto the table. The inside of my head chimes like a belfry. Stocky Agent is staring at me from across the table with these wide bug eyes like my skull and brains are about to pull a JFK all over him.

But then, just as soon as it all starts, the chiming and the paralysis subsides.

With a trembling hand, I manage to pick up the partially smoked cigarette, exhale a very resigned, now smokeless breath and stamp the cancer stick out.

"Everything you wanna know," I whisper. "You want me to tell you everything."

"Everything you remember," Tall Agent smiles. "If that's at all possible."

Stocky Agent pulls a stick of gum from a pack in his pants pocket, carefully unwraps the tin foil and folds the gum before stuffing it into his mouth.

Juicy Fruit. I can smell it from all the way across the table.

By all indicators, it's going to be a long night.

"I think I'll take that cappuccino after all," I say.

For the first time since entering the interview room, I feel the muscles in my face constricting. I know without looking that my expression has turned into something miles away from shiny happy. I'm dead serious.

It all began with a choice.

Rather, not a *choice*, but a really bad decision—the decision to stay with Scarlet Montana for more than her allotted forty minutes. It was the last thing either one of us needed, but the first thing we wanted.

Or *I* wanted, anyway.

In my right mind I'd spend an hour tops on a soothing massage, collect my forty bucks, and make a swift exit. I swear on my dad's cremated remains, that's exactly the way I planned it on my way over through the rain. It's the reason I didn't take the collapsible table with me; the reason I didn't bring my oil belt, opting instead to shove a small plastic bottle into my gym shorts.

Get in quick, get out even quicker.

Just enough time for a quickie massage, while yours truly kneeled over the spot where she lay on her belly on the living room floor, only a white bath towel covering her heart-shaped glutes. In a professional manner, I'd allow my well-oiled hands to do what they had recently been trained (and nearly licensed) to do. At the same time I'd act as a kind of psychiatrist—a well-trusted sounding board to this thirty-eight year old woman who could no longer stand the sight of her life partner, Jake, the man who had given up any possibility of a happy marriage for the title of Albany Chief Detective.

Now instead of a wife, he had a second in command (my former A.P.D. partner, Mitchell Cain); instead of kids he had the South Pearl Street precinct full of upwardly mobile young cops; instead of a cozy suburban home life he had his late evenings, early mornings and more frequent days and nights spent away from home altogether.

As for the beautiful Scarlet, she might have had yours truly at her beck and call. But then instead of a family, she had a huge helping heap of loneliness sprinkled with despair.

Maybe I should have stayed put, ignored Scarlet's phone call. Maybe I should have stayed true to my significant other, Lola, the brown-haired, brown-eyed lovely who was slowly but surely becoming my legit love interest. Maybe I should have listened more closely to my built-in shit detector and not dropped everything to answer the call.

My brain … it couldn't always be trusted to make the right choice.

Braving a violent thunderstorm, I made the mile-long trek to her house on foot in less than ten or twelve minutes. This had to be just around nine o'clock.

Why? Because I'd been right in the middle of my incline presses when I took the call.

Jogging through the downpour across the lawns and suburban driveways in gym shorts, tennis shoes and gray t-shirt, I must have looked like the most insane neighborhood night-crawler you ever saw.

My intentions were good.

I promised myself I would stay with Scarlet for no more than forty, maybe sixty minutes. Considering the way I felt about Lola, I would fight to stay in control. Just a nice massage, an understanding listen, then a quick "Hang in there baby, everything's gonna be just fine." Maybe a hug, a peck to the cheek and then like lightning, I'd be gone in a flash.

Would I ever learn?

Why couldn't I restrain myself?

Why couldn't I just be satisfied with listening to her soft voice? Why did I have to stare into her soft green eyes? Why did I have to gaze upon her ocean of thick auburn hair and picture myself swimming in it? Why did I have to picture my lips touching her thick heart-shaped lips? Why did I have to imagine them running the length of her sweet neck all the way down her back? Why did I have to gently slip my hands underneath the white towel to cup her perfectly carved glutes, to caress her milky white breasts?

Why was it that every time a despairing Scarlet Montana called me over to her lonely home I could not be content with concentrating on my new career while she pontificated upon the horrors of being married to the top cop in Albany?

So here's how it happened with Scarlet inside the living room of my former department superior: our eyes connected, sort of like two deer that hopelessly lock horns. We jumped up from the floor and by the time we made it up to her second floor bedroom not a stitch of clothing was left on our backs.

That's exactly how it went down, only with one further significant fuck-up added to the mix.

That is, a *series* of fuck-ups.

The first being my incessant need to *get down* with Scarlet just because she rang the dinner bell. The second being the stupid decision to suck down one of her husband's tall-necked Buds just before falling into a post-sex deep sleep on her queen-sized Serta. The third being the very sudden and unexplained homecoming of said husband. The fourth being Scarlet's failure to wake me before I was jarred awake to the rattle and hum of an abruptly triggered overhead garage door.

Here's what I did: I jumped out of bed, scrambled about the dark room in search of my shorts and sneakers. All the time I'm doing this crazy one-legged dance while trying to step into my shorts mouthing "Shit, shit, shit" in this sort of screaming whisper voice.

Then comes the back door off the kitchen opening and slamming closed.

"Why'd you let me fall asleep?"

"Relax," Scarlet insisted. "What's he going to do? Shoot you in the head?"

Listen, even from behind closed doors I could see Jake's tight-mustached face, big beefy arms, barrel chest and sausage-thick fingers already reaching for my neck. He didn't have to shoot me. A strangle-hold would do the trick.

And get this: while my life and death were flashing before my eyes, Scarlet calmly lay on her side. What a couple of beats before had been tears were now suddenly replaced with the sweetest smile you ever saw, the white bed sheet covering only her legs, leaving those lovely white titties exposed. I swear, even with the old man marching up those stairs, I almost laid back down with her to kiss her sweet mouth and press her body tightly against mine.

My right mind: it's not always right.

"Are you going home to Lola?" she asked, casually firing up another Virginia Slim. "I think you're beginning to like her more than me."

"I'm about to die," I said, pulling up my gym shorts.

"No one really dies, Richard."

She laughed. I had no idea what the hell was so funny. Especially with the tell-tale footsteps just outside the door, one heavy heartbeat-like clump after the other. But then, that was the thing about Scarlet. You never knew exactly which woman you were getting. Her mood could change as easily as the second hand on a watch face. One minute she might be laughing hysterically and the next staring out into space in an all-consuming sullenness. She could go from sexy to teary-eyed in one point five seconds, especially post-coitus, when lovers should be hugging, not pulling away.

I took one final look at Scarlet before climbing out the second floor window. With my socks and Nike Airs balled up inside my left arm, I heard her smooth voice utter the words I'd never before heard: "I love you, Richard."

Without a response I jumped down onto the back porch overhang. Bare feet slid out from under me so that I landed flat on my ass just a second before falling forward, dropping down onto the rain-soaked lawn on hands and knees.

No time to check for broken bones, no time to feel the pain, no time to consider the sudden stiffness in my right arm.

No time like the present to avoid one of my seizures!

I just bounded back up, caught my breath, and like my fellow Marines drilled me in the first Gulf War, selected a direct line of retreat.

But before I started to run - just in that instant it takes your gray matter to shift from *Stop* to all-out *Go* - I took one last glance up at Scarlet's bedroom window. Through the driving rain I made out her face, her green eyes and auburn hair made all the thicker and richer when the bedroom light was suddenly flicked on behind her.

In that quick second I could tell that she was no longer laughing.

From where I stood in the rain and the quick flashes of lightening, I saw that she was simply smiling. A lonely kind of smile that had nothing to do with happiness. When she raised her right hand, extended an index finger, pressed it to her lips as if to give the sign for *all quiet*, I knew that I could trust her not to reveal anything about our affair to Jake. That no matter how difficult things might get for her that night, no matter how rough, I could trust her *and* her silence. She, in turn, could trust in me—trust in the fact that I would do just about anything for her.

Anything but brave a face-down with Jake in the flesh inside his wife's bedroom.

When Scarlet turned away from the window, I made my swift and stealthy exit from the Montana homestead, praying that a damn good lesson had finally been learned that night and that I would never more be led astray by my other head.

2

Here's how Scarlet first invaded my life: we were both guests at a department fundraiser held every Christmas season inside the Elks Club ballroom. Me having attended the function by department mandate without my first wife—a chief E.R. nurse for the Albany Medical Center who that night was working the four-to-midnight "action shift"—and Scarlet, the guest of her then-fiancé and my department super.

That winter night back in '99 was Scarlet's coming out, so to speak. No one had ever met her before. We only heard rumors about Jake's long-distance love affair with a beautiful young woman from the west coast. But we had never seen so much as a photograph. Considering Jake's wide girth, sloppy appearance and constant three-day shadow, expectations weren't running terribly high. To be frank, we expected a Montana look-alike in drag.

Our expectations could not have been more wrong.

When she walked in arm-in-arm with the top cop, I thought the dance floor might fall out from under my feet. This slim young woman, dressed all in black with thick auburn hair and green eyes, was nothing like I'd imagined. When Jake left her side to get her a drink, she could not have stood more than ten feet away from me. Maybe it was the effects of one too many Jack and Cokes, but I guess I must have been staring, because it was only a matter of a few seconds before her green eyes were drawn to my browns. When they locked on me, I would have sworn that somebody had sucked the oxygen from my lungs.

I remember wanting to say something. Something to put her at ease.

The tight-lipped look on her face, the way she cocked her head, the way she brushed back her hair with a slightly trembling hand, the way she speed-blinked her eyes, it was if she were begging me to say something. Anything at all. Even a simple "Hello" would have been fine, I'm sure.

But instead I just stood there staring, the biggest dolt you ever saw dressed in a blue blazer, wrinkled button-down and blue-striped rep tie, coffee stain painting its center.

By the time Jake made it back with the drinks, Scarlet shifted her focus to him. Gladly. Or so I guessed.

The spell might have been broken, but what had definitely become an *infatuation-at-first-sight* was not.

Jake wasn't blind.

He threw me a silent glare, one that suggested territorial boundaries. The big bear staring down the little bear. I knew my opportunity to introduce myself had come and gone, at least for the time being. Naturally, Jake would make a formal introduction to everyone on his support staff later in the evening.

But then what difference did introductions make? Or more accurately, what difference did my crush make?

I was married to a woman who had recently given birth to our first and what would be our only child together. As far as life partners went, I was locked up till death did us in. But standing there alone on the Elk's Club dance floor, Bing Crosby singing "White Christmas," I eyed the woman who jealously clung to Jake Montana. For the first time in our brief working relationship I would have cut off my left nut to trade places with him.

This is what I learned about Scarlet over the course of the evening: that she was a recent transplant from Southern California. Santa Monica, to be precise. Why she chose to transplant herself to an east coast Deadwood-like Albany might have been anybody's guess.

Santa Monica … the name just dripped off your tongue and lips like sweet nectar. It evoked images of bright sunshine, long stretches of white sandy beach, clear blue surf and killer waves.

Scarlet's bright smile and gentle grace seemed so out of place inside a city like Albany, a place known more for its gray winters than anything else.

There was something else too.

The way Scarlet clung to Jake's beefy arm. Not like he'd become her significant other; more like he'd become her bodyguard. It was as if behind the beautiful smile existed something tragic.

It would be much later on when my own marriage was finally falling apart, that she would reveal the fate of her first husband and only child. They'd been killed in a head-on by a drunken driver, a stockbroker who crossed over the meridian after having passed out at the wheel of his Lexus sedan.

From what Scarlet told me while the two of us lay side by side in her bed, she'd waited up all night for her husband and son to arrive home, knowing that as the hours ticked by she should have been calling the police; she should have been searching for them. But instead she chose to do nothing, because in her heart she already knew that they were dead. She physically felt their absence the same way a person will feel only a cold sensation when a limb is suddenly and unexpectedly severed.

She came east not long after burying her family in the hopes that she could start over, forget the past, begin anew in a different location … as far away from sunny California in geography and spirit as a location could get.

For a while her relationship with Jake represented a brighter future. For a time he became her guardian angel, her protector against what I would come to know as her "psychic demons." But what Scarlet didn't know then was that Jake also had a past as tragic as her own. Like one violent hurricane merging into another, it would be the coming together of those tragic forces that would inevitably spell destruction for them both.

3

But then why did she have to call me on that particular Sunday night?

Or why did I make the wrong decision by answering the phone?

I'd have been better off letting the digital answering service do its job while I kept on pumping out repetition after repetition on my incline bench, filling muscles and veins with precious over-oxygenated blood.

Blame it on the head injury or blame it on plain bad luck. But one thing was for certain, the gods were not with me that night any more than they were with Scarlet. But then maybe the gods had nothing to do with it. Maybe none of this had to do with a damaged cerebral cortex for that matter. Maybe it was just a man thing.

What is it about the deceptive face of lust that taunts us, lures us, tests us? The monster disguised as the prettiest little package you ever saw topped off in delicious auburn hair?

Such were the rapid-fire deliberations that immediately shot through my brain when, later that night, I was startled out of a restless sleep by a fist pounding on my door. I immediately pictured Lola. But then she would never pound on the door. That wasn't her style. Besides, she had a key to the place.

I sat up, rubbed the sleep from my eyes. The gears in my temporal lobe started churning. Thoughts drifted from Lola to Scarlet.

I pictured Scarlet standing outside my front door, the rainwater dripping off her long hair onto chiseled cheekbones and succulent lips. She would have had a knock-down-drag-out with Jake. He came home drunk, angry. He would have landed into her, blackened one of her teardrop eyes.

That's what I imagined.

But it wasn't until I dragged myself out of bed, slid into a pair of jeans, hobbled on down the stairs to the front door, that I realized how false my imagination could be.

The late-night caller was a far cry from Scarlet.

He was just a police officer. The kind of cop you might call "kid" if you were, say, in your mid to late forties. Anything beyond that and you might not notice him at all.

But I recognized him for exactly who he was.

A young cop with barely thirty-six months of experience under his belt, a twenty-something cop with a degree in Criminology from Providence College who went by the name of Joy.

Officer Nicolas "Nicky" Joy.

I remembered him all right.

Just this wiry, nervous little guy with a better-than-regulation buzz and snug-fitting uniform blues, sized thirty-eight short at the max. Actually, a boy/man kind of cop, pink-cheeked where most men his age were bearded. If he didn't look studious enough already, he wore round granny specs over baby blue eyes.

I'd been running into Joy all year long on those occasions when my old partner, Detective Mitchell Cain, called me in on a situation requiring a still-medically-inactive cop who might be willing to work part-time with an overtaxed, or should I say, non-existent S.I.U. (Special Independent Unit).

That night, the blue-eyed Joy stood four-square on the small front portico of my Hope Lane home, the rainwater dripping off the transparent plastic that protected his headpiece and clothing. It didn't take a genius or part-time detective with a constant headache to see that he was breathing unusually hard, bottom lip shaking to the point of trembling. Gripped in his right hand, a heavy black Maglite. As for the palm of his left hand, it rested securely on the butt of his service sidearm.

Looking over the kid's shoulder, I made out the Albany blue-and-white parked up against the opposite curb, a beam of sodium street light shining down upon it, the still-heavy rain strafing the metal trunk and hood. From where I stood inside the open door, I couldn't help but make out the man who was sitting in the back seat, round mustached face looking out onto an empty, rain-soaked neighborhood street.

Jake Montana.

I knew then that something terrible had happened.

I caught my reflection in the door light—my two-day stubble, bald head and brown eyes. My face said, *I need sleep*. But sleep suddenly seemed out of the question.

I told Joy to step inside. He did. The rainwater dripped off his plastic raincoat.

"Jake wants you to come with us, Moonlight," he said.

I began to feel the familiar tightness starting in the back of my head, already working its way towards the middle.

"What's wrong?"

"Jake would rather tell you himself."

I stood there, bare-chested and stone stiff, the cool May mist soaking my skin.

What choice did I have but to go along for the ride? Didn't matter that I was trying to separate myself from police work; reinvent myself as a massage therapist and a personal trainer. I was still a detective. Rather, a private detective still collecting a Council 82 Law Enforcement Union disability pension. Technically speaking, that meant the cops still owned my ass—private license or no private license. By law and by all that was morally right under God and country, I had no choice but to "heed the call" whenever the mighty trumpet sounded.

I said, "Wait for me in the cruiser while I put on a shirt."

But Joy just stood there stiff as a plank, not saying a word, but somehow shouting volumes.

I said, "Let me guess. You think I'm gonna forget you're even here."

"You shot yourself in the head," he said as I started up the stairs. "People say you're not the same."

"It was an accident," I said. "And it's not memory that's the problem."

"Hey, Dick," he jumped in. "Maybe you should explain it to someone who understands."

"The name's Moonlight," I said, slamming the bedroom door shut.

4

Joy opened the cruiser's rear door for me.

I slipped inside, sat myself down beside Jake, my once full-time now part-time superior in the Albany P.D. I held my breath, tried to remain as calm and collected as possible.

The first thing I noticed, besides his sheer mass, was that he wouldn't look at me. From the moment I sat down on the springy back seat, he turned away, focused his gaze outside onto the rain-soaked blacktop.

The cruiser smelled bad; a cross between worms and old tuna fish gone south.

He was dressed in gray slacks with matching suit jacket, white shirt underneath. No tie. The suit was wrinkled, as if he had just picked it up off the bedroom floor and threw it on. Maybe he had. His once-jet-black hair had developed some significant gray across the temples over recent years. It blended naturally with the metallic gray that sprinkled his mustache.

Joy sat up in the driver's seat, blue eyes forward, but on occasion sneaking their way into the rearview.

I had no idea what was thicker: the humidity or the tension, until both were broken by the sound of the chief detective's baritone.

"They almost never leave notes," he uttered in a voice that bore the weight of the world. "Something like ten percent leave notes. That's all."

I swallowed my breath, hoping that somehow it would slow my pulse. It dawned on me that maybe Scarlet had finally left him. That her walking out on him, once and for all, might be the reason behind all of this. In my mind I saw my easy lover with suitcase in hand, closing the back door behind her, stepping out into the night ...

I said, "She'll contact you. Just give her a little time to get her head together."

Jake grunted, like he'd been stabbed in the stomach. He said, "At this point contact would be a miracle."

I turned to him. "What's happened?"

"She's dead," he said. "And that's all."

Off in the near distance, a streak of lightning followed by a slow, rolling thunder.

I pictured the light going on in Scarlet's bedroom not seconds after I'd jumped out the window. Had Jake seen me standing outside on the back lawn in the rain?

I repeated, "Tell me what happened."

He told me to say nothing more. "Not a fucking word."

Up front, Joy put the car in drive. As he pulled away from the curb, I crossed one hand over the other. For the first time that night I felt the tacky, bloody residue that stained the palms of my hands.

5

The ten minute ride from my home to the Pearl Street Precinct felt like it lasted an entire hour. The whole time I was rubbing my palms together as if to erase the thin layer of dried blood that coated them.

Where the hell had blood come from? Had something happened in the night that I could not remember?

Maybe if I hadn't been startled from out of a deep sleep; maybe if I hadn't put my pants on in the dark and in such a rush, I might have noticed the blood before leaving the house.

Riding in the back of that wormy-smelling cruiser, I felt so dizzy I had to swallow slow, deep breaths. Do it without Jake being the wiser.

When Joy pulled up to the old stone-and-glass monstrosity that I once referred to as my home away from home, the big chief turned to me.

He said, "Consider yourself back on the clock. I want you to act as a special independent investigator. For the record, you'll report directly to Mitch Cain. You'll take his lead, corroborate Scarlet's suicide. When it's all over and your report filed, I want you to forget that any of this ever happened. Which shouldn't be too difficult for you."

Memory's not exactly the problem, I wanted to say. But then imagine the time it would have taken to admit the God's honest truth? That because of a bullet fragment barely one millimeter in length lodged up against my cerebral cortex, I sometimes felt the overwhelming need for sleep, or that on occasion my speech became slurred while my right arm went stone stiff, or that when faced with even the simplest of problems I might make the wrong decision.

So was memory a problem?

There were moments I could be forgetful, especially in the short term. But I didn't suffer from amnesia. Technically speaking, I maintained one-hundred percent of my physical faculties. It's just that the bullet fragment sometimes acted like a monkey-in-the-works.

But I remembered Scarlet's face all right.

Sitting in the back seat of that foul-smelling cruiser, I couldn't help but picture the green eyes, the long hair, the milky skin, the full mouth. The face that attracted me to the point of desperation all those years ago. The face that Jake loved, or was supposed to love, anyway. But now that the face belonged to a dead woman, he was dismissing her, not even giving her the benefit of a proper investigation. He was supposed to be her husband; her protector. What I mean is, why not throw every resource available as the captain of the A.P.D. into a hunt for a killer or killers? Why not call in the Staties or even the FBI? Why was he so sure we had a suicide on our hands? I looked into Jake's eyes and saw the past.

I couldn't help but recall the incident that resulted in my forced leave of absence from the cops. Not my attempted suicide, but the incident that occurred not long after my "recovery" when after passing out on an eight-man drug stakeout, I suddenly regained consciousness only to order the raid of the wrong house.

I hadn't been back on the force for more than a week. Despite Jake's objections, I talked him into giving me another shot at my old "Violent Crimes" job. It was a major risk employing a man in possession of my kind of head injury and Jake knew it. But seeing as Albany was outgunned and outmanned, he might see his way to giving me another shot at V.C. But at the first sign of trouble, the first sign of seizure or memory loss or so much as a twitch of my eye, I'd be out on my ass.

Was I clear on the matter? Crystal.

The strings pulled, I was reissued my badge and my service weapon.

It wasn't long before my first shot at a significant collar presented itself. We'd been monitoring a row house in downtown Albany that we suspected of being the base for a major synthetic crack cocaine and crystal meth operation. It had been my job to assemble a team of plainclothes dicks to perform a middle-of-the-night raid in the interest of safety and maybe catching the operation at its busiest. While I took the lead car, Jake and Mitch Cain teamed up behind me in an unmarked suburban. Around the corner awaited four blue-and-whites filled with A.P.D. officers. They would provide immediate backup as soon as the raid was initiated. Everyone was to wait for my signal. Or so it was understood. S.O.P.

And while I aimed night vision binoculars on the bottom floor of the three-story inner-city row house, a radio headset wrapped around my head, the earpiece fitted into the right ear canal, I observed complete silence. But what I didn't know at the time was that the numbness I was beginning to feel in my right arm was actually the telltale sign of an oncoming seizure. Not having experienced one during my convalescence (but having been warned of them), I chalked up the sensation to having slept on it the wrong way the night before. But as the night wore on, the radio silence maintained, the numbness turned to trembling. Flashes of light began to explode behind my eyeballs. Not manmade light, but a super bright white light manufactured inside my brain. I began to feel faint. My breathing grew strained. I tried to speak, but my words emerged from my mouth as a slow, slurred whisper. It was all I could do to hold my head up.

Then a big black nothing.

What woke me from out of my spell was the banter of panicked shouting coming over the earpiece.

"Suspect's fleeing the scene! Suspect's fleeing the scene! Moonlight, you with us?"

With a start I threw open the cruiser door. Pulling my service weapon I shouted "Go, go, go!" into the headset. I was certain that the wood door I was heading for had to be the right one. I'd been staring at it all night.

Even when I kicked the fucker in, I was certain I had the right place.

But then imagine twelve armed cops dressed in black barging into a quiet family flat during the late night, drawing weapons, startling a husband, his wife and their two teenage daughters to the point of tears.

The six-figure false arrest lawsuit that followed pretty much put an end to my full-time work with the A.P.D. As a kind of consolation I was relegated instead to partial Medical Disability and the part-time investigation of "nothing" cases—accident victims, suicides, drug-related shootings, beatings and stabbings. Nothing that required a true investigation per se, other than my John Hancocking a case synopsis.

Not exactly glamour work, but it was badly needed work all the same.

My eyes were back on Jake.

"Since when do you ask me in on something this important?" I said. "I've been assigned to the nobodies that nobody will miss, remember? Scarlet is a somebody. You should know that better than anyone."

"She committed suicide, Moonlight," he said. "She's my wife. I want the case shut before it's even opened. That's why you're here."

But what if it's not suicide? I wanted to ask him. I decided not to. I was the fuck-up who made all the wrong moves, took all the wrong turns, raided the wrong house! He was the captain. Where the hell would I get with him in his present condition, anyway?

I said, "Am I back on the clock?"

He made a sour face. "I just told you that."

He was right. He had. The simplest things get by me sometimes.

Joy got out of the car, opened the door for me. I could tell it wasn't the night for long goodbyes.

I got out of the cruiser just as Joy got back in and shut the door behind him. I lifted the collar on my leather jacket and started up the stone stairs. Maybe I didn't feel the need to empty my bladder, but as soon as I made it through the glass doors, I headed directly for the safety of the men's room.

6

The bathroom was empty.

I locked the door behind me, took my place at the sink, positioned my hands beneath the faucet, allowed the hot water to pour down over them. Didn't matter how hot the water was, how much it stung the skin. Blood-pink water was pouring into the bowl, disappearing down the drain.

Clean hands, never mind a clean conscience. That's all that counted.

I turned off the water, dried myself with the paper towels, discarded them not into the trash bin but by flushing them down the toilet. It was only then that I noticed how much I was sweating. The black t-shirt underneath my jacket was wringing wet. Beads of sweat covered my brow. Turning the water back on, I splashed it onto my face, repeated the drying process.

Then I looked down at my hands. There were no cuts on the tops of them. No scratches, no abrasions. Nothing that could be construed as defensive wounds. No wonder I hadn't noticed the dried blood immediately upon waking.

But then I turned them over.

My palms and finger pads had seen better days. The cuts weren't deep. Nor were they bleeding any longer. Still, they'd been scratched up pretty bad. I moved my fingers, cocked my wrists. The bones, muscles and ligaments weren't damaged in any way. But there was a definite soreness there. Or maybe the dull pain was all in my head.

I swear you could have heard my heart beating inside the empty echo chamber of a men's room.

Why couldn't I recall having done that kind of damage to my hands? What had happened between the time I arrived home from Scarlet's house earlier and the arrival of Joy to my North Albany split-level at two-thirty in the morning? Had I slept-walked, stumbled and tripped? Had I fallen forward onto outstretched hands and not remembered a single detail about the mishap?

Or had something worse occurred?

Scarlet was dead.

Did I have something to do with it?

I looked at my face in the mirror. It was as ashen as a dead man's. The face didn't belong to me. It belonged to someone else. Someone who looked like me. Someone with my face, my voice, my name, my life. Someone who was following me, trying to kill me. The man who had tried to kill me once before but failed. Maybe the same person who killed Scarlet. I had no way of knowing; of being sure about anything.

My mind ... it wasn't always right.

There was a knock at the door. It startled the daylights out me. I took a deep breath, exhaled.

Unlocking the bolt, I opened the door to an old man pushing a cleaning bucket and a mop.

"What the hell you been doing in there?" he snapped.

"I wouldn't go in there if I were you," I said, pushing past him.

7

It was no coincidence that my former colleague, Mitch Cain, was waiting for me inside the hallowed stone walls of the Albany P.D. booking room. Dressed in blue blazer and tan khakis, he was patiently sitting on the edge of one of a dozen identical metal desks set out equidistant from one another inside the wide open space. Gripped in his right hand, a big white Styrofoam cup of Krispy Kreme coffee. In his free hand, a lit cigarette.

An identical coffee cup sat on top of the desk to his left.

Without exchanging a single word I picked up the second cup, cracked the plastic lid.

"Thought you quit," I said.

He stole a quick glance down at the cigarette.

"Blame compulsion," he said. "The more Lynn tries to make me quit, the more I feel compelled to do it."

"What do you expect from a nurse?" I said, recalling the face of my ex-wife and ever tenacious chief nurse for the Albany Medical Center's emergency room. That's right, Mitch Cain was married to my ex-wife, which pretty much made our personal and professional relationship an awkward one, to say the least. It also made for some heavy personal baggage, at least when it came to my love life, that is. What I mean is, while on one side of the spectrum was Lola, the psychologist who was willing to cross over professional boundaries to pursue an as-of-yet unconsummated relationship, on the other side was Scarlet, the secret love that was all about the sex. Taking up the middle was Lynn, the former wife who now regarded me with a hatred best described as palpable.

I took a quick look around the dimly lit room. The place was as hollow as a church.

Two or three comatose cops sitting at metal desks, hands positioned atop computer keyboards … chubby, static faces glowing in the radiant light that shot off their monitors.

Mounted to the painted concrete block walls, numerous plastic signs declaring the A.P.D. a "Smoke Free Workplace." When Cain wasn't around, that is.

Joy stepped in. He approached Cain and me, transparent rain gear still protecting his uniform blues like Saran Wrap.

"They're ready for us, Detective," he said.

Cain shot Joy a silent look. The kid about-faced and exited the room by way of an unpainted solid metal door that led out into the parking garage.

Stamping out his cigarette into a metal ashtray, my old partner set down his coffee. He ran his right hand through cropped hair and down a clean, narrow face.

Exhaling a breath, he said, "I see no need for briefings. You know the seriousness of the situation."

"Dead serious," I said. "Which is why I'm a little surprised you called me in."

"Listen, Moonlight, it's Jake's wife we're talking about here. We can't give Internal Affairs or Prosecutor O'Connor an opportunity to plunge into a full-blown investigation. It just wouldn't—" He raised his right hand as though searching for the right words. "It just wouldn't look copastetic."

"Copasetic," I corrected.

"What?"

"It's copasetic, not copastetic."

He smiled.

"That head of yours," he said, "it's working pretty good these days, old partner."

"I've been taking better care of myself lately. Doctor's orders."

He added, "Well then, just follow my lead and you, me and Jake will get through this thing without a hitch." Grinning. "Per the usual deal there'll be a little bit extra for your trouble."

I listened like a good, pension-collecting, on-again-off-again cop should and sipped my coffee. Until my brain kicked in. I pictured Scarlet lying back on her bed, auburn hair fluffed up against her pillow, tear-soaked eyes wide open, lips smiling wryly. Maybe the reality of her death hadn't begun to sink in. But somehow I knew she deserved better than what I was hearing from her husband and her husband's second in command. Then there was the issue of my hands—the blood, the scrapes, the soreness in the wrists. Just what if I'd had something to do with Scarlet's death? Was I somehow blocking the memory?

One thing was obvious: the question of whether or not Jake had seen me standing on the back lawn outside Scarlet's bedroom window had been answered. No way he would have called me in on the case if he knew I'd been sleeping with the deceased.

But then something else might have been happening.

I gazed into Cain's slate-gray eyes and took a shot.

"You plan on booking Jake tonight?" I said. "Or is all this copasetic stuff about giving him a little head start?"

As stale as it was, the air inside the booking room was sucked out like starlight into a black hole. Cain's grin suddenly morphed into a frown.

"You suddenly grow a conscience overnight, Moonlight?" he whispered, firing up another smoke. "This is an extremely sensitive situation which will require every bit of your professional talents and resources."

In other words, my old partner was asking me to do exactly what he told me to do.

Joy walked back into the room.

Cain exhaled the smoke through his nostrils. First he gave the rookie a confirming nod. Then he looked back up at me.

"I don't mean to be pushy, Moonlight," he sighed. "It's just that your A.P.D. needs you like never before." Pausing for a beat, as if to correct himself, he added, "Rather, I'm asking you, as an old partner and a member in good standing of this most decorated force, to just go along for the ride."

"Part-time member," I interjected. "I made that false bust, remember?"

"We all make our little mistakes," he said. "Besides, your head ...well, let's just say you weren't up for that kind of job."

A frigid sensation enveloped me. Like my pants had somehow just fallen down around my ankles with everybody watching.

I glanced over at the two uniformed cops, their faces never veering from their computer switchboards. I knew they had to be dying to get a better view of our apparently friendly exchange. But I also knew they wouldn't dare.

"No choice," I said like a question. The non-committing part-timer suddenly committed.

He grinned. "Not really."

He checked the pockets of his blazer to make sure he had everything he needed: keys, smokes, lighter, wallet, bullets.

Copasetic . . .

He began walking towards Joy.

"Hey," I called out.

He turned.

I said, "You haven't mentioned a word about my boy."

He said, "Kid's okay. Just started Little League Tee Ball."

Little League, I thought to myself. I didn't know why it hurt so much to hear those two words. Sure I had a visitation schedule with my son, every other Saturday afternoon and every Tuesday evening for dinner. But it was never enough time together. Harrison, or Bear as I nicknamed him, was going on eight years old. Over the past four years Cain had become a dominant force in his life. All it took was half a boy's life for my former partner to replace me as a stable parent. Suicide, successful or not, was not looked upon with a smile by the New York State family court system.

"How's he doing?" I asked.

Cain sort of smirked, nodding over one shoulder and then the other, as if to suggest *not bad, but not great.* "Kids are awkward at that age," he said. "But he's having fun. I help with the coaching." He looked at his watch.

I took one last sip of the still too-hot coffee and set it back down on the booking desk. My hands felt like they were on fire. I lifted them up to my face and blew on them. That's when I remembered the cuts and scrapes. Abruptly I shoved them back into my jacket pockets.

"There's a kill scene waiting for us," my old partner said.

I exhaled a breath. I just could not get it through my head that Scarlet was dead; just could not get over the nagging possibility that I might have had something to do with it.

8

It's been nearly twelve years since my initial meeting with Jake.

It had been only my second night on the job without having to wear uniform blues. Cain and I had finally graduated to the level of Junior Detective. That night we were called in to participate on a drug surveillance op going down inside the Henry Johnson assisted-housing complex located in the south end of Albany's no man's land, not far out of view of the Hudson River. Or as some cops liked to refer to it, the "Garden of Evil."

Considering that this was our second full day on the job as J.D.s, we were ordered to meet up with Lieutenant Montana. He'd recently transferred from the Troy P.D. and was presently assisting a handful of F.B.I. inside the bed of one of those white unmarked command vans with black-tinted windows—the kind of van that just screams *cop*.

I remember Cain dressed all in black—black sweater, black jeans and sneakers, gray eyes covered in narrow sunglasses. And me, dressed the same way. I remember our having to sit on low swivel chairs because you couldn't possibly stand. We said not a single word while the big mustached Jake announced that throughout the op, all he expected of us was to stand back along the staked-out perimeter and "Observe, observe, observe!"

Our target that early evening was a well-known drug dealer. A young man by the name of Cox who was wanted on a three-hundred grand bench warrant for failure to appear in County Court. Seems he failed to answer to charges for the sale and possession of high-grade heroin and numerous automatic assault weapons, including an entire case of 7.62mm Soviet-made A.K.M.s.

We learned that the Albany P.D., along with the F.B.I., had been looking for Cox for more than three months, but with zero luck. That is until Cox's girlfriend, Rachel—a small, wiry, Ivory Soap-skinned kid of seventeen came forward with information about an upcoming deal. From what we were told, the kid had stood before the monstrous Montana, her right cheek recently black-and-blued from a swift Cox left hook, petite size-two body trembling. She wanted to do the right thing from now on. Or so she insisted. She wanted to get away from Cox, change her life for the better. She wanted to become a "good kid."

Of course Jake applauded the kid's decision to turn her life around before it was too late. But first, he needed her help.

The drugs-for-guns deal was to go down in the broad daylight of early evening inside the subsidized apartment complex. Jake would need Rachel to maintain her role as the ever-loyal girlfriend and lure Cox out into the open, whereupon undercover police would then seize him and his home.

Her nervous consent given, the bait was set.

Two days later Mitch and I were standing beside the white van while a dozen plainclothes cops assumed strategic positions all along the brick and concrete complex. We waited anxiously, our eyes peeled on a narrow two-story unit that was flanked on both sides by identical units, each with their own narrow driveway out front. Parked in the middle of *our* driveway was Cox's black Mercury Grand Prix.

Whispered orders were issued over micro headsets.

Time crawled by.

Hurry up and wait!

Until finally Cox's front door opened and out stepped Rachel.

"I got a positive on the bait and the target," the wiry Mitch Cain spoke into his headset. *The tenacious new J.D. already taking the initiative.*

Rachel seemed to be crying while Cox, a six foot, dark-skinned man of about twenty, followed her. He was dressed in baggy Tommy Hilfiger blue jeans that hung low on his hips, baggy boxer shorts puffed out around his waist. His long black hair was braided, his chest bared to reveal a washboard stomach and what looked to be a 9mm Glock tucked inside the waistband of his jeans.

He was swinging his arms in the air, shouting, "What's the problem now, girl?"

But it was only when the distraught Rachel got into the front passenger side seat of the Grand Prix that I got a solid grip on her M.O. Not only was she attempting to convince Cox of her anger, she was luring the armed drug dealer into his car.

A big brave move for such a small person.

While one radio voice observed that a visual had been made on the suspect, a second voice insisted that the rest of us "stand by."

First came a very abrupt "Now!" shouted over the radio.

Then, with Jake leading the frontal charge, four officers converged on the car—two on the left flank, two more on the right. All five of them faced both the suspect and Rachel. With service weapons drawn, beads planted squarely on Cox's head, the officers screamed their demands for him to "Show your hands; step out and away from the car!"

But within the time it took to issue the order, Cox had already removed the Glock from his pants, raised the barrel up high. That's when the call came over the radio: the suspect had "taken away the initiative."

Gunshots rang out.

The windshield exploded.

Cox's driver's side door opened.

Jake, along with the four cops, dropped down to their knees, combat position. Still armed and apparently unhurt, the suspect managed to throw himself over the trunk of the car where he started across the drive. But he didn't cover twenty feet when Jake caught him in his sights, discharging his weapon. The single 9mm Smith and Wesson round dropped the bail-jumping dealer dead on the spot.

Then another tragedy struck.

As soon as the police proceeded to raid the apartment building, Jake peered into the Grand Prix to check on the condition of his star witness. It didn't take but a second or two to see that she had taken a bullet to the face. Just a well-placed shot that could only have come from head on, from where Jake stood during the apprehension. You couldn't help but see it in his face. Jake's face screamed guilt.

You knew right away that her death rested on his shoulders and his shoulders alone. Didn't matter who truly was to blame or not to blame. My department superior was assigning himself with the responsibility.

I stood back by the white van, feeling numbed from adrenalin still pumping through my veins. Jake approached the passenger side of the car. He slowly opened the door, very gently reached inside, ran his hand over the young girl's wide-open eyes. With his thick hand he gently closed her eyelids.

If it was possible to feel a violent silence, I felt it that morning.

I can't tell you for certain, but I'm pretty sure Jake had to be crying when he made his way over to Cox, where the criminal was lying face-down on the grass, and emptied two more rounds into his back.

Didn't matter that Lieutenant Montana was never accused or formally charged with any wrongdoing. Didn't make any difference that he was instead commended for his actions under fire. But I swear that never once did I see him crack even a single smile from that day forward. It was as if, in the accidental shooting of that young girl, a large piece of his own life had died along with her. No amount of forced vacations or department shrinks could change the way he felt about what he'd done.

No one would catch the wrath of his inner turmoil more than Scarlet. Or so I came to conclude not long after we began sleeping together. But don't get me wrong. It's not like I knew her very well. For as intimate as we got, I never really got inside her. Listen, getting to know her was like trying to dig a deep trench in the sand. No matter how deep you dug, the walls kept caving in on you.

But what she did manage was to reveal little snippets here and there, little details of her life with Jake that provided me with at least a little insight. The fact that they had separate bedrooms in and of itself spoke volumes. But then there were also specific events that also revealed the hell Scarlet lived. Like the time she found Jake sitting in his own bedroom with the lights out, a shotgun laid out across his lap. It wasn't the weapon itself that bothered her. It was the look on Jake's face that made her heart stop. The wide-eyed, unblinking expression that shrieked of resolve. You see, I was no stranger to the expression myself, having become intimate with the resolve of the already dead during my own short madness. But I couldn't help be reminded of the short poem she'd Scotch-taped to the top of a strongbox she kept on her nightstand that read:

Could it be Madness - this?
The world has many ways of fooling us and maybe if the soul is dispensable and love is
a combination of chemicals and electric jolts, it doesn't matter much.

Maybe I didn't know her as well as I might have wanted. But I can tell you this: love mattered a great deal to Scarlet Montana. I think it must have mattered to Jake too. Because if love hadn't been important to them, they wouldn't have fallen to pieces when it suddenly abandoned them. I can bet that in all the years she was married to Jake, Scarlet never lodged a single complaint. Not about his long absences or the drinking or the violence.

Not about Jake's perpetually lifeless face.

The same lifeless face that now, like a .22 caliber hollow-point fragment, was hopelessly embedded inside my brain.

9

We arrived at the Montana colonial on Green Meadows Lane just a little after three a.m. Three cop cruisers were parked outside. There was also an E.M.S. "Emergency Response" ambulance backed up into the driveway, the light and sirens killed.

A handful of uniformed cops paced the front lawn in what for the moment had become a kind of light mist. There were two who stood all by themselves, hands jammed inside trouser pockets. A couple of others were smoking cigarettes, kicking at the wet grass with the tips of their black shoes. They were whispering to one another, their eyes peeled on us.

The brutal death of the chief's wife must have seemed like one very surreal situation for them. Not the typical crime scene by any stretch of the imagination.

Under normal circumstances, a carnival-like atmosphere almost always punctuated a crime scene, with bright lights and medical emergency people milling about. People giving orders or taking them while traipsing in and out of the residence, the doors to which are usually propped wide open like a barn even on the dreariest of spring nights.

Usually, you see the rapid-fire flashes coming from the forensic cops and their digital cameras. You see the bright white glare of spotlighting that comes from the television news crews and their shoulder-mounted video units.

You can also count on at least four or five newspaper reporters to shove hand-held recording devices in your face while, as a detective, you do your best to examine the dead and the crime scene that surrounds them. Do it without contaminating it.

But as I exited the cruiser, I could tell right away that the Montana C.S. would prove different. Even the curious neighbors were staying away. Or at least having the good sense to keep their distance, hiding under the cover of darkness and stormy weather. But stepping up the blacktopped drive I couldn't help but feel their eyes cutting into my back as each and every one of them looked out onto the action from behind their living room and bedroom curtains.

I entered the residence behind Cain and Joy.

To my left was a living room that was as familiar to me as the backs of my hands. There was a beige L-shaped couch covered in silk throw pillows. The floor was rich dark hardwood. On the opposite side of the room was a large walnut cabinet that contained a flat-screened plasma TV, a CD player and a DVD player. Behind the cabinet, the wall was covered in original artwork. Big colorful modern pieces. Expensive pieces you would not expect to find inside a cop's house. Not on cop scratch.

Not even the chief's.

In the far corner of the room, opposite from where I stood inside the vestibule, was a wood and glass case, this one antique. Displayed inside were maybe two dozen mail-order dolls. Not the sort of doll you might catch a little girl playing dollhouse with, but expensive one-of-a-kind dolls. Living dolls ... miniature porcelain sculptures with chiseled features and gowns made from expensive fabrics.

From where I stood, I could make out the familiar limited-edition Barbie beside a doll that was supposed to mimic Madonna. Not far down the line another doll had been ordained with a gold tiara, a furry robe and a gem-ornamented sepulcher. A Princess Diana memorial doll for certain. Displayed beside her was a baby blue statue of the Virgin Mary. The Holy Mother's eyes were just as lonely and still as those of the surrounding dolls, and as lonely and still as those of the auburn-haired woman who, until only a few hours before, had owned and cared for them like the children she never bore.

That childless house spoke to me in the eyes and faces of all those lifeless dolls. It spoke to me in a way it never had before. Sure, it was not a happy place. But then, it was more than that too. As I stared into the living room where only a few hours before a very alive Scarlet lay on her stomach on the floor (me kneeling over her), visions of the night shot through my brain like a video on fast forward.

Scarlet lying naked on the bed, blowing smoke rings up to the ceiling ...

Scarlet crying real tears only moments after coming to a screaming climax ...

Scarlet sitting up in her bed, a smile on her face while her husband slammed the door off the kitchen ...

Scarlet frowning, jade-green eyes a million miles away ...

Scarlet laughing while I jumped out of bed, trying desperately to get into my clothes ...

Crazy moments; insane memories.

So maybe this wasn't the first time I had entered the Montana castle, but I had to pretend that it was.

Cain and I climbed the stairs up to the second floor.

Once at the top, he stopped and turned. Slate-gray eyes cut into my own dark brown ones. Behind him, a bathroom. To his left, the second floor hall and the four bedrooms that shot off of it, including Scarlet's.

From where I stood I could see that the bedroom was well lit.

My cut-up hands buried deep in my pockets, I said, "Why you so sure this is a suicide?"

Cain ran the fingers on his right hand over the stubbly hairs on his chin.

"No forcible entry," he said.

Fair enough, I thought. But the response might have been scripted.

I took a step forward inside that narrow second-floor corridor. Out of the corner of my right eye, I made out Scarlet's bare feet where they rested on the edge of the queen-sized bed. They looked like mannequin feet to me—pale, plastic, dead still. For the first time since my rude awakening in the middle of the night, the reality of Scarlet's death lodged itself like a brick inside my stomach. These were not the same feet that had rubbed passionately up against me just a few hours ago. These appeared to be the feet of a stranger.

A dead nobody.

I felt my hands in my pockets. I would have to reveal them eventually. I would have to pull them out of their hiding places.

"Let me ask you something, Mitch," I said. "Is it more accurate to say that no forcible entry has been found, or that no forcible entry has been found *yet*?"

He bit his bottom lip.

"Whole house has been searched and searched again," he responded, eyes half on me, half on the open door leading into Scarlet's room. "By all means, check for yourself."

So what if no forcible entry was found?

Was it possible for me to have lifted a key from Scarlet's bedroom during the course of one of our "massages?"

Of course it was. She wanted to give me a key on more than one occasion. But I'd always refuse on the grounds that this was Jake's home, too. But was it possible that she had somehow slipped me a key and I might not remember having taken it?

I'd be a liar if I said it wasn't.

The point is this: no forcible entry could mean suicide and it could just as easily mean homicide. Not only homicide committed by me, but also by Jake.

I asked, "How about an E.T.D.?"

Cain quickly shoved the sleeve up on his damp blue blazer, gave his wristwatch a sideways glance.

He said, "One o'clock. Give or take."

I'd made it home by one o'clock. I had gone to bed by then. Was it possible that I might have walked in my sleep during that time, made my way back to Scarlet's, snuck my way upstairs, killed her, then snuck my way back out and back to bed?

No choice but to ignore stupid questions like that.

"I'm ready for the body, Mitch," I said.

Cain turned, stepped into the bedroom and came back out.

"Okay," he said.

The adrenalin began to pump as soon as I walked into that room.

Maybe it was the shocking sight of the body, the destruction to the chest and neck, the blood, the still wide-open eyes, the disheveled hair. Or maybe it was the sight of that bedroom window. The same window I climbed out of earlier, my sneakers in my hands. It went through my mind that somebody could have already checked for footprints outside in the soft grass.

Thank God for the rain, I thought. Maybe the heavy rain would erode the prints.

But then again, I reminded myself, that other than sleeping with Scarlet, I hadn't done anything wrong. At least, other than the wounds on my hands, there was nothing to suggest I had anything at all to do with her death.

Why, then, was I so nervous?

I'll tell you why I was nervous.

Because if my fellow officers—not to mention Jake and Cain— found out I was sleeping with Scarlet, they could then implicate me in her death. That is, the suicide turned out to be a homicide. Didn't matter if I had murdered anybody or not. It was the accusation of murder that would make me appear evil in the public eye, that is, once the media got a hold of the story.

That was my overriding problem—avoiding a false accusation.

In any case, there was the game and it needed to be played.

"Whadaya waiting for, partner?" Mitch asked. "Do what you think you have to do, and then let's get the hell out of here."

I sucked a deep breath of dead air and approached my secret lover.

10

My immediate priority was to focus, prioritize my examination, even if I was more or less putting on a show. Cain wasn't about to allow me a proper comprehensive C.S.I. like the forensics boys might get if he were to follow S.O.P. Not with the private deal Jake forced me into. Christ, I'm not sure I wanted to do one. The stuff I needed to pick up on—the stuff that would lead either to a conclusion of suicide or murder—would have to be relegated to the naked eye. As far as they were concerned, I had to make it look like I was going through the proper motions. As far as *I* was concerned, I had to make sure that any homicidal evidence I uncovered did not lead directly to me.

The second goal was to extinguish any torches I still carried for Scarlet; ignore any potential outward signs of anxiety that might give away my personal involvement with the deceased.

It wouldn't be easy.

Not with the low- to medium-velocity blood spatters that stained the baby blue walls and windowpane above the bed. Not with the blood that soaked the mattress, pillow and down comforter. Not with the odor, the sickly sweet smell that filled the twelve-by-fifteen foot bedroom, telling me that Scarlet had definitely entered her second hour of death.

I approached the bed, feeling my feet shuffle across the surprisingly clean carpeting as though in slow motion.

This was not the same woman I'd caressed with my oil-soaked fingertips just hours earlier. Now the human *she* had become an inhuman *it*.

I had to believe in that one distinction if I was going to get through the procedure without passing out. She'd become a soulless shell with a thick, blood-encrusted gash that ran from ear to ear, and numerous puncture wounds marring her bared chest.

This was a body that once belonged to a beautiful woman with wide open eyes, the whites of which were slowly fading to gray, the pupils fully dilated, the head cocked unnaturally to the left, the mouth slightly open in the right-hand corner as if she were about to issue one of her wry smiles.

Cain came back into the room, stepping up behind me. He pulled a cigarette from out of his left breast pocket—slid it out without having to remove the pack. Professional smoker that he was.

I stared down at the horizontal and vertical hesitation slits carved into Scarlet's chest and stomach; at the puncture wounds; at the blue-tinted legs now marbleized with jagged purple and red spider veins. Then a second glance at the window before quickly about-facing to examine the doorjamb behind me.

"You're right about one thing," I said. "No sign of a break-in."

I took a cursory look at the room furniture ... the unbroken table lamp, the tidy table still with its prescription bottle of Ambien and a glass of what appeared to be water, but what I knew had to be Stohly. There was the neatly placed strong box that I had been forbidden to touch, the poem taped to its cover. I found myself once more gazing down at those typed words:

The world has so many ways of fooling us ...

My eyes shifted to the title, *Could it be Madness - this?*

I thought to myself, *Just look at all that madness spattered all over the fucking wall.*

"No sign of a struggle," Cain said, before popping the cigarette into his mouth, unlit.

"Not so much as a footprint or a smear," I added while once more gazing over the tan carpeting.

"A clean scene, Gene," Cain agreed, lighting up the smoke with a silver-plated Zippo. "A clean scene-a-reno."

"Maybe too clean," I said to myself. "We'll need Luminal for prints and smears, and scrape for fibers."

"Not necessary," Cain said.

Joy appeared inside the open door. Cain handed him the still-lit, partially-smoked cigarette.

"Would you mind?" he asked.

I had to wonder where Jake disappeared to. Or maybe "disappeared" wasn't the right word for his obvious absence. Under normal circumstances, he would have remained on site to answer questions.

But these were no ordinary circumstances.

This dead woman was no stranger. She was Jake's own wife and, right or wrong, that was explanation enough for his absence. I knew that the last place he'd want to be seen was here. I knew that the last thing Cain wanted was for me to demand an audience with him. But then, under the circumstances, it would have been the right thing to do.

Joy nervously took the smoking butt into his fingertips, proceeded to carry it down the hall as if it were a lit bomb.

My head was beginning to pound inside its core.

I asked Cain if I could get a drink as I raised my right hand, grabbed hold of it with my left, pinched the feeling back into the flesh and bone.

I opened up the top middle drawer on the large wooden chest pressed up against the far wall, rummaged around the underwear and socks. Maybe by pretending to do some real detective work I might distract myself from having to look at Scarlet and from going into another seizure.

Cain asked, "Hard or soft kind of drink?"

I closed the drawer and proceeded to rummage through the other five, not searching for anything in particular, just giving my hands something to do, my eyes a distraction from my lover's massacred body.

"More coffee," I breathed. "And Advil."

Cain had to chuckle.

Arms outstretched, I steadied myself against the dresser of drawers, regaining my balance.

Joy came back into the room. He was wiping wet hands off on his blue trousers.

Cain turned to him as I finished up the last drawer. He spit out an order for two large blacks, a small bottle of Advil and a pack of Marlboro Lights. He reached into his pocket, pulled out a considerable bankroll, peeled off a twenty, and handed it to the young cop.

He said, "Bring me back the change."

The baby-faced rookie never uttered a single word of objection, even though he'd have to find a place open in the middle of the night in Albany. The town that always sleeps. A Stop-and-Shop maybe. Or a Seven-Eleven.

I turned, breathed in the smell of death once more.

It was while walking back towards the bed that I noticed it. On the floor, rolled up under the box spring, almost entirely hidden by the bed stand. The gray t-shirt that I had worn to Scarlet's just a few hours before.

"You gonna make your evidence search of the body or what, old partner?" Cain asked.

I looked over my shoulder. His back was turned to me while he returned the bankroll to his pants pocket. I never hesitated. I just walked over to the bed, went down to my knees, grabbed the t-shirt, and stuffed it into my jacket.

God willing, no one the wiser.

With heart beating in my temples, I pulled a pair of green rubber gloves from the right-hand pocket of my leather jacket, yanked them on. Then I leaned over Scarlet's body, brought my face within inches of her face.

Reaching out, I touched her tender lips, as if for the very first time.

11

"So these screw-heads put you in the middle of a pretty bad situation," Stocky Agent says. "If you refused the job, you knew they'd come after you. Maybe even with some kind of evidence that would incriminate you; something that would prove you had sex with Scarlet only an hour or two before the hack job that killed her. But then, if you took the job you knew you'd have to lie for them." Eyes wide. "Double-fucking-whammy ... if you'll excuse my French!"

I nod as if to agree. But then just as quickly, I shake my head like I'm disagreeing.

"Yes and no," I say. "Yes, meaning they put me in a bad situation. Yes, they wanted me to do what they told me to do. But at that point, they had no idea that Scarlet and I were intimate."

"So as of that point you were more or less in the clear," Stocky Agent says. "But they still wanted you to lie for them; rubber-stamp their conclusion of suicide."

"Cain and Jake had been paying me a pretty good buck if I did what they told me to do."

"By being a bad cop; by going through the surface motions of an investigation with the intent to issue a bald-faced lie on their behalf."

"I didn't know I was lying for them."

"How can you not know, Moonlight? They told you what to put down in your reports?"

"They issued directives, told me what they expected from me. Time was always tight, so I carried out their orders, quick and painless."

"Nice work if you can get it."

"I've got half a bullet in my brain and divorce debt up to my eyeballs. I wouldn't have had any work at all if it weren't for Montana or Cain."

"Cain's married to your ex-wife and yet you still took work from him."

"Maybe you find this hard to believe, but I never held a grudge against Mitch Cain for what happened between him and Lynn." But then raising up my hand I added "Correction … didn't hold a grudge for all that long."

"Had there been some trouble in paradise, Mr. Moonlight?"

"Lynn and I were over before my affair with Scarlet started; long before she started sleeping with my partner. It was only a matter of time until it broke down the way it did. 'Course, I would have preferred that the breakdown did not include my partner. But by then it was out of my hands."

"Had Lynn wanted out of the marriage while you were still living with her?"

"She'd been threatening me with divorce since the birth of our boy. I just ignored her. She, in turn, gave in to Cain … if you know what I mean."

"Yeah, I know all too well," Stocky Agent laughs. "And in that search she found your partner at the A.P.D. Shit, Moonlight, it all must have driven you a little nuts—the good partner and old friend now becomes the wife's squeeze. Maybe even drove you over the edge."

I try to swallow. But there's nothing to swallow.

"Something like that," I say.

"But you still didn't blame Cain. In fact you willingly took him up on the jobs he offered you as an independent corroborator."

"It was strictly business. I did the jobs and in turn, he gave me the cash I needed to survive."

"By being the human rubber-stamp," Stocky Agent says while his thin partner merely stands on the opposite side of the room, listening, witnessing.

"I never found much reason not to corroborate their reports," I say. "Until Scarlet died, of course. It's then I decided that for once in my life I was going to stick to S.O.P."

"With your lover dead, you couldn't just maintain your status quo with Montana and Cain, do what they told you to do?"

"How could I in all good conscience? If I went along with the suicide just because they wanted me to, then where did that leave Scarlet? Where did it leave her memory? Her life? And what if there really was a murderer out there? Somebody capable of cutting up a beautiful woman? What if that killer really turned out to be her husband? No amount of money could make me turn my head on something like that."

Stocky Agent pauses for a moment, as though to chew on my words. I see his Adam's apple bobbing up and down in his thick neck. I guess my words are none too easy to swallow.

"So it's at this stage you make the transition from simply being the rubber-stamp on the investigation to a real decision maker."

"The major decision being to investigate per S.O.P."

"Now let me get this straight," he continues. "They wanted you to sign off on a suicide, but they had no suicide weapon."

"Here's this brutally cut-up woman whom I had only just slept with. She's supposedly cut herself up bad and yet, where's the blade? She didn't just get up, wash it off, return it to the drawer, get back in her bed and die."

"Could it be that her husband disposed of it?"

"I could only assume he took it, did something with it. Hid it, or got rid of it."

"Which would point to him as a murderer … potentially."

"Or as somebody who was so upset at the sight of his mutilated wife, he just had to dispose of the means of the mutilation."

"People do fucked-up things at fucked-up times. Isn't that right, Moonlight?"

Stocky Agent raises his right hand, makes like a pistol with forefinger and thumb, presses the pretend barrel against his temple. When the thumb falls, he mouths the word "Boom."

I smile, but there's nothing to smile about.

"Listen, I could have done exactly what they wanted me to. But how could I live with myself after that? I'd slept with the deceased. My semen was inside her. I'd left residual evidence lying around the house.

Not just fingerprints, but footprints on the back lawn. Christ, I was lucky enough to find my t-shirt before they did. Who knows what they would have found just by taking a close look at the bed sheets. Hair follicles, DNA, who knows what else."

"But this wasn't all about you," the agent says, voice raised an octave or two. "Just like your old pal Cain said, you did go ahead and grow a conscience."

Stamping out my cigarette, I sit back in my chair, look directly into the face of the agent. In my right hand, the pins and needles begin taking over once more until I grab hold of it with my left.

"I was having a hard time accepting the fact that Scarlet would kill herself, let alone self-mutilate her body with a razor or a kitchen knife or however it was done. Plus I knew Jake and Mitch were not beyond manipulating a crime scene to suit their own purposes."

The agent's face lights up. He busts out laughing.

He says, "Corrupt fucking cops. Well there's something different."

"Listen," I say, "she wasn't just another dead body. She was no rapist or drug dealer who was about to tie up a court system. Scarlet was a nice, lonely kid."

"You'd grown attached to her?" A question the agent poses just when he's beginning to calm down.

"Not attached," I exhale. "But then not unattached either. I cared for her a lot. More than a lot. But she deserved better than what the head cops wanted to give her, whatever their motive. As the independent field man in charge under Cain's thumb, I knew I had at least some opportunity to control three things: first, keeping my name cleared of any and all false charges."

"Second, Mr. Moonlight?"

"Finding out just who or what might have been responsible for her killing. Even if, in the end, I had no choice but to call it a suicide. Just like the bastards wanted."

"And finally?"

"By destroying any evidence that might prove the unthinkable."

"What's the unthinkable?"

"That I killed her and for some reason, couldn't remember any of it."

12

On the ride back to my house, Joy drove the cruiser so silently and cautiously it was as if the road was paved with eggs. In return I sat in the back seat feeling somewhat like the scolded child, running through the events of Scarlet's physical evidence examination over and over again in my mind.

Sitting there with the rain once more coming down steady and hard, I relived the whole thing in my brain. Placing the tips of my Latex gloves to her cheeks, gently brushing the still warm flesh. I recalled how the facial skin turned purple where I touched it, the distinct imprint of my fingertip left behind where the dermis blanched, recalled how the sudden discoloration returned to its natural pale, consistent with the shock that always accompanies massive hemorrhage. I swear I could still smell her sweet, oil-perfumed skin—the sheen from the liquid still visible beneath the blood trails and spatter.

A dead body loses an average of a degree to a degree and a half of its heat per hour. In this case, it told me Cain hadn't been all wrong with his E.T.D. I had conducted the examination (if you want to call it that) at about 3:15. The way I judged it, the body had to have been deceased for less than three hours. Probably no more than two, but definitely no more than three. So between one and two o'clock must have been a fairly good call.

Right hand clutched in left, I looked out the window onto the black, wet night. I saw myself running my fingers down the length of Scarlet's torso. From shoulder to pelvis (avoiding the blood leakage), down along the neck, alongside the rib cage, over the pancreatic region to the hip bone, removing for a moment the bit of blood-soaked bed sheet that covered her sex—pubic hair that looked stark and dark against blue-white skin. I had to look away for a beat or two, gaze instead at the blood spatters that stained the wall. As if this would calm me down.

Ever since we'd entered the house, the bile had been shooting up from my stomach. I had no choice but to swallow it back down.

The whole thing was starting to get to me. Hours before I'd been running these same hands along this very same body, under completely different circumstances. I had been inside her. In a very real way, I was *still* inside her.

When my breathing returned to normal I continued running my hands down the length of her left leg, feeling for any inconsistencies, bumps or bruises that might suggest she'd been beaten. Or maybe bound and gagged, carried into the room not by her own free will.

There was a crucial piece of the puzzle missing.

If I'd had the blade or knife to work with, I could have checked it for prints, latent or otherwise, compared them to anything I might have pulled off the bed frame or the body itself. But Cain was sticking to his story. He told me that Jake had panicked when he found her all cut up. He panicked and disposed of the knife. Where he disposed of it, he didn't know.

That seemed wrong to me. If there was a knife or some kind of razor blade involved, Jake of all people would have been careful to preserve it—to leave it where it lay, untouched. Because if Scarlet had committed suicide as the captain insisted, then it only stood to reason that the blade would have contained only her fingerprints. By disposing of the blade, Jake could have easily turned himself into a potential suspect. In that case, a ruling of suicide would be tossed out.

But then, what about Jake?

Apparently, I wasn't being granted much of an interview. At least no more than I'd already been granted earlier that morning during the drive from my house to the A.P.D.

Jake Montana, my part-time boss.

You don't bite the hand that feeds you. But you might just give it a slight nip once in a while.

Here's how I nipped at Cain: I'm not entirely sure what got into me, maybe it had something to do with my possible involvement in Scarlet's death. Or maybe it had more to do with Jake's possible involvement, but as I raised myself up off the floor and began removing my gloves, I felt a sense of resolve pour over me like the blood that covered my lover's chest. Because at that point I knew for certain that what I was dealing with was a cold, calculated murder.

I directed my gaze at Joy. "Tag and bag her," I said.

Joy turned to Cain, blue eyes gaping open.

"Lieutenant," he said, as if to say *What do I do?*

If this had been a cartoon, Cain's jaw would have dropped to the floor.

He asked, "What are you doing, old partner? You know the score. We just send her on for burial."

"She's got to be cut open before I can make a final decision on your bogus suicide theory," I said. "You know all suicides and homicides go under the knife. And I've got a witness to back me up in my methodology and procedure." I shot Joy a look like *You're it!* "Which means, we've got the lab and toxicology to consider."

Mitch took a step forward, a cup of Seven-Eleven coffee steaming in his right hand.

He said, "Look at her for God's sakes, Moonlight. Look at all the blood. She got drunk out of her mind, cut her own chest open, then finished herself off at the neck. End of story."

He's right. Bury her. Bury the body of evidence. Bury anything that might point to you as a killer.

I said, "Show me a means of death, Mitch. Show me a weapon."

The furrows on Cain's brow were scrunched and deep. His unblinking slate-gray eyes told me he could not believe this was happening.

"Jake panicked, deep-sixed the blade," he insisted. "I don't know where precisely or I'd go get it."

Jake had tossed the very blade that would prove the suicide theory? I wasn't buying it for an instant.

"I want an autopsy, Mitch. I want tox to test for drugs. I want to interview Jake."

"All in that order?" Cain said under his breath. "What if I decide to dismiss you?"

"I go straight to O'Connor," I bluffed.

Cain, nodding, resigned, knowing that for the first time, I was determined to go by the book.

The uniformed Joy, ever in the background, kept his mouth shut, myopic eyes glued to the tops of his shoes. Behind him, two or three A.P.D. cops paced the hall, listening in on our conversation— witnessed it.

"My Lord, Moonlight, you been reading too many mysteries in your spare time."

"I'm just trying to do the right thing."

"Maybe you should think about it this way," Cain added. "Whose side is I.A. gonna take? A part-timer with a memory problem, or mine?"

"Memory's not the problem," I said. "It's a slightly damaged cerebral cortex; an occasional inability to discern what's right from wrong."

He stepped up to my ear. "A simple case of brain damage," he whispered.

I stuffed the rubber gloves into my old partner's coffee cup and walked out.

13

I spotted Lola's silver Subaru parked up against the concrete curb as soon as we made the corner onto Hope Lane. Consciously or not, I knew that I had been looking for it; looking for her. I knew she must have tried to call the house while I was gone. When she got no answer other than the machine, she must have closed up her lab early and made her way over.

Sometimes I couldn't be trusted.

Five after four in the morning. The rain had stopped once more. The air was damp and cold. It had a ripe, gamey smell to it. Probably from the worms that had washed up onto the concrete sidewalk.

My chest and head felt heavy.

I made my way up the slate stairs that led to the front portico of the split-level. Joy took off, headed south back towards the downtown. I wondered if the kid ever slept. Maybe he was an android.

The bile was still bubbling inside my stomach.

Now that I was alone with the night sky, I could plainly feel it. Nausea, sneaking up on me.

Once inside the house, I knew I was going to lose it.

I bolted through the vestibule into the bathroom off the kitchen. I dropped to my knees and retched. All of it was coming out of me. My fear, my confusion. My guilt for what had happened to Scarlet, for denying our past together, for my bolting the scene instead of standing by her side, standing up to Jake. I was sick and sad for her life *and* her death. I was sick and sad that I might have had something to do with it.

I reached into my jacket pocket, pulled out the bloodied t-shirt, wiped my mouth. Some of Scarlet's blood got onto my tongue. The taste of her blood made me sick a second time.

The blood of a woman who was both dead and alive for me.

When I was empty, I tossed the shirt into the dirty laundry hamper under the counter. Then I rinsed my mouth out in the sink. The taste would not go away. I feared it would stay with me forever, like the memory of her touch, her smell, her smile, her soft auburn hair. After a time, I went back to the front door and bolted the lock.

Rather than call up to Lola, I stood at the bottom of the stairs. I listened for the sound of her breathing. It was impossible to hear anything. I pictured her curled up in my bed, long black hair covering the side of her long face, full lips trembling gently as she slept and breathed.

Lola Ross, the psychologist assigned to my case file after my accident.

She'd been assigned on recommendation by my Council 82 Union rep up in Albany to work in close contact with both my New York City neurologist and my local general physician in order to ensure that my brain—such as it was—functioned properly. Or, as properly as could be expected considering the constant threat of occasional blackout, memory loss and/or lapse in judgment. There was only so much that could be expected from white and gray matter that had a bullet frag lodged inside it.

I went back into the kitchen, pulled a clean coffee mug from out of the dishwasher and the bottle of Jack from the wall-mounted cabinet above it. I sat myself down at the kitchen table, poured myself a shot and drank it down in one swift swallow. Then I poured another with the intention of sipping it.

I decided then to try and make some kind of sense out of what had happened last night.

I thought about two different Scarlet Montanas. The first one alive and sexy, kissing me with a full, soft mouth. The other lying naked, flat on her back, throat cut from ear to ear, chest bearing puncture wounds and scrapes.

The first thing I had to do was get it out of my head that I had played a part in Scarlet's killing. What I had to do was relegate my paranoia to ... well ... paranoia. If I didn't start looking at Scarlet's death as a murder somebody else had committed, then I would lose the one chance I had for finding out who the real killer was and how he or she could have done such a thing to such a sweet girl.

Who the hell could have mutilated her if she hadn't managed it herself?

Where was Jake through this whole thing and why wouldn't Cain let me talk to him if they didn't have something to hide or, on the other hand, they didn't have something on me?

Where had the weapon of death gone? Had it just disappeared? Could I possibly trust Cain when he told me that Jake had somehow disposed of it in all his grief?

If Cain wanted me to rubberstamp what obviously required a full police investigation, what the hell could he be covering up?

Questions but no answers.

I did have whiskey.

At times like these, sometimes whiskey was all the answer you needed.

I drank down what was left in my cup, poured one more shot and drank it down. I felt the smoky-tasting liquid coat the back of my throat, trickling down my insides like Mother's medicine. I hoped it would erase the taste of blood in my mouth.

No such luck.

The truth of the Scarlet Montana matter was this: without an opportunity to open her up, I wouldn't know a goddamned thing. Sure, they could go to another dick to corroborate their suicide conclusions. But that might be too risky for them at this point.

I'd already been witness to too many things. They had no choice but to work with me. In turn, maybe I could control the situation for Scarlet. For me.

Whether I followed their rules of engagement or not.

14

Dawn.

I slipped into bed beside Lola, spooned against her, felt her smooth warm skin against my own. I ran my hand down her smooth leg and leaned into her. Maybe we weren't lovers yet, but we had something between us, Lola and me. A trust, a bond. Not that we had to keep our relationship a secret, but she was risking her livelihood by sleeping with me in the same bed. Even if nothing sexual was going on (we were still wearing our underwear!) she'd been there for me—for my head—ever since my accident. We'd developed an attraction. No, that's not right. It was more than an attraction—a kind of symbiosis, like two puzzle pieces fitting together. What we didn't have together was precisely what Scarlet and I had, a sexual relationship.

For now ...

Abstinence, or so Lola claimed, was the one thing that would make our friendship last.

She rolled over and smiled.

"I was worried," she said. "You didn't return my phone calls."

"Jake and Cain called me in."

"Did you eat?"

"I think so."

"Why did they call you in?"

I told her why.

When I was through it was almost full light out. Some of the gray-filtered daylight leaked in around the drawn blinds. Maybe Lola and I were just friends on our way to becoming something more serious, but then sometimes friend-to-friend honesty can still be a real bitch, because she didn't offer up anything in response to my night with Scarlet—before her death and after. No opinion about my apparent lack of control; my decision to do the wrong thing by once more sleeping with someone as vulnerable as Scarlet.

Nothing. Because my right mind, it's not always right.

But then it's not like she up and walked out on me either.

Instead, in typical Lola fashion, she just rolled back over onto her side, facing the opposite direction.

"This is why we don't have sex," she whispered.

Quietly, she got out of bed, put on one of my robes, and went downstairs to make the morning coffee.

15

In my dream I see her.

She is as real to me as she was last night. Flesh and blood and that soft auburn hair.

She comes to me where I'm lying in my bed. She is naked, but no longer cut up or scarred. She bends over, kisses me gently on the lips.

She says, "I'm alive. I'm happy now. I don't need to be rescued."

She turns, disappears …

But then the dream changes.

I'm back inside my kitchen. Outside the big picture window I can make out clear blue sky and leafless trees blowing in a cool wind. Football weather. There's a glass of whiskey set out on the table, the open bottle beside it. Set in between the bottle and the drinking glass are six .22 caliber bullets. But I only need one.

I open the revolver cylinder, slide the single bullet inside, slap the cylinder closed.

I raise the gun up to my head, press the barrel against my right temple, cock back the hammer. I feel my body trembling, the tears running from my eyes, down my face, and dripping off my chin. There's a beautiful red robin perched outside my window. I'm staring into its black eyes. I smile. I begin to squeeze the trigger. But that's when I see the face of my boy. My grip loosens. The pistol begins to drop from my hand at the exact moment the hammer comes down …

When I woke, I thought I heard the rain. But I was mistaken. The shower was running.

Short, sharp rivulets against the old glass-enclosed shower stall in the bathroom. I looked at the empty space that once contained Lola. Now just a dented pillow and a rumpled sheet.

Is there anything lonelier?

I sank down further into the bed, closed my eyes, and tried like hell to fall back to sleep.

It was nearly mid-afternoon by the time I woke up.

I needed my sleep. Doctor's orders. I needed my exercise too. Also doctor's orders.

The running and the weights would have to wait until that night, however. Half the day was already gone.

I was feeling more awake by the time I stepped out of the shower, wrapping a towel around my waist. A few minutes later I was downstairs in the kitchen, washing down a vitamin and an anti-inflammatory with cold orange juice. I mixed my protein shake while sipping on a cup of hot coffee. Decaf.

After downing my shake, I opened the front door to retrieve what had been the morning paper. Maybe the sky was still overcast, but it was impossible not to see him - the white-skinned man standing at the foot of my driveway. A whiter-than-white-skinned man dressed in black jacket, pants and boots. He wore sunglasses as if to protect his eyes from the sun on a rainy day. He looked at me from across the lawn and smiled.

There was a blue Toyota Land Cruiser parked behind him, the engine still running.

I bent over in my towel, feeling the chill in the afternoon air, and picked up the paper. Not knowing what else to do, I smiled back at him.

Then he did something that took me by surprise.

He lifted his right hand and, making a gesture like a knife with extended index finger, ran it across his neck. From where he stood at the foot of the driveway, I could hear him laughing.

I didn't waste a second. I ran back inside, tossing the paper onto the vestibule floor.

Up in the bedroom I found my loaded Browning Hi-Power 9mm in the drawer of the nightstand.

By the time I made it back outside the strange-looking man was already in his car, speeding north on Hope Lane towards the interior of the development.

Hope is shaped like a horseshoe.

I knew there was a chance I might intercept the son of a bitch as he exited the opposite southeast side.

I was dressed in a bath towel, no shoes. I had to hold the towel tight around my waist while I ran along the main road, Browning out front, all the time the wet gravel cutting into my heels and soles.

In the end I wasn't even close.

In the time it took me to cover half the distance between my house and the other side of the horseshoe, the Toyota was already making its way due east along the main road.

I stopped, sucked in a deep breath and passed out.

16

When I opened my eyes, the first thing I noticed was that the blue Land Cruiser was pulled up alongside the road. The second thing I noticed was that the pale-skinned man was standing directly over me. He must have seen me fall to the pavement; must have caught sight of me in the rearview. He was kneeling over me, maybe to get a closer look at my face. I was trying to raise up the Browning and aim it at him. But my right arm was dead.

The albino man dropped down on one knee. He was wearing dark aviator sunglasses, even on a cloud-filled day. He was a man with a bald head, red lips and tongue. Kneeling there, he coughed up a wad of phlegm and spit it out onto the narrow strip of gravel-covered shoulder.

When I worked up the strength to talk, I asked him who the hell he was, why he'd been standing outside my house. He just raised an index finger and pressed it to pursed lips.

"Shhh," he smiled. "Try not to talk, yes?" He spoke heavily accented English.

From where I lay, I could see that his black t-shirt was sticking out of his pants, his jacket pulled back. It was hiked up above his waist, exposing a jagged purple scar along his left side, just above the hip bone. I guess he noticed me noticing him, or his grotesque scar, anyway, because his face suddenly went stone stiff. Reaching down, he picked up my Browning. My hand lifted up along with it. When he let go the whole thing just slapped back down to the ground.

A car went by and then another. The second one slowed down a little as it passed, but then sped up again. The albino man stood up, brushed off his knees.

"You do what you are told, yes?" he said.

Then without another word got back in his ride and burned rubber.

What the hell was happening? Who the hell was the albino man? Was it possible he was Scarlet's killer? Or was he simply some creep I helped put away a long time ago? You never knew in my business. Criminals were paroled. You couldn't fight the system. But then, I think I would have remembered somebody that white; somebody that creepy; somebody carrying that kind of shark-bite scar tissue on his side. Maybe he was a hatchet man hired by Cain or Jake to keep me in order. But that didn't make any sense either. Jake had no reason to threaten me with anything. I was the one man he was counting on to do what he wanted me to do.

There and then I made the decision to start packing my Browning again.

I had been pretty bad about it since my accident. Carrying it only when absolutely necessary, especially in light of my permit being revoked. Even the cops wouldn't allow a man in my condition to carry a loaded firearm. On the record, that is.

Off the record, they insisted that I carry it. Still, I felt better sometimes without it. I don't know why I should feel better, especially when my line of work involved the occasional shoot-or-be-shot. I suppose it all had to do with the death thing. Rather, the proximity of death. As for me, I might have felt healthier than an ox, but with every minute of every day I could see, taste and smell my death as if it were being hastily prepared for me by some higher authority.

A bullet fragment was lodged in my head.

The doctors had assured me that one day the fragment was going to shift and leave me brain dead. Or just plain dead. That would be the day that Moonlight falls for good. That was my reality. It was also my son's reality whether he knew it or not.

Lifting myself up off the damp ground, I breathed in deep and felt the life return to my right arm. A car went by. It was full of kids.

High school kids. They yelled something out the window and whistled. I tightened the towel around my waist, about-faced and began my half-naked march back home.

For now anyway, Moonlight lives.

17

Back inside the kitchen I washed my hands and face, picked out some excess gravel from my knees, the mud from my feet and dried myself off with a dish towel. For a while I just leaned myself against the counter and took a nice quiet breather. I waited for my pulse to slow, my temples to stop throbbing.

When I felt sufficiently calmed, I popped another anti-inflammatory as a precaution and a couple Advils for the inevitable headache that was sure to set in. While doing my best to remove the white pink-eyed image of the albino man from my head, I poured myself a coffee at an hour of the day when I might have been having my first beer.

First I pushed away the mail that had been piling up for some days now. Overdue bills, circulars, catalogues, credit card applications. I spread the *Albany Times Union* newspaper onto the counter between the sink and the telephone and searched for a headline.

I didn't find one. The one I wanted, that is. Big surprise.

What I did find as I freshened my coffee was a small quarter-column that appeared just below the police blotter on page three of local section B, immediately above the five-day weather outlook (rain for the duration). A little sidebar piece penned by crime reporter Brendan Lyons that described what looked to be an apparent suicide by A.P.D. Captain

Jake Montana's wife, Scarlet. The captain discovered the deceased early this morning, said the piece.

I drank some coffee and sighed out loud inside the empty kitchen.

Naturally I couldn't help but feel cheated by the lack of attention and accuracy given to the matter. But like I already pointed out, I wasn't the least bit surprised by it either. What's more, I knew that the story's lack of accuracy or prominent placement had nothing to do with Mr. Lyons. Almost certainly it had to do with an editorial staff who took their orders from much higher service sidearm-toting A.P.D. authorities.

Didn't matter how much dough the publisher was worth; how much political pull he had. Freedom of the press was not necessarily free in these matters. Not when the cops were your friends.

The article went on to state how the thirty-eight-year-old Montana was pronounced dead on the scene as the result of self-inflicted lacerations. No mention that the lacerating weapon in question had not been recovered, as if there were no mystery to the fact that a dead woman is pretty much incapable of hiding the knife she used to kill herself.

The piece closed by quoting the officer in charge of what looked to be—you guessed it—an "open and shut investigation," Senior Detective Mitchell Cain.

"What a tragic loss Mrs. Montana means not only to the chief," he eulogized, "but also to the entire A.P.D. family of law enforcement personnel."

So that was it then.

No mention of my independent investigation. No mention of suspicious circumstances. No mention of a potentially white-washed crime scene or that not a soul other than a few select cops had laid eyes on Jake in the past twelve hours.

Nothing.

Other than what they wanted you to know.

I folded up the newspaper and set it down on the kitchen table next to the Browning.

I turned my attention to the answering machine beside the coffee pot and the little red numeral 3 that blinked on and off.

Raising the machine's volume, I hit the PLAY button. The digital recorder beeped, then spat out the first message. Just another friendly collection agency under employ by my lawyer threatening legal action if I didn't start doing something about my divorce debt.

I punched DELETE.

Next caller. Cain requesting that I meet him downtown at the South Pearl Street precinct in one hour.

"Here's your chance to interview Jake, old partner," were his exact words. "Maybe you're right. Maybe we should proceed a little more carefully on this one."

I deleted Cain. But I had to wonder if he was up to something now that Scarlet's body had been tagged, bagged and shipped to Albany Pathology; now that the press had issued their take.

Caller number three. Like the first two, this message had been recorded while I was either still asleep, in the shower, chasing a smiling albino freak in my bath towel, or lying on the roadside in the same ridiculous getup. It was crime reporter Brendan Lyons. With a soft-spoken, almost monotone voice, Lyons asked if I might spare him a minute or two regarding Scarlet's death. He'd heard through a confidential source that I'd been ordered to assist an over-burdened S.I.U. with the investigation. That said, would it be too much trouble if I met him inside the Skybar on the second floor of the Albany International Airport main terminal at five o'clock that afternoon?

Then Lyons read off his cell number.

I grabbed a pen out of the drawer, jotted it down on the Post-a-Note pad as he read each digit off slowly, clearly, the sound of city traffic flying by in the background.

Punching DELETE for the last time, I stood there for a beat and listened to the newly restarted rain as it strafed the kitchen windows above the sink. I wondered what exactly Lyons wanted to discuss with me if he'd already concluded, along with the rest of them, that Scarlet had committed suicide. I wondered who might have revealed my involvement in the investigation.

Definitely not Cain.

The fact that there was even the suggestion of an investigation would have completely contradicted his earlier statement to the press about this case being *open and shut*. Considering that cops have written as well as unwritten laws that limit freedom of the press, I knew for sure that someone had to have blown a whistle. That is, someone thought the situation important enough to blow a whistle. Anonymous or not.

Either way, I knew that, like me, Lyons had to be smelling a rain-soaked rat.

Then I thought about it from another angle.

I was taking a stand; investigating Scarlet's death for real. A purple-scarred foreign albino man was making threatening gestures. So talking to Lyons might not be a bad idea. Having the press on your side was a distinct advantage, because crime reporters were investigators, too. Investigators who reported their unbiased findings directly to the public. I knew that despite his report, Lyons more than likely hadn't concluded anything. In fact, he must have been working on a theory, or theories, regarding Scarlet's death. Theories that more than likely contradicted his own published story. As the independent field dick, I might have been in a position to substantiate those theories, maybe even expose a murderer or murderers.

I folded the little slip of paper in half, slid it into my wallet.

It was 2:30 in the afternoon. If I got dressed quickly I could make it to the doctor and to the A.P.D. in a matter of an hour. Just like Cain wanted.

18

I was driving the old man's Mercedes funeral coach. The big, black gas hog was all that remained of the mortician business he'd moved out of the Hope Lane house when I was still a teenager. It was a shiny black twenty-year-old station wagon sedan that to this day has logged in less than twelve-thousand miles on the odometer. The black monster was the only prize possession he couldn't bear to part with when eventually he retired and sold the downtown shop along with all the caskets, gurneys, pumps, stainless steel instruments, cabinets, scales and foldable carts. A move he made when he realized that the Harold Moonlight and Son Funeral Service operation he'd so envisioned in his head and heart was not about to happen soon, or any time at all, for that matter.

I still smile when I picture the stocky man with his carefully groomed salt-and-pepper hair and meticulously pressed black suits, black leather shoes sparkling from the nightly polishing. I recall the days when the funeral parlor was still housed inside the Hope Lane home and the way the old man politely greeted the mourners at the front door with a solemn but consoling handshake.

How could I forget the gentle piped-in Muzak and the thick, sweet scent of all those colorful flowers that at times covered the entire back wall from floor to ceiling in the viewing room? At night I'd go to bed knowing full well there was a dead body laid out in a casket just a few feet below me. There were no nightmares, no traumas of any kind. I slept soundly, unaware of ghosts and goblins. If there was a thing that went bump in the night, it was just that—a thing that went bump in the night

I recall dad bent over at the waist, frantically ridding the viewing room of my toys only minutes prior to a viewing—say an army of four dozen green plastic soldiers scattered directly below the steel underbelly of an open casket.

"Richard," he'd bark, while stuffing the army men into his jacket pockets, "we have a family on their way."

The work that took place in the embalming room just off the downstairs on the first level of the split-level home never bothered me. I even got a kick out of accompanying my father to the hospital morgue on the occasional Saturday morning when a body required retrieval.

You might say that living with the dead became a way of life for me from the moment I was born, which made it something I did not fear. But when it came time to decide on a career, I insisted on going my own way.

Around the time I entered the police training academy in Albany, my father sold the Harold Moonlight Funeral Home to another family operation by the name of Fitzgerald. What I never knew at the time was that Dad's sudden weight loss was attributable to pancreatic cancer. When Fitzgerald prepared my father for burial they dressed him in one of his black pinstriped suits and his famous polished leather shoes. They did his hair and then planted a white carnation on his lapel, just like he wore when hosting a viewing. When I was granted a moment alone with him, I knelt at the velvet-covered kneeler and looked upon his formerly stocky body, now skinny and gaunt, his old suit now too large for his ravaged frame.

I was reminded of one of the old man's favorite sayings—something he referred to as the Harold Moonlight Funeral Home motto: "We all owe God a life."

With that in mind, I remember smiling sadly as I stood up from the kneeler, leaned into the casket, and kissed my father's forehead for the very last time. Reaching into my pocket, I pulled one the few remaining little green soldiers left over from when I was a little boy. I placed it into the pocket of his suit jacket. Then, stepping away, I closed the lid and screwed the casket bolts secure. Just like he'd taught me.

I pulled into the parking lot outside the brand new offices of Albany District Physicians for my scheduled checkup. On top of having to head out to New York City for a biannual one-day intensive M.R.I. scanning procedure, I also visited my G.P., Mary Ellen Lane, M.D. every other month for a less comprehensive examination.

Inside her private office, the brown-haired, forty-something doctor made me sit up on the paper-covered examining table while she checked my vitals.

"You're a little thin," she commented. "Have you been eating?"

"Exercising and eating," I said. "Per the good doctor's orders."

"Increase your caloric intake," she said. "And that doesn't mean extra beer or Jack."

The women in my life were as different and individual as snowflakes, but in many ways, just as beautiful. If Lola was the cautious one, Scarlet the passionate one, Lynn the spiteful one, then Dr. Lane was the clinical one.

She proved it by asking all the serious questions.

Did I feel any pain, any nausea?

Did I feel exceptionally tired or dizzy?

Had I experienced any bouts of temporary paralysis? The loss of feeling in my extremities? slurred speech?

How was my appetite?

Was I sleeping?

As for my answers: deny the bad, stress the good, as though my present and future health had nothing to do with reality and everything to do with my skill at fooling my doctor. As you might imagine, my condition was not exactly the easiest one in the world to trust. That early afternoon's confrontation with a strange albino man was proof of that. I'd passed out trying to chase him down. Not that I was about to reveal anything about it to Dr. Lane.

But it was for that reason that I required constant observation, even if I appeared perfectly normal. Since the condition was inoperable, there existed the constant and overriding possibility that the bullet frag could shift at any time, especially under times of stress when the blood pumped at supersonic speeds through gray matter veins and capillaries.

So you might say that Lane's job was not an easy one.

Because it wasn't easy, she demanded that I toe the line, maintain my health regimen at all costs. If I just happened to slip into a coma, it would have affected her on a personal level. Not because she would consider it a mistake on her part as an M.D., but because she genuinely cared about me and the relatively fragile state I was in.

I can't say I was the most agreeable patient for her, but I did my best to follow the program. According to Dr. Lane however, sometimes my best just wasn't good enough. Not if I wanted to go on living, that is.

She looked into my eyes with a laser-guided scope and finished by making me follow her index finger from left to right to left again. Nothing difficult about this procedure.

Dr. Lane didn't just limit her examination to the body. She asked other important questions too. Stuff that had to do with the state of my head *and* heart. For instance, she always asked about my son. Had I been spending enough time with him?

Never enough.

Was I still driving that big black monster around?

Sure, why not?

Didn't driving a funeral coach make me feel morbid?

No, it made me feel like Luke Skywalker - *at one with my destiny*!

Changing the subject: was I working?

I told her I was still hoping to get my masseur license soon, and then my personal training certificate. Until then, I was back to working part time for the A.P.D.

Was I working on anything interesting?

I swallowed something hard and bitter when the name Scarlet Montana fell off my lips.

"I read about that this morning," she said, while placing a cold stethoscope to my chest. "Breathe."

I drew in a breath, felt a pressure building behind my eyeballs.

She said, "Not a very common occurrence. Death by self-mutilation. Have you any idea if she was prone to suicidal depression?"

"Her marriage was pretty bad," I revealed.

"Had she been seeing a doctor, a psychologist? ... Breathe ..."

In with the good air, out with the bad. The pressure behind my eyes, it was causing big tears to build.

She removed the scope, jotted something down in her notes.

I thought about her question, thought about the many late-night conversations Scarlet and I had shared at her kitchen table over drinks or in her bed, our heads resting side by side on her white satin-covered pillows. I wiped my eyes, doing it matter-of-factly so that Lane didn't notice.

"I don't know about any doctors," I said. "But I do know she was part of a group of Psychic Fair people. Meet at the St. Pious school gym every Monday."

Backing up a little …

The Psychic Fair group.

I never really gave them much of a thought until Dr. Lane sparked the connection in my brain. I knew that Scarlet met with the group of mystics once a week. She never did a whole lot of talking about them, other than the occasional snippet of information here or revelation there. Like the previous night when I snuck out of her bedroom and she told me "No one dies."

That was the essence of psychic or mystic theory. The body was simply a vehicle for the soul, which remained alive forever. The mystics did not believe in death and neither did Scarlet. I also knew she was without religion, formal or otherwise. That despite a porcelain statue of the blessed Virgin Mary prominently displayed inside her doll case in the front vestibule of the Green Meadows home, she might not have believed in God at all. Or maybe she'd been religious once upon a time, but somewhere along the way had lost her faith. Maybe if I had suffered the loss of a son and a significant other in the same car crash, I too might have chucked God altogether. But it was possible that mystic theory had taken the place of God in Scarlet's life—filled the spiritual void, as it were. That along with all those aging hippies and their long hair, dangling beads and wide eyes peering up at the starry cosmic infinity was her attempt at finding some sort of meaning in a life that had become full of daytime/nighttime suffering.

I peered into Lane's clinical face. Maybe it was just my imagination an oversensitive cerebral cortex, but I sensed without asking that Lane was suggesting I dig deeper into Scarlet's death. Apparently, without offering her official opinion, she was not buying the publicly reported suicide theory either. Without openly acknowledging it, she had handed me a lead.

The Psychic Fair group.

Scarlet met with the group on Mondays at six. Today was Monday. I could meet Lyons and then take a ride on over there. Maybe grab some free coffee and a doughnut while I was at it.

With a straight, expressionless face, Lane told me I appeared okay.

"Keep up the exercise regimen," she added. "Plus your vitamins and anti-inflammatories. No smoking and limit the Jack, and no more than six codeine a day for headaches. Try Advil instead."

I smiled. She knew I liked my Jack almost as much as I missed cigarettes.

"You've been lucky thus far," she said, sliding my file back into the metal cabinet. "Let's keep it lucky."

I knew exactly what she meant. Anyone who takes a bullet to the brainpan, point blank, should be dead.

Well, it hadn't exactly been point blank.

When I changed my mind about taking my life and the pistol began to drop from my hand, the snub-nosed barrel pointed upwards, the discharged round deflecting and shattering against my skull. In that manner I not only botched the suicide attempt, a small piece of the hollow-point bullet still managed to enter into my head and brain.

I got up off the table, slipped on my pants and strapped my shoulder holster around my chest. I pulled out the Browning, slid back the bolt, made sure the safety was engaged. Then I re-holstered the weapon.

Lane shook her head, throwing me a gaze that would have iced over a popsicle. "You're not supposed to be carrying that thing."

What could I say to that? She was balls-on correct.

She shook her head, opened the office door. "See you in two months," she added.

"Not unless I come to you first."

"Come to me alive," she said. "And next time leave the hand-cannon at home or I'll call a real cop."

19

The funeral coach rolled like a big black tank.

I made my way through the 'burbs" due south, in the direction of Montana's office on South Pearl Street. Per direct order. Running fifteen minutes late. But that still didn't stop me from making a slight detour.

I thought maybe, if I timed it right, I might catch my boy as he got off the school bus.

As it turned out, I could not have timed it any better.

The yellow bus was pulling up in the opposite direction, slowly coming to a stop at the edge of the uphill drive, just as I made the curve past the tall pines that surrounded Mitch Cain's property (my former property) directly to my left.

I'm not sure exactly why I did it, or why I took the chance even, but I pulled the Mercedes over to the side of the road, a good one-hundred feet away from the house to remain hidden by the trees.

Heart beating, I located the vaguest image of my son's head and shoulders through the bus's slightly tinted windshield. The Bear was awkwardly making his way towards the front, his little hand waving goodbye to the other kids who were still belted into their seats, a wide smile planted between a pair of rosy red cheeks.

Happy, not-a-care-on-earth cheeks.

My heart was pounding.

It was over four years ago that I tried to take myself out of his life. But then if it hadn't been for his face—his image—I might not have survived. Of course, we never discussed my accident with him; never discussed exactly what daddy had done to have caused the purple hole in the side of his head. We just referred to it as an accident. Even when the little Bear approached me where I lie in the Albany Medical Hospital bed, all he could muster was a kind of curious glance. After all, I had already moved out of the family home, Lynn having taken up with my partner. So the Bear was growing used to me as the part-time dad. Now I was a part-time dad with a hole in his head. Not that the boy didn't love me. But I think that as time wore on I also became more an object of curiosity for him. Just who was this strange man who came into his life every other Saturday? The man with the purple hole in his head who called himself "dad?"

I gripped the steering wheel while I watched the Bear make it to the front of the bus where he offered a wave to the driver, just as the old man opened up the door. I kept a steady eye on him as he descended carefully down the school bus steps, until he landed with both feet on the dusty soft shoulder of the road. For just a couple of seconds I lost him while he made his way around the front of the yellow vehicle in baggy blue jeans and a hooded navy blue GAP sweatshirt.

He looked so small to me.

Lynn appeared then at the top of the drive, dressed up in her hospital whites. She shouted out for the kid to look both ways before crossing.

With backpack sliding all the way down his left arm, he came to the edge of the bus, looked both ways, heaved the backpack up on his shoulder and jogged his way across the road into his mother's arms. I tried to get a good look at his face, but it wasn't easy at that distance.

I threw the transmission back into drive at exactly the same moment the caution lights on the bus stopped flashing and the miniature side-mounted STOP sign mechanically folded back against its side.

Would I ever learn?

I could feel the tears building up again behind my eyeballs just as the bus passed me by and the Bear skipped his way down the driveway to his home without me. I waited there for a full minute or two, frozen beneath the cloud cover. Then I shifted the Mercedes transmission into reverse and backed the black monster around so that it faced in the opposite direction.

If psychologist Lola Ross were to analyze me, she would tell me there existed a distinct pattern inherent in my actions, a kind of Pavlovian action and reaction. Every time I went to visit Dr. Lane for my checkups, I inevitably made the trip back to this house to see my son get off the school bus. And every time I did it, I vowed never to do it again.

20

The mood inside the A.P.D. South Pearl Street station was downright black and blue.

As always, uniformed cops filled the wide-open booking room while ceiling-mounted fans blew stale air down at the tile floor. And as always, the cops were busy filling out reports, answering phones, questioning the newly arrested, fielding complaints. Maybe it was me, but the place seemed a lot quieter that afternoon, a lot more subdued.

Even the Green Street hookers they brought in through the back door and detained inside the Plexiglas cage seemed to be behaving themselves while the entire department tried to make sense of Scarlet's sudden death. Or so I imagined.

Jake's second floor office was no different.

With the wood door closed behind me, the square-shaped corner room screamed silence. The only sign of life was the slight guttural noise Jake made with his throat when he breathed in and out, as if the action were no longer involuntary but somehow forced.

Only three of us occupied the office. Jake, Cain, and me. In descending order of importance.

Jake sat behind his desk, leaning back in his swivel chair at an angle that allowed him to stare out the window onto South Pearl Street two stories down. Glaring at his profile I could plainly see how entirely exhausted and haggard he was, his thick, gray-streaked hair pressed against the back and side of his head like he'd only just woken up. But somehow I sensed he never went to bed in the first place.

"Go ahead and sit," Cain said from where he was seated in front of the desk.

He was wearing his usual blue blazer and tan slacks, no doubt his 9mm tucked under the left armpit. He was smoking.

"You know why we called you in," he said.

I stood instead of sitting. Mr. Independence. Here was my one chance to confront Jake over the odd circumstances regarding his wife's killing.

I said, "Let me get his straight. Now that Scarlet has been delivered to the M.E., you want me to sign and seal a case synopsis attesting to her suicide."

"We're giving you a chance to do this the right way," Cain said while Jake continued looking out the window. "The way you've always done it for us before, Moonlight."

"The way you tell me to do it."

"On the contrary," he said. "We want a full case synopsis, case management analysis, issue and comparison analysis just in the case Prosecuting Attorney O'Connor gets bored and wants to test your findings against information he decides to collect later on down the road. We also want a diagram of the crime scene. As for disposition and collection of the evidence and photographs, we already have those, thanks to forensics. They will of course be made available for you to examine, so long as you initial the bag tags."

By the sound of it, Cain did want me to go by the book. At least procedurally. But my built-in shit detector told me it was Cain's attempt at sugar-coating the process. Which in the end meant that those procedurally required reports he now requested were still going to jive with his and Jake's theories. Or else!

But then a report detailing suicide as the manner of death would exempt me from any and all involvement in Scarlet's death. I should have been happy about their directives. But I wasn't. I could only assume that even under the most severe memory loss situation, I would never be capable of cutting up a woman like Scarlet.

Okay, then what about Jake? What if he was capable of the unimaginable? What if he had killed his wife and now had no choice but to manipulate the formal investigative proceedings?

"I'll want copies enough for everybody," Cain went on. "Everything on department letterhead. After that, we'll need the M.E. to release the body for burial per Scarlet's last will and testament."

"Then you do want me to proceed with an inquiry," I confirmed. "You got a timeline in mind?"

"Initial paperwork by tomorrow night," Cain said. "Two weeks from this very second for the rest of it." He stamped out his cigarette. Smoke poured out of his nostrils.

"What about the autopsy?" I asked.

Cain's smile faded. "Please, Moonlight," he said, "will you just forget about the autopsy? She cut her throat. We're working with you. Now work with us a little."

I approached the desk. I knew the only reason they weren't firing me on the spot was because I already knew too much. I might have given in, in the interest of protecting myself. But then sometimes you have to take risks in life. Do it not for yourself, but for others. In this case, for a woman who was newly dead. A woman who, under different circumstances, I might have taken as my significant other.

"Where's the blade, Jake?" I asked. He stared out the window. "Where's the blade, Chief?" I repeated. "The blade, Jake?"

"Stop your shit!" Cain shouted.

I looked my former partner in the eye. "I'm still a cop," I said. "And this situation is all fucked up."

"What's that supposed to mean?" Cain asked.

"It means Scarlet was murdered and you and Jake are covering your asses. It also means I'm honestly not giving you anything until I get a pathologist to autopsy."

Jake made a fist and slammed his desktop. The shock wave it created blew through me like a jolt of raw electricity. It almost knocked Cain out of his chair.

"What the hell will it take for you to cooperate the way you used to cooperate?" he demanded. "How much more cash?"

I stepped back like some invisible force had shoved me.

Breathing in deep, I said, "This isn't about money."

"Give us the statement we need, Richard," Cain said, pulling yet another smoke from the pack in his pocket and firing it up with the Zippo, "or think about giving up the A.P.D. altogether."

Cain, my old partner and the stepfather to my son, threatening me. As if threats mattered at this point.

I turned my attention back to Jake.

"Let's say I execute the false statement, play the game," I said. "Word leaks out, I'll be the one indicted. I mean for Christ's sakes, Jake, this is your wife we're talking about here. Not some rogue dope pusher we found belly-up in the South End."

"When are you going to finally understand, Moonlight, that you have no choice but to go along?" Cain jumped in.

"A cop always has a choice," I said.

He nodded for a beat. But then he formed a grin. He said, "Considering what you've already done to contribute to Scarlet's ...how shall we say ... already delicate mental condition, I'm sure you'll decide in the end to make the right choice."

I began to feel the floor shifting out from under my feet.

Jake looked at me with pursed lips and eyes at half-mast, as if to say *don't play dumb*. Then he dropped the atom bomb squarely on my head.

"We know all about your affair with Scarlet," Cain said. "We know you two were lovers and we can prove it."

Now, along with the shifting floor, I felt an invisible noose wrapping itself around my neck.

"All proof aside," Jake said in a surprisingly even tone, "we don't have to prove a goddamned thing. I'm the chief of detectives. I'm popular. I just lost my wife. All I have to do is accuse you of being my wife's fuck buddy, just to get the ball rolling."

Cain said, "That accusation could very well make you a suspect. Maybe even the prime suspect. That is if you don't approve our discovery of suicide."

I was still focusing on Jake. He was doing something I should have been expecting all along. He sat far back in his chair, opened the top drawer on his desk, and pulled out a plastic evidence bag. Inside the transparent bag was a beer bottle. Budweiser was the brand. There was something else too: a small plastic bottle filled with oil—a bottle only a masseur might recognize.

Well, I'll be a sad son of a bitch. Not only did I forget to look for the beer bottle inside Scarlet's bedroom (probably inside her waste can), I'd forgotten all about the oil bottle. My brain … my powers of recall … they weren't all there sometimes.

Cain asked, "Do we need to further this conversation, Moonlight?"

Jake reached into his desk once more, pulled out a plain white business-sized envelope, tossed it across the desk. I caught it in mid-air. Flipping open the unsealed lid, I recognized at least fifty fifty-dollar bills.

"Down payment," Jake said. "Now that we're all on the same page again."

I looked at Cain. He inhaled a deep drag of his cigarette, exhaling it through his nostrils. "Told you he'd come to his senses," he said.

"Despite appearances," Jake jumped in, "we are not trying to cover anything up. You're right, Scarlet was not just another drug dealer. She was my wife. We are, quite simply, expediting the process of providing a reasonable explanation for her death, based upon the existing evidence. With your … ah … recent intimate involvement with the deceased I'm sure you'll see to it that we wrap up the case, ASAP."

"Expediting," I said. "In the interest of what?" I felt the weight of the money in my hand and the weight of the plastic bag that contained the oil and beer bottles set out on Jake's desk.

"In the interest of preserving my wife's memory," Jake said. "The Scarlet I married."

The Scarlet he married. Where the hell was the blade he used to cut her up?

Cash deposit or no cash deposit, beer bottle or no beer bottle, proof of my bedding down with Scarlet or no proof, I knew exactly what an official investigation would do to a man like Jake. It would crack open all sorts of boxes that he and Cain might not want cracked. That was my leverage.

So what's a part-timer with a constant headache to do?

He takes a shot.

I opened the envelope once more, counted out twenty-five-hundred dollars. Then I stuffed the packet into the interior pocket of my leather jacket.

"Since it's the truth we all want, I'll tell you what I'm going to do," I said.

I took a few more steps forward, reached across Jake's desk, picked up the handset on the phone, and punched in the number nine. When the outside line clicked over, I dialed the number for the Albany Medical Center, Office of Pathology. The autopsy room. As expected, George Phillips answered. I asked the Albany pathologist (and my father's former faithful employee) if he had the body of Mrs. Montana scheduled for an exam. He said he had her on ice, pending further orders, and that was it. I asked him if I could get a look at her tonight. He said he didn't see why not.

"Off the record," he clarified.

"Not exactly, George," I said, staring at Jake's face. "The A.P.D. has instructed me to submit a thorough report, which I guess kind of makes me your 'pending further orders.'"

"Come on down, little brother," George said, the former smoker's voice reverberating inside the tiled autopsy room.

I hung up, shifted my gaze to Cain.

Judging by the tight red face and bulging eyeballs, I sensed that his blood pressure was just a few degrees short of rapid boil. I'd never seen him so pissed off in my life. But then, never in my life had I seen Scarlet dead. Never in my life had I considered my feelings for her as I had over the past few hours.

"What the hell do you think you're doing?" he demanded.

"Getting at the truth," I said, patting the thick packet that filled my jacket. "In the interest of preserving Scarlet's memory."

I snatched one of Cain's ballpoints from his chest pocket, then ripped a yellow Post-a-Note from one of the pads on Jake's desk. I penned a receipt for the twenty-five hundred large, signed it, dated it and pasted it back on the desktop. Then I tossed Cain's pen back in his lap.

"There now," I said. "It's official. I am currently in your employ to discover the truth and the whole truth behind the death of Mrs. Jake Montana."

"You, my old partner," Cain said, "are flirting with your own premature demise." He could not have made a truer statement.

"My demise can be expected at any time," I said quietly. "With or without you."

"Oh yeah. Suicide."

"No. Accident."

"Leave," Jake said. "Before I throw you out the window."

I smiled and made for the door.

"Hell of a way to treat an employee," I said, my left hand twisting the brass doorknob. "This keeps up, I'll contact the Better Business Bureau."

Cain whipped the pen at the door.

"We are your Better Business Bureau!" he said.

21

Some thirty minutes later I was pulling into short-term parking at Albany International Airport. International ... as in the puddle jumpers that fly to Canada and Mexico. At the video-monitored entrance gate, I rolled down the funeral coach window, snatched the ticket from the automated ticket vendor and parked as close to the U.S. Air terminal as I could manage.

I met up with Brendan Lyons inside the Skybar on the second floor of the terminal. I recognized his face from the black and white portrait printed in the paper beside his by-line. In person he was a tall, slim, somewhat balding man of about my age. He was wearing gray slacks and a black blazer over a pressed, olive-colored button-down. No tie.

A brown, soft leather briefcase sat on the floor by his feet and on the bar was the same morning edition of the *Albany Times Union* newspaper that I'd read earlier.

He'd already started on a bottle of Miller Genuine Draft by the time I walked in at five minutes after five. As we shook I took a quick look over his shoulder at the wide expanse of tarmac visible through the plate glass wall. Outside, a bright yellow turbo-prop helicopter was warming up its rotors, the giant blades spinning mirage-like circles above the sleek craft.

While Brendan got the attention of the gray-haired woman tending the bar, I sat myself down on one of the seven or so available stools. The gray-haired lady asked for my order.

"Bud," I smiled. I took a look around the small bar. We were the only people to occupy the place. "So what's with the airport?"

The reporter grinned, took a drink of beer. "Albany's a small city," he said. "Pretty much no one knows me here ... what I am, what I do. No one expects me to be working an angle if we get to chatting."

The bartender set my beer down atop a paper napkin. I took notice of the nameplate pinned to her purple uniform shirt. *Anna Mae* it said. I drank some beer.

"That what I am?" I asked. "Angle of the day?"

"Scarlet Montana," he exhaled.

"How'd you find out I was working the case?"

He said, "I called around, checked in with a few sources. Finally I got a cop who told me you were brought in to work the case in place of the non-existent Violent Crimes S.I.U."

"What cop?"

"You know the way the news beat works, Mr. Detective."

He was right, but it didn't hurt to ask. Simple fact of the matter was that people on the inside talked. Their motive was almost always personal gain, for greenbacks. But then, there was also the occasional stab in the back, one pissed-off cop to another. I knew he wasn't about to reveal his source and I wasn't about to push the matter.

We both drank some more beer.

"So how can I help?" I asked.

He never bothered to pull out a tape recorder or a steno pad. No pen or pencil. "I am going to make an assumption, Detective Moonlight," he said. "You believe that Scarlet Montana was murdered last night, or else you would not be wasting your time with me right now." He held his breath for a beat or two. "And, you believe that her husband—the esteemed chief of our very own A.P.D.—has everything to do with that murder."

Sure, it had been more or less my theory for the past twelve hours. I'd even been toying with the idea that I might have had something to do with that murder. There was the issue of my hands, after all. The scrapes, cuts and abrasions. But just hearing the word "murder" come from another's mouth made it seem all the more based in reality—a reality as toxic and frightening to me as cancer.

"Look, Mr. Lyons—"

"Brendan."

"Brendan," I said. "All I know is that I was brought in last night on a potential conflict-of-interest situation that Mitchell Cain and Jake Montana thought important enough to warrant my independent attention."

"What could be more important than the mutilation of one's wife?"

I looked into his face. It looked better in the flesh than in the grainy newsprint.

"Scarlet's death was as gruesome as I've ever witnessed in my life," I said. "That includes the bodies my father sometimes took into his funeral home. County reimbursable jobs. Potter's field burials no one else could or would work with." A drink of beer. "I'm no stranger to the dead, Brendan. To just assume that Scarlet had committed suicide . . ." I threw up my hands. "Well, you get the point."

"So you're saying it is murder."

"No, you're saying that," I said. "That hasn't been determined yet. Thus our little friendly conversation in the airport bar."

Lyons made a crooked kissing motion with his lips and nodded.

"I'm not ruling anything out," I said. "I've got the rules of engagement to pursue before I can determine anything."

Lyons bit his lip.

Outside the big picture window, the chopper body came alive as it bounced up and down on the tarmac with its red, blue and white overhead and undercarriage lights flashing on and off. Beyond that, a U.S. Air 737 was taking off on the main north-south runway.

"My guess is that Cain must be having a real fit over your intention to investigate. That is, if you were to really investigate, because naturally, old man Montana has got to be pissing his pants."

"His own wife," I added. "No evidence of a break-in; no murder or suicide weapon, as in a knife or razorblade."

"Montana can probably feel the County Prosecutor breathing down the back of his fat neck. And you know as well as I do that if O'Connor decides to pursue him, then I.A. will follow. They start pulling out cards at random, the whole place will tumble."

"The only thing they have going for them now is a very weak suicide theory and the fact that Albany hardly registers a blip on the world map," I said.

"Right now, Moonlight, everyone is holding their water waiting to see how things are going to play out. Let's face it, those stiffs at I.A. got no more loyalty than the prosecutor's office. Only to themselves, their own advancement. They're all politicians."

"Go figure," I said.

"Go figure," Lyons chuckled.

Anna Mae brought us another round without our having to ask. Either she was a real good barkeep, or Lyons was somewhat of a regular. A little of both, I guessed.

"Okay," he said, "I'm gonna level with you. I've been ordered by my own editor-in-chief to lay off this one."

"Screw the First Amendment," I said.

"Lay off for *now*," he said. "You have any idea what 'lay off' means to a city desk man?"

I pulled back on the beer. "Lay off," I said, picturing a giant red flag in my head. "Lot of that going around lately. Or maybe she's using reverse psychology on you."

"Nah, my editor's a straight shooter. She wants me to lay off, she means lay off. Last thing she wants to do is piss off the cops in this city."

"Could make things difficult for you when those threats start rolling in."

"Reporters need protection, especially investigative reporters who like to dig up the bad news."

We drank for a while.

"Anything else you wanna ask me?" I said after a beat.

He slid off his stool, reached into his trouser pockets, came out with a twenty, and laid it atop the bar.

"I have a small proposition for you."

I finished up my beer, got up off the stool.

"In the course of your independent investigation," he said, "if you should happen upon any evidence of a, let's say, irrefutable nature that would somehow lead to murder, how's about giving me a little heads-up?"

He said it. Exactly what I wanted him to say. "What about your boss?" I said. "Her gag order?"

"A serious journalist has his integrity to think of."

"And in return?"

"You see justice served."

"What more could I want? Moral payola." I held out my hand. He shook it, then bent down and grabbed his briefcase.

"Remember," he said, "irrefutable evidence or this whole thing will be shot. Looks like that missing blade is a good start."

"We're after the same thing," I agreed, just as the giant chopper rotors went full-blast, so loud you could hear them through the soundproof glass.

Lyons started to leave, but then he stopped to look at me.

"Is it true what they say?" he asked. "About your ...head? The bullet is still lodged inside there?"

"A fragment. I try not to think about it much," I lied.

"A.P.D. placed you on disability over three years ago," he said. "Why work at all?"

"TV sucks," I said. "Besides, I'm learning to be a massage therapist and a personal trainer. But I'm also still a part-time cop. And I like a good mystery now and again."

"Death," he said. "Ain't no mystery in being dead."

"I'll let you know," I said, "soon as I get there."

22

Back on the first floor of the terminal, I couldn't help but take notice of the giant television that took up most of the terminal's northwest wall. Actually not a single monitor, but maybe two dozen digital flat-screens joined together to form one giant electronic display.

The giant T.V. had been tuned to one of the local news channels. They were running a kind of photo montage of Scarlet Montana. From what I could tell, the montage was intended to tell the story of her life through pictures, beginning with when she was just a kid growing up in what I knew were the suburbs of west L.A., to her graduation from a Santa Monica high school, to her commencement from UCLA. There were photographs of her working with disadvantaged youths in Albany's south end and even a photo taken of her and Jake as they walked arm in arm down the church aisle on their wedding day.

No photos of Scarlet drinking herself to sleep.

No photos of the child and husband she lost to a fatal head-on collision.

No photos of her and I having sex.

But there she was again, alive, bright eyes looking out at me from a candid snapshot taken during her high school graduation, donning white cap and gown, clutching a rolled up diploma tight to her chest. She had a future to look forward to.

But then suddenly the smiling face was replaced with a video clip of a filled body bag being pulled out the back end of a black Chevy Suburban and set on a gurney for the ride through the rear doors of the Albany Medical Center morgue.

With the sound muted, I had no way of telling just what was being reported about Scarlet's death, although I knew it couldn't be that different from what Lyons had reported this morning.

Then I saw my own face plastered up on the screen.

The transmission had shifted from the photo montage to the television anchor. Broadcast up on the right-hand corner of the screen, beside the anchor's face, a photograph of me.

The broadcast photo was one I remembered well. It had been taken not long after I'd earned my detective's badge. A nice, professional-quality picture of my clean-shaven image sporting a full head of thick black hair. I was standing in front of a pole-mounted American flag that was set beside the official yellow and navy blue flag representing the Albany Police Department.

For just those few seconds I stood there paralyzed, sure that Jake and Cain had just announced me as their primary suspect. But then, underneath the photo appeared the words I wanted to see: "A.P.D. Special Detective Richard Moonlight: the independent investigator in charge of the Montana inquest."

There, I thought. *Breathe easy, Moonlight. Lyons wasn't kidding. They were making my involvement public.*

I wasn't a suspect after all. At least in the eyes of the media. I was just a paranoid part-timer with a guilty conscience.

My heart was beating inside my throat.

The news report had served as a warning. The sooner I got to the bottom of Scarlet's death, the sooner I could remove myself from the Montana equation and get down to the business of nailing the real killer.

I looked down at my scarred palms.

Cain and Montana knew that I'd been sleeping with Scarlet. My only guess was that Scarlet must have come out and told her husband—point blank—just to burn him up; just to make it hurt. Sure as shit, they were somehow going to use that knowledge against me. That is, if I didn't play by their rules. Therein lay their leverage.

But I wasn't about to play by their rules. If there was a killer out there, I was going to find him. If the killer was Jake, I'd nail him to the wall. In the meantime, if Cain and Jake had it in their mind to make me a suspect, I'd prove them wrong.

If there was any kind of justice for Scarlet, I would dig it up. Even if I had to take out the whole A.P.D. in the process.

I drove across the flat lot in the direction of the manned exit booths where I paid three dollars worth of short term parking fees. Pressing my receipt into the unused ashtray, I might have felt at relative peace had I not taken immediate notice of the Toyota Land Cruiser making its way into the lot, just as I was making my way out.

The albino man was driving the SUV. He made a right-hand turn into the parking lot. He was going so slow along the one-way road, I could make out pink eyes lit up in the glare from the illuminated dash. We eyed one another for the entire few seconds it took to make our respective drive-bys.

I nearly gave myself a case of whiplash trying to catch his license plate number. But by the time I turned around, he was gone.

Behind me, a taxi pulled up. Right on my bumper. The driver hit the horn. I guess he didn't know I was a part-time cop, that I actually did own the road.

No choice but to drive on through the exit to the main road. I peered into the rearview and side mirrors. Nothing ahead of me, nothing behind or to the sides. No blue Toyota Land Cruiser, that is.

But I had learned something: I was being tailed by a white-faced creep with a purple scar-tissue map on his lower torso. Exactly who he was and what he wanted, I had no way of knowing. But I knew it couldn't be good.

Reaching into my jacket, I pulled out my Browning, thumbed off the safety, and set it on the seat beside me.

Browning Hi-Power 9mm, first introduced to US law enforcement in 1935, the year my old man was born.

Both of them my most valuable companions.

23

I'd never attended even a single Psychic Fair meeting. But while Scarlet was pretty closed-mouthed about the subject, she'd revealed enough for me to have a decent idea of what went on in them. For instance, I knew that meditation and mind-freeing played a big role in the proceedings; that the members were mostly leftover hippies from the sixties and seventies; that the seating was mostly lotus style, the dress code something you might find in an old film about Haight-Ashbury circa 1967.

So by the time I entered the St. Pious Catholic Church gymnasium on Upper Loudon Road, right around the corner from my home, I pretty much knew what to expect. In fact, that evening's session was already underway. Sure enough, there were twelve of them sitting in folding chairs, circle formation, legs crossed lotus style.

On the near end of the gym to my left, under the ceiling-mounted basketball hoop, stood a long table. Set upon it were plates of sprouts, tofu, carrots, celery and lots of other mostly vegetarian fare. Plus one of those extra big percolating coffee pots. No doughnuts. No Krispy Kremes; no Dunkins. Not so much as a glazed Munchkin.

As far as I could tell, the Fair was made up entirely of women of varying ages and builds. Except for one man whom I took for the leader. He was a tall, flabby man of about fifty, with long, stark-gray hair pulled back tight in a ponytail. He was dressed in what I can only describe as bright red and yellow pajamas. No shoes. Sandals. Birkenstocks.

His chin and upper lip were hidden behind a thick goatee. Maybe I'd never had the pleasure of this man's acquaintance on any prior occasion, but I knew who he was. Scarlet's psychic leader, her guru or, if you will, her shaman. A man I knew of only as the Reverend Roland Doobie.

He turned to me. "Can I help you with something?" he asked.

"Master Doobie, I presume?" I said.

"That's Dubois." A couple members of the faithful put their heads down and chuckled silently to themselves.

I walked over to the table, poured some coffee into a Styrofoam cup and added a squirt of the only milk to be found, soy milk. No plastic stirrers.

"My psychic gateways need some clearing," I smiled. "I was hoping you could help."

This time a college-age young woman with long hair and a tie-dyed t-shirt chuckled out loud.

Roland "Doobie" Dubois shot her an angry look. "Kismet," he snapped. "Please."

Whatever happened to peace, love and understanding?

"I'm investigating the death of one of your members," I said. "Scarlet Montana."

The entire group, as if on cue, immediately shifted their gaze from me to the floor. Dubois perked up. He shot me a look that told me I wasn't exactly a stranger to him, even though we had definitely never crossed paths before, at least this side of the cosmos. Had Scarlet actually spoken to him about me?

Clearing his throat, he posed, "What is death, Mr.—?"

"Moonlight," I said.

"That's a rather unusual name. Beautiful, but unusual all the same."

"It was my grandfather's name," I said. "My father took it from his father, passed it down to me."

He said, "Tell me, Mr. Moonlight, do you understand the transformation of the soul, the other side of silence, as it were?"

I must have looked as dumb as I felt, because Roland Dubois offered up a sad smirk.

"Allow me to put it another way: how would you describe death?"

"I'm tied to a chair, the lids on my eyes pinned back. On the television, a commercial-free 'American Idol' marathon."

Dubois smiled. "In clinical terms," he said.

I cleared my throat. "Death is achieved via irreversible cessation of circulation of blood in the body of the person or irreversible cessation of all function of the brain of the person."

Raising up his hands, Dubois clapped. "Very good," he said. "As a mortal, you are not without knowledge of life's final mystery."

"Dead people have been a sort of hobby for me my whole life."

Nodding, he turned to a woman on his direct right. A woman of about forty-five, I guessed. Short, rather plump, with thick, round glasses and long black hair streaked with white.

"How would you describe death, Suma?"

The woman raised her head tentatively. Around her neck she wore about two dozen beaded necklaces. She seemed kind of frightened.

She cleared her throat. "Death does not exist," she said in this high-pitched, almost rattled voice. "Death is a mortal term. We are immortal. Therefore death has no meaning for us. It has no place in our vocabulary."

"Thank you, Suma," he said. "There you have it, Mr. Moonlight. Scarlet is not dead. She is merely transfigured into another life form."

"Well I guess that about puts me out of a job," I said while sipping my coffee. It tasted like liquid dirt. In fact, I think it *was* liquid dirt, aka organic mud. I set the cup back on the table.

"Reincarnation," I said.

Dubois nodded.

"Scarlet truly believed in the resurrection not only of the soul, but of the corpus, too," he explained.

All this enlightenment was making me dizzy.

"Can anyone here tell me if Scarlet had been acting strangely over the past few days or weeks?" I asked. It was like asking a group of clowns if they noticed anyone acting funny. Again, the entire group stared at the floor.

Still, I persisted. "Did she seem depressed or angry? Was she acting out in any way that might seem unusual to any of you? Did she—"

"Mr. Moonlight," Dubois interrupted. "As you can see, this is a closed session and you are violating our right of assemblage. I'm afraid I must ask you to leave."

He uncrossed his lotus legs and stood up. All six feet, six inches of him.

Jesus H. Christmas, behold the psychic giant! I knew if I persisted much longer, he might whip my glutes with a bean sprout.

"Take it easy, Father," I said. "I'm trying to get to the bottom of a tragedy."

"There is no tragedy because there is no death. And it's not Father, it's Reverend, if you don't mind."

I backed off.

"Well then, Reverend," I said, "I'll take my leave, back to the world of the mortals." I reached into my pocket for my wallet, slid out as many cards as I had on me, and began passing them around to the circle of ladies. The one named Kismet smiled.

"Richard Moonlight," she said. "Masseur, personal trainer and private investigator. Might you sing and dance as well?"

"Wasn't room for all that on the card," I said. Then, "If any of you happen to recall anything of importance, I urge you to give me a call."

"I'm sure that won't be necessary," the good Reverend said.

By the time I got to him, I had two cards left. I placed them back in my wallet, underneath my silver-plated badge.

"Sorry," I said. "None for you."

He sat back down. "Oh, and why is that, Mr. Moonlight?"

"You're psychic," I said. "You already know my number."

He smiled and laughed a little under his breath. He held out his hand, as though inviting me to place my hand inside it.

"May I?" he inquired.

I felt my stomach tighten up. My hands were scratched up. Inexplicably. But then, this didn't seem exactly like the time to deny the man, give him an excuse to inform a higher authority of my hiding something.

I set my left hand in his far larger hand, palm up.

Surprisingly, he said nothing about the cuts as if they didn't exist. Instead he ran the tip of his right index finger along a thin line that curved its way around the meat of my thumb. After gazing down at the palm for a few beats, he let go of my hand, smiled and shook his head as though puzzled.

"What is it?" I asked, my eyes nervously veering from his to the many women who circled him.

"Nothing's wrong," he said. "It's just that your palm, it's giving me a reading that just can't be."

"What reading is that?"

He laughed again. "It could very well have something to do with those recent abrasions," he remarked. "But if you must know, it says you're already dead."

"I had an accident with a bullet to the head a few years back," I explained. "I *should* be dead. So they tell me, anyway."

"But then, death does not exist, does it, Mr. Moonlight?"

"I guess I'm living proof," I said. "Too bad we can't say the same for Scarlet."

24

I was first introduced to George Phillips back when I was a little kid. Sometime around 1971 or '72, if I remember correctly.

He was a blue-jeaned, crazy-haired, skinny rebel, recently returned from the Vietnam War. In a word, Dad got a kick out of him. Didn't matter how different they were or how George used to bust a gut boasting to my Nixon-supporting old man that he'd fought in the land of the mighty Viet Cong and never once witnessed a single "domino" fall to communism. Dad's attraction to him was immediate.

The fact of the matter was that George grew up a fatherless troubled kid who, had he not possessed "unusual smarts" as my father referred to them, might have ended up a lifetime resident of Green Haven Maximum Security Prison for grand theft auto. But with Dad's encouragement and a full-time/part-time gig at the funeral parlor, George was able to work his way through med school. I've always harbored a sneaking suspicion that when his G.I. bill ran out, Dad had no trouble wiring a payment or two to the Albany Medical College on the Vietnam vet's behalf. In that manner, George became not only a friend to me, but the big brother I never had.

I was standing inside the open double-doorway that accessed the Albany Medical Arts Center autopsy room. My ears pricked up to the soft classical music the pathologist was broadcasting from a rather expensive stereo console system that was set up on the lab counter directly behind the ceiling-mounted weight scale.

I breathed in.

For some people, the pungent odor of formaldehyde and alcohol might make them sick. But to me, the smell reminded me of home. It immediately transported me back to my childhood.

Scarlet's cadaver had already been removed from cold storage and was laid out on the table. From where I stood, I could clearly see the blood and water that was dripping off the body and collecting inside the stainless steel vat positioned beneath the table's drain. Thoughtfully, Phillips had covered her private parts with a green sheet.

He had his back to me while he stood over the body, contemplating it the same way a mad scientist might contemplate a Frankenstein monster. In his right hand he gripped the water spigot which he'd used to wash the body down.

Sensing my presence, he about-faced, set down the spigot, then peeled off his Latex gloves and tossed them into a blue medical waste bin.

"You're late, little brother," he said.

"Sorry," I said, stepping further inside. "I got caught up in a psychic reading of sorts."

We met in the center of the room, directly beside the body-length table. We shook hands and hugged not only like brothers, but like a couple of battle-seasoned crime vets—Phillips, having gained much of his experience with the dead in Vietnam as he did my father's funeral parlor where he'd done everything from assist with embalming to driving the Mercedes coach in a funeral procession.

"So Detective Cain has requested that you solve their little suicide problem," he grinned sympathetically.

I shot a tentative glance in the direction of Scarlet's prone body.

I knew that the sight of her naked limbs and torso had no affect on a pathologist like George. For him, she was just another night's work. The same might have been said for me had I not been her lover. For me she was still flesh and blood. Still a person. Despite the effort, I was having some real trouble referring to her as an "it." Every time I glanced at her for more than a few seconds at a time, I felt a dull drumming in the center of my head and in the back of my throat. There was the nagging pressure against the backs of my eyeballs, the buzzing in my brain.

Had I had anything to do with this?

I could only believe that I hadn't; that on the other hand, Jake had everything to do with it, including motive, opportunity and means.

"Montana extended a personal invitation late last night," I said.

"He wants this one bought and sold right away," Phillips correctly suggested. "Wants the transaction to go down his way, your name and only your name on the sales receipt. Avoid a full-blown internal investigation."

"I *am* the internal investigation," I clarified. "In the interest of preserving his wife's memory."

Phillips grinned.

"He didn't feed you that bullshit, did he Moon?"

"Directly to my bald-headed face."

"The only thing Montana wants to save in a case like this is his own ass. And believe me, that's a lot of real estate to save."

I nodded in the direction of the body. "Along with his freedom," I said. "O'Connor starts flinging accusations, things could get mighty ugly for Albany's finest cop."

If I had to guesstimate, I would have put George's age at around fifty-seven or fifty-eight. But because of his condition—Non-Hotchkins Lymphoma, which had entered into a state of remission some ten years ago but had recently made a comeback. He looked much older. If you didn't know he was an M.D., you'd swear he was an aging rock and roll musician. He was a small, too-thin man with shoulder-length salt-and-pepper hair parted in the middle, a navy blue bandana wrapped around his forehead. That night he was wearing a white smock that buttoned down the front and hung short of his knees.

His sleeves rolled up around his elbows, he wore three silver chain bracelets on his right wrist. He still wore his wedding band even though his divorce went through fifteen years ago, his ex-wife, daughter and granddaughter having taken up roots somewhere outside of Bozeman, Montana. His earlobes supported one silver hoop apiece and on his feet, a pair of worn cowboy boots over which he sported a pair of tight-fitting Levi's jeans with a good-sized tear over the right kneecap.

If I didn't know any better, I'd swear they were the same jeans and boots I'd seen him wearing on the day he arrived at the front door to

23 Hope Lane to answer a help wanted ad. I recall long hair done up in a ponytail, his unzipped Vietnam flack jacket now a loose-fitting vest, right hand raised high, index and middle fingers extended into a peaceful V, gaunt face sporting the widest smile I ever saw on a hippie. Like Dad, I remember liking him right away.

George disappeared into the connecting back office.

A moment later he came back out carrying a neatly folded smock. On top of the smock was placed a pair of green booties, a transparent plastic face shield, a pair of beige Latex gloves and a green cap. He handed the pile to me and told me to get dressed. While I slipped into my hospital costume, he stepped over to the stereo system and proceeded to replace the existing CD with a romantic composition by Vaughn Williams entitled Symphony Numbers 3 and 4, better known as the "Pastoral Symphonies." The same soundtrack he always worked to. Take it from an insider.

He turned to me, just as the lush operatic voices began to fill the white-tiled room. Through his narrow mask I saw him purse his lips as if to say, *Take a deep breath. I know this isn't easy on you.*

Fingering a Teflon scalpel off the tool tray, he brought the razor sharp tip to Scarlet's already scarred sternum.

25

The autopsy proceeded uneventfully.

Having removed the lungs, trachea and esophagus "en bloc" and setting them out on the foldable dissection table, George weighed organ after organ, recording each and every detail of the procedure into a microphone clipped onto his safety glasses.

From the start I had been careful to keep my distance. Especially when he initiated the proceedings by swiping the blade down the center of her chest, following the exact path of the long hesitation scars that, in my mind, anyway, Scarlet did not produce on her own.

After a time however, I found myself taking a good look at her face.

Her open eyes were unusually sunken in. Concave, even. I knew that the eyes of a dead person gradually flattened out, the same way a bicycle tire will lose its air over time (the old man's metaphor). But then, from where I stood maybe four feet away from her face, it seemed as though the eyes no longer possessed any type of reflective sheen whatsoever. Even under the high-powered lamps, the once vivid jade had been reduced to a dull green. Such were the affects of death.

I ran the tips of my Latex-covered fingers over the eyelids, opening and closing them. I noticed then that my fingers were trembling. Taking a step back, I removed them from her face.

Maybe I was just tired and a little crazy, but I shook my head and spit out a little nervous laughter.

I spotted George out of the corner of my eye. He had just completed an examination of her pelvis, using not only his fingers but a stainless steel instrument as well. What he collected from his search he scraped into a small plastic jar the same way you might scrape a dollop of peanut butter off a knife. The procedure completed, he then sealed the lid tightly. After setting the jar down on the counter, he just stood there, staring me down.

"I might be taking a shot in the dark here," he said. "But can I ask you a personal question, Moon?"

I nodded.

"Were you still sleeping with her?"

My wide eyes must have shouted volumes. George was my big brother. I shared and bared many of my secrets with him.

As if to answer his question, I smiled.

"Sheeeeit," is all he said.

26

Scarlet's autopsy was now official pathological history—all Polaroid and digital photos developed and downloaded, the proper opinion form filled out in longhand, the place hosed down, the tissue, blood and stomach content samples tagged, bagged and sent down to Tox for processing.

George was sticking his neck out for me on this one. More than usual. If I got buried alive, he was going to choke on a dirt sandwich right along with me.

The simple fact of the matter was this: some questions had been answered while others remained agonizingly out of reach. In George's official opinion, the mechanism of death constituted traumatic laceration of the throat, which derived initially from asphyxiation and secondarily from massive hemorrhage. The cause of death was a sharp instrument—a razor or a carving knife. More likely a razorblade, judging by the precise "slash" cuts (people tend to stab when using a knife).

The manner of death however, was a different story.

While the scars on her upper body (cuts to the epidermal and upper-epidermal skin layers) and the absence of clothing damage (she was naked) might point to suicide, they could just as easily point to homicide.

The white blanching on her chest and limbs, plus the moderate scrapes and scratches he found along the arms and legs, were thus far the best proof that she might have put up a struggle against an attacker. But then, it was also conceivable that the scratches and bruises could have come from the EMTs who handled her during transport.

The exact time of death? Twelve a.m. or thereabouts. How long did Scarlet live after her throat had been cut? No more than a few seconds. Had she been under the influence of drugs and alcohol? That was for Toxicology to determine, but then I knew firsthand the truth about her love of Stohly and her need for sleep aids like Ambien.

Aside from the hesitation scars, bruises and light scratches, there was no evidence of skin under her fingernails or behind her teeth. No foreign flesh that you might naturally associate with a person struggling for their life. In that sense, with Scarlet acting in the manner of a specific body of evidence, the autopsy served to back up Cain's and Montana's suicide theory. Because if she had been murdered, then by all appearances it looked as though she'd asked for it.

I looked down at my hands. No flesh beneath her fingernails ...no sign of putting up a struggle with an attacker. Good news for me.

But then, what did all this analysis mean? What conclusion could be drawn from the pathological examination? What it meant was the autopsy I so badly wanted revealed evidence that moved me as close to suicide as it did homicide. Which also meant I wasn't about to jump on the horn with Lyons and lay the scoop of the decade on him. Not yet. Not until I had definitive, irrefutable proof concerning the precise manner of death.

The physics question had been gnawing away at me since I'd first laid eyes on the newly deceased Scarlet: "How many pounds of pressure per square inch do you suppose it would take to inflict that kind of wound on a human neck?"

We were sitting around George's metal desk inside the small office that adjoined the autopsy room. A rectangular room with no windows. The long-haired pathologist was looking directly at me, contemplatively, brain matter heating up, gears and belts grinding.

"I once heard about a man who cut himself up pretty bad after ingesting potassium hydroxide. Another guy who stabbed himself to death after drinking an alkaline detergent solution. But in those cases, the poison probably killed them before the hemorrhaging did."

"But we agree that it would take a hell of a lot of strength."

"Abnormal strength. More than a healthy thirty-eight-year-old woman fired up on pills and vodka could work up." George took a toke off a pharmaceutically rolled and distributed marijuana cigarette, held the smoke in while conversing. "I mean, if you're that interested, it wouldn't take much to pull one of the unclaimed stiffs in cold storage, run a blade through its neck, somehow measure the pressure." Eyes as wide as a kid on Christmas morning, he shot up. "Come on Moon, it'll be like old times!"

Fuckin' George. What the hell would he do without dead people?

"I've had enough blood and guts for one day and night," I said as I sat back in the wood chair and stared at the plain block wall behind his desk—a wall that might have proudly displayed his diplomas if he had a vain bone in his body. "Besides," I went on, "I think the answer I'm looking for is obvious enough."

I thought George was turning blue. Finally he released the pain-killing smoke from his over-inflated lungs.

"I guess you'd never get an accurate reading anyway, Moony," he said through a series of coughs and nose farts.

"Unless someone were willing to demonstrate by cutting their own neck open for us," I suggested.

"Totally unrealistic scenario to duplicate."

"Listen George, we both know that self-cutting and self-stabbing is just about the most uncommon method of suicide there is."

He nodded and sat back down. "Something like five percent of all suicides occur from a blade. In almost every case the victim is either schizophrenic or psychotic or drugged up. Usually, all three."

"All the more reason for me to make the differentiation between suicide and homicide. What basic criteria do you gotta establish to prove suicide by knife? Or in this case, a blade?"

Phillips shifted the cigarette into his left hand, then he raised his right hand and extended the index finger.

"To prove it, you gotta first be able to establish at least several possible sites of damage on the front torso for self-inflicted cuts," he said.

"Chest, stomach and neck in this case," I agreed. "Nothing on her back where naturally she can't reach."

Now a second finger raised. "Hesitation scars have got to be present."

"Everything but the neck is a surface cut," I confirmed.

A third and last finger raised. "No damaged clothing."

"She was buck-naked," I replied. "Shit."

The good but cancer-ailing pathologist took another toke from the medical joint.

"So then Jake may have his suicide after all."

"Bullshit," I said. "Because satisfying those three criteria doesn't mean a goddamned thing if it turns out she was too messed up to even hold a blade in her hand, much less run it across her neck."

"Also don't forget, suicide weapons do not have a nasty habit of walking away."

"Homicide made to look like a suicide," I said. "That's what I still say." I crossed my arms over my chest, slipping my hands inside my pits to hide the scratched-up palms.

"Maybe ... almost definitely," George agreed, blowing out more sweet-smelling smoke.

Staring at the white wall, I thought about what might have been the easier alternative, how I might have simply written up the report that Jake and Cain wanted in the first place. The report stating that Scarlet did indeed commit suicide. Christ, I could have collected my money and been on my merry way.

But I chose to go a different route. One part noble, one part save-my-own-ass route.

Still, I had been sleeping with the victim. But now that I was involved and it had been made public, they had no choice but to go with me.

Maybe my reasons for doing what I was doing were so personal, so ingrained, so motivated out of fear, that not even I understood them entirely. Maybe my reasons had something to do with not thinking straight—with once again making all the wrong decisions. But then, I was thinking straight. I had to believe that. My instincts and thought process had to be in good working order. After all, why else would I pose such a threat to Cain if I wasn't in my right mind?

Still, the law was clear in the matter of both homicide and suicide, victims must go under the knife. So at least I had that going for me in my defense should I require one in the end.

What I did not have going for me was the irrefutable evidence I thought I would have had by now. Some shred of forensic proof that shifted the burden of guilt away from myself and that I could use to refute Cain and Montana's suicide theory. For example: latent prints on the murder weapon, DNA samples separate from Scarlet's, hair follicle samples, clothing fiber samples, etc. Something to establish a murder cover-up while using my case synopsis as a smoke screen. Because even though by the looks of things I could make it appear that Scarlet had been murdered, the evidence was still circumstantial at best. Conjecture based upon the interpretation of some weak physical evidence.

Emphasis on "some" and "weak."

"I'll wait for the Tox report," I said. "They tell me she was comatose, then I take you up on your offer to examine the physics implied in suicide by the blade."

George licked his index finger, snuffed out what was left of the joint and returned the roach to his coat pocket.

"They tell me she was only mildly drunk, with enough speed inside her system to light up the city, I go another route," I said. "Which one, I have no idea."

"What about looking into the bruises and scratches?" George asked after a beat.

"Could be something there," I answered. "For all I know, they could be the leftovers from some sex game Jake made her play with him."

"That is, if they had sex at all."

"Maybe he liked to force it on her, in her own bedroom, using his cuffs as an aid."

George perked up. "Now you're cooking with Wesson, Moon. Coming up with a solid theory. Motive, opportunity … "

"Nothing solid about it," I said. "Just another guess in a pile of guesses. There is one thing that's true: if Jake was the one to slice her up, it would have made sense to cuff her limbs to the bedposts."

"Her bed have posts on it?"

It felt kind of funny, him asking me about her bed.

"I can't remember," I said.

"If he did kill her and he did cuff her up, then those scratches would look a hell of a lot more like gouges. And there weren't any."

"Looks like I may have to pay another visit to the Montana bungalow."

George made a scrunched-up, pain-filled facial expression. "Jake is not going to like that," he said. "Move like that kind of goes against his swift conclusion objective."

I stood up. "I don't think he has much choice in the matter."

"While you're at it," George added, "you might search the computer for any emails she might have sent to friends detailing her husband's abusive nature. You might also want to see if she visited any websites that specialize in the proper methodology of killing yourself with a blade. Sick puppy websites. Lastly, little brother, you might look for a life insurance policy."

"Suicide doesn't pay, remember?"

"Nonsense. You pay out enough in premiums the insurance crooks can fix anything."

I pulled my leather coat off the chair back, slipped it on. Then I reached into the interior pocket and pulled out the cash envelope. I counted out ten fifties and handed them over.

"For your granddaughter," I said. "Per the usual deal."

George stuffed the bills into the side pocket of his smock without bothering to count them.

Together we stepped back out into the autopsy room. We took one more good look at Scarlet's body on the slab. I'm not sure I understood why, but I was beginning to get used to looking at her dead body. The pressure in my head had moderated a bit; and as for my right arm and hand, all feeling and sensation were present and accounted for.

"They send over instructions for burial?" I asked.

"As a matter of fact," he said, stepping back into his office and rummaging through his file cabinet until he came out with a manila envelope. He pulled out a thin pile of papers, which he scanned. "This arrived by currier not long before you got here," he said. "Surprise, surprise, they're calling for an immediate cremation."

He handed me the requests. Nothing fishy about them. Standard requests for burial, signed by both Jake and Scarlet Montana back in 2003 when they acquired a living will. I handed the papers back to George.

"They say how soon?"

"Word I got from Fitzgerald's Funeral Home is tomorrow afternoon, four o'clock," he said. "No calling hours, just the bonfire."

"Jesus, George," I said. "When were you planning on letting me in this little tidbit of information?"

He threw his hands up in the air as if to say *Oops!*

"I've got less then twenty-four hours," I thought out loud.

"What for?"

"Before they torch our body of evidence."

"Listen, as a licensed county pathologist I can have it postponed pending your investigation."

I shook my head. "I don't want you getting in over your head until I have the definite proof I need to nail their asses for a cover-up."

"They're gonna destroy the evidence, Moon," he pointed out. "That one cadaver just might be the most important proof you're ever going to get, your body of evidence."

"We have the law and procedure on our side," I said. "You have the Polaroids and the computer disks. Keep them locked up. Do the same with the Tox report once it arrives." I nodded in the direction of Scarlet. "She gets incinerated, that stuff will become as precious as gold."

George walked me out into the dark, empty corridor.

"One thing," he said, eyes not focused on me, but on the concrete floor. "That seminal fluid I collected during her internal."

I knew exactly what he was getting at.

"She definitely had sex with somebody within a few hours of her death."

I hesitated. "You gonna make slides of the samples?" I asked, a little under my breath. Actually, a lot under my breath.

He shook his head. "Wasn't enough material there to get a good read," he said.

"Not enough?" I asked.

"Yeah, not enough," he said, wide-eyed and convincing. "I decided just to toss the shit." He looked up, pursed his lips. I couldn't decide if he was a good or bad liar.

"Why are you so willing to stick your neck out for me, George?"

"You're my little brother," he said. "But I also like the side of right. The law, it's not always right."

"You're a dying breed, George." I said. But as soon as I said it, I wished I could take it back.

"Nahhh, just dying," he said. "From this point on, I follow my heart. 'Sides, I have to sock away all the bucks I can for my granddaughter out in Bozeman."

"You already make good money."

"I go with my heart. Probably would do it even if you didn't contribute to the little sweetheart's college fund. But like I said, no matter what you involve me with, it has to be on the side of right or I won't play the game."

"That's exactly how you should have put it to the draft board when they nailed you for Nam," I said, gazing into his eyes.

He smiled. But as I turned for the door, he stopped me.

"Your hands," he said. "You want me to take a look at them?"

I felt my throat close up.

"I tripped and fell is all," I said.

"Sure thing," George said. "And you and Scarlet were just friends."

A strange guilt weighed heavily upon my shoulders as I trudged back down the corridor towards the freight elevator.

27

Stocky Agent stands and paces the gray room while staring at the concrete floor.

I get the feeling that if this were a Russian spy movie, I'd already be strapped to a metal chair, my eyes blackened, my lips burst and swelled, my front teeth snapped at the roots.

"Let's change the subject for a minute," he says. "Go back in time to October, 2003."

Coming from a G-man, the mere mention of the month and year makes my skin crawl.

"What about it?" I ask.

"According to your testimony, that's the night you had your— how do you refer to it? Your accident."

I reach up with my left hand and pull back my left earlobe, exposing the button-sized scar.

"This what you want to feast your fucking eyes on ?"

"Take it easy, Moonlight. We're just talking here."

I feel my eyes do this crazy roll inside their sockets, as though triggered by a sudden jolt of electricity or pain. Almost automatically, I pull another cigarette from the pack, shove it in between tingling index and middle finger and fire it up.

"I don't see the connection between my accident and Scarlet's death."

Stocky Agent steps back over to the table, sits back down. "I get to decide the questions, remember?"

"I'm a trained dick, remember?"

"Okay I get it," he says. "But what I want to know is, what drives a man to suicide?"

"What drives anybody to suicide?"

"Bankruptcy, clinical depression, terminal disease ...bad marriage."

In my head, I picture my wife ... the way I used to picture her to the point of obsession—fucking Mitch Cain. That one vision is what drove me over the edge, caused me to place the barrel of that .22 to my temple and pull the trigger. But then I never realized that it had been the same for her, her having to imagine what it was like for me to fuck Scarlet. It's the answer they're searching for—the parallel they're trying to make between me and Scarlet. The failed marriage leading to suicide.

I breathe in and out, trying my best to keep head and heart even keel.

I tell him, "If Scarlet wanted to commit suicide, I'm sure she had her reasons."

"Just like you had your reasons."

"Yeah, just like that."

Stocky Agent throws a look at his bearded partner standing in the corner that says *Can you believe this guy?*

The agent sits back in his chair, lets out a breath. He says, "Let me ask you something else. What are the odds of a man shooting himself in the head point blank and surviving?"

I smoke and think. "Ten million to one. Maybe a billion to one"

"More like a one-hundred billion to one if you were to ask me," Stocky Agent exclaims. "Fucking-no-way impossible scenario."

I stamp out the cigarette, exhaling a waft of gray-blue smoke. "So what's your point?"

"What's the likelihood of a woman cutting the shit out of herself, not to mention her own neck, then disposing of the weapon after the deed?"

I laugh. I can't help myself. "Impossible," I say. "But weirder things have happened. Am I right?"

"Just take a look in the mirror, Moonlight," Stocky Agent chuckles. "You fell off the tree of fucked-up-weird and slammed every branch on the way down."

28

I saw the shadow of a figure standing in the driveway even before I made the right turn onto Hope Lane. A sole silhouette standing beside the house like an evil spirit.

I cut the engine on the funeral coach, killed the lights and rolled quietly to a stop. I got out of the car, Browning in hand, and cut across the wet lawn to the slate steps that paralleled most of the split-level's front facade. Making my way down to the drive, I glanced over my right shoulder with the expectation of finding a blue Toyota Land Cruiser parked out front.

But I couldn't see a thing. No Land Cruiser, anyway.

Pressing my shoulder up against the corner of the house, I took a deep breath and exhaled. Then, with pistol aimed directly ahead, I stepped out of the shadows.

"Down on the ground!" I shouted.

"Please don't shoot," came the unexpected plea of a woman. "Please, please, I just came here to talk."

The motion-sensitive spotlight mounted to the stone wall above the garage had picked up our movement. It was now brightly illuminated.

She was one of the Psychic Fair women. The short one with the long gray hair and fifty extra pounds of beads wrapped around her neck.

She was dressed in a long flowery skirt and a matching blouse, all of which were soaked with rainwater.

I pulled up my pistol, returning it to my shoulder holster, safety on.

"Good way to get yourself killed," I said, my heart rate only now beginning to slow. "But what am I saying? You people are immortal."

I sensed her trying to work up a smile, but it didn't seem to take.

"I couldn't sleep," she said. "I thought that if I talked to you, face to face, I could somehow get it off my chest."

"Get what off your chest?"

"Why Scarlet murdered herself."

29

We were sitting at the kitchen table, she sipping a cup of Lipton tea, me slow-sipping a glass of Jack. She'd dried herself with a towel in the bathroom off the kitchen. The long gray hair that draped her pale face made her look quite sad. Her psychic name was Suma, but her real name was Natalie, so she explained.

"I knew if I said anything when you showed up at our meeting, I would have been in big trouble."

"What kind of trouble?"

She pressed her lips together. "Just ... trouble. Maybe tossed from the group."

"I get the feeling your Master "Doobie" Dubois is anything but a live-and-let-live kind of hippie."

"Yes, the master Reverend is controlling," she admitted. She tried to smile, but again it was useless. "But he is not the reason why I am here."

"Why are you here?" I asked, taking another taste of the whiskey. She sipped her tea, sat back in her chair.

"She had no family, you know," Suma-cum-Natalie said. "Scarlet. She had no family. For the past twelve months, we had been her family. She liked to tell us that."

I thought about it. I was well aware that Scarlet's parents had died when she was young; that she had no siblings; that her first husband and only child had died in a head-on collision with a drunk driver. But in my heart, I knew Suma was not referring to that version of immediate family. She was referring to the family she might have had with Jake, but had been cheated out of it.

"She was learning a lot about herself," the pleasant but shy woman continued. "About her inner self. Her dreams were becoming more and more vivid, more luminous, full of flying and astral images. But then, that was also her problem."

I poured some more whiskey and asked her to be more specific.

"You see, Mr. Moonlight, for some people it can take an entire lifetime to reach the point that Scarlet reached in just one year. The point where one becomes so in touch with their subconscious soul, that they can actually control their dreams."

"I dream a lot," I said, "but I guess I haven't reached the point of being able to control them."

"That's because you've probably never tried. But for some people, the separation of the soul from its body is the pinnacle of the mystical pyramid." She paused for a beat, gazing into her tea. "Of course, that kind of power carries with it some risks."

"What risks?"

"As heavenly as the vivid dream state can be, or as hellish."

"Scarlet's dreams weren't heavenly, I take it."

"While they would start out beautifully and wonderfully, they would almost always regress into a nightmare in which several shadow-like figures would appear," she explained. "The way she told it to me, these figures would carry her paralyzed body away to an unknown place. They would strap her down and slice her open. She would experience this dream night after night. It would be so vivid, so real, it was like living her own death over and over again."

I sat back, trying to imagine surviving that kind of nightmare, night after night. Demons and devils pinning me down, cutting me up.

"As far as you know, she never tried to seek out professional help?"

"Scarlet was determined to work through the nightmares. Face them head on, show the black figures in her subconscious that she was not afraid of them. Once she succeeded, they would disappear and forever stop taunting her. No psychologist on earth could have assisted her with that. For Scarlet, her war with the demons had to be fought battle by battle, and only by she and she alone."

Suma finished her tea. I offered to make some more, but she declined. What she wanted was Jack.

I poured a shot into her teacup. She downed it in one swift pull. The psychic teetotaler meets the barfly.

"I'm not being entirely truthful," she confessed, grabbing hold of the bottleneck and helping herself to another shot. "Scarlet did seek out help. Not good help, but something to help her cope all the same."

I asked her to tell me about it.

"I caught her in the bathroom one night at the church. I walked into a stall. She was snorting ... " She let her statement hang as though physically repulsed at what she had to say.

"Snorting," I pressed. "Snorting what, Natalie?"

"It was a brown powder. She was sucking the stuff right up into her nose from off the toilet tank through a rolled up dollar bill."

"Heroin," I said, without raising my voice. "You're sure you saw her snorting heroin?"

"Like I said, it was a powder and it was definitely brown and it definitely changed her mood."

My stomach cramped up. At that point a brick could have slammed me upside the head and it would not have shocked me more.

I thought, if Scarlet was snorting heroin, if this woman was telling the truth, then it was becoming plainly obvious that I had no clue who the real Scarlet Montana was. I relied on my somewhat damaged gray matter to produce a vivid image and pictured my sometime lover leaning over a toilet tank, lush hair veiling her face while she sucked brown shit up into her nostrils using a rolled-up dollar bill for a straw. Sitting there at the kitchen table I ran the image over and over again in my brain. But no matter how many times I played it, rewound it, paused it, I could not get used to it.

But then, I thought about something else. If it could be proven that she had been desperate enough to snort heroin, then it was yet another bit of evidence that would lend itself well to the suicide theory. Still, I was refusing to believe it.

"You have any idea where she might have scored the drugs?" I asked.

Suma drank her shot. Again, just one swift pull. I offered her a third, but she declined.

"Sometimes there was a man who would show up after the meetings," she said. "A funny-looking man with white skin. Whiter than white skin. An albino, I think. He would come pick her up and together they would drive off."

I thought the kitchen chair had slid out from under me. I envisioned my secret albino stalker. "Did this man by any chance drive a big four-by-four SUV—a Toyota Land Cruiser, maybe? Did he speak with a foreign accent? Maybe Polish or Russian?"

Her cheeks were a bit flushed from the whiskey. They looked a lot healthier than when she had first walked into my kitchen from out of the rain.

"A Land Cruiser like all the rich soccer moms drive," she said. "Definitely. And yes, he spoke with a thick accent."

I bit my lip and stood up. I knew that eventually some loose ends would begin to tie up, but I didn't expect these ends to come together.

"Anything else you want to tell me?"

She stood. Together we headed for the front door.

"Nothing. Only that it makes me very sad that Scarlet is gone."

"Don't you believe that she is still alive?" I asked. "Walking around in another's body? Maybe even the body of an animal? Maybe a bird?"

She grinned out the corner of her mouth. "Oh that's just the stuff we like to believe on Monday nights. The Psychic Fair might be good for the soul, but it doesn't make you immortal, Mr. Moonlight. Nor does it pay the bills. It's simply a salve, not a remedy." A sweet smile. "Like a glass of whiskey on a rainy spring night."

"I guess Scarlet could be the proof of that," I said.

"I'm actually pessimistic about the end," she went on. "Rather, not pessimistic necessarily. But let's just say that when we go, there's a good bet that a set of pearly gates will not be waiting for us. When we die it will be nothing. Unconsciousness and that's all."

"Then why frequent the Psychic Fair at all?"

"It provides some kind of balance in my life and inevitable death. Hope without having to resort to the dogma of organized religion which I consider to be the bane of all civilization."

Whoa daddy, I thought, *Natalie would make one hell of a dinner date.*

I asked her if she'd like me to drive her home. Or at least allow me to call her a cab.

She said she only lived on the next block over by the St. Pious church and preferred to walk in the rain. Something about cleansing the mind. But I think she was a little tipsy.

Before she walked out, I stopped her long enough to ask her one more thing.

"Why are you so convinced that Scarlet killed herself?"

"Because she was very sweet and she would never give anyone cause to kill her," she explained. "But she was very, very sad and very, very tortured in her mind."

"It could be that someone wanted her dead," I said.

"Why on earth would anyone want that?"

In my mind I saw Jake; I saw Cain; I saw the black shadows that stabbed her, night after night. Maybe they had their reasons for killing her. Because Scarlet might have known something and was about to use it against them. It would have been motivation enough. It was a motivation stronger than any I could have harbored. It was my job to find out what that "something" was.

"Maybe it's true what they say about nice people finishing last," I mused.

"Perhaps," she said, "but I have this feeling that Scarlet was never even in the race."

She held out her hand. I took it in mine. Without asking, she turned my hand over to expose the scratched up palm, just like the Reverend Dubois had done earlier. I was too surprised to be angry.

"You see anything to dispute your fearless leader's assessment?" I inquired.

She bit down on her lip and let go of my hand.

"It's late," she said. "And all those scratches. It's very difficult to see anything."

"But you do see something," I pressed.

"No," she said turning her head. "Nothing." But she was a sweet woman and all sweet women are terrible liars.

I let Suma out. Or was it Natalie?

She turned back to me, looking into my face with wide, moist eyes. "Moonlight," she whispered. "It's such a pretty, musical name."

"It's just a name," I said. "The name I was born with and the name I'll die with."

She wished me inner peace. I told her all I wanted was a good night's sleep.

"One day, Mr. Moonlight," she whispered, "we'll have all the sleep we ever wished for."

30

Not long after Suma, or Natalie, had exited the carnal reality of Dad's house, I washed down another codeine with a glass of water. Then I went back outside and parked the Mercedes in the garage. Dad might be dead and gone, but I still couldn't shake the feeling that he watched over me like a hawk, especially when I was using his things.

Once I made it back in the house I locked up. When I saw that two new messages had been recorded on the answering machine, I immediately thought of Lola.

Maybe she was on her way over. Maybe it was wishful thinking on my part.

I tapped the PLAY button and listened for a voice. A beautiful voice.

No dice.

Instead I got only the sound of a man's breathing, then a shuffling noise followed by a quick hang-up. As for the second call, same deal.

Since my father's thirty-year-old phone was not blessed with modern caller ID, I deleted the non-messages then punched Star 69 into the handset.

When the operator gave me the number I quickly jotted it down and then dialed. I got a recorded message: "You have reached The

Russo, Saratoga's only traditional Russian restaurant," said a man in a distinctive Russian-accented voice not unlike that possessed by my new white friend. He proceeded to recite the establishment's hours.

I hung up and opened the cabinet that contained my Saratoga region phone book. I looked up The Russo in the yellow pages and found an address for the place on Main in Saratoga's downtown shopping district. Definitely a storefront joint.

I copied the address onto a Post-a-Note and slipped it into my wallet. Then I slid into bed and laid myself down beside my old friend Insomnia.

I finally gave up on the idea of sleep sometime around pre-dawn.

Lying in bed, I stared up at the cracked plaster ceiling, listening to the rain coming down outside. Every raindrop seemed to be calling out my name.

My head was growing tighter, the evil spirits pressing themselves against the backs of my eyeballs.

I knew I had to crawl out of the bed, get the old body moving, distract myself.

Downstairs I made the coffee and wondered why I wasn't nearly as awake on my feet as I was on my back. I listened to the spatter the raindrops made against the kitchen windows when the wind blew hard. I wondered if it would ever stop raining in Albany.

A few minutes later, I decided to call Lyons and leave him an update on his voicemail. I told the crime reporter I was working the case but that I'd still need more time before I could draw up some definite conclusions. Then I mentioned the cremation scheduled for that afternoon. But I also told him that if we met later that evening, I'd more than likely have his answers along with the supporting paperwork.

With that done, I poured another coffee and opened the front door to see if the paper had come yet.

It hadn't.

But from where I stood I looked out onto the thick pines and oaks that separated my front lawn from Hope Lane. The rain was coming down steadily, collecting and running like a small river to the catch basin located at the southeast corner of the property.

I brought the cup to my lips. Once more I saw Scarlet's face. I saw the living face first and the dead face second. Two entirely different people.

I can't say why, but I was reminded suddenly of an old saying that used to hang on my wall above my desk at the A.P.D.

Let conversation cease. Let laughter flee. This is the place where death delights to help the living.

I knew that if Scarlet was to delight in helping me at all, even in death, then she would do her best to lead me directly to her killer.

31

By nine o'clock I'd jogged three miles in the rain, put in a full free-weight workout and three three-minute rounds on the heavy-bag inside the same basement gym I set up back when I was still in high school. Once showered, I treated myself to a pair of clean Levis.

With the Browning strapped to my chest and the Beatle's "White Album" playing in the eight-track cassette player, I was about to take the next necessary step in stopping Scarlet's cremation. Which meant a visit to my old pal and toxicologist, Dr. Norman Miner.

I drove the funeral coach across town to the Albany Medical Center. Having driven in through the entrance gates, I motored all the way to the far west end of the facility, past the concrete parking garage, past the morgue entrance, past the physical plant to a series of three old four-storied buildings made up of brick facades and French-paned windows. At the turn of the twentieth century, Ivy League-style buildings that long ago served as the original Albany Medical Hospital, now were barely large enough to accommodate the labs.

I pulled into the broad parking lot that separated the old facility from the new and parked in a space that, according to a pole-mounted sign, was reserved for Dr. Norman Miner.

I was no stranger to Toxicology, which meant I knew full well that Miner didn't give a rat's ass about his reserved parking space. So riddled was he with gout that it pained him to even touch the gas and brake pedals of his old Volvo sedan with the tips of his swelled toes. Therefore Miner almost always used the local taxi service as his main mode of transport.

I entered the main building, breathing in the old familiar odor—a strange, intense mixture of chemicals, disinfectants and waste that emanated from the many lab animals confined to their stacked metal cages stored in the basement. So much for modern ventilation. But then, if you worked long enough in a place like this, I imagined your nasal passages got used to it.

Upstairs, I stood inside the open doors of the first of three tox labs. It was the usual scene. Dozens of men and women standing around an equal amount of freestanding marble islands with nearly every square inch of counter filled with beakers, clear pots, test tubes, Bunsen burners and laptop computers. Technicians and scientists were so engrossed in their work that not a single one of them bothered to look up at me.

Stepping back out into the corridor I nearly ran him over.

Dr. Norman Miner.

He was a short, squat, curly-haired man who had served as the resident head of S.M.A.C.'s tox division ever since it had a tox division. The same man who had been best friends with my father which, in my mind, made him family. You might say it was a stroke of good luck that he hadn't retired yet. If ever there was a case in which I needed both his medical expertise and his loyalty, this was it.

I peered into his glass-blue eyes and grinned.

"You know why I'm here, old timer," I said in my best imitation of a tough-guy dick. "Whaddaya got for me?"

Miner raised his right hand and quick-slapped my butt.

"Not here, dummy. We'll address your emergency behind closed doors."

It's true, Norman was old. Even by retirement standards.

I watched him as he walked the narrow third-floor corridor, a half-dozen steps ahead of me. Waddled is more like it, with his terribly bowed, nearly stunted legs, bedroom slippers for shoes. He was a short man who had been a good two to three inches taller a good two to three decades ago. Before age and gravity betrayed him.

Once inside his office, he took his place behind a mammoth wooden desk, sat down hard in a leather swivel chair, and released a very relieved breath. The place was as musty as it was cramped. It gave you the feeling that this one room had been left untouched for decades; that as the years passed, the hospital had simply built around it.

Floor-to-ceiling bookshelves covered the walls with what I guessed were about a thousand volumes. So many books and magazines that not a single space of shelf went unused.

Miner ran sausage fingers over a weathered face, then ran them through his full head of stark white locks. I could tell by the thick layer of sweat that coated his upper lip that he was in real pain. The deep set of crow's feet carved into the corners of his eyes proved that he'd been enduring the pain for a long time. As soon as he got hold of his breath and his equilibrium, he asked me how I was holding up, as if the state of my health were foremost on his mind. And to a man like Miner, it was.

"I was about to ask you the same thing."

He smiled as best he could under the circumstances. "It's the damned gout again, Richard," he said. "Getting so I cannot eat or drink a thing without my feet swelling up like balloons."

I was well aware of the good toxicologist's penchant for rich foods and fine wines. A fondness that, at this stage of the life-game, was pretty much killing him. The good toxicologist plagued by toxins swimming around in his own blood.

I sat down in the one wooden chair in front of his desk.

"You should retire to Florida," I said. "Switch to a low-fat diet; take it easy like normal people your age."

He exhaled a breath and looked me in the eye.

"Now let me ask you, Richard," he said. "Just what the hell would I do with myself in Florida?"

I pretended to think about it for a minute, scratching at the tip of my chin with index finger and thumb. "You could chase women, for instance."

"Not with these feet," he said. "'Sides, all the women in Miami are either too old, too married or too rich."

"Rich is good," I said. "And you're mature in years yourself."

"Never married," he said. "Never had any kids, and despite the mileage, I do not consider myself an old man."

"What is it you're trying to tell me, Doc?"

"I'm in full possession of my faculties, feet be damned. And, I've still got my first paycheck."

He pulled out the top desk drawer and retrieved a manila folder, which he laid flat on his desk before flipping it open. From where I sat, I could see that his hands were shaking. Not a lot, but enough for me to notice.

"Mrs. Montana's tox report," he said. "Per yours and Phillips's request."

He ran an index finger across a sheet of eleven-by-fourteen-inch computer-generated graph paper, pausing every second or two to whisper something indiscernible under his breath.

Looking back up, he said, "These are the facts of the matter: not only was the alcohol level in her blood high enough to put most men twice her size into a coma, but she also had a good amount of curare floating around her veins and brain."

"Curare," I said. "Stuff that paralyzes you."

He nodded. "That, Richard, is your smoking gun."

I shook my head. Miner's blue eyes were still glued to mine when he let loose with a painful grunt as he shifted and repositioned sore feet beneath his desk.

"Stuff has been around for years and years," he said. "Emergency rooms still keep it lying around in their closets for the occasional psychopathic patient that can't be controlled."

"I didn't think it was used anymore," I said.

"It's very rare," he agreed. "Or rarely used, anyway. Forty-five years in the business and never once have I come across it in a potential homicide until now." He explained that curare was only lethal when injected directly into the bloodstream, but not when ingested orally, in which case it only caused a temporary total paralysis.

"Edgar Allen Poe suggested the use of curare in his story, *The Premature Burial*," he said with a quick over-the-shoulder glance to the bookshelf behind him. "The story examines the then very real possibility of being buried alive. Poe was petrified of it. With curare you are unable to talk, blink your eyes or move your lips. You can hardly breathe. Yet the mind remains razor sharp, fully cognizant. That was Poe's real fear: being fully conscious of your hopeless, suffocating situation underground."

Miner also revealed that the Nazis had a nasty habit of administering a combination of curare and mescaline on select Jews and Poles in Dachau during their savage wartime mind-control experiments.

"The drug works quickly," he went on. "But then the paralyzing affects can disappear just as fast, depending upon the dosage. So too will all traces of the drug." He shifted his gaze from the tox report to me. "Ten years ago, I never would have found it."

"The miracle of technology," I said. But what I really thought was that it didn't take a brain surgeon or even a toxicologist with forty-five years experience under his lab coat to make a clear determination on how Scarlet had been murdered.

"Somebody fed her the stuff," I added. "Then proceeded to cut her up in a way that would make it look like a psychotic suicide."

"As in self-mutilation," Miner said. "Which is, of course, more believable than if the cuts had been nice and neatly executed."

"The last desperate act of a desperate housewife. That's the theme the killer was after."

Considering this new development, I had to ask myself how possible was it that I would have access, much less the means, to acquire a poison like curare? The answer, of course, was impossible. But then what about Jake? Could he find a way to get the stuff? As the top Albany cop, I knew it was very possible. Standing inside that musty old office, I was beginning to feel my sternum loosen up. For the first time in almost twenty-four hours I was beginning to believe that I had absolutely nothing to do with Scarlet's death. Sure, there were the scratches on my hands, but that's all they were.

Scratches.

"At this point," Miner continued, "I'm beginning to think her heart may have given out even before her throat was cut. But then, here's where things get even more interesting, Richard my boy." Once more, he stared down at the graph. "She also had ingested enough opiate and speed to jumpstart a Mack truck."

"Speed, as in amphetamines," I mused. "Opiate, as in heroin, smack, shit."

He sat back heavily in his chair. I pictured Suma letting me in on Scarlet's nasty drug habit.

"Shit," he said. "Precisely."

"What do you make of all this?" I asked.

"My take is that the sadistic bastard who did this wanted her completely messed up on one hand—"

"Drunk and paralyzed," I interjected.

"But on quite another hand, he wanted her fully awake, fully cognizant." He paused for a quick breath and a painful wince. "You see what I'm getting at here, Richard?"

I shook my head.

"What I'm trying to tell you is that the killer wanted to keep her fully immobile, but also fully conscious while he cut her up."

The silence in the dark room suddenly seemed thicker than the dust that coated the furniture, until I raised the billion dollar question.

"Am I to conclude, Dr. Miner, that in your professional opinion, Scarlet could not possibly have killed herself by slicing her own neck?"

"The only thing she could have managed in her state, Detective Moonlight, was to die."

I sat up straight. The arteries in my head were throbbing.

"You be willing to act as an expert witness in a court of law, old friend?"

Miner made a cross over his heart with his right hand.

"So help me die," he said. "Not that I'm gonna need any."

A beat later, Miner had to excuse himself before hobbling to the bathroom down the hall outside his office. I used the break as an excuse to pull the thick volume of Poe off his bookshelf. Sitting back down I thumbed through the collected works until I came to the story I was looking for *The Premature Burial*.

Alone, inside that dimly lit room, I began to read.

What I learned is that curare could indeed be a very helpful tool for the person who wanted to fake their own death. It could also prove instrumental for the creep who required his victim to become completely incapacitated while remaining fully awake, fully aware. Even if said victim was about to be murdered in the most brutal of ways.

In the tale, Poe recounts the true story of the wife of a prominent Baltimore congressman who one day in the mid 1850s, without warning, was stricken with a "sudden and unaccountable illness." Her doctors, not having the skills necessary to resuscitate, pronounced her dead.

According to Poe, "her face assumed the usual pinch and sunken outline. The lips were of the usual marble pallor. The eyes were lusterless. There was no warmth. Pulsation ceased."

The supposedly dead woman was placed inside the family vault where she remained for three years until it was opened once again. It was then that the widowed husband got the shock of his life. Instead of discovering the decayed body of his wife inside her casket, he found her still clothed bones set beside the tomb's door. Having become fully awake, the woman had somehow managed to escape her casket. At some point during her ordeal, she even managed to light an oil lamp. What she could not manage, however, was to gain anyone's attention before she must have surely starved to death inside that lonely black tomb.

While Poe made no mention of murder or a murderer, it was obvious that the woman had been drugged with a chemical that, while giving away nothing about how or who might have been responsible for administering the mechanism of death, made her appear very dead. Maybe the guilty party had been the woman's politician husband, or maybe it was the woman herself. In any case, the point here was not whodunit, but whatdunit.

Miner came back in. I got up and replaced the volume back onto the shelf where it belonged.

"Pretty scary stuff," he commented.

"If you're still hanging around when I go, promise me you'll make certain there's no gas left in the tank," I said.

"Don't talk like that, son," he said as he painfully slid himself back down into his chair, as if the question had an answer. He sat as far back as the swivel spring would allow without him dropping onto his back.

"Would you be willing to go public with your findings even before a trial begins?" I asked.

He twirled his thumbs. I knew the action helped him to think.

"How far in advance?"

"Today," I replied, with a downward glance at my wristwatch. "Scarlet's body is scheduled for a four o'clock cremation. Phillips has already offered to stop it, but I want to prevent his direct involvement for as long as possible. I might be able to legitimately stop it if you—the toxicologist—go public now."

He nodded for a few seconds while staring down at his twirling thumbs. Then he perked up.

"I have no real reason to withhold my information, if that's what you want. But I warn you, my coming forward now may render my evidence inadmissible in court. Unless there's an order for discovery that I'm not aware of."

"I'm not concerned with the future," I told him. "All I want to do is invite an immediate public inquiry. I do that, I've not only won some kind of justice for Scarlet, but I also start smoking out the real killer or killers."

Sitting up in his chair, Miner once more pulled the center drawer open. He pulled out a second manila folder. A duplicate for sure. He slammed the drawer closed, handing the package to me from across the desk.

"You might find yourself talking to a crime reporter as early as this afternoon," I said. "That is, if I can arrange it. This package doesn't mean a whole lot unless you put yourself out there, offer up a testimony."

"I'll do it," he said, tired face showing hints of yet another wave of pain shooting through his body. "I'll let the public in on the truth."

I felt the slight weight of the package resting against my right quadricep.

"You do this," I warned him, "you act of your own volition. If I.A. suspects you were coerced, they'll crucify us both."

"Look, Richard," he said, "in my professional opinion, somebody messed that woman up real bad. For whatever reason, I don't know. That should be for the police to determine. But if the cops don't want to get to the bottom of it, then I think it's only right that we do it for them."

"No one should be allowed to get away with murder," I growled. "Especially an honest-to-goodness decorated officer of the law."

32

Tox report in hand, I made my swift retreat from Dr. Miner's office.

Outside the building I jogged past the physical plant, past the massive concrete platform that supported the tall, ice-coated liquid oxygen tanks that misted in the gray sky and light rain.

Once inside the funeral coach, I dialed the now-memorized number for Lyons.

"Crime desk," he answered.

"I've got it," I announced. "Smoking gun and all."

"Where are you?"

"Albany Med. And what I've got from tox tells me that Scarlet was drugged, then cut up in her own bed, alive, no evidence of a break-in."

Lyons exhaled. "Holy Christ," he said. "The can of worms has been officially cracked."

"The can of worms runneth over."

"I'll get started on the story now."

I told him about Miner, about his willingness to testify. Then I gave him the phone number to the old toxicologist's office. He said he already had it stored in his Palm Pilot.

"How soon can we meet?" I asked.

"Tonight," he said. "Nine o'clock sharp."

"I need to get to you sooner," I told him. "Scarlet is scheduled for a cremation in a few hours. I need to save her body and I need for it to come from your end."

"I'll contact O'Connor's office immediately after I get Dr. Miner's statement. Believe me, they'll want nothing more than to put a halt to the cremation."

I pulled a ballpoint from what used to be an ashtray full of crushed cigarette butts. "Okay. Nine o'clock it is. The usual venue?"

"Be on time."

I scribbled the number 9 on the back of my left hand and stuffed the pen back into the now ashless tray.

"I never run late," I said, cutting the connection.

33

What all of this meant, of course, was that my intended Russian restaurant visit up in Saratoga would have to be put on hold. For now it was more important to work on how Scarlet died rather than why. As for the albino man, my built-in shit detector told me he had much more to do with the why than the how.

Like most detectives, I had two cameras packed away in a padlocked metal strong-box that I stored inside the back of the funeral coach where once my dad might have stored a wreath. One was a 35mm Minolta with color film that provided day and date imprints, the other a digital camera that I now used in place of the obsolete Polaroid.

Also packed away in the same box, a small black field bag containing scissors, wire cutters, tweezers, pliers, syringes, plastic bags, penlight flashlights, a bottle of luminol and a few other assorted necessities, including fine-haired brushes and magnetic powders for lifting latent fingerprints. Equipment that would have aided my detecting during my first trip to the house had Cain not been supervising.

The Beatles once more cranking from the eight-track speakers, I drove out of the hospital parking lot. I crossed over New Scotland, headed east along Madison until I came to the white marble-paneled Empire State Plaza where I pulled over, ran into the Charter One Bank located on the complex's first floor, and deposited the rest of Jake's cash advance. When I got back in the car I hooked a left onto Eagle, driving past City Hall on my way to New York Route 9 in the direction of the Montana household.

Now was the time to get back inside Scarlet's bedroom, to match the scrapings on her wrists with those on the bedposts. If there were bedposts.

There were other things that needed to be done.

I wanted to pick up any samples that might be stuck to the carpet. These included tiny hair fibers, threads, anything that might appear foreign and/or out of the ordinary. Anything that might have come from Jake, not from me!

I also wanted to get a better look at the blood spatter patterns, spray the room with luminol in order to get a visual on any leftover blood that proved untraceable to the human eye. I had to gather up as much evidence as I could that would corroborate Miner's tox findings—evidence independent of the evidence Albany forensics might have lifted on Sunday night.

The more independent evidence, the better.

When it was done, I might even consider the standard door-to-door interview process. Maybe if I got in the face of the surrounding neighbors I might coerce a statement or two confirming the sounds of violent arguing coming from the Montana household on Sunday night.

Scarlet was to be cremated in six and a half hours. That is, unless Prosecutor O'Connor stepped in to stop it.

I wasn't about to count on anything other than performing the precise and careful C.S.I. that Cain would never have allowed when he first brought me onto the scene as the puppet independent investigator.

"She's not a girl who misses much," sang John Lennon while I cruised up Crumitie along the northern edge of the city where the concrete jungle ended and the suburban sprawl began. I looked over my left shoulder at the Saint Pious parking lot and the big brick church, attached school and gymnasium that loomed in the center of it.

Harrison was in there ... my little bear.

In the center of my brain, I saw him sitting inside one of the painted cement-block classrooms. I saw his face, his closely cropped hair and smooth cheeks. I saw him smiling, laughing, going about his day without me. The vision, as always, was way too real, so that when my attention was diverted by the sound of sirens, I was none too disappointed.

One glance into the rearview revealed at least three fire engines bearing down on my ass end. Without thinking, I pulled over onto the shoulder, allowing them to pass. Sirens blaring, lights flashing, they blew by me in a New York millisecond.

I found myself breathing deep, forehead resting on the steering column. There was the rain falling against the windshield and the swoosh-and-click rhythm of the wiper blades swiping the windshield. I'm not sure why exactly, but I suddenly fell into a fit of exhaustion.

The sleepy sensation poured over me like a cloudburst, from the top of my head to the tips of my toes. I felt dizzy, the fingers on my right hand trembling with pins and needles. I needed to sit down. But then, I was already sitting. All went black even before I closed my eyes.

Scarlet lies on her side. Other than the thin gold necklace that dangles against her white breasts, she is naked. She is smiling, about to break out into a bitter laugh ... I see myself reaching for her; reaching for her neck ...

My eyes opened.

Maybe I was taking on too much with this case. Maybe I should have just signed off on Jake's request. There was a .22 caliber frag in the center of my head, nestled snug up against the cerebral cortex. I knew by now that a whole lot of stress could force the bullet to move.

Still, I was alive.

Scarlet wasn't.

As the sirens faded into the suburban distance, I rubbed my face with damaged hands, forcing the blood up to the surface of the skin. I felt the blood pour back into my fingertips. Gripping the column-mounted transmission stick with my right hand, I threw the heavy funeral coach back into drive and pulled back out onto the road. At the same time I raised my hand, feeling the button-sized entry wound scar behind my ear.

"Happiness is a warm gun," the assassinated Beatle wailed. *"Bang, bang; shoot, shoot."*

34

There was nothing left.

Correction! What was left of the two-story Colonial was completely engulfed in flames and along with it, any hope for further answers, forensic or otherwise, from Scarlet's second-floor bedroom.

Orange-red flames rose and roared out of holes punched into the roof by the fire fighters with their pickaxes, boiled through the blown-out windows. I must have parked a good one-hundred feet away from the inferno, but the heat was so intense it bitch-slapped me in the face the moment I stepped out the car.

The heat didn't let up there. It grew more and more intense as Cain emerged from out of the crowd of sightseers. With the plastic-covered Nicky Joy at his side, he stopped me in my tracks.

"Crime scene all gone," he said. Then, realizing what he had said and how he'd said it, he shook his head in obvious disgust. Joy just stood there, granny glasses streaked with rainwater, transparent raingear sprinkled with black ash.

Together the three of us moved on towards the onlookers and on-the-spot television reporters standing beside their mobile broadcasting vans. Even the firemen who were dressed in full black protective gear—masks and oxygen tanks strapped to their backs—could only come so close to the fire without getting charred. The only visible option for the crews at this stage of the battle was to fix their hoses on the heavy flames and keep them from spreading to the homes located on either side of the Montana estate.

I felt a shove.

Gazing over my right shoulder I saw Brendan Lyons standing there. He was dressed in that same blue blazer and khaki pants combo he'd been wearing the night before when I met him at the airport bar. Gripped in his right hand was a reporter's steno pad.

We'd spoken on the phone just minutes before. There was a number 9 scribbled on the back of my hand to remind me of that night's rendezvous. I knew he'd given me a good look before walking past, nudging my shoulder a little in the process.

"'Scuse me," he said, barely loud enough to be heard above the roaring flames.

For just a split second, I nearly acknowledged that I knew him, but then I caught myself.

He turned his attention to Cain. "Care to make a statement, Detective?"

Cain turned to face the reporter for a full two or three seconds before stating, "No comment."

"Sunday night the Chief's wife apparently committed suicide in this home," Lyons continued. "Perhaps the fire started all by itself as well."

Cain took a quick step forward. "I said no comment."

The cool reporter's expression never wavered. Not happy, not sad. Just Even-Steven. Give away nothing, take away nothing. He began to turn away, but as he did, Cain reached out and took hold of his blazer sleeve.

"Wait a minute," he said. "On second thought, I do want to make a statement."

Lyons did a one-eighty, cupping his left hand over the steno pad to keep the rain off. As if the dinner bell had been rung, five or six other reporters gathered at the feed trough alongside him.

"I would like to go on record with the following," Cain announced. "If it's determined that the destruction by fire of the Montana home was the result of arson, then the responsible party will be prosecuted to the fullest extent of the law. We will also be investigating the possible connection between said arsonist and Scarlet Montana's would-be murderer."

Cain was reversing his conclusion about the manner of Scarlet's death, suicide to murder. Why he had chosen to do it now in public, I could only assume had everything to do with the fire.

Something else was happening too.

My old partner was pushing me out, effectively erasing my role as the independent investigator by calling Scarlet's death a murder. Which meant that now he would have to come up with a viable suspect.

The reporters pushed forward, shoving their way towards Cain with their handheld microphones and cameras.

"Are you saying that Mrs. Montana did not commit suicide after all?" somebody shouted.

"We've reached a new conclusion," Cain said with all the stone-faced confidence of a politician.

"Do you have any suspects, Detective Cain?" a man wearing a Fedora shouted. "And if not, do you have any viable leads?"

"Do you have anyone in custody?" another woman shouted.

"Can you confirm Chief Montana's death?" Lyons abruptly interjected.

The question pierced me like a dum-dum bullet.

"Like I've told you before," Cain said as he and Joy began plowing a path through the media people, "I have no further comment until more answers are made available to me by the arson and on-site emergency technicians. But let me say again, whoever is responsible for the heinous events of the past two days and nights will be severely dealt with." As he passed me, he grabbed hold of my arm. "Let it not be said that the A.P.D. does not take care of its own."

35

It took a good deal of shoving and pushing, but soon enough Cain had pulled us through the crowd and just inside the off-limits perimeter established by a long semi-circular formation of police barricades and yellow crime scene ribbon.

Outwardly, I wasn't saying a goddamned word. But inside, I was screaming!

You torched the place.

You torched the place to destroy crucial evidence that could have been used against you. You torched the place with Jake inside it because maybe he was threatening to talk, to tell the whole truth about whatever it is you're covering up. You destroyed the evidence and a key suspect who was at the same time a key witness, and then you changed your story once you put two and two together and discovered that I was about to prove Scarlet's death a homicide.

I wanted to spit those exact words in his face. But how could I? I had no definite proof of anything.

Now with the Montana home burning to the ground, I wouldn't have enough evidence left over to support a parking violation, much less a homicide. All I had was just a very toxic tox report backed up with Miner's testimony and my gut instinct and growing suspicions about my old partner.

All around us came the roar of the flames and the feel of the steady, ash-filled raindrops that pelted our heads and faces. There were the multi-colored police and fire truck lights and the tinny, indiscernible voices that spewed out of the two-way radios.

Cain slapped me on the shoulder. "Follow me!" he shouted above all the noise. He began walking away from the burning home in the direction of the identical Colonial next door.

I followed.

Standing there, away from the crowd and the burning house, I saw something laid out along the driveway of the untouched home, not ten feet from where an EMT van was parked. The van was white with red block letters printed on the side. It was parked at the top of the drive beside a cop car and a fire department van that had pulled up onto the grass, its tires having dug two parallel swaths out of the moist lawn.

The closer Cain led me to the driveway, the more I could see that the object in question was a body. A person burned so black and beyond recognition that it was hard to tell if it had been a man or a woman. The light rain falling on the charred body caused steam to rise up off the black skin.

Jake.

Having made it across the lawn, Cain and I stood shoulder to shoulder at the edge of the drive, over the burnt remains.

"Who found him?" I asked, kneeling now to get an even better look at a body that had lost at least half its once bulky mass. As expected it had affected all the classical attributes of a burn victim: black, too-tight skin; mouth gaping wide open; arms raised overhead; fists clenched like a boxer in a pugilist's position.

Upon closer inspection, I saw that his right arm was raised noticeably higher than the other. It told me that the right hand had been his dominant.

"Firemen found him inside the kitchen just after the place flashed," Cain said. "In the far end of the room where they also found what they believe to be exploded containers of accelerant."

From down on one knee, I looked up at my former partner. He was dressed in a black blazer and charcoal slacks. He was giving me this hard-as-hell stare. Finally, he spoke up.

"There's something I need to run by you, Dick," he said, voice low and tragic. "The exploded containers, they contained an unusual accelerant…Embalming fluid…Stuff is full of ethanol and alcohol, I'm told. Burns like it too. That's what the fire boys told me."

I stood up, breathing in some of the smoke and ash-tainted air. I knew exactly where Cain was going with his "embalming fluid" crap— the connection, rather, the insinuation he was trying to establish. Because who better to know the highly flammable qualities of embalming fluid than me?

"When are you going to stop the head games?" I demanded.

Cain remained stone-faced. "Please don't get defensive. We have uncovered specific evidence that will link the arson and now the murder to someone who might have access to old cans of embalming fluid. That's all I'm saying."

Cain was playing dodge ball with my head; bluffing; pretending to connect me with Scarlet's death without actually coming out and saying it.

"I was running an independent investigation," I said. "Why would I have destroyed my own evidence by burning down the house?"

He never said a word—didn't have to say a word. My old partner simply smiled.

That was it, then. I was out on my ass whether I liked it or not. The stakes had changed.

Crime scene all gone. More like, *investigation* all gone. It meant that now the fingers of Albany justice were about to point at me as a suspect.

I turned and started back across the lawn towards the still burning home. As I walked, I pictured Cain pulling a cigarette from his jacket pocket and firing it up with his Zippo.

"Your father was an embalmer," I heard him say. "Maybe it's possible there're still some cans of embalming fluid left lying around from his operation. Maybe the arsonist-slash-murderer broke into your home, stole a couple. To make you look like the bad guy."

I stopped, turned back around. Sure enough, the detective was sucking on a fresh butt.

"Let's call all this a pretty bad attempt at the A.P.D. trying to set me up," I growled.

"Jeeze, Dick," he said with a pull on the smoke, "why in the world would I want to do something like that to my old partner? The very man whose own flesh and blood lives under my roof."

Cain, low-blowing. Me, scraped hands clenched into fists.

"Because I'm getting close to finding out who killed Scarlet," I said. "It's why you changed your story from the suicide you so badly wanted to murder. It's why you killed Jake and burnt down his house. You and your little buddy, Nicky."

He released a hit of smoke in the rain. "Personally, Dick, I take serious offense to such an allegation."

I stepped back, lowering my hands. I knew full well the disaster that awaited me should I haul off and wallop him in the mouth.

"Remember," he added, "you were the last one to be with Scarlet the night she died. I've got evidence of your presence at the scene—a beer bottle, a massage therapist's oil bottle. I've even got your DNA. You massaged Scarlet, then you fucked her and then, caught up in some jealous lover's rage, you killed her."

I pictured Jake coming through the kitchen door on that Sunday night. Now he was dead. And along with it, my prime suspect; my entire reason for excluding myself as a possible suspect.

Blue smoke oozed through the narrow gaps in Cain's teeth. "I wonder what Scarlet's autopsy truly revealed?" he mused. "I wonder what the internal showed? Maybe some seminal fluid? Tell me, Moonlight, did you use a condom, or did you fuck *au naturel?*"

In all the years I had known and worked side by side with Senior Detective Mitchell Cain, I had never before been witness to the man who stood before me, just beyond the flames of a burning crime scene. This man was a perfect stranger, a man who had something to hide; a man who was willing to betray the brotherhood of cops because of it; a man who, in my mind anyway, might be willing to kill over it.

I turned back toward the Montana house. By now, it had nearly burned itself out, the building reduced to a pile of charred embers.

I might have stood there in the rain and ash, fighting with Cain till the sun went down. If we still had a sun, that is. There simply was no point. With Jake gone, Cain was the new man in charge. He had the power of the entire A.P.D. behind him and, if I didn't know any better, I.A. in his pocket. If he wanted to set me up, he was going to do it, with or without proof of my intimate involvement with Scarlet.

Welcome to my new world order.

I moved on toward the police barricades.

"Your life is circling the drain, Moonlight!" my old partner shouted. "If I were you, I'd think about getting myself a lawyer!"

I picked up my pace.

"A very good lawyer! Because I believe you're gonna need one pretty damn quick!"

As though heeding my enemy's advice, I ran like hell.

36

With the black plume of smoke hovering over the scene, everything was covered with soot and little gray shards of weightless ash. I took it double-time across the Montana lawn, careful not to trip over the fire hoses. I ran past the firemen, past the uniformed cops and hurdled the yellow barricades set up along the perimeter.

I pushed through the crowd that stood out on the street and made my way to the funeral coach. Falling into the driver's seat I tried hard to ignore Cain's threats. Because for now anyway, that's all they were.

Threats. Head games.

I concentrated only on pulling my shit together while I pulled out my keys and fired up the black monster.

Back home, I downed yet another anti-inflammatory and, right or wrong, I poured a glass of whiskey, setting it down on the kitchen table. I could think of only one more thing to do (again, right or wrong). I had to talk to Lola. Just the sound of her voice would calm me down. Maybe our relationship was sexless, but she was the closest thing I had to a best friend. Cordless phone in hand, I dialed her private line at the State University in Albany.

Mid-afternoon, Tuesday. I knew she'd be tucked away inside her office. True enough, she answered after only two rings.

"It's me," I said. "There's been some complications."

"The fire," she supplied, "it's been all over the news."

"Jake is dead. They killed him too."

"Who's they, Richard?"

"Cain," I said. "Maybe Nicky Joy."

"You know that to be true? You have the proof?"

"I can feel it."

She exhaled some of her frustration. "I saw you and your old partner on the television," she went on. "In the background not far from the burning house."

I brought the whiskey glass to my lips, took a quick sip, and felt the warm liquid against the back of my parched throat. Almost immediately, it relieved some of the pressure in my head.

"He's dropped the suicide theory. Now he wants murder."

"That's what you wanted."

"Yes," I said. "But no."

I stopped right there. How the hell could I explain it?

Lola was right. I had been trying to prove that a homicide had been made to look like a suicide, but at the same time, I was trying to avoid a homicide that would point to me as a suspect.

"Richard, you there?"

I snapped out of my trance; trying my hardest to think straight, logically, cognitively discerning right from all wrong.

"I'm here," I said, picturing Lola sitting in front of her computer in her black jeans and t-shirt, long black hair draping over her face. She'd be working on a paper for publication in a medical journal the likes of *Psychology Today*.

"You're not making any sense," she said.

I looked into my whiskey glass and saw just a hint of my reflection—a distorted face and bald scalp. The pressure inside my head was expanding again. A very specific pressure isolated in the center of my brain that spider-webbed its way out to the surrounding lobes, scratching at the underside of my skull with its claws.

I breathed and told her that Cain was going to set me up.

She told me I should not be alone. Not in my condition.

"Be here now," I said.

37

I punched in the number for Albany Medical, Pathology Unit.

Phillips was taking longer than usual to answer. Or maybe it just seemed that way under the circumstances.

When he picked up I told him, "Cain changed his mind before we had the chance to do it for him."

"Suicide to homicide," George correctly surmised.

"Is Scarlet's body still there?" I asked, freshening my whiskey and downing a quick jolt before posing the question of questions.

"On ice, but not for long. Fitzgerald's people called. They're coming for the body in an hour."

I looked at the clock on the stove. Two-thirty.

Fitzgerald. The largest funeral home in Albany. The very outfit that bought Dad out not long before the cancer cut his retirement short.

"Who gave the order?" I inquired.

"Montana, I assume," he replied. "I guess he must have changed his mind, because they have her slated for the standard send-off instead of cremation."

Jesus, I thought. *He doesn't know.*

"Jake's dead," I told him. "He went up in flames along with his house about an hour ago."

Nothing on the line but dead air. I asked George if he was still there. He said he was.

In my head, I saw him standing inside a windowless four-walled room, some Vaughn Williams playing on the stereo. Total isolation. The way he liked it.

I asked him if he had a copy of Miner's tox report. He said he didn't but that he could get one easily enough just by taking a walk over to the labs. I told him what the report revealed about the drugs, about the curare.

"Cain's right, little brother," he said. "Murder."

"In the first degree."

"What do you want me to do?" he asked.

"A favor. Make that two favors."

"I'm listening."

"Hold onto Scarlet for as long as you can. Don't allow Fitzgerald's people or anyone else to pick up her cadaver. Tell them you've still got a couple of postmortem procedures to take care of now that cremation has been refused."

"What if they elect to wait inside the lab while I perform these … uh … procedures?"

A legitimate question.

"Tell them that you're backed up. That you won't be able to get to her until tomorrow. You're a local Quincy. Your word carries some weight around this town. Maybe you can't go against an order from a top cop like Montana, but you have the right to at least attempt more tests on a possible murder victim. Fitzgerald's people will just have to understand."

"Yeah, but will Cain swallow it now that Jake's dead? What about that second favor?"

"They deliver Jake to your doorstep, do not, under any circumstances, sign off on the body before it's opened up and thoroughly autopsied. Just like you did to Scarlet."

"Not gonna be easy with Cain staring me in the face."

"No matter what he throws at you, you've got to hold the line."

I thought about the curare that Miner found in Scarlet's blood. I wondered if it would be discovered in Jake's blood, too.

"Are we square on all this?"

1

"I don't think I've been asked to play the strong silent type since Tet in '68," he said.

"You can stand up to Cain. I have total faith."

"Faith," he said. "Don't see much of that anymore."

"That's because it's about believing in something you cannot see, feel or prove," I replied.

"Like the truth."

"Something Cain doesn't want you to see."

38

I picked the phone back up and dialed Miner's office. No answer.

At his age, Miner was hit or miss. I suppose it wasn't imperative that I talk with him right away. It was mostly for my own peace of mind; for his reaffirmation in backing me up in the case of Scarlet's murder. Especially in the light of new developments: Jake's death; the arson of the Green Meadows home; Cain's change in Scarlet's manner of death, not to mention his threat to set me up as a prime suspect. Developments Miner was sure to discover by way of the local news while he soaked his aching feet.

Nothing but ringing coming from Miner's office phone.

I pictured a far younger Miner sitting across from my father at the same kitchen table that still occupied the 23 Hope Lane kitchen. The two of them slow-drinking "Coffee Royals." That is, coffee laced with shots of Crown Royal whiskey. I could still hear them laughing aloud while my old man and the good toxicologist tried to outdo one another with stories and theories that almost always revolved around a dead body they'd both had the pleasure of working on—Miner from the medical toxicology end, Dad from the embalming burial end.

When his voicemail clicked on I decided not to leave a message. I didn't know his home number. Miner didn't believe in giving his private number out to anybody. I had it written down someplace, but finding it would be next to impossible. I just could not remember where I put it.

A minute later, I picked the phone back up and punched in the number for Albany Medical Center, Pathology Unit.

Phillips wasn't answering. Or maybe it just seemed that way considering I was once more under the gun. But when he finally picked up, I told him right off, "Cain changed his mind, before you and me could do it for him."

My blood was boiling. I could feel it running, pulsing through my veins, as if my skin had somehow peeled itself back and away from my body.

Just breathing coming from the phone.

"George," I said. "You there?"

"Moon," he mumbled. "Didn't you just call me?"

"Yeah, I'm calling you."

"No, what I mean is, you called me a couple of minutes ago with the exact same information—suicide to murder, keep Scarlet's body in storage, hold off Fitzgerald. Remember?"

I sat back, swallowing a hard breath.

"It's not memory that's the problem," I said.

"Oh, that's good, 'cause for a second or so I thought you might be losing your mind."

"What's left of it," I murmured. But George didn't laugh.

My mind, it wasn't always right. Maybe I wasn't aware of the specific medical reasons for why I suffered from the occasional memory lapse; why they became so frequent during stressful moments (the NYC neurologists used to lob around terms like *cross electrical activation* and *synesthesia*. The lapses could be both frustrating and embarrassing. And what was worse, there wasn't a goddamned thing I could do about them.

"I'll call you back, George," I said.

"Not again, little brother," he replied.

I hung up.

I sat there at the table with the rain having picked up against the roof and the kitchen windows. I poured a whiskey and wracked my aching brain.

What it all came down to was what the hell was Cain hiding? What was so important that he might be willing to murder for it?

I lifted my head, looked out the kitchen window and the gray, rain-filled sky. I knew that in order to get at the real truth, I had to dig deeper. I had to start investigating the *why* on top of the *how*. I had to go back in time to some of the first jobs I'd done for Cain. Not as one of his fulltime staff detectives, but as his "part-timer." It might not have been the correct place to begin digging, but at the moment, it was the only place I had.

I went upstairs into the master bedroom, dug two large boxes out of the closet, and carried them, one atop the other, down to the kitchen table where I began skimming through them.

I'd been placed on disability not long after botching a raid on a suspected drug dealer. The job had been my first since returning to the force after a lengthy recovery. But after the lawsuit that followed, the department relegated me to the part-time projects Cain and/or Jake specifically brought me in on, not as an A.P.D. detective necessarily, but as an independent investigator or a detective's assistant assigned to check and corroborate official police findings. In other words, so long as I did what they told me to do, following their leads from A to Z, there was no problem, no head condition to consider.

Starting with the box marked *'00-'01*, I glanced at my very first part-time assignment dated November 20, 2004 in blue ballpoint. The job involved a teenaged kid who, in a drunken stupor, rammed his motorcycle into a parked car, killing both himself and the woman who was still belted into the driver's seat.

A clear case of vehicular manslaughter. That is, had the kid lived.

At Cain's request I gave the scene a quick once-over, examining both the wreckage of the motorcycle and the car—the former a Harley Davidson and the latter an old model Volkswagen Beetle. In my estimation the kid had been killed instantly when he plowed through the side window and collided head-to-head with the driver, who was also killed instantly.

Even now I recalled taking the time to check out their separate IDs—names, addresses, DOBs and vitals. The fact that they were both organ donors (blood type B and A respectively), didn't surprise me in the least.

So far so good, as far as two unnecessary deaths went. But when I requested the scheduling of an autopsy with my friend George Phillips, Cain swore up and down that it would be a waste of precious time. That if I went "easy on this one," he'd see that I was well compensated. The force, especially S.I.U., was overworked now, he claimed. The result? The A.P.D. didn't always have the manpower or the resources necessary to investigate every little accident or drug-related shooting that came their way.

I remember standing there in the road, little more than a year into my recovery, nauseated as all hell from the anti-inflammatory drugs they were making me take on top of the motion sickness pills and prescription codeine.

I remember Cain, my wife's new sig-other, asking me nice-as-pie to work it out with him at his direction and discretion. If I did that, the whole process might go a lot smoother, including my payment.

"And who knows, old partner," he said, "this is Albany, after all. I can give you a shit-load of work on top of the disability scratch you take in every month."

The golden carrot set before me in the hazy glow of the street lamps, Cain stated that in his own opinion, cause, manner and mechanism of death were obvious: crashed motorcycle; massive head trauma; accident. There was no reason to prolong both family's agonies. Then, with his back to the parked cruisers and the accident wreckage, he proceeded to slide out ten one-hundred dollar bills from the interior pocket of his blazer and stuffed them into the side pocket of my leather jacket.

Did I feel ashamed of myself for taking the money? No.

Correction: yes and no. Yes because, let's face it, it was illegal to accept what amounted to a bribe. No because, financially speaking, I was completely fucked.

At the time, I was still going through my divorce. With mounting law bills, maintenance and child support payments, I couldn't even consider the possibility of not taking the cash. It was either that or sell dope.

After all, I wasn't a regular cop anymore. I was simply a part-time consultant living on the Union's disability. If they wanted to throw a little extra cash at me, I might find myself a little more cooperative in my methods of investigation.

And cooperative I was.

As much as it pained me to harbor a somewhat limited sense of ethics, I simply reached out with my pen, signed off on the paperwork, then went home to Dad's old Olympia typewriter to draw up a full case synopsis of my own.

The second job came a month later. A fifty-seven-year-old widow had jumped from the fifth floor window of her downtown apartment building onto the Grand Street cobblestones in Albany's Little Italy. Murder as the manner of death had already been ruled out by on-site A.P.D. when no forcible entry and no fingerprints other than the woman's own were discovered at the scene.

But when I was brought in I could immediately see that the shattered body was found lying face down in the road only about twelve feet away from the building. Anyone having passed Forensics 101 will tell you that suicides always *jump* out of a window or off a ledge. Homicides, on the other hand, are almost always *dropped* so that they land right beside the wall or the concrete sidewalk below.

Of course, I recalled not being particularly surprised by the fact that this woman was also an organ donor. I didn't think twice about it while I watched Cain pull up to the scene in an unmarked cop cruiser, again with specific underhanded instructions for me to keep my mouth shut about the possibility of murder, despite the position and location of the body. Once more he offered me cash. Twenty-one hundred big ones.

This time however, in the interest of covering our asses, Cain agreed that I call on Phillips to assist with what amounted to about a half hour of bogus pathology paperwork and signatures for the sake of S.O.P.

S.O.P. according to Cain.

I took careful sips of the whiskey, moving through the stacks of notes, records and reports like a man possessed.

Then came the third job. A twenty-year-old black man was gunned down outside TJ's Bar and Grill on South Pearl Street inside Albany's south end not far from where the abandoned railroad yards butt up against the Port of Albany. Cain met me on the scene at two in the morning, again asking me to sign off on their case synopsis and, at the same time, seeing what I could do about securing the necessary paperwork without going to the bother of an autopsy.

"They're just drug dealers anyway," is how he put it, while handing me yet another envelope, this time a mouthwatering grand total of twenty-five hundred.

I sat at the kitchen table and once more ran down the Xeroxed list of the dealer's vitals. His height, weight, criminal record, and how the dealer had bequeathed his body to science. The postmortem request was to take immediate effect upon his sudden death.

"Bequeathed his body to science," I whispered to myself. I guess that's when the realization slapped me over the head.

I flipped through the remaining stack of notes. I had no idea why it hadn't occurred to me earlier, or why I had never noticed it until now. Maybe it had something to do with my condition. Maybe it had something to do with sitting down and wading through the material all at once, because it was only now that the pattern seemed crystal clear. Obvious, even. Or was it just a coincidence that every single man and woman whose death I had "investigated" had consented to organ donation?

I looked through each and every case one more time, starting from the top. Like I said, all of them had organ donor status in common. There was something else, too. Every one of the victims had died from a violent and/or unnatural death.

I sat back and thought about it for a moment. If I were the M.E, would I have bothered to save what was left of those damaged bodies for science and or medicine once I'd completed the autopsy? Probably not.

More than likely, I would have handed over the battle-scarred bodies to the respective families for burial and left it at that. When that happened I couldn't help but picture the old man's face. Organ donation was a relatively new phenomenon that had its genesis in the late sixties and early seventies, concurrent with medical advances and an exploding population. Despite the good it provided for the terminally ill, my father was never keen on the idea of cutting out a corpse's liver or kidney or, Christ forbid, a living, pumping, human heart.

To him there was something spooky about burying an incomplete body, if not sacrilegious. He used to look directly at me and George, the both of us probably stoned, holding back the laughter by biting our tongues. With tight lips and right hand raised high to the ceiling of the brightly lit embalming room, he would say, "Boys, one day some scientist will tell you that to bury a human cadaver is a big waste of organs and body parts. You wait, if we allow the secularists to have their way, one day soon we will all be out of a job."

But of course progress would go on with or without Dad, never mind his or God's opinion.

I inhaled and exhaled deeply. Why hadn't I bothered to step out of the forest before now? Was it possible that I had been so blind that I hadn't even begun to recognize the part I had been playing in what now looked to me like a black market operation to harvest and sell body parts? Was my personal policy of asking no (or very few) questions about to backfire on me now that I had left my name on a paper trail that could be traced all over New York State? Was my brain that messed up?

I took a drink, staring down at the pile of notes, records and papers. Paper tigers poised to bury their fangs and claws into my back. More than two dozen cases of suicides, gunshot and car crash victims, drowning deaths, you name it. Every single one of them organ donors and every one of their case synopses executed by me and in full agreement with A.P.D. findings.

Dick Moonlight, part-time corroborator, big-time patsy, full-time head case.

I thought a little more about Cain's threat to make me the number one suspect in Scarlet's suicide-cum-murder. He had copies of everything at his disposal, I was sure. You see, Cain wasn't the type to overlook things like that. He had been using me all along as the perfect chump for his operation and I hadn't so much as asked a single question about why he wanted to use me.

That is until the Chief of Dicks himself personally brought me in on Scarlet's case. No wonder Cain and Montana seemed so caught off-guard when I refused to be their rubberstamp. For the first time in three years' worth of cases, I was turning my back on them, refusing to follow their line.

Maybe Cain was right when he said that I had suddenly grown a conscience. Maybe not. But then, he was right about one thing: he had the power to nail me to a wall. Power and paper.

He had the ability to establish motive not only in the form of my having been with Scarlet on the night she died, but also for my having engaged in a lengthy affair with her under the pretense of my being the Montana massage therapist. Or so Cain would no doubt assume. And Cain had the beer bottle with my DNA on it to prove it. He had an oil bottle and footsteps in the wet grass. Who knew what other surprises he had stored up his ass? For all I knew, he had a secret videotape stashed away somewhere, showing Scarlet and me doing the wild thing.

Shit!

When I really thought about it, Cain could nail me with motive, opportunity, intent and means. It was as simple as all that.

No murder weapon?

Of course there was no murder weapon because I had been the one to dispose of it. I just had no recollection of my actions. That's the absolute line they would take in a court of law, so help me God or fate.

Okay, Moonlight old boy, take a breath. That's it, breathe easy, get your head together.

I knew then that I needed a lawyer. Cain had been right about that too. There was no time to waste. What choice did I have? None, other than contacting the same man whose firm handled my divorce. Dad's one-time lawyer.

Regardless of the thirty G's I still owed him.

39

Seven God-awful digits I knew by heart. My lawyer, Stanley Rose. His direct office line.

Sometimes I thought Albany should change its name to *Smallbany*, because it was nearly impossible to strike up a relationship with anyone, professional or otherwise, who didn't already have some kind of connection to you, direct or indirect. In keeping with the tradition, Stanley Rose had been Dad's lawyer too, having handled the occasional lawsuit that might arise from clients who, for one reason or another, were unhappy with his services. You'd be surprised at the people who not only expect their loved ones to look alive in death (as if they're just sleeping), but who also expected them to rise up, maybe even sing and dance.

"They're dead for Christ's sakes, Richard!" the old man would shout aloud during an especially frustrating embalming and wake prep.

Like Phillips and Miner, I'd known Stanley nearly all my life, so naturally I retained him to represent me for my divorce. What I didn't know at the time, however, is how badly my income would take a hit after my accident and how difficult if not impossible it would be for me to manage my ever-increasing law bills. So to say my relationship with Stanley had become strained over the years was putting it lightly. Our relationship had become nuclear.

I held my breath as he answered.

"You got a lot of nerve calling me, Richard," he said. "Unless this is about a check."

I tried to look on the bright side, at least he didn't hang up on me.

"I'm doing my best to pay you back," I said, voice cool and calm. "I swear it." It was the truth.

"For more than a year now I've been asking you to take some kind of action on your bill," he said. "You haven't responded once."

I pictured the sixty-something lawyer seated at his wide mahogany desk, horn-rimmed glasses sliding down his straight nose, full head of gray hair groomed to perfection, pale cheeks flushed with anger.

"Listen, Stanley, I'm working on something that will get you paid back in full, plus plenty extra."

For a beat there was only his inhaling and exhaling into the receiver.

"What do you need?"

I started from the beginning, not holding anything back, trying not to repeat myself. After I finished, I asked him if he'd seen anything about the fatal Montana house fire on TV.

"Bits and pieces," he admitted. I knew he had a flat-screened digital television inside his office. It told me he was holding back.

"Then you already know something about my situation," I said. "My predicament."

"A little," he confirmed. "You mind if I call Miner to get his personal take?"

"You don't trust your own client?"

"Who said you were still my client?"

"Don't sweat it, Stan," I insisted. "Miner will confirm my story. Every last detail."

"Then we have no problem."

"Does this mean you're going to help me?"

Stanley might have been a lawyer, but he was also a businessman. If a black market organ harvesting operation existed inside the A.P.D. and if I was being railroaded by one of its principal operators, then he'd definitely want in on the action. A case like that would no doubt make national headlines. *48 Hours* or maybe *Nancy Grace*. National headlines would mean mucho exposure, mucho business. That's what I was banking on, anyway.

"First thing's first, Moonlight," he went on. "Your man, Cain. If he's able to somehow prove you were involved in the organ harvesting operation, no matter the level, you go down right along with him. And that's aside from your involvement in Scarlet's murder."

"Supposed involvement, Stan," I corrected. 'Supposed."

"Scarlet's murder is a whole separate issue. The body parts scheme is another. Your best bet would be to cop a plea with the state for immunity as a material witness."

"Listen, I had no idea what was going on behind the scenes when I signed off on their cases. Cain or Jake would call me in, give me my orders as a part-time investigator, and I did what they told me to do."

"But you knew you were breaking the law."

"My superiors in the department were ordering me to break it."

Stanley cleared his throat. "Let's get one thing straight from the get-go, Richard. You cannot plead ignorance in a court of law. You cannot rely on a perceived disability as a crutch. Maybe you have a little piece of bullet in your head but I believe your ability to determine right from wrong is pretty damned reliable. So let's cut through the bullshit right now."

There occurred one of those deadly pauses, like waiting for the executioner to slide the needle in the vein.

He asked me if I had access to the original records. I told him that the originals would have to be stored in the A.P.D. warehouse. Microfilm copies would be available at the City Hall Office of Records. Not to mention Cain's personal file.

"Then it will be impossible to cover over the paper trail," he surmised. "All you can hope for is that the state will buy your argument of being strong-armed into producing those phony case synopses." He paused. "I'll be truthful, Cain and Montana, I've always known them as pretty good guys. Honest, decent, hardworking."

I thought more about it. "They didn't exactly put a gun to my head. But I also knew they could make my life pretty miserable if they didn't get their way."

"Let me ask you something," Stanley went on. "You didn't take any off-the-books cash from either Cain or Jake, did you?"

Me, once more staring into the whiskey glass.

"Guess how you got paid for as long as you did during my divorce?"

"You really are a fuckup, Moonlight, you know that?"

I thought about the old man. Stanley never would have referred to him as a fuckup. Especially to his face. But then, dad didn't have a problem with his brain. Nor did he have a damaged cerebral cortex. Okay, I'll admit it, even if he did have a bullet lodged in his brain, he'd still be able to function on all cylinders. I on the other hand had always suffered from a faulty cylinder or two. Bullet to the brain or no bullet.

"You gonna help me or not, Stan?"

"No more pro bono," he said. "What do you plan on using for money?"

"What ever happened to client contingency?"

"Borderline clients that already owe me thirty large automatically relinquish contingency status."

For a moment I was stumped, until I quickly glanced at the old wooden placard that hung above the old G.E. stove. The one that read "God Bless This Home!"

"I'll mortgage the house."

"There's a bullet in your head could shift position at any time," he pointed out. "What's the probability of the bank giving you a thirty-year note?"

I paused for a beat.

"You know, that's what I've always liked about you, Stan. Your sensitivity."

"I'm a businessman," he said. "And I'm not in the business of making friends. You want sensitive, call Dr. Phil."

"Tell you what," I said, knowing I was treading micro-thin ice. "I'll sign over the deed."

He cleared his throat again. "Get the deed to my office. I'll be in touch after that." He hung up.

I tried to think like my father. If I were him, where would I have kept the deed to the house? It was impossible to think like Dad. He was smarter than me, more together. Didn't matter that he was dead. He was still more on the ball. In the months immediately following my accident, it was painful even to work up a simple thought. Since then, my condition had steadily improved. But that didn't mean I was out of the woods. Or would be anytime soon. I had trouble with certain things now. Important things versus unimportant things. Right versus wrong; logical versus illogical.

The deed to 23 Hope Lane. Even if I had stored it in a safe place for just such an emergency, I would never be able to remember where I put it.

40

I got out the phone book and looked up the Albany County tax assessor in the blue pages. When I got the woman who ran the department, I asked her what I needed to do in order to come up with a copy of the deed to my property. She told me I needed to come into the county courthouse where the county clerk would make a copy of the original, which should be on file. The copy would cost me twenty-five bucks. Cash. No credit.

She asked me for my address. She could look it up for me on the computer, verify my information, then send word down to the clerk to begin processing the paperwork. Save me some time. I asked her if she would be so kind.

"Is the property registered in your name?"

"It was transferred in my name after my father's death."

A moment or two passed. Long enough for me to have a quick swallow of whiskey.

Suddenly I heard a deep sigh.

"Oh my," she said. "Mr. Moonlight, is it?"

"Yes," I said. "Richard Moonlight."

"I'm not sure if you are aware of this, but a lien has been placed on your property."

My head ... an invisible vice was squeezing it.

"No one's notified me of a lien."

She checked the date of the lien, told me it had gone into activation only this morning.

"By whom?"

"By the Property Tax Department, claiming a fifteen-thousand dollar back-tax deficit, Mr. Moonlight."

I sat back in my chair, trying to breathe even and steady. Had I paid my tax bills? I mean, my life wasn't a complete train wreck. I recalled that I had paid the biannual bills, even recalled writing the checks at the kitchen table, stuffing the envelopes and licking the stamps. Maybe it was possible I was behind by a payment or two, but not fifteen Gs.

"With whom do I speak to straighten this out?"

"Well, that would be me," she answered. "Oh, pardon me, I'll have to put you on hold."

She did.

I drank.

The phone disconnected.

I called back.

The same woman answered. "Tax Assessor."

I told her who it was, that I had been disconnected. She hung up. I called back again. She hung up again without saying anything. I called back again. Nothing but a busy signal.

Then Lola walked in through the back door off the kitchen.

Standing in the frame of the still open door, her dark hair was wet with rain. Her somber face glowed in the dull white light that shined down from the light fixture.

"Dr. Ross," I said, lifting my glass high, "how's about a drink?"

She leaned against the doorframe, shooting me one of those tight-lipped slanty-eyed looks that spoke far louder than words. Without a whisper she crossed the kitchen floor and grabbed a glass out of the cabinet above the sink. She rinsed the glass out with cold water, than dried it with the dishtowel draped over the faucet.

Approaching the kitchen table, she leaned into me. For a quick and hopeful moment, I thought she was about to kiss me atop my head. Instead she brushed her fingers gently over my scalp, then set the glass down, pouring herself a half shot. She beamed at me with a tan face draped by long brown hair and matching brown eyes, and downed the shot in one quick swallow. Placing the glass back down on the table, she poured another drink and sat herself down.

"You're about to become a prime suspect in a homicide case," she whispered. "And you're celebrating?"

"Not celebrating," I said to her. "Commiserating."

"With yourself," she said. "How very pathetic of you, Moonlight."

I proceeded to tell her everything starting from the top, even re-treading the stuff she already knew, and the hot-off-the-press stuff like the sudden lien on my property when in fact, I'd paid my tax bills. Or most of them, anyway. So I thought. When I was through, Lola sat back in her chair, staring into her glass.

"On one hand I think you might be overreacting." Her voice was soft, low, almost inaudible. "Despite the terrible unpleasantness between you two, Cain had always been a decent partner to you and a supportive stepfather to your son. But he also has a talent for manipulation."

"Like you said, my boy lives with him. In there lies his advantage."

"Yes, but after your forced leave of absence, when you needed money the most, you were ready and willing to do what he wanted you to do, no questions asked. You were going through a divorce. You had alimony and child support to contend with. You needed the cash. And he gave you the full authority to act in the name of the law so long as you took his or Jake's lead. And don't give me any nonsense about the A.P.D. making your life miserable if you didn't go along, because they never told you that or else you would have told me. You made that up just to make things sound more dramatic for Stanley."

"I'm raising the stakes," I said, biting my lip.

"At whose expense?"

"My own."

"Wrong," the psychologist said. "Maybe you've sufficiently challenged Cain, but in the end, he believes that you will back down. You will do what he tells you to do, because that has always been the specific nature of your relationship. Your symbiosis. Cain is as much a control freak as you're all over the place. He believes that sooner or later you will cave. Because in a very real and very strange way, he believes you need him. Not because he lives with your son, but because he actually sees through all the skull and gray matter, sees that bullet inside your head as clear as day. He believes it makes you vulnerable, naïve, almost. Certainly, easily manipulated."

"But he's mistaken," I said. "I'm not backing down on this one."

"You're breaking the pattern," she replied. "Divorcing yourself from him in more ways than one for a good cause. I applaud you for it. But for a man in your condition, it will not be easy."

"He *will* try and put the finger on me," I insisted. "His threats are serious."

"Take a minute to think about it, Moonlight. If he tries to implicate you in his body parts operation—if there is a body parts operation—he risks implicating himself. Inevitably, he would also be tied in with Scarlet's murder and now Jake's."

"Maybe he's willing to take that chance. He's now the top cop by default. I'm the part-time head case."

"But you are not invisible," she insisted. "Even if yours is the only traceable name on the paper trail, it will lead to Cain, no matter what. He's the one who hired you in the first place, even after Jake forced you into medical leave. That very connection will raise the red flag."

"Unless that is, he's got all his excuses, smoke screens and alibis in order."

She got up from the table, went into the freezer, grabbed a couple of ice cubes, dropped them into her drink, and sat back down.

"Cain is more afraid than you know," she went on. "I think his world came crashing down when Scarlet suddenly showed up with her neck cut open from ear to ear."

"Assuming Jake was alone in killing her," I said.

"Then they invite you to come along for the ride, the one constant they think they can control and manipulate into supporting their conclusion of suicide. And yet, you suddenly turn on them."

I listened to the rhythm of the rain, looking at Lola's face, at her dark teardrop eyes. I asked her what else she had spinning around inside that clinical brain of hers.

"What if Jake and Scarlet were in on this organ thing more than you know?" she said.

"Whaddaya mean more?" I asked. "My gut instinct is that Scarlet didn't know about it at all."

"Suma already attested to witnessing Scarlet doing illicit drugs—snorting heroin, for God's sake. She'd been involved with some albino man who's been harassing you since Monday morning."

"Not exactly harassing," I said. "But I am about to insist on a little face time with the pink-eyed Q-Tip in the next day or so, clear things up a little."

"Listen," she went on, "what if, for whatever reason, both Jake and Scarlet wanted out? Or, even better, what if Montana didn't kill anybody? What if he just wanted out of his deal with Cain now that he could see how wrong he'd been; how his involvement with this thing was just eating away at Scarlet? Perhaps he had become overwrought with guilt or maybe he found Jesus. Maybe he wanted to try and clean Scarlet up, get his marriage back before it was too late. Anyway, maybe when he confronted Cain with this all hell broke loose. Cain felt he had no choice but to get rid of them both just to shut them up."

"If that were the case, he'd have no choice but to place the blame on me and hope that Johnny Q. Public would buy into it. I'm the logical chump because it's not only my name plastered all over the case synopses, I also had a track record of taking off-the-books cash from them."

Lola went tight-faced again.

"And don't forget," she said, "you were sleeping with Scarlet."

I felt a lump in my chest. "Oh yeah," I mumbled, "there was that too."

"What about the lien? Have you balanced your checkbook lately, Richard?"

I smiled the smile of the guilty. To be honest, I wasn't even sure if I could find my checkbook.

We didn't say anything for a minute. Then Lola took one more sip of her whiskey, got up from the table and set her glass in the sink.

"You said that the firemen found some old embalming solution containers in the burnt remains of Jake's house."

"That's what Cain told me."

"It's your nature to take him at his word. But did you actually see the containers?"

I shook my head. "They're probably hidden inside the same closet along with Scarlet's murder weapon and suicide note," I joked.

Lola didn't laugh.

"Your dad left a few cans of the stuff lying around downstairs along with his tools," she pointed out. "Did it ever occur to you while you were having your little pity party to maybe check and see if any of them were missing?"

"Kind of slipped my mind."

She shook her head and smiled. The first smile since arriving earlier. Not a cheery smile. Sardonic, frustrated.

"Shall we?" she asked, heading for the stairs.

"Lola," I said.

She stopped, her back to me, inside the vestibule off the kitchen.

"I'm sorry about getting you involved in this thing."

"Sometimes I'm sorry we ever met," she said. "But only sometimes."

Then she walked downstairs.

41

We were standing inside the old embalming room, now turned TV room, just off the space reserved for laundry on the bottom floor of the split-level. In a far corner, inside a closet that ran the length of the narrow space, was located a stack of old five-gallon plastic embalming fluid containers my father left behind when he moved his business downtown back in the 1970s. The stuff was comprised primarily of formaldehyde, methanol and ethanol, along with a few other toxic carcinogens tossed in the mix. It made sense to use it as an accelerant. As it was, you might find the occasional pot smoker who liked to dip their ducktail joints into the pink fluid to make the bone burn longer and more intensely.

At Lola's insistence, I groggily went ahead and counted the containers, but it was really a wasted effort since I had never bothered to count them in the first place. Whether it was ten or twenty I had no idea. It was simply a stack of toxic chemicals I had no way of getting rid of without having to find a dump that wouldn't charge me both arms and a leg for disposal.

We checked the room top to bottom for evidence of a break-in. We checked and rechecked the windows. Then we checked the back door that led out onto a concrete patio. We found no indication that suggested Cain or maybe Joy had somehow broken in and stolen a couple of cans of embalming solution. But if one of them had, the only way it would have been possible was by using a key to get in.

The only people with keys were Lola and me.

We went back up into the kitchen and sat back down at the table.

"I guess it doesn't matter if a can from your personal embalming fluid cache was used to start the blaze or not," Lola pointed out. "How difficult can it be to get the stuff? You can probably locate it online just like anything else."

"eBay," I nodded.

"Craigslist."

"So what do we do now, Doc?" I asked as I got up from the table. "In your professional opinion."

She crossed her arms and legs. "Just keep on doing what you're doing," she said.

I turned to her, leaning back against the counter. "And what have I been doing?"

"The right thing," she said. "The purpose behind your being hired by the A.P.D. in the first place. As a detective attempting to find the true cause behind Scarlet's murder. Find out how she died, you've done your job. In the mean time, you discover who done it, you win the grand prize."

"The 'why,'" I said. "You also have to establish the 'why' in order to derive a total understanding of a case."

"Precisely," Lola agreed.

I walked over to where she was sitting. "What's the grand prize?"

"Justice," she said. "Redemption."

"For me?"

"For Scarlet. If your going by the book has Cain so frightened to the point of arson and homicide," she continued, "then there's no telling what kind of grave he could be digging for himself."

"Nice choice of words," I said. "But then, I don't want to be his next homicide. I'm already a short-timer ... speaking of graves."

As soon as I said it, I knew I shouldn't have. Lola had spent the better part of a year counseling me on the reasons behind my suicide attempt. As a professional and as a friend she had talked me out of my funk, my death wish. She gave me reason to live, or at the very least, to move on with my life, as precarious as it may be. So any funny talk of death never failed to just plain piss her off.

She sat back in her chair, running open fingers through her long brown hair. I looked down at my hands folded in my lap. For a split second I thought about revealing them to Lola. But then something inside held me back.

"Maybe you think your life and death is a big joke," she said after a time. "But I am a part of you and I don't think it's a big joke at all."

She was right. Maybe the bullet was inside me, resting, waiting, but it was Lola who felt the pain.

Outside the kitchen, I heard the rumble of thunder not far in the distance. Perfectly, ominously timed. Then the lights went out.

"Now what?" I grumbled, looking around a now powerless kitchen.

"Power outage," Lola correctly surmised.

She got up and looked out of the window above the kitchen sink, I guess to see if any of the neighbors were also out of power. She said she couldn't really tell from where she was standing.

It wasn't the first time the power had gone out inside the old Moonlight homestead. Which meant I wasn't going to worry about it. Not with more pressing matters at hand.

She looked down at my left hand, pointed to the number 9 hastily scribbled upon the skin. I told her that it was a reminder to meet Lyons at the airport at nine o'clock. She glanced at her watch.

"I have a class to teach in thirty minutes," she said, standing up. "And you, my *Moonlight* friend, have four hours."

"Four hours to do what?" I asked, feeling two separate pressure points—one expanding in my head, another inside my sternum.

"To sober up before your meeting with Lyons."

42

My pockets were bone dry.

Lyons had picked up the tab the last time I met up with him at the Skybar. It would be a gross injustice for him to pick up this one too. Reciprocation was important in matters of shared information.

I pulled into a Mobile gas station and went inside to use the ATM. There was a young kid behind a counter that displayed cigarettes, candy, chewing gum and dirty magazines still protected in transparent plastic. He was wearing headphones attached to a white iPod hanging by a thin cord around his neck. He had short hair, a hoop earring in his left ear and a peach-fuzz chin beard. No pimples.

He'd barely gazed up at me when I came through the door, approached the cash machine, slipped my card into the required slot, and typed in my four-digit PIN number.

When the card shot back out along with a receipt that screamed "Insufficient Funds," I knew there had to be some mistake. Sure, money was tight, but I had already deposited what was left of the cash down-payment Jake had handed over. The money should have been readily available.

I slid the card in one more time and got the same result. This time I waved my hand at the kid. He looked up from his magazine and pulled off the headphones.

"Yeah?" he grunted.

"Something wrong with the machine?" I asked.

He shrugged. "I just do the register."

The door opened. A teenaged girl stepped in. Her dirty blond hair was tied in braids. She was wearing tight hip-hugger jeans and a tight boy-beater, the word JUICY stretched across an ample chest.

She approached the machine, threw me a bright Pepsodent smile.

"Are you still … using … ?" She let her words trail off.

I took a step back. "By all means," I offered.

She put in her card and punched in her number. After a second or two, the machine spit out three fresh twenties. The girl made it look easy.

She retrieved the card and her cash and exited the store.

"See," the kid said. "Machine works good."

Smart kid. Speak the English very well.

I decided to give the plastic one more shot. Same humiliating turndown.

Fuck it, I said to myself. I pulled out my near maxed-out Visa, popped it in, and began hitting the buttons that would authorize a two-hundred dollar cash advance.

But it was another turndown.

I tried again and again and was turned down again and again. By now, the kid behind the counter was growing suspicious. So was I. I might have been a head case, but I was beginning to get the distinct feeling that somebody somewhere was fucking with me. Fucking with my life. First Jake's sudden demise, then the tax lien, then the power outage, and now insufficient funds.

Cain.

It had to be somebody with pull and power. Somebody who could mess up another individual's life and get away with it in the name of the law.

The counter boy stared at me hard. "Listen man, machine just doesn't like you."

I glanced at my watch. Ten minutes till nine. Already I was running way too late. Conspiracy to destroy my life or no conspiracy, I had a mission to accomplish.

Lyons is buying again, I told myself as I departed the Mobile.

43

Just like the last time, I parked the funeral coach in the short-term parking garage across the street from the main terminal building. I unstrapped my shoulder holster, slid it out from under my jacket, and stuffed it and the Browning it housed into the glove box.

With the autopsy and tox report tucked under my left arm, I jogged across the two-lane, one-way access road that spanned the entire half-moon-shaped perimeter of the brick and glass structure. Once across the road I moved on past the nervous couples and families pulling luggage from the trunks of yellow taxis that pulled up along the curb and the even more nervous security guards looking on with a kind of tentative suspicion.

The automatic glass doors split open, allowing me entrance to the terminal.

I glanced over my shoulder in the direction of the huge multi-television monitor that was broadcasting a panoramic scene of Niagara Falls. New York State tourist propaganda. Maybe they should broadcast a short feature about our being the most taxed state in the nation. That would attract people to the Empire State. I shot past the few travelers lined up around the adjustable ropes set just a few feet beyond the U.S. Air counter and the two female attendants dressed in identical polyester suits who occupied the ticket booth and fed the baggage conveyor belt.

I stepped onto the escalator. It moved too slow. When I began to feel the badly timed pangs of dizziness setting in, I bounded the metal treads two at a time until I reached the mezzanine. No choice but to fight it.

On the second floor people walked past me in both directions along the carpeted corridor just outside the security scanners that marked the entrance to the second floor flight gates. When I picked out Lyons standing there at the entrance to the Skybar, shoulder to shoulder with Cain, I knew that I'd walked straight into the hornet's nest. Instinct told me I should about-face and select a direct line of retreat—the emergency exit stairwell directly behind me.

But that shit wasn't happening.

Plainclothes FBI and uniformed cops emerged from out of the woodwork. It took only seconds for them to surround me. They came at me from behind the reception booths and portable counters; came at me in their windbreakers with FBI printed on the back in big yellow letters, handguns aimed at my head. They sprung at me from out of the men's and ladies' rooms. They came at me from out of the Skybar. Cain had his 9mm drawn. Rather than aim it at me, he allowed the short barrel to bob against the side of his right knee.

He approached me casual as all hell, slate grey eyes peering into mine, the lips on his hollow cheeks forming a smile that shouted "I got you now, old partner."

Behind Cain, Lyons just stood there, both hands stuffed into his trouser pockets, looking down at the tops of his shoes.

From behind, a cop ordered me to hold my hands up high where he could see them. "Do it now!" he shouted.

A voice I recognized plain enough. Officer Nicky Joy.

I raised them slowly, knowing full well that I was about to expose the cuts and scratches on my palms to both the A.P.D. and the FBI.

Cain stared at my palms and smiled. "Where's you get those?" he asked.

Joy ordered me to drop down to my knees. I hesitated. Then instinct kicked in and I dropped my hands.

The barrel of Cain's pistol, I never saw it when he whacked me across the head with it, putting me down on my face like a rabid dog.

When I came to, I found myself flat on my stomach.

My wrists were cuffed tight behind my back, the crown of my skull pulsing with pain. My right arm went stone stiff, my fingers dead.

"You saw him reach for a weapon," Cain insisted. "Did you not see the suspect reaching for a weapon, Officer Joy?"

Cain's words sounded distant and hollow, like they were being spoken through a tube. It was the same when Joy started telling me to stand while holding tightly to the cuffed wrists behind my back.

"Sure thing, Detective," Joy said, but his tone lacked conviction. Fact is, the kid looked gaunt, nervous, almost like he was about to break out in tears at any moment. "The suspect appeared to be going for a gun."

I couldn't speak. My fucking head throbbed.

Cain in the lead, Joy began escorting me toward the escalators.

"Mr. Richard Moonlight, you have the right to remain silent," Cain recited. "Anything you say can and will be used against you in a court of law. You have the right to an attorney . . ."

He read off a Miranda I knew by heart, pushing me while I tried to maintain my balance. Reaching the top of the escalator, a barrage of flashes and video spotlights slapped my face, stinging my retinas. There was a sea of media crowded along the first floor where all the travelers should have been. Someone had to have tipped them off.

I had been caught up in a sting, plain and simple.

Lyons had been the bait and I was the sorry-ass fish that bought into it, hook, line and fucking sinker. By the looks of things, my built-in shit detector was on the fritz along with the rest of my head.

Christ, would I ever learn?

As we stepped onto the escalator, I couldn't help but view the wall of television monitors to my direct right. That's when I saw my handcuffed image being escorted down the mobile staircase, live and Johnny-on-the-spot!

"I know my rights," I said to Cain. "I'm an officer of the law."

"Tell it to your maker," he said.

44

Stocky Agent stands over me, slams his fist against the table with such force that even his silent partner standing off to the side jumps a mile. He bends down and gets in my face.

"You expect me to believe you had no idea about the body parts operation until the day they nabbed your ass at the airport?"

I smell his sour breath and stare back at him.

"You want me to believe that until Tuesday, May seventh, you never once put two and two together? Even after rubber-stamping all those case synopses?"

I shake my head, reach into my chest pocket with a trembling hand for another smoke, pop it into my mouth, and fire it up.

"I told you, man, my head." I exhale the white smoke. "Sometimes my judgment's not what it should be. My choices get confused. It's why they won't let me carry a gun, officially. It's why they wouldn't give me my son. Goddamned choices."

"What choices, Richard?"

"The choice not to ask questions when Cain told me to look the other way; the choice to take his money and run; the choice to keep coming back to the trough for more work when I could have told them all to go to hell; the choice to sleep with Scarlet when I should have stuck with being her masseur."

"Yet when Scarlet is found cut up in her own bed, you choose to take the moral stand even if it means implicating yourself in the murder. It doesn't add up."

"She deserved more. She was important."

"So then you can tell the difference, can't you, Moonlight?"

"What difference?"

"Between what's right and what's wrong."

"I guess I never looked at it that way."

Stocky Agent takes a step back, stuffs his hands into his pockets, pulls them out again, and sets them on his hips.

"You know what I think, Moonlight?" he says, glancing at his silent partner. "I don't think you're nearly the head case you make yourself out to be. Or maybe it's you who's playing the head games after all. Maybe you're the one with something to hide, because not only did Scarlet trust you, you were the last to be with her."

"Jake Montana was the last to be with her."

"Okay, Richard," Stocky Agent corrects himself. "You were the last to f-u-c-k her. Do I always have to spell shit out for you?"

I smoke. Tall Bearded Partner stands off in the corner, ever silent, ever the procedural witness.

Stocky Agent comes up on me from behind. He sets thick hands on my shoulders and begins to massage my traps. How funny: the FBI agent acting the role of the part-time masseur.

"Tell me something, Moonlight," he says in a far softer voice. "As a cop, would you consider yourself guilty of criminal indiscretions? Or do you merely consider yourself a sad victim of circumstances?"

Great. Another one of those *fucked if I answer, fucked if I don't answer* kind of questions.

Shrugging the agent away, I say "I tried to do something about it. Even after they arrested me; even after I managed to get away. So if you'll let me finish, I'll tell you why I kept trying to prove my innocence. Even when I knew that if I was caught they would shoot to kill. Why would a guilty man put himself through all that?"

"Because people do fucked-up things in fucked-up situations," Stocky Agent points out for the second time that late afternoon.

"Yeah, well, that was one pretty fucked-up situation."

The agent sits himself back down. "Well by all means, explain to me the situation," he insists. "No bullshit. Begin with your preliminary hearing in front of Judge Hughes."

45

The two of them stood there like human figures out of a bad dream.

Joy and Cain, the arresting officers, standing to the right-hand side of the bench, only about seven to ten feet in front of the long table where I sat shackled and cuffed, directly beside my lawyer, Stanley.

This was the morning after my airport arrest.

Per S.O.P. I'd been called before the county court for a prelim hearing. For the show they'd decided to keep me dressed in my blazing orange county lockup suit. Albany was in an uproar so they sped the process up, made a circus of the whole thing.

With all the media attention the show was already getting, they weren't about to allow a former Albany cop arrested in connection with two possible counts of Murder One to be arraigned in his best suit. They wanted me to appear the ruthless killer.

"Mr. Prosecutor," the balding, ashen-faced Judge Hughes announced from high up on his bench, "you may proceed with your action."

I sat there, careful not to rattle my chains. I didn't want the noise to draw more unwanted attention. Like the attention I was getting from the spectators and media people allowed inside the hearing; like the hordes of angry Albany cops perched outside the courthouse. Maybe they were already building a gallows out in the parking lot.

Stanley tapped his feet. I heard the nervous clip-clop, clip-clop coming from under the table. The noise was unsettling.

For the hearing he'd dressed himself sharply in a charcoal three-piece suit. His full head of thick gray hair was parted neatly on the side in a kind of wave that draped over his left eye, almost touching the rims of his eyeglasses.

To my immediate right sat the special prosecuting attorney for Albany County. Beside him sat an entourage of assistant D.A.s, lawyers and clerks. Every member of the team had their own personal laptop computer opened and glowing before intense young faces.

O'Connor stood. He smoothed out the creases in his black suit, lifted a yellow legal pad off his desk, and started walking my way. He faced me, not three feet away from where I sat, little brown eyes cutting into me like lasers.

Until he turned towards the bench.

"Your Honor, the defense is requesting bail, but the county would like to present the argument to counter such request, based upon evidence of two counts of capital murder, the first of which we plan on proving beyond a reasonable doubt."

"State your case, please, Mr. O'Connor."

My head pounded from the tension; my wrists and ankles nearly bleeding from yanking and pulling on the shackles and cuffs.

"In the weeks ahead, we will make evident beyond the shadow of a doubt that A.P.D. Detective Richard Moonlight deliberately and intentionally set out to murder Scarlet Montana, after which he murdered her surviving husband."

Stanley shot up. "Objection, Your Honor!" he shouted. "Might I remind the prosecutor that the law defines the defendant as innocent until proven guilty. Mr. O'Connor seems intent on passing sentence on my client even before the bench has granted a hearing with the grand jury. And might I add that Mr. Moonlight is presently accused of one offense, not two."

"Very well, Mr. Rose, we'll strike that from the record," Hughes announced for the court stenographer. "Your objection is duly sustained." He tapped something on the keys of his own laptop computer which was set to his right-hand side. "However I am going to allow Mr. O'Connor the opportunity to state his evidence."

Stanley the gunslinger sat down.

O'Connor stepped over to his table where he was handed a stack of eight-by-ten color glossies from one of his young women. Once more he approached the bench, handing the photos to the judge. Having slipped on a pair of reading glasses, Hughes began shuffling through them. When he was finished, he handed the photos back to O'Connor.

"Of course, Mr. Prosecutor, you will make these pictures available to the defense by two o'clock this afternoon," he instructed.

"Naturally, Your Honor," he agreed. "Per the order of discovery."

Hughes sat back hard in his swivel chair, removed his glasses. "You realize, Mr. O'Connor, Mr. Rose, that I have no choice but to accept most of your evidence as factual. I am talking about the defendant's cut up palms, also his prints and the blood spatter patterns discovered on the scene. Also I'm referring to the footprints found in the backyard of the Montana home and the so-called oil bottle. However, I'm curious as to the inclusion of the beer bottle. What am I supposed to make of it?"

"We believe the bottle to contain Mr. Moonlight's DNA as well as latent fingerprints," O'Connor explained, "sufficiently placing him at the scene of the crime on the night of May fifth."

"What I'm trying to say is, where is the actual bottle, Mr. O'Connor?"

The prosecutor went tight-faced. He cleared his throat. "We seem to have lost track of it, sir."

Stanley shot up again. "Your Honor, beer bottles and prints may indeed point to my client having been present at Ms. Montana's house before she died. They were friends. Mr. Moonlight often performed message therapy on her for which he received financial remuneration—"

"And apparently quite a bit more," O'Connor blurted out to a courtroom that exploded in laughter.

But when Hughes slapped the gavel, the room went silent.

"Please continue, Mr. Rose," an annoyed Judge ordered.

Stanley brought a fist to his mouth and cleared his throat. "It's not at all unusual for a massage therapist who makes house calls to leave something as insignificant as an oil bottle behind. Nor does it suggest that my client had anything whatsoever to do with Ms. Montana's death. And may we respectfully remind the prosecution that photographs of beer bottles do not qualify as viable evidence."

"Overruled, Mr. Rose," Hughes said. "It will be your job to prove that none of these items, photographed or not, point to murder. May I also remind you that the wounded palms look especially intriguing, convincing me that deviation from the bond process will be the way to go after all."

My skull wasn't just pounding, it was splitting open.

"Your Honor, might I remind the court that my client suffers from an inoperable physiological condition. A .22 caliber bullet is lodged in the center of his brain, directly beside his cerebral cortex and thalamus, causing on occasion an inability for rational thought."

Stanley, the Moonlight family lawyer, exploited my condition, knowing that in the end he could own my house.

"He looks fine to me, sir," Hughes said, not without a slight smile. "I am told he is well enough to play cop, and anybody well enough to play cop is also well enough to pose himself as a substantial flight risk."

"He is well enough in relative terms," Stanley said. "However, the stress of lockup carries with it the potential to create problems with the condition, increasing his risk of stroke and/or seizure for which the state will bear the ultimate responsibility."

"Save it for later, Mr. Rose. While Mr. Moonlight lives, I've got two dead people to think about, one of them my chief detective."

Hughes looked me directly in the eye, asked me if I understood the nature of the charges filed. I said I did. He asked me if I was aware of my constitutional rights as an accused offender.

"Yes," I told him.

"There will be no set bail," Hughes went on, "as is consistent with capital cases in my court of law. I am ordering the defendant detained to Albany County Correctional Facility until a hearing with the grand jury."

The courtroom exploded in cheers and jeers. *So much for the side of right.*

Then the judge set a date for a grand jury hearing. He slammed down the gavel and that was it.

I watched Cain as he turned to me and smiled. Son of a bitch actually cracked a grin before he walked by me on his way out of the courtroom.

Joy, on the other hand, approached me with a face so distraught you'd have thought he was the one facing a death sentence. He asked me to turn around and step out and away from the table. When I did, he grabbed hold of my jumper collar and asked me to walk. It was then, as we were moving past the judge's bench, that he dropped something. I didn't know what until I looked down.

It was simply a pen. A Bic ballpoint.

He ordered me to stop. I did. He went down to retrieve his pen. When he did, I felt the sensation in my foot. Something sliding inside my orange slipper. Something small, cold and hard.

I said nothing about it.

When we stepped out into the hall and began our march toward an awaiting county armored vehicle, I knew it must have had something to do with what Joy whispered in my ear: "Hotel Wellington. Room 6-5-7."

I made not a sound. I simply repeated the words and numbers over and over again in my head as I shuffled forward. *Hotel Wellington, room 6-5-7. Hotel Wellington, room 6-5-7. Hotel Wellington, room 6-5-7.*

Just what the significance room 6-5-7 carried I had no clue, only that it represented to me some kind of hope in an otherwise hopeless situation. But then there was something else I managed to figure out: sometime between my arrest and arraignment, Officer Joy had made the conscious decision to piss on Cain's parade.

46

The concrete-and-razor-wire Albany County Lockup was located across the river from Albany on what used to be a riverside crude oil processing plant. In order to get there, we had to cross over an eighty-foot high steel expansion bridge that supported four lanes of Interstate 90 traffic— two going east towards Boston; two going west to Buffalo.

There were two county deputies escorting me to the jail in a black Chevy Suburban with tinted one-way glass. I guess the deception had been orchestrated in the interest of my safety. As a supposed cop killer (or the killer of the head dick's wife, anyway), there existed the very real possibility that someone—angry cop or no angry cop—might try and take a shot at me.

Funny how they didn't provide me with a Kevlar vest; funny how the Suburban contained no incarceration cage. Not to keep me in, but to keep would-be attackers out.

I sat in the middle of the back seat with only a seatbelt securing me. The two deputies up front didn't bother with theirs even though buckling up is the law. Being a deputy has its perks.

The big blond-haired guy driving the Suburban must have been doing ninety when he hit the on-ramp for the bridge. Everything in the vehicle shifted to the left, including me.

"Jesus, Paulie," said the second, smaller, dark-haired guy. "You're gonna get us killed."

"You think I wanna die?" said Paulie. "Maybe we ought to burn one, Timmy? Calm me down a little."

Timmy made a nod over his left shoulder, to bring attention to me. "What about him?" he asked, as if I were blind, deaf and dumb.

"What about him?" Paulie repeated as the entrance to the bridge loomed ahead. "He's gonna fry soon enough. You think our burning one is gonna make a goddamned difference? 'Sides, stupid fucker can't remember a goddamned thing."

It's not memory that's the problem.

Timmy paused to run his hands over his clean-shaven cheeks. I could tell he was thinking it over, coming to a definite decision. Then, as if I weren't even there, the county law officer reached into his shirt pocket and produced a fat bomber of a joint. He flipped it into his mouth, lightning it with a transparent yellow Bic lighter.

"That's a boy," Paulie said with a big-ass grin. "Light the sucker up."

The bridge approached.

A laptop computer had been installed in the center of the Suburban console directly below the two-way radio. The computer was turned off and the radio was so low you couldn't hear the dispatcher's voice at all. Maybe the guards didn't care. Secured between the two bucket seats was a riot shotgun. I had a hard time keeping my eyes off of it while Timmy had a hard time making fire with his lighter.

"Fuckin' childproof lighters," he complained.

We were on the bridge now, heading directly over the river. Looking out the window, it seemed a long way down.

"Let me try," Paulie said, reaching across the console for the lighter.

"I've got it, man," Timmy insisted, thumbing the mechanism with a vengeance.

"Let me," Paulie insisted.

The suburban began to swerve. Paulie tried to grab hold of the little lighter, but his partner insisted on doing it himself. Paulie wasn't keeping his eyes on the road.

When we crossed over into the far right lane, he wasn't aware of it.

I decided then that the time had come.

Because I was sitting down, there was more than enough slack in my waist restraint for me to unbuckle my seatbelt.

No one noticed. Not when I bent down, retrieved the key out of my slipper, and tucked it inside my mouth under my tongue. We were half way over the bridge when I reached up and over Paulie's head with my cuffed hands, wrapped the chain restraint around his fat neck, and squeezed as hard as I could.

It wasn't like the movies at all.

We didn't swerve all over the road while a major struggle ensued inside the Chevy. There was no time for dramatics. The whole thing took no more than three seconds, tops.

It was all a matter of my wrapping the restraint around the neck and squeezing and the wheel on the Suburban cutting all the way to the right and then the open-mouthed expression on Timmy's gaunt face as we slammed into the concrete barrier.

47

Fully conscious, I lifted up my feet and kicked out the door window. Climbing out head first, I dropped down onto the concrete, managing to break the fall with my cuffed hands. All around me, cars and trucks were skidding to a halt, not to avoid the smashed Suburban, but to get a look at me.

I didn't give them a chance to get a good look.

I hobbled over to the side of the bridge in my shackles and cuffs and climbed up onto the steel railing.

"Don't do it!" somebody shouted.

I jumped.

An eighty-foot drop, feet first into the Hudson.

I gathered up my bearings and bobbed in the slight chop, fighting the weight and restriction of the chains, shackles and cuffs. I pumped like a mad dog to keep my head above water. The fast current propelled me downriver. The key still tucked under my tongue, I tried to breathe without swallowing river water.

I tried to glance over my right shoulder. There was too much distance between me and the bridge to make out the Suburban, much less the guards. Maybe they'd bought it in the collision. Maybe they went over the side of the bridge along with me. I wondered if they could swim.

I had to get to the riverbank before I drowned in the current.

To my direct right, the Port of Albany. A freighter was docked parallel with the port, beside a mooring with a big number 6 painted on its concrete base. To my direct left, the county lockup with its guard towers and searchlights beaming down upon chain link and razor-wire fencing. I must have covered a half mile or more in just a matter of a half a minute.

The damp air smelled like rotten fish.

I tried treading water, but the pull on my legs and feet was too strong. Gazing back at that freighter, I could see that it was getting smaller. The current was pulling me farther and farther away from the port, along with the stunted Albany skyline behind it. I couldn't last forever in that chop. I had to make a run for the bank before my body was dragged further south, where the river opened up almost like an inland ocean.

I was beginning to sense the onset of exhaustion. Was I about to undergo a seizure? If I passed out now the chains and shackles would carry me to the bottom. I had to get myself to the riverbank now.

Without the complete use of my arms, I propelled my body along like a seal, all the time trying to hold off the seizure as though I had any control over it at all. Finally I made it to a large culvert that emptied out onto a patch of gravelly riverbank.

I crawled up onto the bank, stuffed myself into the aluminum tube, and hid my body among the foul-smelling dead and bloated fish. I wanted to move, but I couldn't. My left arm felt numb. There were brilliant flashes of light coming from inside my brain. No choice but to surrender. I laid my head down atop the damp corrugated metal and, for better or worse, passed out.

By the time I woke up, the afternoon was gone.

I crawled out onto the bank and laid there in my orange jumper, soaking wet from head to toes, hands and feet still bound in shackles and cuffs.

I spit out the key. Curling my legs into my chest, I reached down with my left hand and started unlocking. A few moments later, I was free.

I dug a hole in the wet sand and tossed in the chains and cuffs. Then I filled the hole back in. I looked up at the sky. Thick gray-black clouds stared back at me.

I judged the time to be about five o'clock, five-thirty. It was hard to tell. It was hard to believe that nobody had located me by now. The current had carried me a great distance from the bridge in a very short time.

Just up ahead, a concrete dike wall was situated maybe ten feet above the shoreline. In the far distance to the north came the mechanical drone of a giant dock-mounted crane that was lifting and setting fifty-gallon drum-filled palettes into the docked freighter's hold. With the quickly fading cloud-filtered daylight, I knew that the crane would soon be stopping, the workers who manned it heading home.

Until that time, I would have to crawl back into the culvert and sit tight.

It didn't take long for full dark to settle in.

I emerged from out of the culvert once more and made my way up the narrow stretch of riverbank towards the dike wall. The port crane had stopped, its mechanical drone giving way to the high-pitched straining and stressing of the freighter's steel hull bobbing up and down in the river's wake. Out beyond the docked freighter, I could make out the bright pier-mounted beacons of light shooting out across the wide river.

That's when I saw the barge coming from out of the north along with the current. A flat, brightly illuminated diving barge with maybe half a dozen men and women standing on it. From where I stood, I could make out two black, rubber-suited divers who were just then dropping into the black river, no doubt in search of a possibly drowned fugitive. I knew that when they eventually came up without my body, I would be considered alive and dangerous.

Standing wet and cold on the riverbank, I felt very alone. Soon I heard a voice and the clap of footsteps coming towards me from the direction of the dike wall. When the narrow cone-shaped light began to strafe the beach, I knew that it had to be the police.

I went down onto my stomach and crawled my way across the beach to the concrete wall. Stuffing my body between the wall and the beach, I tried to make myself invisible. Rather, tried to *will* myself invisible. Facing the river I saw the bright white flashlight shine upon the very spot I had been standing in just a couple of seconds before.

The A.P.D., my former brothers and sisters in arms.

Had they not announced themselves with their chest-mounted radios and flashlights, I'd already be back in custody. Instead I held my breath, lying there perfectly still until the flashlight moved further south along the dike wall. When the light had all but disappeared, I got back on my feet and started jogging in the opposite direction towards the port and the longshoreman locker rooms.

The time had come for a change in wardrobe.

48

I walked alongside a brick monster of a building that stretched the entire length of the main pier—a two-story warehouse with maybe thirty separate docking bays closed off by identical metal overhead doors. As a detective, I knew that the port office was located somewhere in the general vicinity. I found it located at the far north end of the structure.

The solid metal door was padlocked, but there was a chicken-wire-reinforced warehouse window that had been left slightly ajar. I pushed in the window, pulled myself up and stuffed my body in through the opening.

I went down onto the wood plank floor hard. I didn't waste a second of time. Picking myself up, I made my way through the front office to the back where the showers and locker rooms were located.

The locker room was windowless, with only a large louver for ventilation. There was a bathroom and a gang shower. Out beyond that was a closed off area designated for the machine shop. Every available space was filled with metal lockers covered in graffiti and Scotch-taped *Penthouse* and *Hustler* nudes. The place reeked of worms and mold.

I stood there sopping wet with only the outside dockside spots to light my way. I rummaged through the few lockers that had no locks on them. By the end of my search, I found a pair of workman's khakis, a white t-shirt and a pair of steel-toed Timberlands that fit good enough.

So far so good. I was alive; I had new clothes and a destination in mind. *Hotel Wellington, Room 6-5-7.*

They were coming through the machine shop doors when I spotted them. Two state troopers. One man speaking to the other in a slow whisper voice, the narrow beams of light coming from their hand-held sticks bouncing off the block walls and tin lockers like twin Tinkerbells.

I pressed my back up against the lockers and held my breath. I waited until the troopers made it past the showers and stepped into the locker room. There were no windows to crawl through. The only way out would be back through the office. I would somehow have to get those two gray-uniformed troopers behind me.

I waited until they passed me by. Then I moved on toward the office, taking slow, silent steps while they searched the locker room.

I must have been halfway across the floor when I noticed that the office door leading out onto the pier was no longer padlocked. It was wide open. Somebody had to have opened it. Maybe the same man who, right then, stepped out of the shadows and pointed an old black-plated service revolver in my face.

The night watchman raised a silver whistle to his lips and started to blow. The high-pitched whistle was piercing.

He was an old man, maybe somewhere in his mid seventies. A tall, uniformed, crooked branch of a man with scraggly gray hair, a gaunt, stubble-covered face and wide, wet eyes.

"Stop!" he spat.

The whistle hung off his neck by an old black shoelace. The pistol trembled in his right hand, too heavy for his skin and bones. Looking into his bloodshot and blistered eyes, I knew he had to be frightened out of his wits. I looked for the index finger on his right hand. Was it pressed against the pistol trigger? It was impossible to tell in the half light, even from a distance of only five or six feet.

"Hands!" he insisted. "Raise your goddamned hands!"

Slowly I raised them, shoulder height. It must have been the cue the two troopers were waiting for. They came up on me from behind. I didn't require eyes in the back of my head to know where they stood.

One of them shouted "Down on your knees!"

I knew he could not have been more than three feet away from me. So close I could almost feel his hot breath against the back of my neck.

I hesitated for only a second or two before I started bending my knees, collapsing my body, careful to go slow, not give the old man a reason to shoot me in the face, not give the troopers a reason to shoot me in the back.

As far as they were concerned, I was already on my way back to county lockup, ready to stand trial for the Montana murders. Me, Richard Moonlight, part-time cop turned cop killer; fulltime head case.

But then I was no killer, and all semblance of fair-and-squareness had skipped town the deep, dark morning Joy and Jake pulled me out of bed and ordered me to head up a smokescreen independent investigation.

I lowered my body.

"Get down!" came a voice from behind.

"Easy boys," I said. "We're playing on the same team, remember?"

The old man's pistol barrel followed the tip of my nose every inch of the way down. To my right, the flashes of red, white and blue trooper cruiser lights reflected against the wall. I knew that it was just a matter of seconds until the empty cruiser attracted the attention of any trooper or cop who might have been dispatched to the immediate area. Just a matter of time until these two men and one over-the-hill night watchman turned into an entire makeshift squad.

I started lowering my hands. I didn't stop lowering them until they were almost level with my knees and the floor. Then I leaned all my bodyweight onto my left arm and, just like that, extended my right leg, swinging it against the old man's legs like a battleaxe.

His feet were cut right out from under him. He dropped like a sack of rags and bones.

The revolver fell out of his hand and bounced off the floor. I rolled over onto my right side, brought the pistol up, pressed the barrel against his bald head, and cocked the hammer.

I had no choice but to do it. I'd been screwed from the start, ever since those cops had decided to check out the locker room. Christ, ever since I'd washed up on the riverbank; ever since the night watchman decided to play hero.

~ 195 ~

I got up, telling the old man to lie flat on his stomach, to not make a sound or I'd have to shoot him.

"Don't test me," I said. The troopers just stood there, side arms in hand I told them to toss me the guns, then remove their utility belts and toss me those too.

"Do it," I said.

Outside, the sound of sirens was getting louder.

First they exchanged part confused, part frightened glances. Then together, the two bent down and slid their pieces over to me. Standing once more, they undid their belts and tossed them over at my feet.

I confiscated both of the officers' .38 mm Smith and Wesson automatics and stuffed one of them into my pant waist, while keeping the other on the cops and the old man.

I pulled the extra clips off their utility belts and stuffed them into my pockets. Then, reaching out, I pulled each of their radios off their chests and threw them down hard onto the concrete floor, shattering their plastic casings, strewing radio parts all over the floor.

A fifty-gallon drum filled with old motor oil stood only a few feet away from me, on my left-hand side. I sidestepped over to it, tossing in the old man's revolver along with his walkie-talkie.

Just for the sheer hell of it, I ordered the larger trooper to hand over his Kevlar vest.

"You planning on being shot?" he asked, as if it were the time for jokes.

"Exactly," I said.

He pulled it over his head, heaved it my way. I told them to go flat onto their bellies. They didn't argue.

Pulling the cuffs from the belts, I handed them to the old man.

"Lock them up," I said. "You lock yourself to the big one."

The old man moved painfully slow. Or maybe it was my imagination. But in the end, he got the job done.

When they were secured, I pulled off my t-shirt and strapped on the vest. I did it while holding the piece on all three of them. Then I pulled the t-shirt back over the Kevlar. You never knew when a bulletproof vest might come in handy. Especially when the entire State of New York had a gun pointed at your head.

The sirens were so loud now they made my brain hurt. It seemed everything made my brain hurt.

Making my way to the open door, I stuck my head out, surveying south, then north.

All clear.

I stepped out into the night.

49

The chopper pilot must have spotted me exiting the warehouse office.

The Huey must have been following the route of the river when it caught me rounding the corner of the warehouse and out onto the parking lot. It wasn't one of ours. The A.P.D. couldn't have afforded a chopper even if they'd fired every cop on the payroll. It had to belong to the state troopers. A spotlight was mounted to its belly.

It shone a bright beacon down upon me. I had no way of escaping the big round spot. Not out in the open like that. No matter how much I tried to shake it, the circle of light followed my every step as I shot across the lot toward the city.

I pictured the gates of the Saint Agnes Cemetery located just across the road at the edge of the port lot. With the chopper still hovering overhead, I bolted across the empty road. Coming upon the stone cemetery wall I went over the top, dropping down onto the other side. I hid myself in a thick bed of overgrown weeds and brush.

The rain started coming down hard. Lightning flashed over the mountains to the east. The thunder followed just a few seconds later. The police sirens went silent.

Down on my belly, curled up against the old stone wall, I waited for the chopper to make another pass with its bright beacon. Then I got back up on my feet and made one more run for the wooded glade that bordered the west side of the cemetery.

Once inside the protection of the thick cover I dove down flat on my belly again.

I was soaking wet again. Burrs and thorns dug into the flesh on my arms and legs, but I didn't have the time to care. All I wanted to do was catch my breath and wait for the chopper to disappear. Only then would I think about my next move.

50

A half hour later, I was moving on through the woods, climbing over more chain-link and wood fences than I cared to count. It took more time than it should have, but I managed to make it back into the city's south end without being sighted.

I was cold, wet and hungry. I estimated the time to be close to nine o'clock.

Keeping inside the shadows, I kept a steady pace down Green Street, passed a boarded up Saint Joseph's church, passed the old movie theatre that now was used as a plumbing supply warehouse, passed the old townhouses where the nineteenth century lumber barons and steel mill owners lived. From there I moved on through the rain along Broadway, past the old Greyhound station and on past the brightly lit, aluminum-paneled Albany Civic Center.

Soon I was climbing the desolate back side of the State Street hill in the pouring rain, cutting through the now abandoned parking garage and out to what had once been considered the rear garden entrance to the Hotel Wellington. A forgotten garden from a forgotten era that had evolved into a jungle of thick weeds, heavy vines, scattered bits of trash and shattered concrete.

I made my way into the alley and waited there under a concealing curtain of darkness and rain for as long as it took. I waited until I was certain that no cruisers were prowling the State Street side of the hotel. It was then that I slipped out of the alley and approached the boarded-over front entrance to the once majestic Wellington.

Grabbing hold of the plywood that covered the old revolving door frame, I ripped one side away, allowing myself just enough room to slip inside. I wiped the water from my face and eyes and combed back my hair with open fingers. I pulled one of the automatics from my pant waist and took a quick look around at what remained of the old lobby. A circle of light that leaked in from the street lamps shined down upon an old reception counter. A long, rectangular cabinet finished at one time with what I guessed must have been cherry wood panels. Or maybe mahogany. The panels had been pulled away, exposing only a rough wood skeleton.

I took a few steps forward, tickling the trigger guard with my shooting finger as I made my way through the rest of the lobby, my feet shuffling over soot-covered black and white marbled tiles.

I came to a large center stairwell. Inside the stairwell was an old Otis elevator that made the vertical run up the entire twenty stories of the hotel all the way to the ceiling-mounted skylights. The elevator carriage had an accordion-like door that opened and closed manually. Most of the machine's guts had been ripped out.

From the bottom of the wrap-around staircase I looked up at the electric spotlight that leaked in through the skylights and shined down upon the naked stair treads like dull yellow tracer beams.

I climbed the stairs.

There was the cracking of the treads and the wet moldy odor from the rain that seeped in through the roof. When I made it to the sixth floor landing, I faced a dark corridor. The automatic gripped in my right hand, I walked over empty beer cans and wine bottles, over down pillows with feather stuffing oozing out, gray-brown and clumpy, through long gashes torn in the cases. I stepped around piles of papers, over mattresses, discarded clothing and ripped up sections of carpeting.

Midway along the corridor, my eyes running over the numbers tacked to the wood doors, I heard a rustling sound. Looking down at my feet, I saw a rat sneaking its greasy black head out from under a pile of crumpled up newspaper. I jumped back when the cat-sized rodent scurried over the tops of my boots.

I moved faster then, reaching out and grabbing hold of the occasional brass doorknob along the way, turning each one, surprised to find them all locked.

Then I found Room 657.

Like all the others, it too was locked.

Taking two steps back, I raised my right leg and kicked the door in. Both hands gripping the pistol, I stepped through the open doorway. I waved the barrel from one side of the dark room to the other crouched, taking short, rapid breaths, not caring about the smell, feeling the hot blood rushing in and out of my brain.

"Joy?" I called out, surprised at the sound of my own voice. "Nicky Joy?"

The room was thick with sweat and darkness. I couldn't see the pistol in front of my face. I couldn't see anything other than the streetlight that shined in through the square window behind the thin shade that covered it.

I was convinced then that Joy wasn't coming, that he'd lied to me; that this whole thing was some kind of bizarre setup.

But then a flashlight popped on.

My throat closed in on itself, mouth dry.

I recognized Joy's puffy red face in the severe white light. I could tell by his wide, wet eyes and shaking lips that he was afraid.

I held a bead on his face, in the very spot where he was shining the flashlight, but he didn't seem to care.

He was crying.

"What is this?" I demanded.

But before he could answer, the bathroom door opened. Out stepped a man with a pale, pink-eyed face.

51

The wood door opened and the albino man showed himself.

He was smiling. The smile grew wider as he raised a sawed-off shotgun to chest height and fired at Joy's head, point blank.

The whole thing could not have taken more than a half-second from start to finish, so that Joy's body had not even hit the floor before the man turned the weapon on me and pulled the trigger.

There was a quick flash of white light, like a flash fire, then the immediate force of the blast against my chest and the driving-nail feeling of buckshot piercing my left arm and the back of my head bouncing off the plaster wall behind me. Then there was the warm blood that dribbled down my arm as I slowly slid down onto the floor and lost consciousness.

The first thing I noticed when I opened my eyes was the white streetlight that poured in through the narrow window in the bathroom to my right. The light reflected off what was left of the medicine cabinet mirror mounted to the wall above the old porcelain sink. It also reflected Joy's exposed chest, his split-open ribcage and the blood-encrusted void where his heart had been. There was blood all over the floor and a blue medical specimen transport box sitting out not far from where the dead Joy lay in his own fluids.

An identical specimen box sat on the floor beside me, its lid removed, exposing a translucent plastic bag that had been stuffed inside it. I was staring at it when the albino man approached me, his white face full of smiles and spattered blood. He held a scalpel in one hand and a bloodied towel in the other. He bent down over me and positioned the knife over my lower right side, exactly where my liver was located. He pressed the blade at the precise moment I raised the .38 with my good hand and jammed it against his head.

"Motherfocker," I heard him whisper.

"This is for Scarlet," I said, before I squeezed the trigger.

I pushed his deadweight body off of me. Then I touched the small pellet wounds on my left arm with the tips of my fingers. The wounds were stinging, bleeding. For some reason, there was no paralysis to speak of in my left arm, no pins and needles that tingled the extremities.

I slid myself up along the wall. The pain shifted from the front of my skull to the back. It latched onto my spinal column like a pair of vice grips, then bolted all the way down my back to my toes. Even without the added weight of the dead albino man, my chest felt crushed, as if I'd dropped three-hundred pounds worth of Olympic weights on it.

I managed to get back up on my feet, pausing for a few beats to regain my balance. Using the back side of my t-shirt, I wiped the .38 clean of my prints and shoved the grip into the albino man's left hand, his index finger wrapped around the trigger. The deception complete, I stood back for a minute, viewing the scene.

A classic murder-mutilation-suicide gone bad, sort of. My little hoax—such as it was—would have to do.

Was this the place where the body parts were harvested from the victims I'd signed off on? Had the albino man cut up Scarlet? If he had, why didn't he take any of her organs?

I stared at the room, the two bodies, the blood, Joy's split ribcage. I wanted to vomit, but I couldn't. I could only wonder what the Albany P.D. would make out of the whole thing. That is, if they ever thought to search this rat trap in the first place.

I stood over Joy. Aside from his missing heart, the top of his skull was gone, vaporized by the shotgun blast. Only his lower jaw was left, the loose skin on his forehead flapped over at the hairline so that it looked more like the hide of a furry animal than the skin of a human being.

I had to wonder why he slipped me that key, called me out here in the first place. Maybe this one room had served as some kind of safe-house for him. Maybe it wasn't a place for harvesting organs at all. Maybe it was simply a place only he knew about, a place apart from his coconspirators. Somewhere he could go to escape the heat of Cain's and Jake's illegal operation. He would have slipped me the key because this would have been the only safe place where we could meet in all of Albany. With the entire city on my tail, this wretched place made perfect sense. As for the kid's motivation, maybe he wanted to turn himself in to the FBI with me by his side. Or maybe he wanted to kill me, take my organs, shut me up before my trial began for Scarlet's murder and I spilled the beans about everybody, including himself. Or maybe he was just a confused kid who was way over his head in deep shit.

One thing had become painfully evident; the albino man had somehow beaten him to the punch. The albino man must have suspected that the kid was up to something and tracked him here. And as for the second painfully evident reality that there would be no fact-finding interview with the white-skinned man now. Not in his condition. No names or places that might shed light on the specific nature of his associations with Scarlet, the heroin, and the body parts operation.

My mouth was parched and pasty. It tasted of blood and gunmetal. The bleeding in my left arm had slowed, but I knew I had to get myself to a doctor. Do it soon before infection set in. Which meant I had two choices, get a hold of Dr. Lane or George.

Didn't make sense to implicate Lane in this mess. If word got out that she'd assisted a fugitive, her license would be pulled. Not that George's wouldn't be if he got snagged. But then, he was already in on things, which meant I had to make an appeal to him whether I liked it or not whether he liked it or not.

Bending, I patted the pockets of Joy's size thirty-eight uniform. I didn't come up with anything other than a key ring that contained maybe a dozen keys. Not car keys, but the kind of keys that might go to your average household locksets.

Pocketing the key ring, I walked to the nearest window. A window that accessed an alley. I pulled back the shade. There was an old fire escape mounted to the brick exterior. Exactly what I had hoped for.

Before I took off, I thought about checking to see if the albino man had any ID on him. Of course he wouldn't. He was a professional, after all. Just what the hell did I expect to find on him anyway: a calling card?

Turning to get one more good look at him, I saw that his shirt tails were pulled up around his chest, exposing the bottom of his torso. A thick purple scar circumnavigated his right side where the kidney should be and a jagged depression in the flesh, as if a shark had taken a bite out of the son of a bitch. Above that was the tattoo of a skull. The ink was black, including the eyes. Eyes that looked right through me.

Pulling my eyes away from the tattoo, I reversed my earlier decision and searched his pockets. As expected I discovered no ID, but what I did find was an envelope full of cash and a plane ticket. I pulled the items out of his pockets, stuffed it inside the tattered Kevlar vest and backed away.

Standing up straight, I took a quick glance around the place like I normally do before checking out of a hotel room. For a quick second I thought about taking Joy's boxed heart with me, putting it to good use. Who knew what poor soul was waiting for a heart? But then what the hell was I thinking? I also thought about maybe wiping the place clean of prints. But then, what the hell was the use? My blood was all over the place, for Christ's sake.

My blood, Joy's blood and the blood of the albino man—this harvester of body parts; this heroin pusher; this killer.

At that point, I knew Cain would take great pleasure in nailing me with both their deaths, whether it looked like a murder-suicide or not. Because that's the way things had been going for me. Just one more nail in the coffin for old Richard Moonlight, *Captain Head Case.*

I was losing blood.

I walked back over to the window and tore away the shade. Taking a deep, painful breath, I raised up my right leg and kicked out the glass pane. Then I crouched my way through the opening, stepping out onto the metal grate. From up there on the landing, I looked out onto downtown Albany. Nothing was moving in the abandoned alley of the Hotel Wellington other than the rain.

52

Stocky Agent and I face one another across the long table. Tall Witnessing Agent stands silently in the brightly lit room's far corner.

"This man you killed," he says. "Did he ever give you a name?"

"No, he did not."

Stocky Agent looks up at the thin bearded man. "Get me the sheet," he says.

The thin man walks out of the room and after a brief few beats comes back in. He hands Stocky Agent an 8.5x11-inch poster with front and side mug shots of the albino man printed on it beside a list of vitals. At the top of the sheet is the word WANTED in bold black letters. Just below that are the words IN CONNECTION WITH DOMESTIC AND INTERNATIONAL SMUGGLING ACTIVITIES.

I stare at the poster, recall jabbing the .9mm barrel against the man's head, recall pressing the trigger and the sudden dead body-weight pressed against my bruised ribs. I recall the purple scar that wrapped around his kidney area, the tattoo of a small skull above it. Did the motherfucker actually have one his own kidneys cut out to pawn off on the black market? I read the man's name off the sheet: Joseph Surikov. I roll the name around in my brain for a few seconds; until I spit it back out. Metaphorically speaking, that is.

"Did you know that we'd been tracing this piece of shit for more than four months?" Stocky Agent says. "Do you know what Joseph's untimely death did to our operation?" He pronounced Joseph like Yoseph.

"Let me guess," I say. "One less Russian mobster is going to get away from the big bad FBI."

"Keep wisecracking!" the agent explodes, slapping the sheet onto the table and bounding up from his chair. "We wanted him alive. You made him dead. We could make you do time for putting a cap in his ass."

I pull another smoke from my chest pocket. He's got to be fucking kidding if he expects me to buy that shit even for a second.

"Son of a bitch tried to kill me," I say, going for the Zippo laid out on the tabletop, but not before Stocky Agent snatches it up first.

"Kill or be killed, is that your defense, Moonlight? I wonder what a Federal judge would have to say to that."

The unlit cigarette dangles from between my lips. I know exactly what a Fed judge would say: *Mr. Moonlight, you did what you had to do under the circumstances.*

"I've been near dead and I've been very alive," I say. "Believe me, alive is better. So yes, I would indeed plead self-defense. Now may I please have my lighter back?"

"It's your life," Stocky Agent offers while striking up a flame. "Now why not use it to give me some real information before I decide to hold you overnight?"

53

I called George's number from a payphone at the bottom of the State Street hill.

"The whole city is looking for you, Moon."

Nothing but dead air on the line and the rain that strafed the concrete sidewalk. I made a tight fist with my right hand, looking all around me. Not a soul on the street. Just the occasional taxi flying past, the drivers either not bothering to give me a second look or not seeing me at all in the darkness and the rain. No cops, no troopers, no marshals. But I knew my luck wouldn't last.

"Tell me what to do," George said.

I looked over my shoulder at the red-lettered neon sign mounted over the door to a bar called "Red Square" on the corner of State and Broadway.

"Get your car," I told him. "Meet me outside Red Square in ten minutes."

"The whole town is buzzing with pigs," he said. "And you want me to pick you up outside a bar?"

"Pull up and wait. You won't see me but I'll see you."

54

Less than an hour later, I was sitting on top of the dissecting table in the AMC basement autopsy room.

George had locked the lab doors. He'd also brought in a television, set it on the counter beside the stereo system, and run a cable to it from outside his open office door. It was tuned to one of the local early morning news programs. They were showing some video footage shot the previous afternoon. The scene of the car crash that had resulted in my escape from county authorities who'd been assigned to escort me to jail.

There was the banged up Chevy Suburban, its front end smashed in and the large gouge it put in the metal rail and concrete safety wall. There was the shattered windshield and the kicked-out side window that I squirmed out of immediately after the collision. Standing bewildered beside the smashed up Chevy were the two sheriff's deputies who'd been fighting over the childproof lighter. Paulie and Timmy, if I remembered correctly.

The two brainiacs were being bandaged up by a couple of EMTs. Their faces were wide-eyed, filled with shock. According to the reporter on the scene, they'd been brutally attacked by yours truly.

"It's a miracle we're still alive!" Timmy Ferguson was quoted as saying.

"Yeah, a real miracle," added the tall blond-haired Paulie Rabuffo.

Conveniently they left out the part about firing up the joint.

In a moment the video feed shifted to Cain. He was dressed in his blue blazer and pressed white shirt. He was wearing sunglasses in the cloud cover and the rain. He said he was putting all other duties aside to concentrate on one task and one task only: "The apprehension of Richard Moonlight."

When the news continued on to another story, George turned off the set.

For maybe the fourth time since he'd escorted me into the autopsy room, he was checking the double doors to make sure they were locked. We both knew it was only a matter of time until Cain came sneaking around. Meanwhile, the good pathologist wasn't taking any chances.

The formerly white, now blood-soaked t-shirt I had taken from the port locker room was lying on the floor beside the damaged Kevlar vest. The money-filled envelope I'd stuffed into the vest was now stuffed into my pants pocket, along with the plane ticket.

Destination? There wasn't one listed. It was an open ticket. By the looks of it, the albino man was about to skip town as soon as he cleaned a little house. I wondered if Cain had been on his list of "things to do."

My ribs had been wrapped with gauze and surgical tape while the dozen stitches George had sewn into my left arm were already beginning to itch. Resting inside a small stainless steel bowl to my immediate left, in a tiny pool of blood, were two steel BBs.

George stood beside me with his long, mostly gray hair hanging over the collar of his white smock. For a change, the stereo was turned off while we kept eyes and ears open for any trouble that might come our way in the form of the A.P.D. For the past twenty minutes I had managed to fill him in on everything that went down on the sixth floor of the Hotel Wellington while he patched me up.

The only thing that remained were questions. Lots of questions.

"If you think Cain killed Jake," he said, picking up the bloodied t-shirt and vest off the floor and stuffing them into the bio-waste can, "might we also assume Cain killed Scarlet?"

"We might assume it," I said. "That is if the albino man didn't kill her."

"But no body parts had been harvested from her. Seems to me any man willing to cut out his own kidney isn't about to waste an opportunity like Scarlet would have been."

"Cain," I said.

"Cain," he agreed. Then he said, "Tell you what, Moony. Let's take a look at Jake. He's in a drawer on ice, right next to Scarlet."

"The funeral home doesn't have her yet?"

"It took a little doing," he said, "but I held the Fitzgerald Funeral Home off. Just like you told me to. I spoke with Mrs. Fitz herself. She's doing it as a personal favor to me and your dad."

Loyalty. It was one of Mrs. Fitzgerald's qualities. Clearly the old gal had a long and good memory of us Moonlights.

"You know what this means," I said.

"Not one body of evidence, but two."

"No way in hell anybody else is gonna get their hands on them but us."

We made our way out of the autopsy room and down the hall to the morgue. When we stepped inside, George locked the door behind us. Paranoia maybe, but for good reason.

The morgue was a large, rectangular room. It had a tile floor with a drain in the center. The wall to your right as you walked in was filled with drawers. They looked like file cabinet drawers. Only instead of papers, they contained dead bodies. To the left was a Corian counter and glass-faced cabinets filled with various chemical solutions. Beside it was a walk-in cooler, usually where new arrivals awaiting autopsy or embalming were stored.

The smell of the place was anything but foreign to me.

George made his way to two side-by-side drawers, both marked Montana. He opened the one to the right, the one with the name Jacob penned on the white ID card along with Case Number 33 (Scarlet was 32).

When George slid him out I could see that Jake had been positioned headfirst. I could also see that his arms, which had previously been rendered in an overhead pugilist's position, were now broken in order for him to better fit inside the drawer. He smelled like a burnt pot roast.

First George slapped on a pair of latex gloves, then he reached inside the drawer and lifted up Jake's charred head. He felt around with his fingers until he found something.

"There she blows," he said. "Looks like the old chief took one hell of a wallop to the back of the head."

I slapped a glove on my right hand, reached inside and confirmed the walnut-sized divot in the back of the dead man's skull.

I slipped off the glove. "Somebody hit him," I said. George shut the drawer. "I can bet dollars to diamonds he did not die in the fire. I can bet somebody snuck up on him from behind, whacked him over the head, then torched the place to cover his or her tracks."

"Papers said his body was found curled up on the kitchen floor of his home."

"Makes sense," I said. "There's a door off the kitchen. Cain could have broke in and taken care of business."

"We're getting closer," George replied. "You match up the divot in the back of his head to the barrel of Cain's pistol, you got a winner."

"But it still doesn't do us any good about Scarlet," I said. "There's nothing to prove that he had anything to do with her death."

George nodded.

I asked him to pull her out one more time. "I just want to take one more look at her. See if we might have missed something the first time."

He slid her out.

There it was again, that organ-slide sensation in my stomach, the pressure in my head and behind the eyeballs. If I just looked at her auburn hair, closed eyes and red lips she might have appeared to be sleeping. But then, by glancing downwards a couple of inches you couldn't help but see the lacerated neck and the dozens of cuts and hesitation marks on her chest. There were the crude sutures from George's autopsy.

The pathologist pulled her all the way out. I stared down at her. Like every time when I looked at her in this condition, I tried to remain as clinical as possible, not letting my emotions get to me. Maybe I had liked her more than I thought. Maybe I loved her, just a little. But then I thought about murder. What were some of the things that would lead me to believe another person had stabbed her to death?

First, there would be "defensive" cuts visible in the dorsal or palm side of the hands. In the drawer, she was lying palms up. They were as clean and undamaged as a baby's whistle.

Secondly, a murderer would stab repeatedly. Okay, there was something. Scarlet had multiple stab wounds. But then, it was the wounds themselves that bothered me. Other than the neck wound, the cuts were shallow.

Thirdly, the wounds were all relegated to the chest, belly and neck area. A murderer would almost surely have stabbed her in the shoulders or in the pelvic region or even in the back.

Now what about suicide? I thought. Were there any tentative stabs? Something Scarlet might have inflicted to see how much it was going to hurt before she worked up the courage needed to pull off the entire deed? There were dozens of them. Did she remove her clothes before she stabbed herself? She had. Were there any defensive wounds on her arms or on the backs of her hands? Not a damn thing.

I took a step back.

"Homicide made to look like suicide," I said.

"Damn good job of it too," George agreed. "Because it almost looks like Scarlet wanted to die."

"She certainly didn't put a fight," I said. "It's almost like she could have scripted it herself."

George slammed the drawer closed. "Might have been perfect, Moon, if only the killer thought to leave behind a note and a blade."

I nodded. "Still, she's the best body of evidence we have and quite possibly, my only way out of this thing. If only we can manage to hold onto her, which at this point is going to be pretty impossible."

That's when it came to me.

"George, pull both bodies. Let's bag them and get them the hell out of here."

He looked at me and laughed.

"You can't just remove them from the deep freeze," he said. "They'll start to thaw."

I thought about the old man, how during the 1965 blackout that ravaged the entire state for two days, he was forced to store two cadavers in each of the Hope Lane bathtubs, one upstairs, one down. All it took to keep them from rotting was plenty of ice, so my dad bragged to George and I on more than one occasion.

"How many bathtubs you got at your place?" I asked.

"Why my place?"

"How many?"

"Two," he surrendered.

"Perfect," I said. "Exactly what we'll need."

He laughed again. "I see what you're up to, little bro. Your dad's blackout story, which I'm not sure I ever believed. Funeral homes, even in the sixties, came equipped with generators. In any case, it's gonna take an awful lot of ice."

It took only about five minutes to get them bagged and laid out onto two gurneys for transport in George's old El Camino.

Outside, I knew daybreak was coming soon. I wanted to get going while we could still depend on the dark for cover, get the bodies safely inside George's downtown townhouse, get them into the tubs and packed with ice. We would have made it without a hitch too, if only it hadn't been for that knock on the morgue door. A pounding fist, followed by Cain ordering George to "Open the fuck up!"

55

Scarlet's empty drawer was still open.

"Get in," George said.

"Jesus," I said.

I looked inside the drawer. It was dark and cavernous.

"George, I can't☐ "

"Don't argue!" he insisted, his voice a whisper-shout. Skinny old George practically picked me up and threw me in himself.

When he closed the door my world went black. I was locked inside a morgue drawer that only minutes before held the body of a woman I'd slept with. Had I hidden inside caskets back when I was a kid? Yeah. But this was different.

I tried to hold my breath, but it was impossible. No choice but to breathe the cold death smell in through my mouth while George unlocked the door to the room, allowing Cain inside.

"What can I do for you, Detective?" I heard George say, nice and polite.

"Where is he?" Cain asked.

"Where is who, Detective?"

"Your friend, Dick Moonlight."

As far as I could tell from inside that drawer, Cain was all alone. But then, I had no way of being sure. The voices were difficult to pick up through the drawer's steel paneling.

"Don't insult me, Detective," I heard George go on. "Mr. Moonlight is a fugitive wanted for the murder of Mrs. Montana. I, for one, would not hesitate to alert the proper authorities if I were to come upon him."

That's when Cain laughed. One of those loud smoker's laughs that comes from deep inside toasty lungs followed by a couple of lung-ripping coughs.

"That was beautiful, Dr. Phillips," he said. "You really missed your calling."

I began to hear something else now. Like a banging noise, only not a banging noise. More like a mechanical sliding sound followed by a slamming sound. Cain, opening and closing the drawers.

"Let me tell you something, Doctor," Cain said. "If I find out you're lying to me, I will revoke your license. I will see to it that you do time."

"Like I've already told you," George said, cool and collected, "I'm not the type to harbor a man suspected of murder. I have my reputation to consider."

"And what a hell of a reputation it is, George," Cain said. "When was the last time you saw the light of day? You know, it's true what they say about you."

"What do they say about me, Detective?"

"That you're really just as dead as the stiffs you slice up down here."

"Is that what they say?"

Cain laughed some more. "That's what I say, Phillips."

"Sticks and stones, Detective," George said. "Sticks and stones."

Cain was treating George like common dirt. I understood then why my big brother went out of his way to help me whenever I asked for it. This wasn't only about extra money for his granddaughter. It was about giving it back to people like Cain who considered the pathologist the lowest rung on the medical ladder. As if working with the dead made you incompetent when it came to dealing with the living.

Vincent Zandri

A few more drawers opened. The noises were getting louder. He was coming closer. Lying inside there, stone stiff and still, I knew he could not have been more than a drawer or two away from me.

I closed my eyes, waiting for it to slide open.

But the drawer didn't move.

Instead I heard Cain ask about the two tagged and bagged stiffs laid out on the gurneys.

"You're the inquiring detective," George said. "You tell me."

I heard what I thought was the unzipping of the body bags.

"Why do you have them laid out like this?" Cain inquired.

"They're both on their way to Fitzgerald's," George said. "For embalming and for burial per the deceased's instructions." He paused a beat. "Please don't hesitate to give the funeral directors a call if you'd like to confirm. You may use the phone in my office."

I heard the zipping back up of the bags. At least, I thought I could hear it.

Loyalty ... Fitzgerald's... If Cain called George's bluff and made the call, I knew that Mrs. Fitzgerald would not be able to lie for us. Nor would I want her to.

"In a little while I'm heading north," Cain said. "I'll be back in town by noon. I'll call then. If the bodies aren't there by that time, I'll send my own people out after them."

"I certainly won't stand in the way of law and order, Detective," George went on. "Is there anything else you need from me this fine morning?"

I heard the door open.

"Just remember what I said, Phillips," Cain insisted. "You hold back on me with anything, anything at all, and I will take you down right along with your old buddy. Do you understand me?"

"So help me die, Detective."

"You have a very morbid sense of humor, Dr. Phillips."

At least he's got one, I thought from my grave.

The door slammed behind Cain. A second later the drawer opened. I couldn't jump out fast enough. I had a bullet in my brain. Who knew when I'd be renting one of those things for real? While I scrubbed my face and hands in the sink, George went out into the parking lot to make certain Cain was gone for good. When he came back in his face looked tighter than a tick.

"It's still raining," he said. "But the sun hasn't come up yet. We can go now, we can make it to my house before full dawn."

"George," I said, "if you do this, there's no turning back."

"Listen, Moon, I know what I'm doing ... in an *us-against-the-world* sort of way."

I finished drying my face and made my way back into the pathologist's office. Opening up the top drawer of his file cabinet, I pulled a folder that contained the name and case number of a job I had worked on for Cain just a short time ago. I shoved it under my arm and met George back out in the hall, gazing into his tired blue eyes.

"Got what you need?" he asked.

"An acquittal would be nice," I said. "And maybe a new brain."

56

On the way uptown we stopped at a Stewarts convenience store. While I waited sunk down in the passenger seat of the El Camino, George proceeded to clean the place out of its ice.

A few minutes later the sun was coming up over thick gray clouds. First we transported the ice, then we carried the bodies in through the back door off a dark, narrow alley.

We set Jake's bagged body into the tub inside the downstairs bathroom off the kitchen. After packing my former boss in ice, we then carried Scarlet up to the second floor bathroom and repeated the process.

Having packed them with ice however, we both knew that their state of preservation (such as it was) would not last. Maybe thirty-six to forty-eight hours at most before things started getting ripe. Even then we'd have to change the ice two times per day, minimum.

By the time we were through, daybreak was in full shine through the usual gray filter. Maybe the day was entirely overcast, but this morning at least the rain had taken a breather. George was good enough to find me a pair of Levis plus a green-and-black-checkered shirt. The jeans and the shirt were a bit snug in the waist and chest, but at least there wasn't any blood on them.

"Now what?" George asked from inside his galley kitchen, a cup of coffee in hand.

"You got a wire tap hanging around?" I half joked.

"How's about an old hand-held tape recorder?"

"What about a video camera?"

"Super-eight home movie camera," he smiled. "My old man bought it right after the war. I used to make crazy trippy movies with it back in the late sixties."

"Get it out. And don't forget film."

"Whaddaya you got in mind?" he asked.

"While I pay a visit to my ex-wife, I'll need you to go north, get some footage of Cain."

"How can you be sure he's not home right now, catching up on his beauty sleep?"

"Because people in his position do not sleep. And don't forget, we were partners for a hell of a long time. I know how the motherfucker thinks," I growled.

"So what's the mofo thinking?" George asked.

"He mentioned going north. I think I can provide you with the specific Saratoga address."

I asked him for a phonebook. When he pulled it out from a drawer in the kitchen, I once again looked up the stats on the Russian cuisine restaurant called The Russo. I wrote everything down on a slip of scrap paper and handed it to George. I asked him how he felt about using his credit card to rent a Ryder van for the day while I commandeered the El Camino. We'd need the van later on, anyway.

"If I have to," he said.

I told him he had to.

"Christ, Moon, to think I used to order your skinny ass around."

I instructed him to meet me back at his house at noon sharp.

He said he could be ready to rock 'n' roll in five minutes. Then he said, "Ain't got much in the way of scratch, Moony, other than what you fed me after the autopsy."

I got his point loud and crystal. That dough was his dough. No, that's not right. It was his granddaughter's dough.

"Color eight-millimeter film takes a week to ten days to process. But I produce enough working capital, I can get a guy I know across the river to develop it one hour."

I reached into my pocket, pulled out the albino man's envelope, opened it, and slid out five one-hundreds for myself and ten for George. There were fifteen more one-hundred dollar bills left over, which I stashed back in my pants.

"Will that do?"

"Plenty," he said. He stuffed the goods in his chest pocket and left through the back door.

57

I parked the El Camino three lots down from Lynn and Mitchell Cain's center hall Colonial. As expected, Cain's BMW wasn't parked in the drive.

Rather than ring the bell, giving Lynn the chance to eye me from the upstairs window, I decided to backdoor it. I couldn't have made a better decision.

The way the house was set on a decline, the back door off the basement was accessible at ground level. The finished basement also served as a playroom for my boy, who was sitting on the carpeted floor playing Xbox.

First I pulled out my shirttails, draping them over the automatic stuffed into my jeans. Then I tapped on the window beside the door with my knuckles. When the scrappy little kid looked up from his game, he saw my face and smiled. From outside I couldn't help but notice that his baseball mitt was set in his lap.

"Daddy!" I heard him say through the glass.

I motioned with my right hand for him to unlock the door and let me in. Without missing a beat, he tossed the glove onto the floor, got up and opened the door. A second later, I was in.

When I bent down to kiss him, I felt my head go light, my throat close in on itself.

"We were supposed to be together last night," he said, a little pout forming on his face. "What happened?"

"Daddy sort of got tied up," I said. "But I promise, I'll make it up to you next week. How about we take the canoe up to Little's lake, catch some bass?"

"Cool!" he said, with a little jump. "So long as I don't have a game."

"You don't always play ball, do you, Bear?"

His Batman pajama bottoms were falling down his skinny body, so he hiked them up.

"I saw you on TV," he said. I felt my heart race when he said it.

"How'd I look?" I asked.

"All dressed up in orange like that guy in *The Fugitive*. Mitch and me watch that movie on DVD."

My stomach sank at the thought of my son cozying up to Cain.

"I look good?"

He snickered. "Mom said it was about time you got what you had coming."

"That's Mom," I said. "Always joking around." I ran my hand through his hair. "Speaking of Mom, is she up?"

"She's on her treadmill, I think. I'm not supposed to disturb her when she's exercising."

I took a quick moment to listen. I made out the sound of the treadmill belt winding its way around the rollers.

"I think I'll go up and say hello," I said.

"Okay, but Mommy's not going to like being disturbed."

I told him I'd proceed at my own risk.

"That's what Mitch always says," he said. Then he asked, "Daddy, will I see you on TV again?"

I smiled. "Yes, you will, and when you do I won't be wearing an orange jumper. But I will, however, be wearing a smile. Just for you."

"I can't wait to see it," he said.

"Neither can I."

I took the stairs up into the kitchen, two at a time.

I didn't stop there.

I pulled the one hand cannon I had left from out of my jeans, made my way into the front vestibule, and up the center hall stairs. On the way I noticed that the wall was covered with photos of the whole

Cain family. Smiley-faced pics of Mitch, Lynn and my son sitting on a sunny Cape Cod beach. Another of just Lynn and Mitch holding hands on their wedding day.

At the top of the stairs was a picture of Mitch and my son, each of them down on one knee, smiling for the camera. Mitch was wearing a red baseball cap that said "Joe's Grill" on the brim. It matched exactly the red t-shirt and cap my son was wearing. Further down, another photo revealed Mitch all dressed up his uniform blues, his hair cut just as short as it was now, but without the gray. As for the smug cop smile, it hadn't changed one bit.

At the top of the stairs, the rolling thunder noise coming from the treadmill was almost deafening. I made my way down the narrow hall, past the bathroom, past walls covered with more family snapshots, past the master bedroom until I came to a room that contained the treadmill, a television and nothing else.

I stepped inside, tapping the pistol barrel on the doorjamb. Lynn looked up quick. If this had been a Loony Toon, she would have shot straight through the ceiling. She pulled off her headphones and yanked a plastic red safety key from the readout panel that instantly stopped the rolling tread.

"How did you get in here?" she demanded, breathless voice barely a whisper.

"You shouldn't leave our son alone in the basement," I told her.

She stepped off the now idol treadmill. "I'm calling the police."

"I am the police," I said, thumbing the hammer on the .38. "Besides, it's your husband they really want. They just don't know it yet."

"You're crazy."

"No, I'm in my right mind for a change. Mitchell is the crazy one. Believes he can get away with murder."

Lynn was wearing black spandex biker shorts, ped socks with Nike emblems on them and Nike running shoes. Her hair was bleached blonde, trimmed butch-short. When I was married to her it was sandy brown and shoulder-length. Like Martha Stewart.

"Mitchell is an outstanding officer and a decorated detective," she said. "He would never do anything to jeopardize his reputation and the reputation of his family." She actually seemed genuine, her eyes filling with tears.

~ 225 ~

"I saw what they said about you on the news. About how you killed Scarlet Montana. You're the criminal now. The screw-up-everything-you-touch son of a bitch. Knowing you, you probably have no recollection of it. Or at least, that will be your story. Won't it, Richard?" She rattled the whole thing off without taking a breath.

It made my skin shiver to be the subject of one of her tirades, especially one accusing me of murder. Maybe she knew something more than I knew. Something from the inside. In any case, I wasn't there to argue. I was there to get information. Which is why I slid my hand inside my shirt, hitting RECORD on the tape recorder I'd duct-taped to my already bandaged chest.

"Mind if I ask you some questions?"

"You're the one with the gun," she said.

I asked her the standard questions that I knew would either go unanswered or just relegated to *I don't know what you're talking about.*

Did she know that Mitch was engaged in illegal black market activity, namely the illicit harvesting and sales of body parts? Did she have any idea how long he had been participating in the operation? Why, in her opinion, would Mitch want to risk his own life by killing Scarlet and Jake?

I asked her everything I could think of. But the most I got out of her was the tight angry face I recalled so well. The face that told me, if she could, she would tear my eyeballs out and swallow them whole.

The face that wasn't entirely her fault. Not by a long shot. Because I wasn't exactly being fair, was I? In a real way, she had every right to be angry. I was the one who'd decided to put my career before my family. I was the one who'd decided to sleep with Scarlet. Then, when I discovered that Lynn was sleeping with my partner, I'd decided to play the role of the suicidal cop. As if that would have solved everything.

So who could blame Lynn now?

Now that she was about to be screwed over again. Not by a man, necessarily, but by a goddamned cop.

"Now if you do not plan on shooting me," she said, "I have a child to get off to school. You do remember our son, don't you, Richard?"

Memory, it's not the problem.

She approached me. I thumbed back the hammer, lowered the weapon to my side. I couldn't help but feel deflated and defeated, as if my life were nothing more than a badly played board game.

"I don't blame you for not talking," I said. "I hurt you once."

"You gave me a world of hurt, more than once. And to believe I tried to help you when you needed it most, and you refused."

"Maybe it's Mitch who's hurting you now."

That's when her eyes went from wide and angry to heavy and hurt. The mere mention of Mitch and hurt in the same sentence seemed to knock the wind right out of her. Having shared my life with them both, I knew Cain and I knew Lynn. There was something more to her distress than met the eye. I decided to go with my intuition.

"He's cheating on you, isn't he?"

"That's none of your business."

"But what is my business is this, I'm not going to prison for a murder I did not commit."

She lowered her head for a second. When she came back up, I could see that she was crying. Really bawling. If I had to guess, they were more the tears of frustration than sadness. In any case, I let her cry it out for a while.

"That Scarlet Montana," she said. "Nobody deserves to die that kind of death. But she was no good, Richard. She was big trouble."

Her words hit me hard. It also kicked my built-in shit detector into overdrive. Because it was then that I knew for certain, Cain was fucking Scarlet. Or should I say, fucking Scarlet right along with me. The pressure behind my eyeballs suddenly shifted, dropping into my stomach like a lead weight. Scarlet might have been clinically dead, but for the first time ever, I was beginning to feel a genuine animosity towards her.

Lynn was right. Scarlet was a boatload of trouble, even in death.

"Mitch," I said, a rock-sized lump in my throat. "Mitch and Scarlet. For how long?"

"Since last summer."

"I'm sorry."

"We have a son," Lynn went on. "We will always have a son, no matter how we feel about one another."

"Yes," I said. "We have a son."

"I would prefer that his father stay out of prison. He needs you. He needed Mitch too, once upon a time. But now he needs you again."

"Then for our son's sake, Lynn, give me something. Anything I can go on that will set this thing straight."

She looked into my eyes, nodded her head. "If I give you something," she said, "will you make certain that nothing happens to our boy?"

I told her I would make sure.

"Promise me, Richard!" she insisted, her voice verging on a shout.

"I promise, Lynn," I said. "You know I do."

She nodded with tight lips and wet eyes.

"That's exactly what worries me. Not knowing if you will keep your promise. You have a habit of not paying attention to certain matters of importance."

What could I possibly say to that? I felt the weight of the pistol in my hand. Suddenly I felt ashamed of myself for thinking I would need it. For shade of a second, it was as if we had never divorced as I watched her walk into her bedroom where she opened a drawer, dug her hand deep inside, and produced a stack of envelopes. When she came back out she handed one of the envelopes to me along with a pen and a blank yellow Post-a-Note. It had the name of a bank on it. A Swiss bank.

"I'll give you exactly ten seconds to write down the user name, password, social security number and account number," she said. "Then I want you out of this house."

I scribbled everything down. Then I handed her back the envelope.

"Just leave," she said.

I started for the stairs. But before I took them, I turned back to her.

"I'm sorry," I said, "about the way things turned out between us. I'm sorry for what I did with Scarlet."

"I'm sorry for our son. I'm sorry for you and I'm sorry for the sad son of a bitch I replaced you with and yeah, I'm sorry for Scarlet too. May God have mercy on her poor fucking soul."

She took a staggered step back, looked me up and down, and shook her head. For a moment, I thought she was going to pass out.

"Are you really going to call the cops, tell them I was here?"

She wiped her eyes with the backs of her hands.

"My God, Richard," she sadly laughed. "You just said it yourself. You are the goddamned cops."

§

58

I navigated the less-populated secondary roads all the way back to George's townhouse. The route took me through narrow alleys flanked on both sides by the backs of the old brick row houses. I motored steadily past overfilled dumpsters and countless burnt-out cars that had been stripped of everything but their steering columns. The drive took me ten more minutes than it would have had I gone the usual, out-in-the-open route. Which meant that as soon I arrived at the townhouse, I wasted no time.

Out in George's living room, I sat at the computer, bringing up the Google search engine. When I typed in "www.bankvonernst.com," I came up with a website that was housed in Liechtenstein. Post-a-Note laid out before me, I typed in the necessary user information in the spaces indicated.

The online spreadsheet appeared before me in a flash. Scrolling down, I discovered thirty-two separate transactions dating back the past four years to early 2007, all of them adding up to a grand total of $400,806 US. Unless Cain had come into some money from some recently deceased aunt or uncle, he was making one hell of a payday as a detective for the Albany cops.

I printed a hardcopy of the statement. If I'd possessed Mitch's passwords, I might have cashed the damn thing out, sent all proceeds care of the Attorney General. For now, the bank statement would have to do.

Inside the galley kitchen I pulled George's phonebook back out from the stand below the wall-mounted telephone. Since I couldn't very well go to the police with my discovery, I located the address for the local FBI. In another drawer I found an envelope and some stamps. Addressing the envelope, I penned the word URGENT beneath the zip code and stuck it sideways under the lid of George's mailbox as outgoing mail.

That done, I pulled the duct-taped recorder off my chest and set it on the coffee table. Setting my aching body down onto the sofa, I laid back, head against the springy cushion. To say that I felt very heavy and tired was an understatement. The Smith and Wesson resting on my chest (easy access), I closed my eyes and drifted.

There was a slam.

I shot up, pistol in hand, pointing it at the front door.

"Take it easy, Moon. It's just me." George was holding a white plastic shopping bag. He seemed to have an energy about him I hadn't seen in a long time. He was an outlaw again, and enjoying it.

I took a minute to catch my breath. How long had I been passed out?

"Did you get the shots?"

"Haven't let a Moonlight down yet," he grinned.

59

The super-eight film had been shot from across a rather dusky early-morning side street somewhere near Saratoga's downtown business center. It showed Cain and a thick, black-clad (Russian?) man standing outside the back service entrance door to what looked like a restaurant.

The Russo.

Smartly, George took a quick shot of the rental van's dashboard-mounted digital clock at that exact point in time. It read 7:30. It wasn't exactly an official *time-stamped* photo, but it would have to do. When the film once more focused on the two men, there seemed to be no doubt that they were arguing. Maybe there was no sound to go with the old 8mm, but clearly the dark man was holding a silenced automatic on Cain. They were moving their mouths rapidly and at certain points, waving their arms at one another. I had no idea what they were saying. Although I could not see their faces, there was no doubt that they were fighting, face to face, nose to nose, and seemingly oblivious to the pistol as they were the steady rain that soaked them.

But then Cain suddenly turned, tossing a burning cigarette to the wet concrete sidewalk and stormed off across the road.

Another shot at the rental truck clock showed 8:20. Cain had been negotiating with his buyer for nearly an hour.

That was it. The visual eyebrow-raising evidence I needed.

The end of the five-minute film ran through the projector, causing it to flap with every spin of the top reel. George killed the power and hit the lights.

"Okay?" he asked.

"Yeah, okay," I said.

He folded down the screen, took a look outside.

Still all clear in Albany, he reassured. As luck would have it, the townhouse had belonged to his long deceased mother. It was still deeded in her name. As for the telephone directory, George was conveniently unlisted. But the safety cushion, such as it was, wouldn't last very long.

"What now?" he asked, turning back to me.

I told him about my little talk with Lynn, about how she had led me to the Swiss bank account, how the bank statement was on its way to the FBI now that the mailman had made his rounds.

"She did that for you?" he said, as if surprised.

"Scarlet and Mitch," I said. "It appears they'd been bedding down."

He pursed his lips and shook his head. I got the feeling he wanted to make a comment; maybe something about Lynn's bad luck at having lost two husbands to the same auburn-haired, green-eyed beauty. But he let it go.

Instead he said, "It's official. Detective Cain is now our primary suspect in the murders of Scarlet and Jake Montana. Hands-fucking-down, little brother."

I ejected the mini cassette tape from the recorder and put it with the film, my copy of the Swiss bank statement and the case file I'd pulled from George's office earlier. I told him that if we had a brain and a half between us, we would lay low until dark. That would be the safe thing to do. But then, we couldn't afford the convenience of safety.

George went back into the kitchen, grabbed a Diet Coke, and sat down with it on the chair across from the couch. He made a tight-lipped grimace. Maybe he didn't say a word about it, but the expression told me he was experiencing pain.

"There's one more job we have to pull off before I decide to end this thing," I said.

He pulled a half-smoked joint from his shirt pocket, lit it with his Bic lighter, and took three or four tap-tap drags on it, careful not to burn his lips on the fiery nub. He silently held it out for me, to offer me a toke. I shook my head politely.

During the trip up to Saratoga in the rental van, he had tied his long hair back into a ponytail. His face was covered in gray-black stubble. He looked older than his age. But then I also knew how much pain George had to endure day in and day out.

"What's on your mind?" he exhaled.

I stood up, tucking my 9mm in the waist of my jeans.

"I'll explain as best I can during the ride to the Home Depot."

The plan, as I relayed it to George went something like this: time was short, which meant we'd have to backdoor the operation. Rather than confront the body part buyers (or what was left of them) up in Saratoga, we'd go after the product itself. Or in this case, the "host" of the product, the dead and buried victims.

What I had in mind was to put George's and my talents for dealing with the dead to good and practical use. The two of us had worked the death trade as assistant morticians. I had the mortician business floating around in my veins. George had graduated to the level of pathologist. Who better than us to undertake a mission to resurrect the dead?

More specifically, my theory revolved around locating just one of the harvested bodies, attaching it to Cain and Jake either by means of procedural association (the police report) or better yet, by physical contact.

"The point is," I told George as he drove us toward the Washington Avenue Home Depot in the van, "I don't really have to prove anything. All I need to do is prove that a conspiracy exists."

Eyes on the rain-soaked road, George shrugged his shoulders.

I told him that the mere suggestion of a conspiracy would naturally lead the FBI to believe that a cover-up was in the works. The cover-up would lead them to the frame job that Cain and Montana had been pulling on me all these months and years. I told him that Cain, acting in the position as the chief investigating officer on the unnatural deaths he'd called me in on, never recorded the fact that he pulled organs from the bodies. That deception alone, if it could be proven, was definitely going to raise the attention not only of Prosecutor O'Connor, but also the victims' surviving families.

"But what's to prevent Cain from denying everything?" George asked. "He'll just say he had no contact with the bodies once they left the scene of the crime or accident."

"No way he can deny everything."

"And how's that?"

"Because as you well know, a police report that requests either partial or no autopsy, by its very definition, must already be thorough and conclusive as to the cause, manner and mechanism of death. Gonna look a little suspicious if he overlooked a missing kidney or two. If there was no autopsy, how's a set of kidneys missing?"

He nodded. "It's the can of worms trick," he said. "Poke a hole through the tin lid, get the prosecutor to peek inside."

"I'm gonna do better than that," I told him. "I'm gonna shove a fistful of night crawlers down his throat."

"Nasty," George said with a sour face.

The yellow van cruised west along the long stretch of highway. After a long beat, George spoke up again.

"Let me get this straight, Moon," he said. "You want to dig up one of the bodies Cain chopped up for spare parts?"

I turned to him. "You and me, brother. We're the perfect candidates for this kind of job. The last thing he wants is for one of those chop jobs to suddenly show up six feet above ground."

George shot me a look. "The last thing he wants is a postmortem evaluation," he added.

"That's where you come in," I said. "You perform a postmortem from caudal to clavicle. We do it in front of a video camera, prove without a doubt that the body was cut after it was pronounced dead."

I could tell George was thinking about it.

"The cadavers all gave consent for organ donation," he pointed out. "What if the court just assumes the bodies were cut up in the interest of science or medicine?"

"You and I both know that anybody under the age of twenty-one must have their family notified prior to going under the knife. Regardless of driver's license permission. If the family had been notified there would have been a clear paper trail leading up to the recipient." I picked up the manila folder I took from his office file cabinet earlier, thumbing through it to exaggerate its thinness. "Look," I said. "No paper trail."

"Not the first time I've laid eyes on those folders," George said. "Just the first time I've realized how stupid they are. If you're gonna cut up bodies for spare parts, you might as well fill out the false paperwork to cover your corrupt ass."

"What Cain and Jake must have been counting on was the reactions of the families involved. As far as the families are concerned, the bodies of their loved ones were buried just the way they looked in life. You know how funny people can be about death—"

"Hermetically sealed caskets," George jumped in. "Stainless steel-lined concrete burial vaults. Nonsensical when you really stop and think about it."

"Ah yes, but remember the philosophy of the great Harold Moonlight: it makes people feel calm and collected inside to know that their beloved dead and buried are protected from the worms."

"I see where you're headed, Moony," he said. "Any of those families get word their little boy or girl's body has been messed with and select members of the A.P.D. may be responsible, they'll create a shit storm so thick even a slick operator like Cain won't escape it."

60

We drove in silence while the afternoon wore on and the rain came down heavier. Soon the Home Depot loomed on the horizon like a giant metal-sided, neon-lit hardware and home supply Oz.

"There's just one thing that bothers me," George said as we passed signs that directed us towards the parking area. "We go digging up a body illegally, they'll not only add that to our laundry list of crimes, they'll toss any evidence we come up with out of court."

I gazed at George's profile—the gaunt nose, the long ponytail, the worn jean jacket that replaced the white smock just before we escaped Albany Med's basement.

"We're not doing anything illegal," I said.

"Unauthorized exhumation is not punishable by law in New York State?" he needlessly asked. "You have to consult with the cemetery authority and get permission from the family."

He pulled into the massive parking lot, made a beeline for an empty spot up close to the glass entry doors. He threw the transmission into park and killed the engine.

"We're gonna get permission," I assured him, lifting the file folder once more, then setting it back down on my lap. "From the family." My voice sounded muffled and thick with the engine off and the windows shut against the rain.

Taking his hand off the keys, George left them dangling in the ignition.

"We don't have that kind of time."

"I didn't say when we'd get it. I just said we'd get it. Sooner or later."

"You're counting on this sooner-or-later permission," he said like a question.

"When the family sees what we've done for them," I explained, "they'll be sending us roses."

"What about getting caught?" he asked. "You can't just expect to drive into a cemetery and start digging away."

"You remember Albany Rural Cemetery?" I asked.

"You know I do," he said.

He and I had personally assisted with the burial of dozens of Moonlight clients at Albany Rural back in the seventies.

"The body we're going to take is buried in the center of that ten-square-mile, heavily wooded plot of real estate," I pointed out. "We'll be fine."

"Risk," George murmured with a shake of the head. "There's some serious risk in what we're doing."

"Risk is our middle name," I replied, pulling out a small list of items I needed him to pick up.

"I'm changing mine to Stupid," he said, snatching the list from my fingers.

My reason for choosing the teenaged body of Kevin Ryan was not indiscriminate.

His official manner of death had been listed on the thin D.C. as suicide. I was aware of that fact without having to consult the D.C. itself. After all, I was the one who had filled out the form (which George, at my request, later co-signed as the county pathologist).

I also knew for a fact that Ryan's death had actually resulted from an accidental hanging inside the walk-in attic of his parent's suburban home. So did Cain at the time. While I'd wanted to list "accidental death" instead of suicide in order to avoid any investigation at all, Cain insisted I go with the latter.

Maybe the general public isn't aware of it, but many so-called "child suicides" are really just accidents. The "suicides" often involve teenage boys who have hanged themselves while trying to enhance their solitary sexual experience. They realize that by hanging themselves from the neck while masturbating, they can achieve one powerful orgasm. Ugly to contemplate, but a fact all the same.

I guess it all starts somewhere in the adolescent experience (and possibly the world wide web). Kids somehow discover that by applying a pressure to the carotid artery you severely diminish the oxygen supply to the brain. The more oxygen that gets cut off, the better the climax. Which is exactly why so many of these kids end up dead. The grief-stricken parents, not wanting to live with the pain and stigma attached to "death by experimental self-gratification" almost always opt for the no less tragic, but more understanding, suicide. Some are even willing to pay a cop like Cain for the slight change in the manner of death.

Suburbanites have their reputations to think about. Which, as far as I was concerned, is exactly what Cain had been counting on when he called me in on the job. I remember looking at the eighteen-year-old's body, which had been hanging from an attic rafter for less than an hour when his father discovered him.

Cain insisted I call it a suicide, despite the evidence that his entire lower body was naked, his right hand raised high overhead, clutching the leather belt he'd wrapped around his neck and buckled to the overhead rafter while his left hand was still grasping his organ.

"Fuck the autopsy," is how he put it. "Just get George to sign away."

When I asked him why the presiding A.P.D. officer on duty didn't sign it himself, he said he had his reasons. In the end he simply insisted on utilizing my part-time "expertise" on this one, backed up by a pathologist's signature as well as a comprehensive C.S. for which he was prepared to pay handsomely in cold, hard scratch. The department was crazy, backed-up with pending cases.

The usual Cain-Montana police story.

I took a look around the lot to make sure we weren't being followed. That's when a strange feeling began to swim over me. A cold up-and-down-my-backbone sensation that told me maybe we hadn't been careful enough; that it would only be a matter of time until I was connected with George; until somebody discovered that he hadn't shown up for work today; that the now missing bodies of the Montanas hadn't made it to the Fitzgerald funeral home after all.

As strange as it sounded, I had to wonder what the hell Cain was doing with his time. Why hadn't he picked up on me yet? Albany wasn't big. Maybe forty thousand souls. Maybe he was so busy reassuring his body part buyers that he wasn't paying attention to the chase, the re-apprehension of Albany's "most wanted."

The rush of ice-cold anxiety was so bad I couldn't feel my feet. I locked the car doors. Turning the keyed ignition, I powered up the dash. It was the top of the four o'clock hour.

It didn't take a lot of searching to find an AM station that played only news. After a commercial for a place called the Tire Warehouse, they read the lead story.

"The search for escaped A.P.D. officer-turned-murderer Richard Moonlight intensified late this afternoon. State Police, in cooperation with U.S. Marshals and FBI, have set up perimeter checkpoints within a fifteen-mile radius of Albany city limits. Traffic along the Thruway and Interstate 90 has begun to back up in all directions while choppers are combing the rural and outlying areas for any signs of the forty-year-old detective officially charged in the gruesome killing of thirty-eight-year-old Scarlet Montana.

"Speaking from outside the sealed off doors to the Albany Medical Center autopsy room, Albany P.D. detective Mitchell Cain was quoted as saying, 'We are closing in on Mr. Moonlight. We know he was here in this hospital within the past hour because we've recovered both a t-shirt and a stolen Kevlar vest with his blood on it. The materials had been discarded as refuse inside a medical waste bin. We now also suspect that Dr. George Phillips, hospital pathologist, may in fact be aiding and abetting Moonlight.'

"This afternoon a shocked Albany remains on full alert while a man accused of first degree homicide roams the streets and byways.

This is Megan Baker reporting—"

I turned off the radio and killed the ignition. So that's what Cain was doing. He hadn't been bluffing when he told George that the Montana bodies better make it to Fitzgerald's funeral home by noon or else face the consequences.

My brain was buzzing. Too much adrenalin, too much blood. Synapses and nerve endings overheating, glowing. I made a fist with my right hand, then released it.

I knew then that we had to go back and get the Montana bodies before the police obtained the warrant necessary to raid George's home. We'd have to grab up the bodies, exhume Ryan, then get the hell out of Albany. That is, we'd have to leave town long enough to put our case together. When that was done, I was fully prepared to turn myself in, not as the state's number one suspect, but as the state's number one witness.

I wiped the steam off the windshield, watching for George. What was taking him so long?

For a split second, I pictured his cuffed and shackled body being yanked out the front double doors of the Home Depot, a pair of gun-toting cops on either side of him. But it was my imagination playing tricks on me again.

Lola ... I had to talk with Lola.

We had no cell phone. That meant getting out of the car and exposing myself in broad daylight. It was raining again. I had that advantage. There was a payphone mounted to the side of the building. I could see it from where I was sitting. No one was standing near it. No one in their right mind would want to be outside on a day like today. Only head cases who don't know enough to get out of the rain.

I opened the door, exited the car, and felt the cool, hard spray on my face.

61

I slipped the quarters into the slot and waited for the dial tone. Then I dialed the number for Lola's office at the university. She answered almost immediately.

"It's me," I said.

No voice, just breathing, the sound of chairs and furniture sliding around in the background. Like her laboratory office was being ransacked.

"Not now," she said.

"Cain," I guessed. "Cain is there, isn't he?"

"Yes."

I'm not certain how I knew that Cain would come snooping. But then, having worked with him almost my entire adult life, I wasn't entirely unaware of his M.O. And then there was my intuition; my built-in shit detector.

"Did he present a formal warrant?"

"Yes."

I knew that Cain and Lola had met a couple of times before, however briefly, during my post-accident treatment. Their business together had been of an official nature. I also knew that Lola never quite took a liking to Cain. You might say she saw right through him, or at the very least saw another more black or sinister side of him that I didn't see until way too late.

I turned away from the wall, gazing out upon the parking lot. Just scattered trucks and cars pulling in and out. People running, not walking towards the doors, jacket collars pulled up over their heads. Nature's wrath; Cain's rage.

The senior detective (and now "acting" South Pearl Street chief by default) had produced the warrants he needed in record time. Who knew what judges he had stuffed in his hip pocket? Maybe even Hughes.

"Don't tell him anything," I said. "Call Stanley, tell him what's happened; what they're doing to you."

"Richard ..."

"What is it?"

"Are you feeling okay?"

Lola, always thinking of me, my health. Not thinking of her own well-being.

"Never better," I lied. "What about you? Can you handle this?"

"He's coming back in," she said. "I have to go."

"You won't hear from me until this thing is over. One way or another."

"Live," she said, and hung up.

62

As soon as George got back in the car I told him exactly what I knew. Did it as calm and collected as possible. There was no time for panic. Now that George had been fingered by Cain, we had to get the off the road. That didn't stop him from racing out of the parking lot.

We drove back to his townhouse as fast as we could without running the risk of a pull-over. The home's brownstone exterior was quiet and calm, but that didn't mean we weren't walking into a trap.

Pulling out the .38, I followed George up the back steps to the rear entrance. Once inside we scanned the place up and down. No one was there. No cops in the closets; no marshals on the rooftop; no troopers in the basement. Just the dead bodies in the bathtubs.

Immediately we loaded the Montanas into the cargo bay of the Ryder rental van, salvaging what we could of the ice, tossing it all into the mix. The whole operation took about twenty minutes. As George locked the joint back up, we began to hear sirens in the distance. We had no way of knowing if the sirens were intended for us. Neither of us wanted to wait around long enough to find out.

"You take the van, I'll take the El Camino," George said. "I need you to follow me downtown to a guy I know who owes me a favor. He'll put my car up for a while, give it a fresh coat of paint while we take care of business."

We were off, each of us behind the wheel of our respective rides heading downtown in the direction of the river. I didn't say anything about it, but I could see that George was careful to drive the minor roads, keeping away from the main avenues and thoroughfares. If we got nailed now, with the bodies in the back of the van, we'd be toast.

Soon we came to a downtown warehouse area that was situated maybe a hundred feet from the river. Just one of those old brick monsters that used to serve as an industrial mill in its prime.

George pulled up in front of a pair of roll-up doors and got out. He walked up to a metal door that was positioned beside the roll-ups and pressed the bell. After a beat or two, a man dressed in oil-stained overalls showed himself. The man was wearing an old Yankees baseball cap and was holding a towel in his grease-stained hands.

I watched them talk for a minute. Then I saw them both turn around, getting a look at me. I felt weird. Paranoid and weird. I saw the man nod his head while he wiped his hands with the towel. He closed the door behind him. As George made his way back to the car, the overhead door began to roll up.

George got back in and threw the El Camino in drive. "Don't say anything to these people, Moonlight. Doesn't matter that you're a fugitive. You're still a cop and they know it. Just stand off to the side while they do their work. My thinking is we chill out here for a while until full dark. Then we can go to work."

He pulled the car into a mechanic's garage. Behind us the roll-up went back down.

The place was brightly lit with two separate bays that contained hydraulic jacks and grease pits underneath. There was a fire-engine-red Porsche Carrera situated on the raised rack to our right. The guy with the Yankees cap was working underneath it. There were racks and stacks of tools and tires piled one atop the other. The walls were covered with old Sunoco and Mobile tin signboards and posters of half naked busty models, wrenches gripped in hand like big metal phalluses, the words "Sears Tough" printed below their bare feet.

We drove straight over our empty bay and into a separate wing behind the pits. When I got out of the car I could see that the concrete floor was stained with layers of paint. There were so many colors of paint, it all seemed to blend into a kind of orange-gray. I wasn't out the door before two equally paint-stained grease monkeys began taping black plastic to the windshield and side windows.

George told me to grab a cup of coffee in the outer office. He said to wait there with the door closed until his people were done.

"What are you going to do?" I asked him.

"Haircut," he said before walking out of the shop.

63

What shocked me was not the new dark blue paint job on the El Camino. What shocked me was George's new 'do.' But then *'do'* wasn't the right word for it.

His head had been shaved bald, his thin beard trimmed down to just a goatee and mustache. The jean jacket was gone as were the jeans, replaced now with a black turtleneck sweater, black wool pants and black cowboy boots. In his left ear was a diamond stud earring. Strapped to his belt was a small holster or sheathe that housed two black-plated scalpels.

Standing outside the shop office, he opened up his wallet to show me a new driver's license, the name Gerry Horn printed under the photo ID.

"It'll take us forty-five minutes to get into Poughkeepsie and over to the hospital," he said. "There are roadblocks and checkpoints going in and out of the city—off the Thruway, off the Taconic. We get stopped; I don't come close to matching the description of Dr. Phillips. They would have cut your hair too but, well …" He didn't finish his thought because there's not much you can do with a bald head.

I took a look around the shop, at the man still working on the Porsche, and the separate men pulling the black plastic off the El Camino's windows, scraping off the old registration and inspection stickers, slapping on the new.

"We're gonna store the El Camino here until this thing is done," George added while shooting a glance at his watch. "Time to resurrect that kid."

I exhaled a breath, making my way toward the Ryder van parked inside the garage.

"You're driving," I said, tossing him the keys.

"You can ride up front for now, Moon," George said. "It's not the back roads I'm worried about. It's the highway."

I opened the passenger-side door, hopped up inside, and closed the door behind me. George got in behind the wheel. The overhead door was raised.

Taking a glance at himself in the rearview, George threw the tranny in reverse.

"Let's hope this works," he murmured.

"No choice but to work," I told him.

We backed out.

64

I knew that Kevin Ryan's plot was located five miles inside the dark, heavily wooded Albany Rural Cemetery. It was set beside a newly transplanted catalpa tree that was now in full spring bloom with big white flowers. I knew the tree was meant as a metaphor for Kevin's life. Rather, the memory of his life, the memory that would never die.

Some of the petals from the tree had fallen in the wind and the rain. The leaves had scattered about the newly laid sod. In the dark they looked like big snowflakes. Ryan's headstone had been recently quarried. It was polished smooth. It glistened from the rain and from the hand-held battery-powered lamp that I shined upon it. It rose out of the ground maybe two and one-half feet high. An inscription read:

Kevin Dubin Ryan
September 2, 1988 - June 6, 2006
Loving Son
May Your Spirit Bloom Forever

I knew I couldn't have been wrong about that tree.

George had temporarily traded in his new black cowboy boots for a pair of rubber lineman boots, his black trench coat for a yellow rain slicker. I had on the same getup and for good reason. Pretty soon we'd be playing in the mud. He was carrying a pickaxe in one hand and a shovel in the other. Tools I'd asked him to pick up at the Home Depot.

He tossed them onto the grass.

"We're gonna need more than this, Moon," he pointed out.

I told him I was banking on a backhoe that would surely be on site. I knew from firsthand experience that it had to be housed inside the maintenance garage not far from where we were standing. No cemetery was complete without a backhoe. That was a given.

"You have the keys to said backhoe, little brother?"

"Key should be on the wall."

"What if it's not?"

"What'd you do prior to taking up shop with Harold Moonlight?"

Some rain dripped off his nose onto his chin beard.

"My little hotwiring career almost cost me seven-to-ten in Green Haven," he said. "Thank God for Vietnam."

"At least the government was kind enough to give you a choice," I said. "Or else you'd be scrubbing down pathology instead of working it."

He might have asked me where the garage was located, but having worked for the old man for as long as he did, he knew exactly where to find it. It was our good fortune that nothing much ever changed in these old cemeteries.

George and I had been trained in the art of proper burial procedure and, along with it, the art of proper exhumation. In our time as employees of the Harold Moonlight Funeral Home, we'd performed at least a couple dozen exhumations on bodies that had to be relocated due to eminent domain issues or bodies that required further examination by the police and/or FBI.

Fact is, working both the burial and exhumation detail had been a good way for one-time rookies like George and I to "get our feet dirty." Or so the old man liked to say with a sly smile. For reasons of cemetery protocol, almost the entirety of the burial/exhumations we'd worked on at the Albany Rural Cemetery was performed during nighttime hours under artificial lamplight.

With all this in mind, I had no doubt that George and I could safely exhume the body of Ryan, have the casket loaded into the rental van, have the hole filled back in and be back on the road in an hour's time. That is, if we hadn't lost our touch.

I stood there for a while with the light turned off, just listening to the rain that fell on the plots until the rattle and hum of a tractor engine filled the night. The cemetery backhoe.

Thank God for George. He had talent in those fingers. More talent than the hospital administration gave him credit for. He pulled up to the plot and pushed down a lever that retracted and set in place the two hydraulic stabilizers.

"It's pretty amazing what you can do with one of these," he said, holding up a scalpel with his right hand. Even in the rain and the dark, I could easily make out its smooth black, Teflon-coated surface—a surface as sharp as the smile planted on George's face.

"You might have pulled the key from off the garage wall," I told him.

"Where the hell's the fun in that, Moon?" he grinned. "Besides, the maintenance people around here are smarter than they were in our day."

"No key, huh?"

He pocketed the scalpel into the leather sheath attached to his belt and pulled back on the lever that raised the bucket high.

By the light of both the van and the backhoe, the whole exhumation took just fifty minutes from start to finish. Managing a quick and efficient exhumation isn't exactly like riding a bike. But then we hadn't lost our touch. I actually got the feeling that the old man was watching our backs.

Staring up at George seated in that little black chair like a cowboy atop a mechanical dinosaur, I sensed that, to him, exhumation was about as much fun as you could have with your clothes on. We'd shared a lot of laughs all those years ago working side by side in the dark of a warm summer night, music playing from a transistor radio, one of George's perpetually burning joints keeping our spirits sky high.

He operated the separate handles of the machine like a pro, gingerly tickling the sticks until he got the bucket to dig precisely where he wanted, all the time his eyes filled with rain water, but still glued to the open plot.

We weren't in any real danger of being caught. Relatively speaking, that is. Ryan's plot was well out of the way of the main road

(Route 378). To a group of innocent kids looking for a quiet spooky place to smoke pot and drink beers, I knew we'd just appear to be another night-shift in action.

We located the chain in the cab of the backhoe. Having attached it to the backhoe bucket claws, we were able to support the weight of the casket while carefully sliding it into the van's storage bay, to the left of the stacked Montana cadavers and the bags of dry ice preserving them. A few minutes later we had the hole filled back in, the sod replaced and the backhoe parked back inside the brick maintenance shed.

In a matter of hours it would be daylight.

Ryan's remains would be autopsied and his illegally harvested body revealed, the proof I needed to nail Cain.

65

I rode in the back of the van while George drove.

I sat on the metal pan floor and sensed the weight of the bodies beside me. There was the motion of the vehicle as it sped south along the Thruway towards Poughkeepsie. Minute after grueling minute of doing nothing but taking slow, steady breaths with bruised lungs and ribs, listening to my heart throb inside my temples.

Luck was with us.

We encountered only one security checkpoint along the way, just before exiting Route 90 onto the north-south Thruway. And even then we weren't ordered to stop. We were merely waved on by the presiding state troopers, or so George told me later.

This is what else he told me: that he had yet another friend who owed him yet another favor. That this friend was also a pathologist. That he would allow us one full hour inside the autopsy room of the Saint Paul's Medical Center not a mile down the main road from Marist College. One hour, no more. This person would be there to greet us at the door. He would ensure that no one would disturb us. But after one hour, we were to leave the same way we came. Don't ask questions, don't bother with cleanup, don't so much as take the time to pee. Just get the hell out.

Once inside the Saint Paul's basement morgue, we wheeled the mud-strewn casket into the Decomposed Room, which was located down the hall from the much larger Autopsy Room. The windowless space was specially ventilated not only because of the horrific odor an exhumed body gives off once the casket lid is cracked, but also because of the contagious diseases it might carry.

Located in the center of the room were two steel tables. Each table had hand-held spigots attached to its edges that provided running water for the pathologist and his deceased patient. Stored inside the wall-to-wall glass cabinets were dozens of jars with screw-on lids, all of which contained body parts of one kind or another. There were eyes, ears, livers, appendixes, hearts and even one jar that held an entire premature human fetus…a boy.

The whole place looked like some sanitized version of Dr. Frankenstein's laboratory. But then, this was a place where the dead did some real talking to the living.

George had set up the facility's video camera on a tripod and slipped in a fresh tape. From its position in the far corner of the room, it would easily capture the entire procedure he was about to perform. Once we both put on our green gowns, protective eye shields and respiration masks, he hit the RECORD switch on the remote control that was set on the stainless steel instrument tray by his right-hand side. When the little red light lit up on the camera, I felt my stomach began to quiver, my whole body start to tingle.

Because it had been laid inside an air and watertight cement vault, the casket had been perfectly preserved. The same could be said for the body. Maybe I had held my breath while George cranked open the lid, but I breathed a sigh of relief when I caught my first glimpse of Kevin. Despite the mold that covered his face (a common fungal reaction that I knew from experience, occurring in most air-tight compartments), the flesh and bones were completely intact. Even the navy-blue suit his parents had buried him in was still in good shape, as was the somewhat withered single red rose clasped between the folded fingers of his right hand.

It didn't take long to hit the jackpot.

Once the suit jacket, shirt and undershirt were removed, we could plainly view the hasty incisions that had been made over the places where the organs were harvested. There was one on the right side of the upper pelvis and two more on the left side. And if we could plainly make out the incisions, so could the video camera.

Both kidneys and the liver had been extracted.

Whoever had performed the butcher job had not even bothered to fill in the hollow places left behind where the organs had once filled them out. Just a cursory needle and thread job.

Even the devil has more respect for the dead.

It dawned on me that whoever prepared him for burial might not have questioned his condition. It led me to believe that it was possible that more people were in on Cain and Montana's black market operation than I initially believed.

George worked fast, precisely describing the details of the post-burial autopsy as if it had it been officially commissioned by the state. With the procedure concluded, and the two of us certain beyond any doubt that someone somehow had cut out the kid's organ's immediately after death and without the necessary notification from the family, we dressed Kevin back up and laid him once more inside his casket. Securing the lid, we then rolled him back out to the van, slipping him inside with the other two bodies. That accomplished, we went back inside to remove our scrubs and to retrieve the videotape. The entire process took only forty-five minutes from start to finish.

Heading back out to the car, I made a mental note of the accumulated evidence.

I had the Montana cadavers and I had the exhumed body of Kevin Ryan plus his recorded postmortem examination. There was the Swiss bank account and there was the paper trail in my possession that described victims I'd rubber-stamped for Cain, each one of them organ donors.

There was the film of Cain entering and leaving a downtown Saratoga Russian restaurant and there was Dr. Miner's toxicology report that had picked up on the curare, not to mention evidence that proved Scarlet had been drugged way beyond the possibility of committing suicide with a knife.

There was taped testimony from Lynn suggesting that Cain was sleeping with Scarlet. If what she told me was true, Albany's newest police captain could be nabbed with murder and the motive with which to execute it.

Then there was George's testimony and mine. Not that it would count for much.

I felt all the air inside my lungs escape like suddenly deflated balloons. I reached out with both hands, balancing myself against the van.

"You ready to do this, little brother?" George shouted, grabbing hold of my shoulders.

"Yeah," I lied, my voice hardly more than a whisper. "Yeah."

Climbing inside the back of the van, I laid myself down beside the dead.

66

Once past the Thruway checkpoint just south of Albany, George pulled over onto the shoulder and killed the lights. The danger gone, he helped me out of the back bay. Then I joined him inside the cab. He reached into the pocket of his black trench coat and handed me a cell phone.

"Thought you didn't believe much in modern technology?" I said.

"It came with the haircut," he explained just as he pulled back out onto the highway, hitting the gas.

The traffic was light. The checked line-stripes zipped past the white headlights like machinegun tracers. Hypnotic and quick. It was one o'clock in the morning. My job wasn't finished. I decided to get right back to work.

I dialed Cain's cell phone. There was a quick pick-up. Cain wasn't sleeping well these days. Who the hell was?

He barked out his name.

"What ever happened to a polite hello?" I asked.

Dead air told me he was trying to swallow a brick. "Tell me where you are, Moonlight. I can come get you. No cops, no press. Just you and me."

Not a word about Joy. Not a word about the albino man. Could it be Cain hadn't found them yet? I was counting on it.

"I know everything about everything," I told him. "About you, Jake and Joy running the body parts. About Scarlet threatening to go public with it. About you killing her even though you were fucking her. I know she was being fed heroin from some albino Russian, and I know about a grief-stricken Jake going turncoat on you. I know you killed him to shut him up. I know you tried to burn up all trace evidence along with his house."

"You're crazy," he said. I remembered Lynn saying the same thing.

"You pinned the whole thing on me because you had my signatures on all those case reports; because you found a beer bottle with my prints and spit on it up in Scarlet's bedroom; because you might have proof that Scarlet and me were occasional lovers."

There was a shuffling noise. I heard the pop-top on his Zippo lighter. It told me he was firing up a smoke. I pictured the top cop sitting at his A.P.D. desk, bottle of scotch by his side, shirt sleeves rolled up, with only the white bulb of his desk lamp to light up the blue cloud of cigarette smoke.

"And I suppose you can prove all of this."

"The evidence I have at my disposal is indisputable and irrefutable," I said. "Would you like me to give you an accounting?"

"What do you want from me?"

"Call a press conference with the powers that be," I told him. "Internal Affairs, O'Connor, the mayor, the fucking governor, for Christ's sakes. Call it for noon today so that the local news broadcasts it live and uncut."

Straight ahead of me lay dark, open road. On the cell phone, the sound of Cain breathing and smoking.

"You announce that your department, along with the DA, have made a grave mistake in accusing me of the Montana murders. You tell all of Albany that I am now a free man, that I need not find myself in legal jeopardy any longer."

"What am I supposed to tell the press when they ask me for a new suspect?"

"That's your call," I said. "I just wanna live out whatever life I got left."

I glanced over at a smiling George. He pulled his right hand off the wheel, made a thumbs up.

"Second request," I said. "You and Lynn draw up a letter transferring primary custody of my son to me. I want you to fax it immediately to Stanley Rose's office."

Nothing on the line but silence.

"What if I say a big *fuck you* to all of this?"

"Then I happily go public with the bodies of evidence."

"The Montanas," he said. "You took the bodies."

"I'll do you one better. You remember that kid Ryan you pinned with a suicidal hanging a while back? Seems his liver and his kidneys showed up missing during our post-burial autopsy."

"We," Cain said. "As in you and Phillips."

"And did I mention the footage we shot of you going in and out of The Russo Restaurant in Saratoga long before the lunch or dinner hour? Either you've acquired a taste for Russian cuisine or you've got Russian mob buddies who partake in the illegal heroin and body parts trade with Albany's best. You want more?"

"You, blackmailing me," he said. "Go figure."

"What goes around comes around," I replied. "And by the way, what's with this fascination with sloppy seconds on every woman I sleep with?"

Beside me, George was driving, grinning, trying not to burst out laughing.

Cain growled. "In the end, it'll be your word against mine, Moonlight. The fugitive versus the new chief detective."

"Correction," I chanced. "Your word against mine *and* Nicky Joy's."

Dead air for a beat. "Joy is with you?"

There, I thought. He said it. *Exactly what I needed him to say.*

"Let's just say he's very safe and very sorry for the crimes he's assisted you with committing against humanity."

"Sorry for himself," he said, "or sorry for you?"

"Sorry for you, actually," I told him, "and the hard time you're gonna be doing when all this is exposed."

Cain's tight face seething, veins popping through the skin on his brow, I could see it so vividly in my head I could almost reach out and touch it.

"I'll call for the conference," he said. "But how do I know I can trust you? How do I know you won't turn yourself and your so-called evidence in to the FBI?"

"Send the letter of custody out tonight and go through with your conference tomorrow," I explained. "Then we'll decide what to do about my evidence."

"How do I get in touch with you?" he asked.

"You don't," I said, cutting the connection.

67

We turned off the highway, pulling onto the main rural road that would lead us back into the heart of Albany.

George was no longer grinning. Nor was he saying a single word about anything. As for me, the *maybes* were beginning to pile up in my brain like a multiple car wreck.

Maybe I should have been heading straight for the FBI. Maybe I should have been on the horn with Stanley. But then, maybe Stanley wanted nothing more to do with me now that I'd become a fugitive on the run from a crime I "supposedly" did not commit. Maybe he'd prefer that I throw myself at the mercy of Judge Hughes. Maybe he'd decided to ditch me now that I had no way of producing the deed to my house.

I felt my stomach going sour on me, my head pounding in its core. I knew that if I started thinking too hard again, I'd risk another seizure. Goddamned nerves. Or should I say paranoia?

I stared out the van window at the yellow road signs that flew past, illuminated for just a split second in the van's high beams. I listened to the *swipe-swipe-swipe* of the windshield wipers and for a second I glanced at George's newly groomed image.

If it were possible to stop the world and jump the hell off I would have done it in a heartbeat. Instead I'd have to content myself with stopping something else.

"Stop the van, George."

He turned to me. "What do you mean stop☐"

"Just stop the fucking van!" I shouted.

He pulled off to the side, killed the lights but kept the engine and the wipers running.

"We're not going to Albany?"

"Who the hell are we fooling?" I asked. "There's nowhere for us to go, no place to hide."

"I know some people☐"

I shook my head. "Hear me out," I said. "Cain has no intention of calling for a conference."

"You think he just told you what you wanted to hear?"

"I know Cain," I told him. "I think he's going to stall me. I think he has no intention of letting me off the hook for this thing anymore than he intends to transfer custody of my kid."

"You're thinking like a detective again," he commented. "Nice and logical, without the usual crippling effects."

"Cain thinks Joy is working with me now," I said. "If he believes the kid is siding with me, he's going to go looking for him. He'll try and kill him to shut him up. Just like Scarlet; just like Jake."

"Impossible," George said. "Joy's already dead."

"But Cain doesn't know that. He probably just assumes that Joy is lying low until this thing somehow blows over."

George nodded his head. Steel blue eyes told me he knew where I was going with this.

"He'll start looking in the most obvious place," he said. "The kid's house."

"If I know Cain, he's opening up the trunk of his prized Beamer and setting a container or two of embalming fluid inside it. He's getting into the car and setting out to Joy's house right now."

"Why don't you call him back, save him the trouble?"

The rain strafed the hood and the trunk. The wipers swished. My heart beat, my belly caved.

"Because no matter who's dead, Cain's not about to deal with me."

"There's not gonna be any conferences," he agreed. "No admittance by the A.P.D. or the prosecutor of making a mistake."

"Instead there's going to be another murder," I said. "And it's going to happen now, this very night."

"Joy is going to die twice," George surmised.

"And if Cain has his way," I continued, "the kid's blood will be on my hands. But if I have *my* way, I'll catch him in the act."

68

First George pulled into a gas station, checking out Joy's home address in a plastic-encased phonebook that was attached to the payphone unit by a thin cable.

"How's the pain?" he asked as soon as he got back inside the car.

"I'll manage," I said, touching the stitches on my left arm through my shirt.

"Want a painkiller?"

"I'll tough it out for now."

He pulled back out of the station and together we barreled our way toward Albany along Route 5. In the meantime I called Miner's office. Naturally he wasn't there. Aside from Lola, he was the only one I could call, tell him where I was going, where I would be in case I didn't make it out alive. I left him a detailed message, including Joy's address.

Next I dialed Lyons' cell phone number. It rang for a quite a while before he picked up.

"Lyons," he said in a sleepy voice.

"Guess who?"

A pause. Maybe he confused me for a dream.

"I heard ...you could ...be dead," he stuttered, voice sounding thick and slurred like he had a sock stuffed inside his mouth.

"I'm like that pink bunny," I said. "I keep on going and going."

He didn't laugh. "Tell me where I can meet you." His voice noticeably perked up. "We still have time ... to get this ... get this story out."

He sounded out of breath. He mumbled something away from the phone.

"You alone, Lyons?" I asked.

"My wife," he said. "She's asleep next to my daughter."

"Irrefutable evidence," I told him. "I finally have it. Enough to prove me innocent of murder."

"Tell me where to meet you."

"I'll get to that," I said. "But this isn't going to be about the original article. Instead I want you to witness something."

He didn't respond.

"You there?"

"Yeah ... here. Witness what?"

"Another murder."

He cleared his throat. "Whose murder?"

"Doesn't matter. Just get your ass out of bed and get some clothes on."

Another pause.

"What's this all about, Mr. Moonlight?"

"Just know that the evidence I've collected will point to you as an accessory for taking a kickback from Cain," I said. "So don't fuck me over by going to the cops."

That had to jerk him.

"I'm no accessory to any—"

"Cut the bullshit, Lyons," I growled. "I know you set me up. You and Cain. I saw your face at the airport, remember? How much did Cain pay you to stab me in the back?"

He was back to saying nothing.

"Get a pen," I commanded. "Write this down."

I gave him Joy's address without mentioning the dead kid's name.

"That it?" he asked.

"Bring a camera," I said before terminating the call.

69

Joy lived, or had lived, in a just-add-water, prefab condominium complex just two miles outside the Albany city limits. One of those white, vinyl-sided units set inside a complex of one or two-hundred identical condo units.

George and I pulled onto Woodside Drive, straining our eyes, stretching our necks trying to follow the numbered sequence mounted to every identical mailbox along the way. In the end we didn't have much trouble finding the place. Not with the four-door Ford Explorer parked maybe thirty feet down from Joy's place.

Printed on the side panels of the SUV in big red-on-white letters were the words *The Albany Times Union.*

Could the vehicle be any more conspicuous?

"The reporter beat us here," George pointed out as he pulled the van over to the side of the road, just a few parcels up from Joy's postage-stamp front lawn.

As far as we could see, not a sign of life was showing itself outside 52 Woodside Drive. Nothing was stirring. Not even a goddamned rat like Cain. Were it not for the garage-mounted lamplight coming from the two identical condos that bookmarked Joy's unit, the place would have been completely blacked out.

I told George to wait in the car while I checked around back.

Turns out the back was just as black and dead as the front.

No Lyons, no photographer.

No nothing.

Back at the van I suggested to my big brother that maybe Lyons was still waiting inside the Suburban. The rain had all but stopped by then. The air was moist and cold, even for the spring.

We took it slow and easy along the gradually declining road, both of us knowing full well that Cain could have set a trap for us. Thumbing the pistol safety off, I peered into the driver's side window of the Ford.

The SUV was empty.

I suspected then that it was quite possible, if not probable, that somehow Lyons had let himself into the condo. But then, how the hell would he have gotten in if he didn't already have a key?

One thing was glaringly obvious: something wasn't right.

I had to power up my built-in shit detector. Cain was planning something. Exactly what he was planning I would have no way of knowing until it decided to jump out and bite me in the face.

George followed me around the garage to the wood-paneled front door. Because I was the only one holding a gun, he was careful to stay close. A foot or two away from me at most.

At first glance the door appeared to be undisturbed. All quiet on the suburban front. For a split second I thought about the doorbell.

With my pistol tucked into my pant waist, I pulled the ring of keys from my left-hand pocket, inserting them one at a time into the lock. The first four out of a dozen keys, while sliding easily into the lock, did not turn the tumblers. That is until I got to number five. Slipping the smooth metal key into the slot, I felt the mechanical release of the tumblers. Holding my breath, I turned the knob clockwise, gently pushed the door open and I was in.

I looked over my shoulder at George. There was this look in his eyes that somehow I knew would be there. This look that said *this is an unhealthy place.*

We stepped into the dark vestibule. Looking up, I could see the vague lighting that leaked in through an arched picture window mounted above the front door. The wall to my left was decorated with a giant poster. Some fully-framed half-man, half-lizard. A bright green devil with a long pitchfork tail that smiled at me with dog-like fangs and piercing red eyes that reminded me of the albino man. The creature was holding a bottle of liquor in his left hand. Some kind of booze that was supposed to bring the devil out in you.

To my direct right, a staircase followed the perimeter of the exterior wall. From where I stood I could see that the stairs led to a second floor loft and some bedrooms beyond it. The wall to my right was covered in original artwork. Abstract modern stuff that looked a hell of a lot like the pieces Scarlet and Jake had displayed inside their house before it burned. Expensive art. Not the kind of thing a rookie cop would be acquiring on rookie pay.

No family photos, no snapshot of Joy with a girlfriend or boyfriend or with parents or siblings, for that matter. It was like he hadn't really lived there at all.

One before the other we tiptoed into the kitchen, just past a door that led out to the garage and another door that led to a bathroom. My pulse was pounding in both temples, the pressure in the center of my head intense.

Fuck it, I told myself. I called out for Lyons, but got no response. Not from anywhere inside the house. Nothing but silence and a buzzing-hum that came from the motor of the white G.E. refrigerator.

We moved on a few more steps, me with the 9mm raised at chest height, barrel pointing at the ceiling.

The narrow kitchen ran almost the entire length of the first floor living space. At the very end of it was a sliding door that accessed a wood deck. The wet deck glistened in the little bit of light that shined onto it from the next door neighbor's exterior spots. The same bit of light that leaked in through the plate glass doors and vaguely illuminated what at first looked like a crumpled bundle set on the kitchen floor, like a plastic Hefty bag.

A sweet smell hung in the air.

I would have recognized the odor back when I was a kid; an odor that reminded me of the old man; of home. It was a smell George must have recognized too.

The smell of death.

I reached out with my left hand, ran it along the wall, found a light switch, flipped it on.

You could not miss him now, nor could you mistake him for a plastic Hefty bag filled with garbage.

Lyons lay face down on the floor in a pool of his own blood.

70

I knew then that the newsman had made it here too fast, taking the bullets meant for Joy, George and me. I didn't know if it had been Lyons who'd jimmied the door or if it had been Cain. But then what did it matter at that point? He was dead. So too was my witness and my newspaper story.

I cocked the pistol hammer. I wanted the mechanical noise to serve as a warning. I knew Cain was there. Christ, I'd known he was there even before I'd hit the light switch, even before I'd seen the jimmied door lock. I should have known anyway. From that point on everything seemed to move in this kind of slow, stuttered motion. Like a DVD when it's slowed to a fraction of its normal speed.

Then came a quick *POP!* just before George dropped down to his knees. I tasted the salty blood on my lips and tongue. The blood coated my mouth at the precise moment my big brother collapsed flat onto his chest and face, the quick thump of Cain's silenced pistol barely registering.

It was like a dream, it all happened so slow and quiet, but then fast and violent at the same time. While I definitely felt the quick slam against my head, it was followed by the sensation of nothing at all. As the world shut down and numbness ensued, everything inside my head went black.

71

When I came to I opened my eyes and saw one body at my feet. And a second to my direct left. The blood that covered the tile was so thick and rich it appeared more black than red. I could feel it soaking into my pant leg.

I tried propping myself up onto my elbow. It was then that I sensed a weight shift in my head and the pain settle in like two separate ice picks lodged directly behind my eyeballs. I sat up straight, felt my stomach constrict. Everything came up on me.

"That's it," Cain offered. "Out with the bad."

When I was through, I sucked in a deep breath and used my left hand to push myself back up against the refrigerator. I tried to stand, but it was impossible. The spirit was willing, but the brain was near dead.

I sat there, knees tucked into my chest, head between my legs. Cain had cold-cocked me twice in the same place, in the same week, with the same goddamned gun. He'd seated himself up on the counter beside the sink. In his right hand, a 9mm law enforcement service pistol. Set beside him on the counter was what looked to be a black skullcap. He was dressed in a long black leather jacket, black pants and sneakers.

This much was certain: my fragile life must have been a testament to how much Cain needed me alive to take the rap for everything. Sitting there on Joy's tiled floor, head splitting, stomach reeling, ribs busted up, I might have welcomed death. Maybe death offered me only blackness and nothingness, but it was also painless.

Cain fired up a cigarette. He smiled.

"You really have no idea about what's going on, do you, old partner?" he posed. "You don't have a fucking clue about what comes next?"

"This is the part where you set me up for three more murders," I growled, the words coming out like they were ripping themselves away from the back of my throat.

He stared down at me with those slate-gray hawk eyes.

"How can you be sure you didn't kill them? Why have you been assuming all along that I set you up? Why are you always screaming conspiracy?"

I tried to hold my head up, tried to stand again, but it was useless. My chin kept bobbing against my sternum.

"Pull the clip on your piece," he said. "Smell the barrel."

I swallowed a breath, peeled the automatic from my right hand, pointed the barrel up at my face, and took a good whiff. It smelled freshly fired. I thumbed the clip, felt it drop into the palm of my scarred hand, and looked into it. Three rounds were missing. Then, looking down at my feet, I could easily make out three spent brass shell casings sitting in a blood puddle.

Something began to happen to my body then. Rather, to my head. This electric vibration and buzzing began to sound, as if my brain had been somehow plugged into an outlet. I knew then that the orchestral music that blared inside my skull was just getting started.

"You're just a one-man wrecking crew, Moonlight," Cain said. "No regard for the sanctity of human life whatsoever."

"I have this problem with my head," I told him.

"You're on a death march, which is why, consciously or not, you went on a killing spree. If you ask me, you couldn't stand watching all these people around you having a life."

In my head, the music was getting louder, the symphony pounding on their strings, blowing into their trumpets, banging on their drums.

I gazed up at Cain sitting on the counter, smoking, his tongue shooting in and out of his mouth snake-like while he talked, the smoke clouding above his head.

"I know what you're thinking, old partner," he continued. "That I'm a liar. Maybe I am, maybe I'm not. Because in the end, how can you tell what's real, or just a figment of your imagination? After all, you haven't been acting in your right mind. You've got a bullet in your brain. You've been accused of murder one with a second count to follow. Your powers of recall may be warped because you're not in complete control of your faculties. Fuck, Moonlight, for all you know, this whole thing is an illusion."

The .38 back in my right hand, six rounds left over. It was so heavy, I could barely lift it off the floor, much less plant a bead on Cain.

"Let's go further back, shall we?" he said. "Picture Captain Head Case, that's you, fucking Scarlet Montana in her bed. Then when it was over, after shoving a whole bunch of drugs and booze down her throat, he runs a blade across her neck in a way that would strongly suggest suicide. Because after all, Scarlet was an unhappy woman. Less than a day later, the man comes up on Jake Montana from behind, cracks the big guy's skull with a pistol barrel. He leaves him lying on the kitchen floor to burn up with the house he's soaked in embalming fluid, because that shit burns nice and long and slow, almost like kerosene. The man torches the Montana home where he committed not one but two murders in order to destroy the evidence.

"But that's not enough killing for the head case. Now that he's been arrested, he's got to figure a way out; a way to escape. But Nicky Joy has already done that for him. Nicky wants to help him because Nicky wants out of the madness. Nicky wants to make an appeal. So he arranges for the man to have a key to room 657 at the Hotel Wellington. It's the safe house for their organ harvesting operation. Nicky has no doubt the head case will make it there because he will do anything to get free, even if it means killing or being killed. So when the two guards transporting him to county deps are attacked inside their car, it's no surprise. It's also no surprise that Head Case has escaped by doing something insane like jumping off an eighty-foot-high bridge. Most people would think twice about making that kind of jump, but the head case had a habit of making wrong decisions.

"From there he breaks into a longshoreman's locker room, shoots a night watchman in the back, then locks up two state troopers. Heading out to the hotel, he finds room 657, finds Nicky Joy and an old Russian partner by the name of Joseph. Head Case doesn't hesitate to kill both men, then manipulate the scene to make it look like an organ harvesting gone terribly wrong.

"I wonder, Moonlight, did Nicky scream when you cut his heart out?"

My head was vibrating like a gong; my breath coming and going in little short spurts. Cain had known about Joy all along. He'd only bluffed to get me out in the open. I swallowed some blood. It was then I saw it standing just outside the sliding glass doors. The solitary figure, the silhouette.

"Now picture our head case sneaking around the back of Joy's condo, slipping into the kitchen by way of the sliding glass doors, and pumping two rounds into an innocent crime reporter's head."

I had to believe then that he'd swapped pistols with me. We carried identical 9mm Smith and Wessons. He must have cleaned his prints and switched the pieces when I was out cold. He must have made the switch. I was sure of it. Or, I had to be sure of it. I had to believe it! Maybe I wasn't in my right mind all the time, but I knew he made the switch. I didn't have to see it happen to know it was true. I just had to believe it.

"Now picture the head case pumping a round into Dr. Phillips's chest just as he entered the dark kitchen. I mean, the poor bastard, the poor innocent pathologist you dragged into this mess. Your mess. He must have had no idea what hit him in the dark when you tried to silence him."

Framed inside the sliding door I could see the figure as he stepped forward ... a squat bulldog of a man.

Cain slid down off the counter, approached me, reached down, and pulled the 9mm from my hand.

"So what happens now?" he asked. "Do I call in my people and take a chance on having you arrested once more? Do we arrange for a trial, giving you the chance to escape again?"

He aimed the pistol not at my face, but at the right-hand side of my head. At my temple. In the same place I shot myself four years before. Cain let out a small laugh as the glass slider slowly opened behind him. In stepped a man, quiet as all hell, Cain not having the slightest clue.

"Tell me something Moonlight. Do you realize how sick you are?" Shoving the pistol barrel behind my ear, he pressed it up against my button-sized scar. "Come on, Moonlight, you've been here before. What's it feel like to die?"

I closed my eyes. That's when I heard Dr. Miner's voice clear as day.

"Mitchell Cain," he said. "Put down the gun."

That's when my old partner pulled the pistol back away from my head. He straightened up, looked at Miner. My dad's old buddy was standing there in a black rain slicker, baggy khakis, work boots and a round-brimmed fisherman's hat pulled down tight over a full head of curly white hair. He was sopping wet from head to toe. In his right hand, an old black-plated revolver, like the kind cops used to carry before there was color TV. He was striking a bead on Cain.

"Don't do this," Miner said. "He's not well."

Cain turned the 9mm on the doctor, aimed for his face.

"You have got to be kidding me, old man," he growled. "You gonna let this one-man holocaust go free?"

"Who you calling old?" Miner demanded, a split second before the blast.

72

"Let me get this straight: Jake and Cain decided they had you right where they wanted you, desperate and short of cash." Stocky Agent pontificated. "They pulled you back in as a part-timer, asked you politely to rubberstamp a few of their open-and-shut cases. They told you the force was understaffed and you believed them. You were a cop. Now they needed you again. But you were different somehow. The bullet fragment had changed you, made you more naive, let's say. You had difficulty telling the difference between right and wrong sometimes. You already fucked up one major arrest, gotten yourself busted down to forced medical leave. Which made you the perfect candidate for Cain's operation. But even after willingly completing false document after false document, you make matters worse by getting in bed with the police captain's wife."

"It all seemed like the right thing to do at the time," I say.

"You realize what I can do now?" Stocky Agent asks, eyes peering not at me but at his silent partner. "I can book you on multiple counts of conspiracy to falsify police reports, plus multiple counts in the complicity to commit the illegal harvesting and sale of organs and body parts. Not to mention fraud and grand larceny. Then there's all those murders, all that carnage. People connected directly to you."

I pull the pack of cigarettes from my shirt pocket, set them on the table.

"You're not believing all that bullshit Cain laid on me?"

"What's not to believe?"

We stare at one another for a beat, until I say "Let me guess. You'll book me for multiple counts of murder unless I give you something else."

"You want your only child to know that his father is going to spend eternity in hell? Or would you rather he knew that for once his dad did the right thing?"

"My head ... it can't be trusted."

Stocky Agent leans up, getting right in my face again. Nose tip to nose tip.

He says, "You said that you and Dr. Miner fled the scene at Joy's condo. Albany was still looking at you as an escaped murderer. What'd you do next?"

"I did exactly what I should have done when I collected the bodies of evidence in the first place. I turned myself in." I slide another smoke from the pack.

"Before all that, Moonlight, before you turned yourself in. Miner did more for you than just neutralize Cain. He helped you out with your story. Because ..." He pauses.

I look down at the cigarette burning between my fingers. It's trembling. Behind my eyeballs, I feel a great pressure. I feel tears. I can't help the tears. "Because ... my head ... it's not right."

"And now you needed help."

"There's a bullet frag in my head. It makes me do all the wrong things sometimes."

"Tell me Moonlight. Was Cain right? Did you in fact make the decision to commit murder? Right or wrong?"

73

As soon as the single round hit him, Cain fell backwards, what was left of his head smacking against the bloody linoleum. The .38 caliber bullet from Miner's old revolver had pierced his right eye. That kind of entrance wound told me he was already on his way to hell before he hit the floor.

I was still sitting on the floor not three feet away from him, back pressed up against the refrigerator door when Dr. Miner handed me the revolver. He bent down, checked Lyons's pulse, and shook his head almost sadly. But when he came to George, he looked up at me with piercing blue eyes. It was a good look.

"He's alive."

He then pulled a white hanky from his back pocket and wrapped it around his hand. He picked up the phone and dialed 911, urging the dispatcher to hurry with an ambulance. Then he gave the dispatcher the address. He hung up without revealing his name.

Next he grabbed the .38 back out of my hand and stuffed it into his pants pocket. Then he did something horrible. Careful to step over the bodies and the blood, he reached down and stuck his fingers into the palm-sized section of Cain's blown-away skullcap. He dug around the brains for what seemed like a full minute until he stood up with what he wanted.

From where I was seated I could see it in his hand, a blunted cylindrical lump of .38 caliber slug. He slipped it into his jacket pocket. With that hanky once more wrapped around his hand, he pulled the 9mm from Cain's death grip and blew another round into the eye socket entry wound where the .38 had pierced it minutes before. The deed done, he replaced the piece back into Cain's hand, only this time positioning the pistol barrel towards the dead man's face, the right-hand thumb pressed against the trigger.

I sat there staring at him for a minute, the man who became my ex-wife's husband, the stepfather to my kid.

Miner asked me if I was okay. It was impossible to answer.

He stood there beside me for a beat, maybe two. He said nothing at first until he offered me his hand, telling me it was time to get the hell out of there.

By the time we made it back out the sliding glass doors, we could already hear the sirens.

74

The temporary paralysis in my right arm was just that. Temporary.

Still, it required a maximum effort to follow Miner in his blue Volvo to a Seven-Eleven located about a half-mile up the road. Pulling into the lot, he parked it behind the dumpster. After grabbing a crowbar from out of his trunk, he told me to scoot over while he took the wheel of the van, gout be damned. Six cop cars, a fire engine and an E.M.S. van blew by the store. They appeared to have no clue about us.

So we hoped.

Knowing that the dry ice might not be enough to keep the Montana bodies from decomposing beyond the point of viable physical evidence (Ryan was sealed in his casket), Miner bought up a whole lot of ice and packed the bagged bodies well. He also bought up a handful of Snickers candy bars. I wasn't sure why. We then drove across town to the banks of the Hudson River where he got out, hobbled over to the concrete dike wall and tossed both the .38 revolver and the .38 automatic into the drink. From there we proceeded to the last place I thought we'd ever go.

My house on Hope Lane.

With crowbar in hand, Miner led me around to the back door off the kitchen, where he pried off the lockbox the cops had installed some days before. He then jimmied the door lock and we were in.

In a word, the place was a wreck.

The cops had ransacked it. Not a single drawer hadn't been pulled out of the kitchen counters and overturned ... spoons, knives and broken plates strewn about the floor. It was the same story with every room in the house. Just what they were looking for, I had no idea.

I pulled a broom from the closet and started sweeping the glass and broken china into a pile. But Miner ordered me to sit down. He packed a plastic sandwich bag with ice and told me to keep it pressed against the back of my head.

"Where do you keep your pain killers?" he asked.

"Codeine?"

"Codeine will put you to sleep, son. Advil or aspirin."

I told him he could find a bottle of what he was looking for in the cabinet above the Lazy Susan, directly beside the prescription codeine.

He set the Advil on the table along with a glass of water. I swallowed two tablets while he went back out to his car, then came back in with an old black leather bag. The same kind of leather bag doctors used to carry with them when they still made house calls. Opening it, he pulled out a blood pressure kit and another instrument that he said would measure my blood sugar levels.

"I thought you were a toxicologist?" I said.

"I'm an M.D. first," he stated.

His examination completed, he put the stuff back into the bag. Hobbling away from the table, he opened the refrigerator.

"Just what I thought," he murmured.

I turned and gazed into the empty fridge. Well, not completely empty. There was some beer in there, a bottle of vodka and some French's mustard.

"When was the last time you ate a proper meal?"

I looked Norman in the eye. "I honestly can't remember," I answered.

"Have you ever thought about why exactly you might be experiencing these episodes of dizziness and passing out? Ever thought about why you make a lot of wrong decisions? Ever wonder why there are things you can't remember doing?"

I recalled Cain sitting up on the kitchen counter inside Joy's townhouse. I recalled the list of murders he said I'd committed— murders that I could not have possibly committed. That's what I believed, anyway. It's what I had to believe.

"I have this condition," I said.

"Maybe you have a bullet frag in your head and maybe it is directly responsible for your condition, but it certainly does not help that you remember to drink but forget to eat."

His face turned stone cold as he pulled the Snickers bars from the right-hand pocket of his rain slicker and dropped them before me onto the table.

"Eat up, Tiger," he ordered.

Tiger. It's what the old man used to call me when I was still a kid. It felt good, him calling me Tiger. Sweet, like the candy.

Miner looked relieved when he was finally able to drop himself in the chair across from me. We sat there in the dark while I ate the candy bars.

I started telling him everything that had happened since I'd escaped. At least, I told him my first-hand version. About Joy's murder, about the albino man cutting his heart out, then wanting to take my liver. I told him about the exhumation, about the post-burial autopsy that revealed the illegally harvested organs. I told him everything.

When it was done, I looked into his gentle old face.

"How the hell did you find me?" I asked.

"You called me, remember? You gave me Joy's address."

I suddenly remembered. "But that was two in the morning," I said. "Your office line."

"I couldn't sleep," he said. "Not with what I was finding out about your case."

"Why are you doing this?" I asked. "Why are you willing to kill for me?"

"First of all, you're the closest thing I have to a son. Second of all, your dad and I were pals. Third of all, proof of suicide is the only thing that will save you. Fourth of all, Cain was going to shoot you in the head ... I was your last line of self defense."

I sat back, let out a breath. I wondered why Cain would bother reciting a list of people he thought I'd killed if he was only going to blow my brains out in the end anyway. Must have made him feel good to expound on his version of the truth.

"You do believe I didn't kill Scarlet, don't you, Doc?"

Miner averted his eyes, got up from the table, reached inside his rain slicker once more, and pulled out a transparent plastic evidence bag that contained a beer bottle. He pulled out his bloodstained handkerchief, then opened the bag, grabbed hold of the bottle, and set it on the table beside the bottle of Advil.

I just looked at the long-necked bottle, the tinted transparency of the glass, the red, white, blue and gold label, the big cursive letters that spelled out *Budweiser*. I pictured the photograph of the bottle Prosecutor O'Connor produced at my hearing in place of the real thing. I knew then that it had to be the one.

I asked him how he managed to get it.

"It was sent to me," he said, "from Nicky Joy. Probably after it had been processed at the fingerprint lab."

I couldn't believe what I was hearing.

"There is no way Nicky would have willingly turned that over to tox," I said, "unless he meant to cooperate with us. Knowing our relationship, he never would have done it unless he was throwing in the towel on both Scarlet and the body parts operation."

"I think it was the beginning of the end for Nicky Joy," Miner said. "First he hands this bottle over to me, knowing full well that you and George would also have requested a tox analysis of Scarlet's poisoned blood. The action completed, he slips you a key to your shackles and cuffs, knowing you'd get away from the deputies because you had no choice but to get away. And had your rendezvous at the hotel turned out differently, he would have turned himself in to his own people, told the whole truth about how and why Scarlet died. As he reveals the whole truth, Cain would go down right along with him and you'd be free and clear of all charges. Least, that's how I think it was supposed to work."

"You found something on the bottle besides my saliva," I guessed.

"Zolpidem tartrate," he said. "What you and I know as common, everyday Ambien. It was mixed in with the small amount of backwash."

"How much Ambien?"

"My guess is she must have crushed up three or four of her own ten milligram pills into a fine powder, then slipped it in the beer after she opened it for you." He paused a beat. "She did open it for you?"

I held the icepack against the back of my head. I recalled that night, lying in her bed while she made her way down to the kitchen, then came back upstairs with a bottle of beer for me, a Stohly on the rocks for her. It's what she always did after we made love. It was the routine. Knowing what I know now, I couldn't help but wonder if Scarlet had used her short time away from me down in the kitchen to snort a line of two of the heroin before she returned with my beer. Maybe that would explain her sudden if not erratic mood shifts—her going from sullen to giddy happy in what seemed an instant. I never gave it a second thought until now.

"That would explain why I fell asleep so quickly after drinking the beer," I said. "Why I would always fall asleep."

"The Ambien would perhaps trigger a seizure," he suggested.

I set down the icepack and got up from the table. Reaching up to the cupboard above the sink, I pulled down the bottle of Jack, pouring a shot into the water glass. Then I raised the bottle up, as if to offer some to Miner. He shook his head.

I took a sip of the warm whiskey, let it sit against the back of my throat before I swallowed it. *The beer bottle explains a lot,* I told myself. *The reason why Joy slipped that cuff key into my slipper. Nicky must have realized the whole thing was about to crumble now that I'd revealed my intention to pursue the real truth behind Scarlet's death.*

Sitting there at the table, I pictured skinny Nicky getting into one of the A.P.D. blue-and-whites and driving to the hospital, leaving a package outside the door to Toxicology. A package marked URGENT with Miner's name scribbled on it.

"You have a new death theory," I said.

Miner sat back, focusing his gaze on the empty beer bottle.

"A theory backed up by solid evidence," he answered with a breath. "You ready to listen?"

I drank down what was left in my glass and poured another. Then I sat back in my chair, grabbing hold of my right hand with my left. "You talk," I said. "For a change, I'll listen."

75

He removed his fishing hat and set it on the table. Despite his years, his hair was thick and white as opposed to gray. It seemed to make his blue eyes even more penetrating.

Speaking in soft tones from across the table, he transported me back to the night of nights—Sunday, May fifth.

His professional opinion based upon what he called "the totality of the collected evidence": was that not long after I'd left the house through her window, Scarlet began to drink heavily.

"Maybe she drank with Jake. Maybe she drank by herself. Maybe they argued and fought and drank. Who knows? Fact is, her binge drinking was not a symptom of some depression. That night it became a deliberate, calculated act. She was anesthetizing herself by bingeing to a point where she could do some serious stabbing, serious cutting to her flesh and not feel all the pain."

I sipped my drink and pictured Scarlet—her long auburn hair and rich green eyes. It was easy picturing Scarlet. But what didn't come easy was seeing her cut herself up.

Miner said that at some point she began to ingest a mixture of speed and heroin. Not speed-balling, but snorting the stuff in lines. Alternating between the drugs and the drink. When she reached the point where courage and pain were no longer an issue, she began to stab at her torso, self-inflicting the surface wounds.

He said that she must have continued making the cuts for some time, alternating between the drugs and the drink. What's even more incredible, Miner noted, is the quiet she'd have to maintain during the entire procedure so that she didn't wake her husband.

I looked at him, listening to the nearly clinical way he was explaining his theory.

"But is all this physically possible?" I asked.

"Given the right conditions," he said, while once more standing, reaching for his jacket, and retrieving a folded sheet of paper from an interior pocket.

"Especially if her husband was passed out from too much drink."

He handed the sheet to me. I glanced at it as he sat back down.

It appeared to be Xeroxed from a medical textbook. Diagrams of human bodies with black Xs printed on their torsos where self-inflicted cuts would be found. The single sheet detailed eight "self-cutting or self-stabbing" suicides. Suicides who, much like Scarlet, had managed to cut themselves from naval to throat.

"When do you think she made the fatal cut?" I asked.

"At one point," Miner went on, "the booze and drugs would have become too much for her. She would have been bleeding heavily by now, and she would have been growing weak despite the speed. I think it was then that she took one final massive dose of the speed/heroin combination, then drank down as much vodka as possible along with a dose of the curare."

"But the curare would have paralyzed her," I told him, recalling our conversation inside his office of a few days ago.

He said it would have taken more than a full minute for it to kick in. In her toxic condition, perhaps even longer. She ingested the curare, laid back down on her bed, then slashed her throat immediately after.

"Unlike the heroin, speed and alcohol," he went on, "the curare laid heavily in the blood. It hadn't circulated though the major organs—namely, the liver and the kidneys. In order for this to happen, she would have had to ingest it after she cut her throat. Since that is a physical and practical impossibility, she must have taken the stuff only seconds before she cut her throat."

"That is, unless Jake did it for her," I said. "Or Cain."

He shook his head.

"That was the whole point of the curare," he said. "To make it look like Jake or Cain or the whole goddamned A.P.D. was there, doing these horrible, mutilating acts to her while she was still awake. But I doubt that any of them were there at all. From what I saw in Phillips's report, the hesitation wounds were too precise, too consistent with self-stabbing."

"It was a suicide after all," I said.

"No one except God can know if she planned it this way, but in the end I believe she performed a brilliantly executed suicide that suggested homicide—a suicide that pointed directly to her husband and maybe even to Cain and their organ harvesting."

As for Joy, he explained, he wasn't the good little cop he appeared to be either. "I called the academy up in Albany and they had no one by the name of Joy on record for the years 2005 or 2006. I did some further investigating. Fact is, the kid was dismissed under suspicious circumstances from Providence College's pre-med program sometime during his senior year."

"Pre-med," I said. "It's not inconceivable that he would at least know how to cut a body. Rudimentarily speaking."

"In my own opinion he was the surgeon who performed the illegal harvesting operations on the dead bodies. Or most of the more recent dead bodies, anyway. He and the albino man you shot. They must have done it from the safe house in the hotel. And as for that condo, it wasn't deeded in the kid's name at all, but in Cain's."

"And Scarlet exposed it all at the expense of her life," I murmured."

"If what you've revealed to me is true—that Scarlet hated her husband and probably hated Cain just as much—then her suicide might be considered her swan song; a way for her to enact an ironic revenge on the people who had been systematically ruining her life for a long, long time."

I slow-sipped my drink and ran it through my mind for minute, contemplating all the nightmares Scarlet had been having. The ones Suma had told me about. The dark demons and figures that appeared in her vivid dreams; the devils that would strap her down and cut her up night after night. By killing herself, Scarlet had recreated her nightmare in real life. Only this time, the demons were not dreamed. They were real people. They were Jake, Cain and Joy.

But then couldn't she have found a better way to get back at them? Did she have to enact her revenge by taking her own life? It just didn't make any sense. Or did it? After all, people do fucked-up things during fucked-up times.

Looking up from the table, I saw my reflection in the picture window. I quickly turned away. I just couldn't bear to look at myself knowing that I too had tried to take my own life. Not out of despair, but out of revenge.

Pure revenge.

"None of this still explains the disappearance of the blade," I said. "It couldn't have just disappeared like that. And wouldn't there have been traces of heroin all over her bed sheets?"

Miner shrugged. "My guess is that Jake found her in her cut-up condition, panicked, picked up the blade, and got his bloody prints all over it. He probably cleaned the place up, disposed of any drugs he found lying around, the booze and the blade. Then, instead of following S.O.P., calling 911, he simply calls in his colleagues." He sighed. "Naturally, I can't be certain of anything, but the scenario seems logical enough to me for a head dick fearing reprisals from his own A.P.D. and the media."

I nodded. "That would explain the more than one hour between the E.T.D. and my initial investigation of the crime scene. And now we have both Montana bodies in our possession."

"Thank Christ for that," he said. "Further tests will be required. A full autopsy for Jake and another autopsy for Scarlet, just for starters. Not to mention an independent re-examination of that kid you pulled up out of the ground. Have you contacted the parents for permission to exhume?"

I told him that I hadn't; that I was counting on their support later on when tests showed positive for illegal organ harvesting. But Miner shook his head, telling me it was a mistake not having made contact with them—that at this point, he would call them as soon as we left Hope Lane, beg them for their understanding. We'd deal with the cemetery authority later.

He also told me he'd been in contact with Stanley Rose. Turns out the Moonlight family lawyer was working on a reconvening of the grand jury and Judge Hughes. He also had a meeting with Prosecutor O'Connor that afternoon. If all went well, I would be acquitted of all charges pending the introduction of the new evidence and theory regarding Scarlet's manner of death.

"All that needs to happen now," Miner said, "is for you to turn yourself in to the FBI. Back door only; no press passes."

I finished my drink, got up, and put back the bottle. It was getting low. Hopefully I would be able to buy another soon. But what I was even more hopeful about was the condition of my big brother George. In my mind I could only assume that the E.M.T.s had successfully transferred him to the hospital from Joy's townhouse; that his wounds were not entirely serious.

I went upstairs, changed my clothes, and put on a jacket. When I came back into the kitchen, Miner was standing by the back door.

"You ready to tell the truth?" he asked, repacking the empty Bud bottle and pocketing his hanky.

"Looks like Scarlet's already done that for me," I said, the tension behind my eyes now fading.

I once more pictured Cain sitting on Joy's kitchen counter; heard him reciting all those murders. For a while, I was beginning to believe him.

As soon as we walked out the back door, Norman purposely dropped the bag and the bottle it contained onto the concrete landing. Then, painfully bending down, he picked the plastic baggy back up. The glass inside it had shattered.

Turning to me, he asked "Would you care to do the honors?"

Taking the bag from him I heaved it into the thick brush that adjoined my back property. With any luck it would never be seen again.

76

Dr. Miner's expert testimony, the three bodies of evidence which were placed back inside the A.M.C. morgue to await further examination by the state's chief medical examiner, Cain's Swiss bank account statement, the super-eight film of him entering and leaving The Russo restaurant, Lynn's taped statement about Cain's affair with Scarlet, Kevin Ryan's postmortem video (along with his family's consent), Stanley Rose's renewed faith in my innocence … all of these things and more combined to make my second grand jury appearance last only an hour before Judge Hughes had no choice but to toss out the charge of Murder One in the case of Scarlet Montana.

As for the prosecution, they had no choice but to drop their indictments. The bad news was that the Judge referred all further investigations of my apparent complicity in the illegal body parts operation to a team of FBI agents who were present at the convening.

At the conclusion of these proceedings Hughes stood up, telling me I was free to go. When he brought the gavel down hard against the wood block I thought my heart would explode through my chest. Stanley stood up, grabbed hold of my hand, and pulled me away from the table as if the judge might change his mind. He led me down the center aisle of the courtroom out onto the marble steps where a wave of reporters, journalists and TV crews converged upon me.

"Mr. Moonlight, are you planning on bringing suit against New York State for malicious prosecution?"

"Mr. Moonlight, if you did not kill Mrs. Montana, can you offer us a theory as to who did and why?"

"Mr. Moonlight, where will you go now that you are a free man?"

Stanley continued to pull me away from the courthouse, through the media gauntlet, microphones jabbing me in the face, against my mouth, cameras flashing in my eyes, hands clawing at my shirt and jacket.

Until finally, Stanley stopped.

"Mr. Moonlight has no comment at this time as his ordeal has been a very trying one. For now, he wishes only to return home for a much deserved rest."

I spotted her at the bottom of the marble courthouse steps, out of the corner of my left eye. A woman dressed all in black, wearing a matching black hat and veil covering her face. She stood on the sidewalk, a little girl beside her pressed up against her leg, holding tightly to the hem of her short skirt as if for dear life.

I was aware that Lyons had a wife and a little girl. My gut instinct told me these two people were them.

When we reached the bottom of the courthouse steps, I stopped. Stanley nearly tore the sleeve off my jacket, he was so anxious to leave.

"What are you doing, Moonlight?" he shouted above the collective roar of the reporters. "We have a car waiting for us."

I pulled myself from his grip and made my way toward the woman and her little girl.

She raised her veil, exposing a young face swollen by sobs and sad brown eyes. Eyes that seemed like they would melt if so much as one more tear passed through them.

I stepped closer to her. As I did so, the little girl pressed herself into her mother even tighter. The kid trembled.

"Ask me anything," I said, forcing my words not from my mouth and lips, but from the back of my throat.

She offered me three words.

"Did he ... suffer?"

I exhaled a deep breath. "No," I said. "He didn't suffer."

I had no idea if he had suffered or not. I hadn't been there when Cain shot him in the head. But then a detailed explanation of events wasn't necessary. I'd already given her the answer she needed.

First the woman nodded. Then she turned away from me. Her husband had double-crossed me. That wasn't her fault.

She took hold of her daughter's hand, led her back down the sidewalk towards an awaiting taxi.

77

After more than a week of seclusion, the reporters seemed to have gotten the message and decided to stop hounding me. I wasn't about to say a word to them. Not with the body parts investigation still pending. Stanley's orders.

One afternoon, the camera crews, photographers and newspaper people simply packed up and drove away. I have to admit it though, I felt kind of bad about their splitting the scene. Kind of lonely. But then I imagined that in terms of current events, the news of my innocence in the Montana murder case was no longer fresh.

Lola took to making me three squares a day and within a week, I put on some badly needed pounds. But that still didn't mean I wouldn't experience more seizures, more memory lapses, more bad decision making. Only time would tell.

Lola and I shared dinner almost every evening. Sometimes she slept over. But all that swiftly ended. Why? Suffice it to say that with the crisis behind me, we had a little more time to focus on our friendship. Too much time, it turns out.

Case and point: one night after dinner we both went up to my bed to lie down and watch a little television. We held hands like teenagers. She cuddled into me. We kissed. Her big brown eyes, soft brown hair and tan skin made her look as sweet as she tasted. I kissed her neck, sensing her body growing warmer and warmer as I found her breasts, suckled her pert nipples, until I felt Lola's hand gently massaging the smooth skin on my head and I felt her pushing me further and further down. When I came to that special place I kissed her bare thighs and moved in time with her every motion as she opened up for me and, using both her hands, pulled my face into her.

After she came with a near silent convulsion, I raised myself up onto my hands, brought my face up to hers and with her hand guiding me, I entered into her. I kissed her gently and I knew then that I loved her more than anything else in this world.

So that was it, then: Lola and I had sex.

We broke the barrier from which neither one of us would ever return. And I loved every precious minute of it.

Would I ever learn?

The next morning, Lola was sullen if not downright sad. The sadness left me feeling nervous and self-conscious.

Our wonderful friendship was behind us.

"Everything will change now," she said in her soft voice, dark eyes tearing up. "You just wait and see, Moonlight."

I told her to take some time to think it all over. She did. That left me spending most of my days and nights alone.

I took advantage of the time by running and lifting weights, sometimes twice a day. I made sure to regain my strength, even before I paid a visit to Dr. Lane, who removed the stitches from my left arm and checked over my beat-up ribs. While it wasn't quite yet the time for a full checkup, she made sure to give me a thorough going-over about being more responsible for my health.

"At least I'm not smoking," I told her. But she didn't find anything funny.

While Kevin Ryan was reburied without legal reprisals from his still grieving parents, so too were the Montanas. Because of his involvement with the body parts operation, Jake was denied a pomp-and-ceremony funeral. In fact, most of his department stayed away from the proceedings entirely. Or so I'm told. I too did not attend the ceremony.

The one person I did leave the house for was George. The E.M.T.s had indeed done their job and done it well.

It turns out that he was well on the mend, his prognosis a good one. Although he had been knocked entirely unconscious by the close-range shot, the 9mm round had only wounded him (however severely) when it entered his chest and lodged itself somewhere up inside his right shoulder. Considering his already fragile medical condition, the state had immediately approved him for more pharmaceutical marijuana.

I visited him inside his third-floor private room at the Albany Medical Center, having made sure to bring plenty of paperback mysteries and a surprise pint of Jack that I stuffed into the bottom of the paper bag. It was like going back thirty years, back when he worked for Harold Moonlight, George and I sneaking a couple of shots apiece when an attractive blond-haired nurse named Heidi wasn't looking. But I knew that eventually, George would be offering her a swig or two, along with a nice, warm, cozy spot for her to rest her feet on his hospital bed. If I knew George like I thought I did, I knew he wasn't about to waste even a single moment of his ninth life.

He toked gently off a medical joint and tried to introduce us not long before I took my leave.

"This man here is my little brother," he said, a mild stoned-drunkenness already settling in to his bedridden skin and bones. "We used to be in the death trade together, but now we fight crime."

The young, well-endowed nurse gave me the once-over. She wore a low-cut nursing outfit that also showed off plump thighs. I guessed her hair to be natural blond. The way it was pinned up under her little white hat showed off the smooth skin on the back of her neck.

"Which one are you?" she asked, not without a sly smile. "Batman or Robin?"

"Superman," I said, unable to resist the temptation.

"That's funny," she explained. "That's what Twiggy said."

"Twiggy," George repeated with a Cheshire Cat grin. "I think she likes me."

I looked at the attractive young nurse. I wanted to ask her if she knew my ex-wife, Lynn. But of course, she must have known her. Lynn was the big boss, after all. Still, I decided not to bring the subject up.

As for the black market operation: like I said, it was still in the hands of the FBI. Aside from a phone call or two, I had yet to be called in for an interview or an interrogation or whatever was being planned. But then, I knew that it was only a matter of time until my name came up. Until then, I wasn't even going to think about looking for work. But sooner or later it would become a necessity, since I pretty much could discount any further employment with the A.P.D.

If the massage therapy, physical training or private detecting didn't work out, I could always ask the Fitzgeralds for a job, because once in the death trade, always in the death trade.

The power was turned back on, the place cleaned up, my credit and cash accounts restored, the lien on 23 Hope Lane revoked. I still had bills to pay, including the thirty G's I still owed Stanley from my divorce. Curiously, he hadn't been bothering me about it. Nor had he mentioned the deed to the house. Not even the collection agencies were knocking down my door. What's more, I hadn't so much as received a bill for my more recent representation. But then I can't say I was all that surprised. With all the attention Stanley was getting out of my case, including a possible book deal and a television appearance on *48 Hours*, he would be rolling in the cash.

There was still the matter of Scarlet's death, which as far as the A.P.D's newly reinstated S.I.U. was concerned, was officially being classified as a suicide, especially in the light of the grand jury's decision. Truth be told, I still couldn't help but feel uncomfortable about the whole thing. There was something gnawing at me, like an itch I couldn't scratch. I was convinced that there had to be more to her death, more than met the eye besides a woman who gave up her own life in order that she might trash a few others or kill off a few nightmarish demons.

In my heart, I knew there had to be another reason behind it all; something she'd never shared with me that maybe only she knew, or perhaps just she and Jake knew. And if that were indeed the case, that Scarlet and Jake shared some horrible secret that caused her to take her own life, then by all means they had taken it with them to their separate graves.

Finally, a funeral was held for Mitch Cain.

The department also refused to offer him the standard twenty-one-gun sendoff. Not even Lynn showed up for the event, making his farewell a fairly frigid one. Frigid air: something that might come in handy where he was headed.

One thing I did notice, however, during one of my flybys in the Mercedes funeral coach, was that a FOR SALE sign had gone up outside the Cain house. Obviously, Lynn was making definite plans with her newfound widowhood. Which prompted me to place a call.

She picked up the phone the same time my son picked up on a separate extension.

"It's okay, babe," she said. "I've got it."

"Okay, Mom," he replied before clumsily hanging up.

"Hello?"

I said hello and dispensed with the pleasantries, asking her if she would consider granting me at least half-custody to our son. "Now might be a good time for me to share responsibilities," I said.

I can't say why, but when I said it, I thought my entire insides were going to spill out onto the floor. Maybe my anxiety had something to do with the chance I was taking by calling her. I knew that she would probably say no. I realized that with Mitch gone, his pension denied and the house up for sale (the proceeds of which were almost surely going to be seized by both state and federal agencies) that the only thing she had to hold onto was her work as a nurse and our boy.

Still, it was worth the shot.

Initially, she said nothing. She just sort of inhaled and exhaled. For a beat or two it was as if she no longer possessed the strength necessary to make words. Maybe she didn't.

Imagine my surprise when she told me she admired Scarlet for what she had done. Admired her courage, her guts. How she managed to extend the ultimate fuckoff to them all. How she could not have scripted it better herself even if she were a Hollywood writer.

"As much as I despised Scarlet Montana for what she did to me, to you, to Mitchell, to my family," she confessed, "I was only too glad to help in my own small way."

Of course, that's when the realization sank in.

In my mind I shouted *You gave Scarlet the curare! Scarlet let you in on what she was planning and you gave her the curare and the speed. You're a nurse! You'd have the access inside the E.R. You hated her because she was sleeping with your second husband after having slept with your first husband!*

I shouted it out in my head instead of over the phone because I really did not want to know the truth. If my instincts were right on and Lynn had indeed assisted in Scarlet's self-demise, then I could not begin to face the reality of it all. We had a son together, after all. Lynn, no matter who she was or what she had become, would always be his mother. I would prefer to think of her as someone who would not assist in a killing, even if that killing did turn out to be a suicide.

I was relieved when, after a few weighted silent beats, she proceeded to say something else. But then it didn't have anything to do with the curare or the speed. It had everything to do with our son. In no uncertain terms, she was transferring half-custody to me. She was heading out to Los Angeles for a while. She'd already arranged for a position at the Mount Sinai Medical Center in Los Angeles. For the time being, she wanted me to look after our son. Upon arrival in the City of Angels she would email me with her new telephone number. For now I could expect the proper papers to be drawn up by her lawyer and delivered to me for signature as soon as they were completed. As for the boy, he would be dropped off on the following Monday morning. She wasn't sure how long she'd be gone. She had a lot of soul searching to do; a lot of patients to heal. But until she made it back to the east coast, the boy would remain with me fulltime.

"And please," she added, "keep your guns locked up."

Any questions?

None whatsoever.

I hung up before she had a chance to take it all back.

78

One calm, cool night I did something completely out of character for me: I fell asleep early. The rain that had been falling on Albany for almost three weeks straight had shifted out to sea a few days earlier. Now the late May nights were warm, breezy and dry. Summer was coming.

I can't tell you how long I'd been asleep, but when the phone rang, I was startled awake. For a fleeting few seconds I didn't know where I was, nor did I know the time.

I answered the phone.

I didn't recognize the voice right away, but when he identified himself as Reverend Roland Dubois, the Psychic Fair Master of Ceremonies, I no longer had to think about it.

"I need to see you," he said. "Get something off my chest."

"Now?" I asked, not at all sure I wanted to hear what he had to say.

"Please," he said. "It's important."

I hesitated for a beat, then I gave him my address. What else could I do? Avoid him like the bubonic plague for the rest of my days?

When I hung up it struck me as kind of funny that the good reverend needed me, of all people, to hear his confession.

Twenty minutes later he stood before me in the kitchen of my home looking like an over-sized Jesus. When he sat down across from me at the table, I looked up at him, at his full gray goatee and equally gray locks. There was something about his brown eyes. Instead of appearing tight and cynical like they did during my visit to the Psychic Fair some weeks back, they seemed sad now, sedate almost. Judging by his solemn expression, I could tell that the reverend had been indeed holding onto something for a long, long time.

First he inhaled a long silent breath. Then after an equally long exhale, he started in with something I already knew. Christ, something everybody knew by now! That Scarlet was addicted to the heroin her husband's body parts buyer provided for her free of charge. Almost free of charge, I should say Silence was Scarlet's currency. The need for her to turn her back on her husband's illegal activities.

Next he told me something I didn't know, but that I might have suspected all along. That the good reverend had been in love with her too. Although they never slept together, he would often visit her in the night when she was most alone and very lonely.

"Mostly she wanted to talk," he said. "In private; away from the group."

"What about?" I asked, as that all-too-familiar pressure began building up behind my eyes.

"Her sadness," he replied. "You see, her depression ... it wasn't because her husband was just another whacked-out cop, if you'll pardon the expression."

"Don't worry," I said, "I'm not a cop anymore."

"The depression was the result of something much more devastating."

He got up from the table, went over to the window above the sink, and looked out onto the night.

Some years back, he continued, Scarlet got pregnant. It happened just a few years after Jake had accidentally shot and killed that young woman in the south end, the one who had been working with the Albany police in order to apprehend her drug-dealing boyfriend.

"If you recall," the reverend said, "Jake took the whole thing very badly."

"I recall," I said, picturing once again my first afternoon as a junior detective, seeing Jake empty his pistol into the dealer's car.

He went on. According to Scarlet, Jake refused to speak of the episode. He retreated into himself along with the bitter memory. At times his depression was all-consuming. For days and even weeks, he'd hardly look at Scarlet, hardly speak or interact with her in any way. What started out as a union between two people who needed one another as protectors, suddenly broke down.

"They did have their moments, however," the reverend added. "Breakthrough moments. Or so Scarlet referred to them."

"Is that when she got pregnant?" I asked. "During one of these breakthrough moments?"

He said she'd carried the child well into the second trimester without telling a soul. She didn't have a job and her social life was almost nonexistent. She never even visited the precinct, so the knowledge of her pregnancy was pretty hush-hush. In the meantime, Jake was getting worse. Staying away from the house more and more, drinking heavily. And when he did come home he was often filled with rage. Sometimes he took the rage out on Scarlet. As she grew deeper into her pregnancy, the drinking and the rage escalated.

The reverend stared out the picture window onto the darkness and a set of silent chimes that hung by the eave.

"The way Scarlet told it to me," he said, "it happened the night of Easter Sunday, nearly ten years ago now. The two had taken a drive up to Saratoga for a late afternoon dinner."

He explained that Jake and Scarlet were having a nice time for a change. A breakthrough moment. Jake not thinking about the past; Scarlet not thinking about anything, just being with her husband while they drank and ate, never once taking her left hand off her small belly, as if to protect it. It would have been a time she cherished, a real breakthrough in their marriage; just a tiny block of time when they were on the same page, protecting and needing one another in the same way they had when they first met.

But then something happened.

A family walked into the restaurant. Just an average family dressed up in their Easter Sunday best looking to celebrate the resurrection with a little steak and wine, just like everybody else. A small family, the reverend said. Mom, dad, a teenaged son and a teenaged daughter. Unassuming, you might say. Were it not for the distinct resemblance the daughter had to Rachel, the blond girl Jake killed.

"Scarlet caught him staring at the girl from across the table," Reverend Dubois went on, hands stuffed in his pants pockets. "She could see Jake's eyes swell and fill with tears while he gazed upon this innocent teenaged kid."

"Breakthrough moment quickly ended," I supposed.

"Jake just got up and made his way over to the girl. Imagine this huge, strange, teary-eyed man approaching this young girl, her parents watching all of this as it transpires, him taking the girl's hand in his, kissing it, telling her how God-awful sorry he was. He tried to hug the girl, literally lifting her off her feet. When she screamed, the father went after him. Several waiters had to intervene before it was over."

I pictured the scene in my mind: big Jake wrestling with this girl's father while trying to apologize about a young life accidentally snuffed out in the line of fire. But then I couldn't imagine what had to be going through Scarlet's mind at the time, what kind of panic.

"Well, the parents of the girl were just about ready to call the police when Montana pulled out his badge, told them he was the police. Then he simply left the restaurant without paying.

"Scarlet did her best to explain what the commotion had been about. After a few minutes the family understood perfectly. They felt so badly for Jake and for Scarlet, they picked up the tab for two Easter dinners barely touched.

"That night, Jake got terribly drunk. He paced the house carrying his service pistol, mumbling something about how screwed Albany really was. The whole business of Albany law was a house of cards built upon a foundation of lies and deceit. He was no better than the criminals they housed at Green Haven and Sing Sing. He was a criminal. He was a killer, a murderer. He was a traitor to the cause. He had made a separate peace with God by selling his soul to the devil.

"Scarlet tried to console him. She asked him to stop, to go to bed, to sleep it off. In the morning, he'd feel better. But this just made him angrier. Still she persisted, begged him to stop drinking. Because it just made him worse.

"And then she said it. She told him if he didn't stop, she was going to leave him. She was going to leave him and he would never see the birth of his child. She said it over and over again until she was screaming at him."

The good reverend paused for a beat, hesitant to reveal what happened next. Until he had no choice.

"It worked," he finally went on. "Jake stopped. He set down his glass on the kitchen table. He capped the bottle, went over to the sink, washed his face and dried it with a dishtowel. But instead of putting the dishtowel down, he wrapped it around his right hand and with a smile plastered on his face, proceeded to beat Scarlet until she was unconscious."

I sat there, watched the big, gray-haired man turn away from the window, locking his brown eyes with mine.

"That night," he whispered, "she lost the baby. Spontaneous termination, I believe they call it. Miscarriage. It happened right in her bed. She was alone. Jake had already left the house. No one ever knew about it, until she told me. Not even Jake asked about it. Not once did he bring the subject up again in the months to come. As if she had never carried his child in the first place."

I stared down at my hands folded in my lap. They felt cold and sweaty. My head was reeling. I felt slightly nauseated from the bitter taste of bile in my mouth.

"So you see, Mr. Moonlight," Dubois spoke, grave-faced and sullen, "Scarlet had a lot more to die for than just a bad husband. She had a final revenge to enact, a final showdown not only with her maker, but also with the one man who had destroyed her and her child. Why did she kill herself? In dying, she could somehow free herself of the pain while avenging her son's murder. That might not be the truth, but that's the truth I want to believe, anyway."

"It was a boy?" I asked.

"She was going to call him James."

I ran my hands through my hair, cleared my throat.

"Why are you telling me this now?" I asked. "Why didn't you come forward when the investigation was still active? Why not come forward when Cain originally arrested me for her murder?"

"Because I was afraid and I didn't want to betray our secret," he said. "I made a solemn promise to Scarlet that I would never tell anyone about the baby. Not even you."

"You didn't know me until she was dead."

"But I did," he said. "You see, Scarlet used to talk a lot about you. She loved you. She felt bad about your condition. But then, she admired the way you always laughed about it, made jokes about it. Jokes that made her laugh and made her sad at the same time. She felt something for you that she didn't feel for me."

"What about Cain?" I asked. "Did she feel anything for him? Did she love him too?"

He vigorously shook his head, like I wasn't getting his point.

"When she slept with Cain, it was purely to get back at Jake. He didn't even have to know about it. It was simply the act that made the difference for her. But you weren't like that. She said you never sought her out. That she sought you out and that you were always there for her when she needed you."

I watched him swallow a breath. I thought at any moment he might break down along with me.

"She told me something once not long before she died that should put the whole thing into perspective for you."

I wasn't sure I wanted to know.

"She said she never had sex with you. That she made love to you."

I groaned. "You had to tell me that, didn't you?"

"Yes," he said. "I thought you should know, even though God knows how I wished she would have made love to me."

He formed a smile, but I could tell he wasn't the least bit happy or relieved. If I could have read his mind, I knew what it would have said: *If only she could have loved me, I could have saved her.*

My God, if I could have read all their minds, dead or alive, they would have said the same thing. Cain, the reverend, who knows who else. They all must have thought the same thing—*If only she loved me, I could have made things right for her.*

I was the one man she had loved, and I ran away from her, allowed her to die. If only I had stayed by her side that Sunday night in May when Jake suddenly and unexpectedly came home. If only I hadn't run away like a coward. If only I'd stayed by her side, to defend her, defend what we had together, then Scarlet might still be alive.

Without another word the reverend got up from the table and made his way to the door. But before leaving, he turned back to me.

I couldn't help but notice the squinty-eyed look of inquisitiveness on his long face.

"Is this where it happened?" he asked. "At the kitchen table?"

I felt my heart drop into my stomach.

"Your suicide?" he added. "You tried to take your own life at this very table." He said it like a question, but I was sure that he knew the truth without my confirming it.

Had I ever spoken to the man about my suicide attempt? Never. Other than Lola, I tried never to speak about the details of that long ago spring day with anybody. Not even Scarlet. I guess the reverend had his psychic powers after all.

He worked up a sad smile, like he sensed I was about to melt into the linoleum right before his eyes.

"Pardon me if I never wish to see you again," he said.

"Permission granted," I replied.

He saw himself out the back door.

A few minutes later, I was lying back on the bed once more, falling in and out of sleep, until an uninterrupted sleep—a sleep not plagued by demons—looked next to impossible.

During one of the awake times, I was staring up at the dark ceiling. I had a clear vision of Scarlet's Green Meadows home. I'm not sure if I had somehow dreamed of the place, but I sensed myself back inside her bedroom. I actually felt myself back in bed with Scarlet, her soft body pressed up beside my own, her bare feet rubbing up against my toes.

When I opened my eyes I knew I should have stayed in bed, but something was gnawing at me. Maybe I was finally experiencing my own psychic breakthrough, because I heard a voice speaking to me inside my head. A voice I recognized; a voice that haunted me. Scarlet's voice.

"I love you, Richard," it said. The voice made me want to get up, throw on my jeans and a jacket, and make my way back over to her house in the rain.

I never would have believed it, but Scarlet was speaking to me from the dead.

79

I went around back of a rectangular, concrete-walled hole that had provided the foundations for a house that once stood there. A house that was now reduced to an open basement filled with charred timbers and ruined furniture. That's when it caught my eye. The rear patio, I mean. The small concrete patio butted up against the back lawn, directly below what had been a back porch overhang. The overhang had been located directly below Scarlet's bedroom window.

I must have slapped the palms of my hands against the concrete in effort to break my fall after having slipped off the back porch overhang. In all my adrenalin-charged rush to get the hell out of there, I must have never noticed it until later—later when I could only assume that the scratches and abrasions on the palms of my hands must have had something to do with Scarlet's death.

I'm not sure what possessed me, but when I shined the flashlight into the hole I saw something I recognized. Funny how pristine it still seemed. Or maybe it just looked that way from where I was standing above ground, breathing in the wet, musty charcoal smell. The baby blue porcelain statue of the Madonna, the Christ mother lying on her back, glazed eyes looking up at me, as if truly watching me, calling me to her.

For a split second I saw Scarlet's face in her face and I felt my throat close up on itself. The whole thing was too strange for words. Still, it took an almost superhuman effort to peel my eyes away. But before I did, I noticed something else stuffed in the rubble just below the statue.

The strongbox.

Dropping to my knees, I extended my arms, reaching for the box without falling into the exposed basement. Clutching the metal box with my fingers, I managed to pull it out. Of course I recognized it right away as the strongbox Scarlet kept directly beside her bed on the nightstand—the off-limits box with the "madness" poem taped to the top that now had been burned away in the fire.

Climbing to my knees, I set the strongbox on the grass before me. As I thumbed the lock release, I realized how badly my now-healed hands were trembling. The box was locked and I didn't have a key.

I looked all around where I knelt, shining the flashlight onto the wet earth until I found a rock half sticking out of the mud. I dug with my hands and freed the stone. Then, using both hands I raised them up high and brought the rock down hard onto the box's lock. The one collision was all it took for the lid to pop open. Setting the rock aside, I opened the lid all the way, shining the flashlight inside.

That's when I saw them. Three items, the first, a business-sized envelope placed inside a plastic Ziploc bag for protection; the second, a leather pouch with a drawstring top; and third, a small leather-bound baby diary.

I took out the plastic-enclosed envelope and immediately stuffed it into the right-hand pocket of my jacket. Then, placing the flashlight under my armpit so that it shined on the diary, I began to thumb through the pages. I thumbed from blank page to blank page, until I came to one single entry scribbled on the final page of the diary. Written in what I recognized as Scarlet's handwriting were these words:

James Montana, April 17, 2000 – April 17, 2000

It was the strangest sensation. Me, positioned on my knees, staring down at the identical birth and death dates of Scarlet's baby. My hands went from trembling to outright shaking when I set the diary back inside the box and picked up the leather pouch. Drawing back the string, I reached inside and pulled out a bone, then another and another.

I felt something break inside of me and my tears fell hard. But I wasn't sure who I was crying for. Whether it was for Scarlet, her child or for me. One thing was certain: I wanted the memory of James to be forever buried beside his mother, if only in spirit. I set the bones back inside the bag, and the bag back inside the strongbox along with the diary.

Digging with my hands in the same hole from which I freed the rock, I set the strongbox inside and covered it up with the loose, rain-soaked soil. As a final gesture I set a patch of loose sod on top. Then, standing, I did something extraordinary, even for myself.

I made the sign of the cross for the first time since I could remember.

Pulling my eyes away from James' small grave, I turned my back on the Montana home. If anyone knew enough not to disturb the dead, it was me.

I was about to head back to Hope Lane when a set of headlights broke through the damp darkness. I killed the flashlight, gazing in their direction.

Lola, driving Dad's funeral coach.

She must have followed me here. I had no idea how much she might have witnessed, no idea how long she'd been out there watching me in the dark before she decided to pull up front. I guess it didn't really matter. All that mattered was her presence.

Crossing over the front lawn, I made my way to where she parked up along the curb. When she rolled down the window I was struck by how beautiful she was with her long brown hair, brown teardrop eyes and soft red lips. For a change she wasn't wearing her lab coat.

"Did you find what you were looking for?" she whispered.

I smiled, wiping my eyes with my muddy hands. "There are some questions better left unanswered."

She smiled back. "Some questions are better left un-posed."

I slid myself into the Harold Moonlight funeral coach and she drove me back home.

80

I'm seated at a long metal table inside a windowless interrogation room.

Just as they have been for more than three hours, Stocky Agent is seated next to me, while his bearded partner stands in the far corner, witness to the exchange.

I put out my cigarette, sit back in my chair.

"How do you suppose she was able to keep her child's remains?"

"Scarlet never went to the hospital after her miscarriage," I say. "She must have buried the child out back and later on, dug him back up. It's the only explanation."

"What about the letter inside the plastic bag? Where is it?"

"When I opened it, it disintegrated in my hands. Must have been the effects of the fire."

"You didn't see anything written on it at all? It might have contained the suicide note everyone was looking for."

I shake my head.

"Just paper, and it disintegrated. I'm sorry."

Stocky Agent nods. He sits back in his chair and sighs.

"Well," he says in a resigned voice, "I guess maybe in the end, you have learned your lesson after all, Mr. Moonlight. You're not the head case you make yourself out to be. You're not the killer, either."

I cross my arms over my chest and exhale. Stocky Agent stands.

"That's it," he says, turning toward the giant mirror, running his right index finger across his neck in a slashing motion, like someone slicing their own neck.

"So you're not going to book me for anything?" I ask.

"You're cooperating," he tells me, while his partner moves away from the wall to stand beside him. "No charges are to be filed for now. You're a free man, pending further questioning, of course."

"You have no one to arrest now," I add. "The way I learned it, someone always has to pay when it comes to murder. Especially a cop's murder."

"Believe me, Mr. Moonlight," Stocky Agent says, "someone will pay. Sooner or later, justice will be served and someone will go down for this mess. The body parts op alone extends way beyond the boundaries of Albany and Saratoga." He rolls his eyes. "And of course, there is the inevitable hellfire." Stocky Agent is a God-fearing man.

"Cain and Montana were just cogs in a much larger machine, weren't they?" I inquire.

"Cain, Joy and Montana tapped into a lucrative market," the agent offers. "But you took a real chance getting so close to them. They were dangerous men who risked life, limb and reputation by directly connecting themselves with a mob-sponsored black market operation."

"Moonlights aren't afraid of dying," I say.

"How wonderful for you."

I find myself nodding, as if finally someone besides Dad and George understands. But I know it's only wishful thinking on my part. Standing, I make for the exit, but turn back around when the agent calls out my name once more.

"Yeah?"

"You forgot your cigarettes," he says, holding up the pack.

"I'm the last jerk on the earth who should be smoking. How 'bout you keep 'em."

"I quit three years ago," Stocky Agent says, grinning. "But I suppose I can find the second-to-last jerk."

I pick up the pack and stuff it into the bottom right-hand pocket of my leather jacket.

Going for the door, I get this cold feeling in my feet, a numbness in my right hand, a pressure in the center of my head. The sensations speak to me, alarming me, just like my built-in shit detector.

They tell me these FBI agents won't ever see me alive again.

81

Outside, it was raining again. I wondered if it would ever stop for more than three or four days at a time.

Pulling the collar up on my leather jacket, I started walking toward the old man's Mercedes. It was parked up against the curb on Broadway. From where I stood I could make out Lola in the passenger seat. Seated on her lap was my boy. I wasn't really sure, but it looked like they were playing some sort of tickle game. She was smiling and laughing, waving her hands up and down. I couldn't see it of course, but deep in my head I imagined their smiling faces, their laughter.

The rain intensified. So much rain I was practically blinded. For a few seconds all I could make out was the blurry red and blue light that glared from the neon signs hanging over the windows of the downtown gin mills. More doors and signs than I could count.

But then I saw it lying in the road, directly beside a storm sewer drain that had backed up and was overflowing in the heavy rain. A red robin lying on its side on the soaked macadam. The bird was struggling to lift its wings, its beak opening and closing helplessly, black marble eye reflecting the streetlight. I stood there, watching the bird watch me. It was all alone in the open road, suffering, its scarlet feathers trembling, as though begging me for help.

For just a split second I was tempted to walk into the road, pick the bird up with my bare hands, and slip it into my jacket pocket.

But I did nothing.

What could I possibly do for this creature other than put it out of its misery? And somehow the thought of killing, no matter how easy, just didn't seem like the right thing to do. Because all that's born dies, one way or another. It's just a matter of how much time you've got. Like the old man used to say: we all owe God a life.

But there was one thing I had to do.

Stepping out into the road, I reached into my pants pocket and pulled out my wallet. Unfolding it, I slipped out a folded letter and a razorblade that had been pulled off the t-shirt I snatched from the floor in Scarlet's bedroom on the night my ex-wife, Lynn, killed her. Just one of those loose razors construction people use for scraping away old wallpaper. A paper-thin, super-light blade soaked in sticky blood that bore Lynn's fingerprints and only Lynn's. Fingerprints that checked out with the prints the A.M.C. security office still kept on file. The blade was the one that Lynn had used to kill Scarlet Montana at Scarlet's request.

Standing in the rain, I pictured my wife entering the Montana home by using the key she took off her husband's key ring—a key Scarlet surely would have given him. I saw her quietly climb the stairs, enter Scarlet's bedroom, just the way Scarlet scripted it in the epistle I took from her strongbox—the plastic-encased letter addressed to Lynn Cain, "Personal and Confidential," that described what would become the suicide of Scarlet Montana, detail for detail.

I saw Lynn pull a syringe from her jacket pocket, saw her inject Scarlet with the curare. Then returning the syringe to her pocket, she pulled out the blade. I then saw Scarlet's green eyes looking into Lynn's. I saw Scarlet nod and close her eyes. It would have been her way of telling Lynn to do it now; to destroy the demons that haunted her by inflicting the cuts and the pain.

That's when the blade must have come down, the blood spatter hitting Scarlet's face and the walls behind and beside her. I saw big tears falling off Lynn's face as she performed a perfectly scripted homicide to resemble suicide by self-cutting.

Scarlet and Lynn. They were a match made in hell.

Scarlet wanted to die and Lynn wanted her to die for what she did to me and later on to Cain.

I looked down at a blade that had gotten stuck to my t-shirt when Lynn dropped it beside the bed, her grisly deed done. That blade did not reappear again until last week's laundry day when I discovered it at the bottom of the hamper.

I guess stranger things have happened.

For now I held the blade in my fingertips, felt its near weightlessness, witnessed Scarlet's rain-diluted blood washing away from the blade, pink and cloudy. I dipped my finger into the blood and I pressed it against my lips and I felt my heart stop and my mouth go dry. Then I bent down, dropping the blade through the sewer grate along with the suicide letter.

Standing there in the downpour, I wiped my palms clean against my pants. Then I made the decision to do something else.

Bending at the waist, I cupped my hands under the injured bird and lifted it up in the palms of my hands. I felt its feathery wet heat against my skin, little rapid heart beating against my fingers as I made my way back across the sidewalk, setting it down onto a dry piece of awning-protected concrete.

I made sure not to look back.

In the near distance, my fragile family waited for me inside the old man's pride and joy Mercedes funeral coach. Pulling a cigarette from the pack in my jacket, I cupped my hands around it and fired it up. I wasn't sure how much time I had left. But then life is full of surprises.

Exhaling blue smoke, I tossed the cig to the pavement. I stuffed my hands in my pockets and made my way toward the laughter in the deep, rainy night.

You are invited to visit ***Vincent Zandri*** on his website:
www.vincentzandri.com

Made in the USA
Lexington, KY
23 May 2010